A Woman's Business

A Woman's Business

Tracy Mungo

MUNGO PRESS

A Woman's Business / Tracy Mungo
1. Fiction / Historical
2. Fiction / African American
3. Fiction / General
4. Fiction / Urban Literature
5. Fiction / Women's Literature
6. Fiction / Family Drama

Cataloging-in-Publication Data is on file with the Library of Congress

ISBN: 979-8-9934711-0-5

10 9 8 7 6 5 4 3 2 1

DEDICATION

*F*or the girl who once sought love and approval outside herself, and for the woman she became — finally learning to give both freely to herself. This book is my love letter to me.

For me. For every time I was told I wasn't enough, every time I placed others above myself, every time I silenced my own needs. Today I rise, unashamed, and claim this story as mine. This book is my victory — and I gift it first to myself.

TABLE OF CONTENTS

ACKNOWLEDGMENTS

First, I thank **God** for walking with me through every word.

To my daughters **Tiffani Jackson and Wayada Hollins** — You are my heartbeat, my lifeline.

To my grandbabies **Quentin, Christian, Bella, Kimaya, Kaniya, Daisi, Kimani,** and great-grandbaby **Kimani K.**— You are my joy and inspiration.

To my siblings **Lorraine, Dennis, Kevin, Dana** — Our memories breathe through these pages. Our shared stories, laughter, and sometimes tears have all found their way into these characters.

To my nephew **Logan R. Mungo, III** — Thank you.

To my oldest niece **LaShawn** — Who came to see about her auntie when I needed her to help nurse me back to life. Your love for me is undeniable.

To my nieces and great-nieces **Paris, Alaziah, Sydney, Logan** — The blooming branch of our tree. Keep reaching toward your own truth. There's power in your story waiting to be told.

To my great-nephews **Shaun, Jayden, Sevyn** — This, too, is your legacy. You will keep my spirit alive by just saying my name. I'm proud to know you will always remember me.

To my great-nieces **Zhuri and Zoey** — Learn the power of words. The words of this book hold power. Some of these words about a woman's business were actually spoken by your ancestors. Be wise and apply them.

To my beloved **Aunt Eleanor Carter** and **Uncle Raymond W. Harris** — My mother's cherished siblings. You are the living branches of our family tree, the keepers of stories that shaped who we are. Your laughter, wisdom, and unwavering love have carried the spirit of our ancestors forward. At 84 and 85, you remain a testament to endurance, grace, and faith. Thank you for the memories, the lessons, and the warmth that continues to guide us all.

To my loved ones who have gone home to glory — My precious **daughter Paula Jackson**; my devoted **parents Logan Robert Mungo, Sr. and Marlene Martha Mungo, who without I would've been nothing. They are the roots of my strength**; my dear **Irish twin brother Logan R. (Bobby) Mungo, Jr., who I know is smiling down on me with great pride**; my two **nephews Kevin L. Mungo, Jr. and Tevin J. Mungo, both gone too soon**; my beautiful **great-niece Tyler Gabrielle Lewis, also gone too soon**; my **special great-aunt Flossie Jones Gray, whose essence lives on**; two of my dearest **divine tribe of special girlfriends Ramona Epperson and Vivian Bledsoe-Brown**, all who now became my ancestors.

All of your spirits walk with me in every page I write. Though your earthly voices are silent, your presence speaks through the rhythm of my heart. This book is part of your legacy, too — born from the love, laughter, and lessons you left behind.

To my **tribe of girlfriends** — My circle of divine women. You've been my laughter in dark days, my prayer warriors, and my living proof that sisterhood is sacred.

To my **literary mentor Joylynn M. Ross** — Your guidance gave me courage and confidence to claim my voice. You helped me polish my craft while protecting my heart, and I'll never forget that.

And to every **reader** — Thank you for holding my story in your hands. I hope it moves you like it moved through me. It was written with love — for you.

A special thanks to **Lorraine Mungo and Author Nikita Lynette Nichols** — Who had taken on their God-given assignment to facilitate my meeting my literary mentor.

— **Tracy Mungo**
A Woman's Business

Chapter 1

CRAZY AFRICAN SISTERS

"Florence, get your high yellow ass out that front door and quit letting the flies in the house. Ain't nobody come calling on you," said Ginny, shooing away invisible flies to hammer in her point. A typical exaggeration of the oldest of the three Jones daughters.

"You go straight to hell, Ginny!" Florence growled back. She wasn't about to let her sister, older or not, be the boss of her. "Besides, I rather be yellow as the sun than as dark as your black ass."

"Ooooh, you betta watch your mouth before Momma gets wind and takes a switch to your behind," Ginny teased. "And you know them marks gon' show up real good." Ginny chuckled. "And like Momma always says, 'You ain't too big to get your tail beat.'"

"And that includes you, too," Florence spat, closing and turning away from the rickety screen door she'd been peeking out of. A screen that had a hole in it so big, the door didn't even need to be open for flies to make their way into the three-bedroom, two-story home the family of five lived in. "Just because you about to be a teenager don't mean you gon' be running things. Momma still the woman of this here house."

"Yeah, but I'm still going to be a woman in this house, and don't you forget it, little sis. In this family, a girl becomes a woman at thirteen, and in less than two weeks..." Ginny's words floated off with such conceit.

Florence loaned her attention to Ginny. "Yeah, well, age ain't nothing but a number. It ain't gon' make you better than me." Florence let out a harrumph, crossing her arms over her chest.

"Well, you the one who already think you're better than me because you got Daddy's color. He's just as much my daddy as he's yours." Ginny was not going to let her sister insult her, which was exactly what she took Florence's reference to her dark brown skin color to be.

Ginny wasn't as light-complected as her two sisters, which often made her silently and painfully question her paternity. Willie Jones was still the man all three young girls in the home called Daddy. Ginny did have his height, though. And that was just enough of a mustard seed to give her hope that maybe Willie really was her biological daddy.

Most folks assumed that Florence had taken her daddy's complexion and her mother's shorter stature, while Ginny inherited just the opposite: her mother's dark, beautiful African skin and her father's height. But with Florence on the cusp of turning twelve years old, she still had plenty more inches to grow. And that was the mustard seed Florence needed to know that one day soon, she could kick Ginny's behind good.

Florence's five-foot frame took a step toward Ginny, who was both older and taller. Even so, Florence had Ginny by about ten pounds.

"He probably ain't even your damn daddy. He was probably just kind enough to say he's your daddy," Ginny snapped back, not the least bit intimidated by Florence's charge toward her. She remained snugged in her daddy's—their momma's husband, Willie's—favorite blue chair, her eyes buried in the book she was reading. "He didn't want you to have to grow up thinking you're the bastard that you are." She chuckled under her breath as she turned a page.

No matter how many times Ginny and Florence went at it, that dig never got old—one or the other reminding each other that *somebody* had a different daddy—but for some reason, it stung Ginny worse than it did Florence. And Florence could tell by the way it always brought Ginny's words to a sudden halt, giving her pause before she shot back. As if struggling in her thoughts whether she should argue about the truth. Either way, her failed attempts to hide the proverbial wound on her face let Florence know she'd won the battle regardless of whatever Ginny's comeback was.

May Rose, the girls' mother, hollered from the kitchen where she was cooking up some neckbones with cabbage and hot water cornbread. "Both of you quit trying to talk my business when you don't even know what you're speaking on." Other than being their mother, thirty-six-year-old May Rose was her daughters' referee for all their bickering matches.

"I do know, Momma," Ginny said, slamming the book shut. "Nana and her sisters were talking about it when I was at Nana's house last Saturday getting my hair pressed." Ginny vacated the chair, dropping the book in it to hold her place. She marched into the kitchen so that her mother could hear her real good and see the truth coming out of her mouth. "Nana always saying that we would be better off if you had pursued Mr. Claypool because he was a hard-working old fool of a man. And unlike Daddy, who thinks he done gave you everything in the world, Mr. Claypool probably would have since he actually had something to give. More than a raggedy piece of land with a couple raggedy dwellings and a raggedy cow." Ginny spoke matter-of-factly, as if everything Nana said was bond.

"Is that so?" May Rose asked, twisting her mouth while also impressed at how well Ginny was able to imitate Nana's tone, facial expressions, body gestures, and demeanor. "And just what else did that nana of yours have to say?" It was clear by the tone in her voice that May Rose's only mission was to find out exactly how much of her business her own mother was putting in her daughters' minds.

This was a sign to Ginny that everything Nana said was true, as May Rose had yet to ever deny any of the news pertaining to her children's fathers, and the way she handled men in general, that Ginny ever carried back from Nana.

Ginny was glad to continue spilling the beans as she sat at the pea-green kitchen table to get good and comfortable. Although it was always hard to get too comfortable due to the wobbling table that May Rose had been saying forever she was going to get Willie to permanently fix. The book that had once been there as a temporary fix to keep it somewhat stable was now sitting in Willie's blue chair.

"Nana said you didn't do your work—a woman's business," Ginny continued. "Not to mention you fell in love with Daddy, being he's mulatto."

May Rose swung around from the stove and commanded in her high-pitched voice, "The fact yo' daddy's skin is damn near white ain't—"

"And that he got good hair," Ginny added with an air about her.

"If you repeat that shit again, I'm going to knock your teeth out your damn mouth," May Rose said with such fierce and force that spittle came flying out of her mouth.

Ginny was a bit taken aback. Just two seconds ago, her mother all but extended her teacup, insisting Ginny pour into it the words Nana had poured into her ears. Then just like that, she was barking at her like she was a dog, when all Ginny had done was carry the bone.

"Florence!" May Rose shouted so that her voice would carry loud and clear into the next room. "Hand me the—"

May Rose didn't even have to finish her sentence, as Florence cut her off when she appeared in the kitchen doorway.

"Already got it, Momma. Here you go." Florence handed May Rose the freshly picked switch that Lynette, their youngest sister, had pulled from the tree that morning when she got her butt lit up for talking fresh. It was 1925. Not only did the grown folks have the authority to beat a child into submission and the respect of authority, but they gave them the courtesy to handpick the means with which to do it.

"I oughtta knock your teeth out your mouth," Ginny said to Florence with venom in her voice and her eyes.

If Ginny could have balled her fist and knocked that smug look off Florence's face, she would have. But time didn't permit, as May Rose got to swinging on Ginny the moment the transfer of the switch was made from Florence's hands to May Rose's.

"I'm the lone person knocking out teeth around here," May Rose said as she whipped Ginny from the kitchen to the living room.

This was one of the very few times when Ginny appreciated her dark skin. There would be no proof of the beating. Whenever Florence and Lynette got beat, however, proof was sure to show up nice and clear as red welts.

Ginny ran like an Olympic hurdle jumper, hopping over anything in her way to get free of that switch May Rose was wielding like a crazy woman.

"Hey, watch it," Lynette said, more concerned about Ginny stepping on her dolls than the fact that she was getting beat half to death. After all, it was just another Tuesday in the Jones's house.

Ginny leaped over Lynette's leg while she played on the rotten, uneven, wooden floor with her handmade doll. It was her favorite, the one May Rose had made with scraps from the dress she'd sewn for First Lady Ramona, the town minister's wife.

Grateful that Ginny still had respect for her indoor playground, even in the midst of getting her tail beat, Lynette thought she might offer her older sister that same type of grace.

"Momma, Ginny ain't lying," Lynette said. "Nana always tells me the same thing. She tells all of us, don't she, Florence?"

Although she was enjoying the fact that Ginny was getting paid back for the mess she had just been talking about her, Florence wasn't about to break the sister code. When the truth could set one of them free, it had to be told. And right now, the truth could set Ginny free from that licking she was taking from May Rose.

"It's true, Momma," Florence regretfully confirmed, which made May Rose halt mid-swing from laying a good one on Ginny. "Nana often recounts when I'm leaving her house, 'Flo, baby,'" she mocked Nana just as good, if not better, than Ginny. "'One of the principles of a woman's business is *not* to fall in love…like your crazy momma did.'"

May Rose's chest rose and fell as she caught her breath, listening to her middle child recount her own mother's words against her. May Rose's eyes encouraged Florence to continue.

"I asked Nana what she meant by that...a woman's business and all," Florence said. "'Just tarry,' Nana told me. 'Your turn will come to learn the business.'"

The atmosphere relaxed. May Rose lowered her switch-wielding hand. Ginny stood still behind the couch, hopeful the obstacle course had ended, and Lynette's full attention was back on her dolls.

Florence continued. "Nana told me that the ladies, the Crazy African Sisters, will get me back in those woods, where they will teach me how to catch babies, catch those white boys, and catch those colored boys that got a daddy with money like preacher man Smith, who can also heal the sick."

May Rose snarled her next words. "They can go back to their damn country."

Nana and her sisters had been taken from the Fulani tribe in Ghana, West Africa, in 1865 at the end of the transatlantic slave trade. They were in their early teens and had completed the family's rites of passage into womanhood not too long before that. So, everything they'd learned was fresh in their minds.

Nana never knew who May Rose's daddy was because she and her sisters were bought by the slave owner, Bristow Cantor, for the purpose of breeding. Nana only bore May Rose because she remembered how to prevent the dirty suds from going inside her to keep her from becoming with child when they tried to force her and her sisters to breed. The African men knew the plan. No dirty suds in these women. The act, sometimes, got good to Nana with some good-looking Fulani men, which was how she slipped up and got May Rose caught up in her womb. Nana's hips gripped their big wide backs, and she let all the dirty suds explode in her. Then here came May Rose.

Nana and her two sisters became known as the Crazy African Sisters because they fought the white men on the plantation, even knowing they would be whipped. They would stand toe-to-toe with them, nonetheless. The plantation owner would charge the townspeople money to come watch them fight. Their eyes would stay swollen, and lips cut. They were determined not to be broken.

The Crazy African Sisters' father was a king of their tribe and had prepared the sisters for this. Had even taught them the language of the white man. Old Man Cantor decided since he couldn't breed them, he would make money fighting them. He's the one who actually gave them the name "Crazy African Sisters."

Even in the Jones household, Nana and her sisters were referred to as the Crazy African Sisters depending on who was referencing them. Because if it were Willie, the word 'crazy' would be somewhere in the description as well. "They're worth more trouble than they're worth. And they ain't worth a damn," May Rose said.

Ginny let out a chuckle that contagiously spread throughout the room. In a snap, they'd all gone from yelling to roaring with laughter.

"I know they our elders," Ginny said, "but some of the stuff they do and say do be crazy."

"Tell me about it," Florence cosigned as they spent the next few minutes declaring how they felt about the Crazy African Sisters.

May Rose said under her breath, "Thank God Willie ain't here." The last thing she needed was for him to hear her agreeing with him about how crazy her momma and aunts were.

May Rose picked up the book from the chair that Ginny had earlier abandoned, placed it on the glass end table with a built-in lamp, and sat down. "Willie has such disdain for Momma and her sisters," May Rose voiced. "I guess I can't half-blame him. They are time and time again making mischief in our home."

May Rose was accurate. Even though the three sisters shared the little house just a hundred feet or so from the big house where May Rose and her family lived, as far as Willie was concerned, they might as well have been all under the same roof. At least twice a week, May Rose and Willie were in a disagreement about something her mother and aunts had said or done.

"Why they do so all the time, Momma?" Lynette asked with inquisitive eyes as she made her doll dance.

May Rose exhaled. "The bottom line, honey, is they don't believe my Willie is good enough for me," she confessed. And ironically, they weren't all the way wrong about their assessment of her husband. She then let out a harrumph. "While none of them have a husband at all, worrying about me and my man."

May Rose loved Willie and couldn't care less what anybody—her momma and aunts included—believed. This was displayed in her actions each and every day. Yeah, he got on her nerves good, but he was her husband. And American women stood by their man. And in this moment, it was displayed in her eyes as she stared off, thinking about Willie, allowing his favorite chair to hug her as if it were his very arms comforting her.

The girls loved the love May Rose had in her eyes for their daddy the few times they detected it. They also loved Nana and their great-aunts dearly. This was why the young girls were so often torn when it came to love.

May Rose didn't seem to be on the same team, or even the same playing field, as the Crazy African Sisters when it came to love—the love between a woman and a man, anyway. As far as Nana and her sisters were concerned, that's something that should never exist. Love should not flow from the woman to man. As a matter of fact, if they were hearing their Nana's message loud and clear, it was a woman's business *not* to love a man.

May Rose and Willie knew their daughters held their Nana and great-aunts in high regard. They suspected how torn they must be when it came to their differences. They also suspected the girls had such fancy mouths because of their maternal female elders. That was why on more occasions than they should, they gave them grace. It just so happened that May Rose was running low on grace fumes today, as she'd ripped into both Lynette and Ginny already.

"I wish Nana and our aunties weren't so mean when it came to you and Daddy," Ginny said, sinking down into the couch across from where May Rose sat.

"I know, baby, I know," May Rose said, now softening up with her, "but the history of that runs deep." She leaned back and thought about her mother and her aunts. Before May Rose knew it, a minute smile crept across her lips.

"The sisters sure do know how to light a room up, though," May Rose said her thoughts aloud. They always wore the most beautiful fabrics in the brightest of oranges, greens, yellows, purples, and blues. And she loved how they would sit and teach her daughters all about the fabrics of their garb, which were mostly Ghanian Kente cloths. Each color and print was worn for different occasions.

Elma, May Rose's mother—aka Nana, and the middle child of the Crazy African Sisters—didn't have a husband, but she had a man who provided for her dearly. Anything Elma dreamed up, he had for her before she could even wake up from the dream. And he was responsible for all the beautiful African clothing Nana wore, as he traveled to Ghana often and always returned with gifts.

He was a giving man.

He was a white man.

A white man from America.

A white man who Elma despised dearly because, as with most of the white men she'd encountered in her years, she believed he was just another one traveling through the country of Ghana to continue to steal their riches. So, she figured being in a relationship with him was her way and means of getting some of the riches back.

On his most recent trip, he bought Elma back some red and black Kente cloth for funerals, and black and white for the burial celebration. Elma would tell all the women of the community she would at one point in the future wear the funeral and celebration Kente cloths to celebrate the white man's death. He didn't deserve her Fulani beauty.

Her mother was a beautiful woman. May Rose couldn't argue that. She was a small-framed woman with waist-length, curly hair. Her eyes were almond-shaped, and she had a pointy nose that was the perfect size for her oval face. The men in the town used to say her and her sisters had the beauty of a fox. Little did they know they were just as sly.

Elma and her sisters often did their native Fulani woman dance called Apatampa. It involved a lot of fast feet motion, shaking of the hips, and chanting. This dance was performed outside as the women circled the house. The purpose was to call on the ancestors for the protection of their home and family. The dirt rising from under their bare feet would be like a dust storm with strong winds making it circle and swirl like a tornado. Another way to describe it was like having horses racing through the yard and kicking up dirt. Most of the time, as May Rose watched in awe, she couldn't tell if it was their feet or hips causing all the commotion.

Elma had no filter when it came to sharing her business with the white man with her granddaughters. "I'll witness the white man's house crumble, coupled with witnessing his death right before my eyes," she warned. That's not all she would share with the girls as part of what could have been referred to as "pretraining to woman's business," which was their family business.

She showed the girls another dance called the Mapouka with the flutters. It was a very gracious dance executed by a woman in the privacy of her room for the sole delight of a man. The woman would shake her behind vigorously from side to side, as if it were shivering without the rest of the body.

Willie witnessed some of the dances the sisters did on an occasion or two but made it clear that he could do without them.

"When they do all of their dances, they look just plain dirty," Willie would say with disgust lacing his words. "You can do all that gyrating and kicking up dirt if you want," he told May Rose, "but my babies—not a single one of 'em—will be doing those dances."

May Rose heard Willie loud and clear, but whether she'd adhere to his wishes was yet to be determined. It was tradition for the women in her family, and with Ginny turning thirteen in less than a month, she would be the first of the girls to experience this generational rite of passage...*if* May Rose decided her daughters would be a part of the family business.

This was important to Elma and her sisters, Bertha and Etta. Coincidently, these were names that the Oyinbos, aka white men, named them when they snatched them from the home-land they loved so much and took them to Bedford, Virgina. Now years later, with the sisters being in their sixties, they still used their Fulani names. Nana's was Sangaré, Aunt Bertha's was Bocoum, and Aunt Etta's was Diallo. Even May Rose had a Fulani name, which was Olawale.

May Rose had to admit that despite her frustration with how her mother and aunts felt about her straying from the family business, so to speak, she hadn't completely abandoned the excitement she once felt for it. She recalled how powerful and in control it had made her feel. And a part of her didn't want to rob her daughters of experiencing that same control and power. So, what if she decided to skip a generation and, as an only child, stray from the business? It was a decision she got to make for herself. But was it fair for her to make that decision for her daughters? Was it fair for her to take away their choice?

"A woman without a choice is like a man with too many," Nana always said.

The more May Rose thought back to her own ceremony of learning a woman's business, the more she leaned toward allowing Ginny to have her own—choice, that was.

The rite of passage experience for May Rose was spiritual, insightful, and loving. It was the first time she had felt that sort of emotion all compressed into one. It was the first time she'd experienced the real power of womanhood.

May Rose recalled her mother and aunts spending hours in the woods teaching her that her true love should only be herself, her children, her elders, and the homeland from which her ancestors came. That was what her mother's tribe taught.

One profound thing May Rose learned from the ceremony was that love in a relationship revolves around a woman's vagina. It must cost a man to call it his own. Perhaps in money. Perhaps in material things. Or even perhaps in blood. But there was a price to pay. Sometimes, the dilemma was who was going to pay it.

May Rose was always taught to question whether it was the woman or the woman's vagina a man had love for—or perhaps even the love of the ownership of it.

"At the end of the day," Nana had told young thirteen-year-old May Rose, "it is a prize, and a man must win as many prizes he feels he wants. And as long as you know the truth but make him believe the lie, you will always stay in control. And the women in this family, all the women in this family, must be taught this and live by this. It is our family business."

Those words ripped through May Rose's soul as she recalled them and knew right then and there what had to be done.

The fire.

The blood.

The drum.

The spirits.

The ancestors.

Yes, May Rose's mind was made up. Ginny would not be denied her rite of passage into womanhood...into a woman's business. But what Ginny decided to do with her job and resume would be up to her.

The corners of May Rose's mouth rose into a smile. She thought that perhaps if Ginny turned out to be a good worker, she could make up for where the women in the family felt May Rose lacked. Which was with her decision to choose to fall in love and marry...and actually being in love with the man she married. Maybe the Crazy African Sisters would spend so much time molding and training Ginny that they would get off

May Rose's back. They'd finally let her be. With Willie. Happy and in love.

Too bad she'd have to sacrifice her own daughters to get that peace.

"The axe forgets; a tree remembers."

African Proverb

Chapter 2

❧

THE CEREMONY

he ceremony for Ginny began at midnight, the first full moon after her thirteenth birthday. Putting together the ceremony was nothing compared to keeping it a secret from Willie, which was why—for added measure—May Rose ordered Ginny not to whisper a word of it to her sisters, wagging a switch in front of her to remind her of the consequences of doing so.

And now the moment was here. It was difficult to tell who was most excited: Ginny, May Rose, or the elders.

The Crazy African Sisters were dressed in their finest Kente cloths with matching headwraps. They were adorned with beautiful necklaces, bracelets, and ankle jewelry made with colored glass beads and cowrie shells, plus what looked like human teeth. May Rose was dressed identical to them. It had been a while since she donned clothing to represent her heritage, and it made her feel good. Proud, even.

May Rose was helping Ginny dress for the occasion. Ginny held onto her mother's shoulders to balance while May Rose kneeled in front of her, helping the teenager step into her bed slip. The bed slip was what Ginny and her sisters would sleep in at night or wear under their Sunday dresses. It was made out of a white sheet with elastic that hugged the waist. May Rose made the girls matching little, white shirts. Some she made were just one piece, like a dress.

But the bed slip Ginny wore for her ceremony was special. It was knee-length, made with white satin and white lace on the hem. Dainty, white, satin bows were strategically sewn around the hem. The top of her body remained bare.

"Momma, Daddy is going to get you," Ginny said. "He thinks we're catching a baby tonight two towns over for a white missy."

May Rose, her mother, and her aunts were all midwives. Learning to "catch babies" was part of the African culture and part of a woman's business. Now that Ginny was a teenager, she would also become a midwife. She'd already been in training for a couple months. Prior to training, Ginny always pictured the babies shooting out the womb and across the room, then the midwives having to catch them like an umpire catches unhit balls. But even after having helped catch three babies already, it still wasn't that much short of what she'd imagined. The baby didn't shoot across the room, but some of those babies shot out their mother's womb all the same.

May Rose shooed off her oldest daughter's comment with the flick of her hand and continued making sure nothing was out of place on Ginny's big day. She stood up and gave Ginny the once-over. She then licked her index and middle fingers, using the saliva to pat down a piece of Ginny's hair that was, in fact, out of place. "Girl, hush about that. Besides, he has the other two girls to distract him," May Rose said. "Now go on." This time, May Rose shooed Ginny with a loving push. "They're ready for you."

Ginny turned away, heading in the direction of a ring of fire made out of dried cowhide and grass that the elders had been setting up. Not fully knowing what to anticipate made Ginny pause her steps. She allowed her mind to travel back to the conversation she'd had with her mother moments before.

"There is nothing to be afraid about," May Rose had said. "You'll experience some things you might not understand, but it will all make sense in the end."

Sensing Ginny's hesitation, May Rose stepped up close behind her. So close, Ginny couldn't tell if it was her mother's breath or fear of the unexpected making the hair rise on the back of her neck.

May Rose placed her hands as strategically on Ginny's shoulders as she'd placed the satin bows on the bed slip. She held on gently and whispered in her ear, "You heard me. I said get. You got this." She pushed Ginny away by her shoulders. On the outside looking in, one might have thought she was angry. The real fact of the matter was that May Rose was struggling to keep her eyes from filling with tears. She couldn't push Ginny away soon enough so that she could tend to wiping the disobedient ones that insisted on showing on her face.

Ginny slowly walked away into the arms of her elders, which consisted of Nana and Nana's two sisters. May Rose quickly brushed her tears away before they could escape her eyes and immediately took to the drum.

The elders carefully led Ginny through a small opening in the circle. They helped her lie down in the center of the fire ring while they remained standing.

The drum, called a Djembe in Africa, was said to consist of three spirits—the spirit of the tree as the body, the spirit of the animal whose skin covered the drum, and the spirit of the drum maker. It was used as a source of communication and could be heard from long distances. May Rose beat the drum during the ceremony to notify the ancestors that another girl-child had crossed over into womanhood

May Rose closed her eyes as if calling on the ancestors for guidance, assistance, and permission to proceed. After a few seconds, she inhaled and then exhaled deeply, taking in and letting out the smell of all the ingredients that made up the rite of passage ceremony.

Smoke.

Incense.

Dirt.

Cinnamon.

Sweat.

And even tears.

May Rose opened her eyes and began beating the hand drum.

Thump. Her left hand hit the goat skin of which the drum was made.

Thump. Her left hand again.

Thump. Now her right.

Thump. Her right hand again.

Then her left. Left. Right. Left.

Slow at first. Then faster every few thumps.

The rhythm was hypnotic.

The elders began doing the cheerful Apatampa dance. They started off by slapping their hands on their thighs twice. On the third beat, they clapped piercingly twice. They then raised their arms and began to wave their hands in the air. This was repeated several times. Next, they began to moan a deep myste-rious moan. It was as if they were communicating in a language that only the spirits could interpret.

Once the moaning started, Ginny was sweating and shaking. The sweat could have been from fear of the unknown or the heat from the fire. Whatever the cause, the effect was glistening beads of perspiration sliding down her body and onto the ground. The wetness formed a small puddle beneath her. Ginny's body trembled in sync with the rhythm of both the drum and the women's hips.

Sangaré threw some seeds in the air. Some escaped over the fire, while the majority landed at Ginny's feet, which was the intended target. At Sangaré's right foot was a bucket full of goat blood, which she butchered earlier that day for dinner. The three dancing women went down to their knees near the fire and began rubbing the goat blood all over Ginny's chest, arms, and legs. Their dripping sweat mixed with the blood, but they did not flinch even once from the heat of the fire.

Sangaré started praying, powerful and bold. "Dear God, we bring before you another one of our girl-children. Please give her the spirit, strength, and courage to uphold herself, family, community, and nation. Please let her clearly understand a woman's job will allow her to rule her temple in order to protect her temple. Please give her your kingdom knowledge to pass it down to all of the women generations behind her. God of all heavens, please accept our Ginny into womanhood."

The elders began chanting like they were in gut-wrenching pain.

"Praise God," Sangaré concluded. She then spat at the fire.

From Ginny's vantagepoint, the flame rose as high as Nana's house, as the ceremony was taking place in the back woods right behind the little house the Crazy African Sisters resided in.

After the flame was reduced, May Rose threw water over it. As part of the ceremony, buckets of water were kept on hand to put out the flames and to clean the blood off the girl-child for whom the ceremony was being performed.

The women stripped Ginny of her bed slip, drenched her with water, and then helped her to her feet.

Ginny stood still with her arms straight down at her sides. Bocoum started draping strands of orange beads, seeds, shells, and teeth around Ginny's small waist, then tied them in place.

Diallo said aloud with power in her voice, "Abdebowale." She bestowed Ginny's ancestral name upon her. "Our ancestors said that your name shall be Abdebowale. The crown has come home."

"Abdebowale," Ginny said softly under her breath to acknowledge it. "Abdebowale," she repeated to accept it.

"You have been directed by our God of all ages to return to your native land of Ghana," Bocoum said. "You are to leave something of all of your elders behind since we have not been able to return."

Abdebowale was sitting on what looked like a wooden throne. She remained there, sitting in complete stillness, as the elders began circling while singing.

"No man will own your temple," they sang as May Rose hit the drum. "You are always in control. In the end, you will rule. You will rule. You will rule."

As their voices faded, so did the sound of the drum. Each elder stopped dancing.

Bocoum bent over and whispered to Abdebowale, "So, it is done."

Sangaré confidently boasted, "I see you mastering the woman job." She winked at Abdebowale and smirked at May Rose. As the closing of the ceremony neared, Sangaré stood in front of Abdebowale with the other ladies alongside her. Sangaré began recounting the history of the waist beads adornment. "This, child," she started, fingering some of the beads between her fingers, "is deeply rooted in the Ghanian culture. These particular beads signify womanhood, spirituality, sensuality, beauty, social and wealth status, on top of being a reminder of your body size." She looked into Abdebowale's eyes. "You will feel when you have eaten too much. The strands will start to tighten." She slightly pulled on the waist beads to show Abdebowale how little room she had.

Abdebowale nodded her understanding.

"You must stop eating as soon as the strand starts feeling tight." She grabbed Abdebowale's face and squeezed her cheeks tightly before declaring forcefully, "Not after the next bite of fried pork chop, but right then and there. You stop!" She softened her body language and her tone. "You must wear at least three strands at all times, but you can wear as many as you desire. Most of all, no man should ever touch them. No matter how good he makes you feel, he must not touch them. You control that part of your body. That's your job as a woman."

A woman's business had existed and was passed down in May Rose's family for more generations than could be documented. Abdeowale had taken so much in and honestly had no idea of some of the things Sangaré and the other elders had instilled in her. Yet everything had been relayed to her with deep emotion and intensity, as if life depended on it. Not just Abdebowale's life, but every woman's life for generations to come. Abdeowale would be sure to ask her mother to further explain and clarify her grandmother and great-aunts' words.

As the ceremony ended, Sangaré gave Abdebowale some final instructions. "Child, you have two weeks from tomorrow to gather all the questions that will be dancing about your pretty little head about what just happened here this evening, and what it means to the future." She bent down and gently grabbed Abdebowale by the chin. "And the future of any other girl-child that come out of that there womb of yours." She used the same hand that had just gripped Abdebowale's chin to point at her lower stomach. Sangaré stood up straight. "And you have that same amount of time to prepare for part two of the ceremony."

Olawale stepped in. "There will be questions answered." She nodded to her oldest daughter and gave her a reassuring look that she'd be there to answer them. "Baby, go think about your questions."

"And don't say you don't have any," Olawale said. "All women do." She gave Abdebowale a disapproving look. "Then try answering them yourself. God has given you the smarts of your African ancestors. If you don't have answers to some questions, that will be fine. But when we meet in two weeks, we will go over all your questions and answers."

Abdebowale nodded her understanding.

"Do not be surprised by your questions or answers. You're now beginning to think like a woman," Olawale said.

May Rose said, "We'll have more and plenty of womanly discussions." She then leaned in and reiterated, "Don't say a word to your sisters at all if you don't want to feel the sting of the strap."

Once again, Abdebowale nodded her understanding.

May Rose and Ginny cleaned up and changed from their ceremony clothing back into their regular clothes. They gave their good-bye hugs and kisses to the elders, and everyone departed in their respective directions. The sun was coming up as Ginny and May Rose started walking up the dirt road to their house. Ginny had her arm around her mother's waist as they walked. This was the first time she felt May Rose's waist beads to know what they actually were. Every time she'd asked as a child, she was always told, "Your time will come." And indeed, it had.

Ginny grabbed her mother tighter as they walked through the door. She was bursting with excitement, but she was also shaking from the inside out. Her head was spinning with the thought of keeping a secret from her younger sisters and her father. Her mind was also flooded with some of the questions she would ask for part two of the ceremony. Some of the questions were so grownup that she worried her mother would be angry at a girl-child even having such thoughts. But she wasn't a child. Ginny was a woman now.

The first person to meet them when they walked in the door was Florence, who had been peeking out of the living room window, waiting to see them coming up the road. She was grinning from ear-to-ear. The mischievous look on her face hinted that even though Willie may have bought their story about catching babies for some white lady, perhaps Florence hadn't.

Ginny had already expressed her concerns to her mother about Florence having some type of sixth sense.

"All the while I was packing my clothes for the ceremony," Ginny had told May Rose worriedly as they headed toward the elders' little house so Ginny could get dressed, "Florence kept giving me this look. Like she knew we wasn't going to catch no babies."

May Rose wasn't worried at all, telling Ginny, "Let your little sister think whatever she wants, but it will be your tail if you confirm it."

So, Ginny brushed off her paranoia and acted normal.

Florence had a look of anticipation on her face as if she just knew Ginny was going to tell her what her and May Rose had really been up to. Little did she know, Ginny was sworn to secrecy. Florence would just have to wait another year until it was her turn to enter into womanhood. Plus, in Ginny's mind, she wasn't into small talk with little girls. Not when she was now a woman.

"About time two of the most beautiful women in my life made their way back home," Willie said, coming out of the kitchen with a glass of whiskey. He kissed May Rose on the lips. "And I just know, woman, you got some damn money for a new hog as long as your ass been gone catching babies." He smiled and winked at his wife.

"You pipe down, old man." May Rose playfully pushed Willie on his chest.

"Oh, never mind me," he said. "I'm in a mood because we had to listen to them crazy bitches in the back doing that African shit they do."

Ginny was used to her daddy complaining and fussing about her Nana and her aunts, but now it hit her differently. Before, Willie's words would roll off her back, but this time, they stuck to her chest like glue. "Now, Daddy, that is not nice. They are Africans, and we are part African just like them."

May Rose pushed Ginny back a few steps. "Don't you go minding her," she said to Willie with a flirty smile. She then shot Ginny a knowing look. "It's just going to be a matter of time before I'm going to have a serious talk with you, Ginny, about that sassy mouth of yours."

"But, Momma—" Ginny started before May Rose cut her a look that threatened the switch would get pulled out if she did not catch on and play along. Ginny took a step back from the fight she was about to put up.

May Rose continued to play out her strategy, turning her attention back to her husband. At that moment, she told Willie,

"And for you, mister…" She planted her nail in the middle of Willie's chest. This time, not so playful. "I have told you before to keep my family's names out of your drunken mouth."

By then, Lynette came into the front room. Her eyes were as big as the moon that lit up the dawn sky as she wiped the sleep out of them. "What's going on in here?" she asked.

"Mind your business and your manners," May Rose told her youngest daughter. "And how many times have I told you to stay out of grown folks' business? What you doing up out of bed anyway? You should be calling hogs." She looked at Florence. "You, too, missy."

Willie took the conversation right back to where he'd left off with it. "I built that house back there on my land that your people just live on."

"Your land?" May Rose screamed. "I took care of your mammy until she took her last breath. She left that land to the both of us. Not just you," May Rose spat. "This here is *our* land."

This was a fight Willie and May Rose had had a hundred times, and all the past hundred times, it ended the same. With May Rose putting Willie on Front Street about how she cared for his sick momma while he cared for the whiskey bottle. And he had no reason to believe the hundred and first time would pan out any different. He threw the last of his whiskey down his throat and then raised his arms, letting them fall to his side in defeat.

"I tried," Willie said. "Can't say nothing 'bout this woman's people without her going all up in arms." He shook his head. "I'm going to bed." He turned back in the direction from which he'd come.

"Same here," May Rose said.

"I'll be damned if you do," Willie spat over his shoulder. "You're taking your ass in that kitchen and fix me and these children breakfast."

"That sho nuff must have been moonshine in that glass," May Rose said with an attitude, throwing her hands on her hips. "Moonshine somebody done pissed in and got your mind crazy. 'Cause you sure talking crazy. I'm going to bed." May Rose was exhausted, as if she really had been up all night helping somebody give birth to a baby. But that had never stopped her from taking care of her man—taking care of her family— before. So, everyone in that room knew that she was going to bed, but not until after she went in the kitchen and prepared breakfast.

Florence and Ginny turned and looked at each other.

Ginny mumbled under her breath to Florence, "Nana is going to hit the roof when she hears how Daddy just talked to Momma, and how she accepted it."

"Not if she don't know," Florence mumbled back. "Besides, Momma always do what Daddy says. Those her wifely duties." The latter was something she'd heard May Rose say on occasion.

"Yeah, but it ain't a woman's business," Ginny said, then had to remind herself that there was no need going back and forth with her sister. Florence was still thinking like a child. And Ginny was a woman. Her rite of passage ceremony into womanhood had just proved it.

"No woman should take that from a man is what Nana would say." Ginny couldn't help but express the thought aloud in a whisper to her little sister. And as if the spirits were controlling her, she couldn't help expressing it to her father as well. "Man, don't you have no respect for your woman?"

Ginny had been known to be fly at the mouth. Heck, all the girls had. Something Willie blamed on the Crazy African

Sisters. But even that comment took everyone in the room by surprise.

Willie balled his fist and looked at May Rose. "Rose, this girl keeps trying me."

And trying Willie, indeed, Ginny was.

Ginny struggled with treating Willie like a real daddy since so many seeds had been planted in her heart that he wasn't. On top of that, Ginny simply felt that Willie treated her differently, especially when he got to drinking. May Rose had told her time and time again not to let what Nana and her sisters said—and more importantly, what Florence teased her about—get the best of her.

But at the same time, Ginny's comeback would be, "You know what Nana says about a drunken tongue. A drunken tongue speaks a sober mind."

Nonetheless, May Rose did her best to keep the peace.

"Willie, you just go on to bed," May Rose said, walking over to Ginny and grabbing her by the arm. "I'll handle this one right here. You go on now, Willie, and I'll go on in the kitchen and get breakfast started." May Rose feigned a smile while she tightly gripped Ginny's arm.

"But, Momma," Ginny started.

"'But, Momma' my ass," May Rose murmured through gritted teeth. She then shot a hard whisper into Ginny's ear. "I'm going into the kitchen more so out of not wanting you to get your smart ass beat by your daddy, not because I'm following orders."

Smelling herself, a bit more than she ought to, Ginny shot back, "Momma, if that man even tries to lay a finger on me, let alone a whole hand, I will run out back to Nana and the elders' house and tell 'em everything that's going on right now."

May Rose might not have believed that Ginny would make such a threat, but what she did believe was that Ginny would see the threat through. And she knew what that meant. It meant that the Crazy African Sisters would call up spirits from hell, if need be, to remove Willie from her and the children's lives.

"Ginny, what are you trying to do to your daddy, my husband?" May Rose whispered, shaking Ginny's arm. "Lord have mercy on this man if you go get them old biddies involved."

May Rose was right, which was why Ginny had made the threat in the first place.

But not wanting to ruin what would be the most memorable day in Ginny's life, May Rose decided to continue trying to keep the peace. "Let's consider it your celebration breakfast," she whispered. Her grip turned into a soft squeeze. "How's that sound?" She softly brushed the back of her hand down Ginny's cheek.

Ginny put a winning smile on her face. "I think breakfast sounds good after all, Momma."

> *"It is the women who make some men succeed*
> *where others fail."*
>
> African Proverb

Chapter 3

CLOSED MOUTHS GET US FED

May Rose hummed while making the biggest breakfast she could gather up. She fried some catfish, boiled some hominy grits, fried potatoes, toasted some freshly baked bread in the wood stove, and made some homemade peach preserve she had just canned a couple of days ago.

Willie went and lay back on the bed in his drawers and tee-shirt. All three of the girls remained in the kitchen to help their mother. Each girl did their part in helping May Rose, except for Ginny. She was too busy huffing and puffing about how Willie had tried to ruin her special day.

"What's so special about it?" Florence asked as she set the table. "Feels like just another day to me?" She shrugged and continued her task.

May Rose shot Ginny a look of death as she put her index finger over her lips, reminding her to keep her mouth shut about the ceremony.

"Momma, you know a woman's job," Ginny said. "I'm not sure of all what it is yet, but I'll bet you it's not this." She looked around the kitchen with a frown.

"Ginny, go hang those wet clothes on the line until I call for you for breakfast," May Rose said, assigning her oldest daughter a task that would get her out of her hair and out of the kitchen. Limiting the chances of her slipping up and saying something about the ceremony.

Ginny rolled her eyes and headed for the back door.

Before Ginny could get to it, May Rose grabbed her and whispered in her ear, "Nana or none of the other sisters better not hear about what just went on in my house. You hear?" She stared Ginny in the eyes.

Ginny giggled. "Then you better grab the other two up along with me." Her eyes darted from Florence to Lynette. "They're the ones more likely to run their mouths."

"Whatever." May Rose turned her loose. "You heard what I said."

Ginny stomped toward the door, and May Rose went back to cooking, but the teenager turned and paused before exiting, watching her mother do whatever it took to care for her man and children. Although a part of Ginny pitied her mother for going against everything she'd just been taught and would be taught about the role of a woman, she envied her, too. In spite of what everyone thought, she was a wife and mother first. And something told Ginny it was probably tougher than just being a woman.

She abruptly ran over and kissed May Rose on the cheek.

Her mother halted in shock. "Ginny." She rubbed the very spot her daughter had just planted a loving kiss. "What was that f…" Her words trailed off because she'd already gotten the answer from Ginny's eyes.

"I love you, Momma," Ginny said. And she didn't even have to wait around to hear her mother say it back. She'd already gotten the answer from May Rose's eyes.

Later that morning, Willie got up from his previous evening's drunken binge. He went into the kitchen, where May
Rose was finishing up breakfast. The girls had gone on to bed
with the promise that their mother would wake them once the
food was served.

Willie blocked his eyes with his hands from the sun that
blared in from the window over the water basin. "Damn it!" He
went and snatched the curtain shut.

May Rose shook her head at the sight of him. "I'm the
damn one cooking breakfast in all of this damn sun. I don't
know what you growling about."

Willie sat at the table and scanned the settings. "What good
is all these plates and utensils laid out if ain't nothing to use
them for? Where the hell is the food?"

May Rose sucked her teeth, put her hands on her hips, and
whipped around. "Breakfast is not all the way done yet, Willie.
What the hell do you want in here? Go on and sit in your chair
or something and get out of my way."

"I ain't even in none of your way," Willie declared hoarsely.
"Besides, I need to talk with you."

"I'm listening." May Rose continued grumbling about Willie's complaining with a complaint of her own. "If you'd see
about this old stove like I been asking you to, maybe it would
get a little hotter and the food would be done."

"You know they have these things called coal mines under-
ground over in West Virgina, right?"

"I believe I have," May Rose assured him as she started placing the food in serving bowls. "But what good is some lump of
coals gon' do us with this here old oven?"

"Will you hush up and just listen up? Damn," Willie huffed.
"They take the colored men over there to go get the coal out of
the mines."

May Rose said sarcastically, "Yes, but I still don't understand what the hell does that have to do with me?"

"Would you miss me in that bed, rubbing on all my good stuff you are carrying around, if I went off and did some work over in them mines?"

May Rose paused. She looked over at her husband to see if she could determine how serious he was. Just what was this man getting at? She wished he'd hurry up and get there already.

"I mean, I would probably come home on most weekends and some holidays. The money is supposed to be favorable." He looked around the kitchen, eyeballing the paint chipping from the ceiling and the loose windowsill over the water basin. "We could fix up around here and get the girls things they need. They can wear pretty dresses to the schoolhouse. You are the schoolteacher, and your daughters dress in scraps. And most importantly, your loudmouth mammy will not be able to say I could be doing better for us."

May Rose remained silent, not sure if Willie was trying to convince her or himself as to whether this was a good opportunity for him and the family.

"What do you say, May Rose?" Willie asked after sitting long enough in her dead silence. When May Rose did not respond, still pondering everything Willie had just dumped on her, he continued. "You'll have to take full charge of this farm on top of all the other things you do." And just in case that wasn't enough, he added the cherry on top. "And never mind fixing that old stove. I'll get you a brand-new one." Willie smiled widely, the brightness of his white teeth hitting May Rose in the face harder than the sun. Thank goodness he was missing a tooth or else he might have blinded her.

May Rose thought about all the work on the farm that Willie currently did that would end up being her chores. They grew cabbage, collard greens, turnip greens, tomatoes, corn, and okra. They had chickens, one cow, and hogs from time to time. Then she thought about what her, as Willie said, "mammy" would think about her working like a mule. She'd probably be disowned not just from the family business, but from the family!

Willie continued with May Rose's verbal to-do list. "And plus, still fit in sewing for Minister Smith and his family, teaching the children in town, catching babies, and most of all, steering our daughters in the right direction." He cleared his throat, figuring since he was on an uninterrupted roll, he might as well keep on rolling. "I have to let the bossman know this evening."

May Rose had been staring off as she took in Willie's words, but now her head snapped up to look at him. "You already been considering it?"

Now it was Willie who had been bitten by the silent bug.

May Rose turned off the stove and went and sat down across from him, the unbalanced table rocking as she did so. She stared out the kitchen window, several thoughts flowing through her mind. She thought the house would be peaceful most of the time with Willie gone, except for the girls making their usual fuss. Her mother and the elders would not have reason to talk negatively about what Willie wasn't financially able to do for the household because he would have extra money from mining. However, he would be leaving all the farmwork to May Rose. Something the elders would definitely frown upon. And it would 100% fall on her because she had to raise hell to get them daughters of hers to work.

Plus, the thought that stayed in front of May Rose's mind was who was going to keep her bed and her body warm at night. After all, Willie was a good-looking man with his wavy mixed-gray head of hair and his long arms and legs. His body of a man in his twenties didn't reflect his true age of forty-one, but neither did the gray hairs. May Rose loved a tall man, and God had blessed him with six feet and seven inches in height. She looked her husband in the eyes, grabbed his hands from across the table, and said, "William H. Jones, we're going to miss you."

Willie exhaled, in shock that May Rose didn't even put on her boxing gloves, let alone put up a fight.

"You're doing this for the betterment of our home. All I can do is support you." She shook his hands. "Just promise me you won't be drinking moonshine under them grounds."

Willie let out a chuckle and pulled his hands from his wife's. "Woman, you crazy." He laughed again and then took on a serious demeanor. "The bossman will be bringing the papers for us to sign this evening."

"Is that so?" May Rose inquired with a raised eyebrow. "How did you know I would agree?"

"Because I know my woman." Willie grabbed May Rose's hands and planted kisses on them.

She started to reminisce back to the day she first laid eyes on Willie. She was in the town's general store picking up some vegetable planting seeds for Mr. Claypool, the old man that her momma and her two aunts lived with at the time. He allowed them to live there as long as they cleaned, cooked, and occasionally allowed him to hump on them. Mr. Claypool, of course, took a liking to the youngest of the women, which was May Rose.

Willie walked into the store, right after May Rose paid for her seeds and was headed out. He stood so tall that he had to duck to get in under the doorway. He stopped, stood right in front of her, and said, "Close your mouth."

May Rose looked around to see who he might have been talking to.

"Yes, I'm talking to you. And, yes, you have just seen the most handsome fellow in Bedford." Willie started popping his collar with a conceited grin that showed all thirty-one of his teeth. "Let me guess, you up in this here store trying to buy some sugar." He leaned down and almost in a whisper said, "Do you want some of this good sugar?" He stood back up tall and winked at her.

May Rose painted a rose-colored smile on her face and then stood toe-to-toe with him. "Listen here, colored boy, you will have dreams about me every night if I let you taste my sweet lips and nightmares when I don't."

Taken aback by May Rose's own confidence and boldness, Willie snapped his neck back and said, "Where you come from, girl? I know every woman in this town, and I ain't ever saw you. Cause I'd remember." He looked May Rose's small frame and small waist up and down while licking his lips. "What man in their right mind could forget a face like that and skin as choco-late as a box cake?"

May Rose feigned shy, slightly blushing. "My African beauty ain't for everyone. So, I keep myself under wraps until the right man comes along and can handle the vision." She licked her lips and batted her eyes, thinking, *If I can rope this one in, Momma would be so proud. He's nice, clean, dressed nice, and looks to have money. Hell, maybe even some land.*

Willie chuckled. "You sure have a strong tongue for such a little girl."

The shopkeeper walked over and tapped Willie on the shoulder, growling, "Willie Jones, pick up the bag of animal feed there on the floor that you came to get." The shopkeeper pointed to the order Willie placed every week. "And take your mannish self out of my store."

Willie did as he was told. "Put it on my credit," he requested.

The shopkeeper turned to face May Rose. "Young lady, I am sure Mr. Claypool would not understand you flirting with Willie." He wagged a disapproving finger at her. "Take those seeds and get on, gal. Do your courting on the outside of my shop."

May Rose went out the door first, and Willie went running behind her. He set the feed down and said, "Miss Claypool with the sweet lips, what's your first name?"

Rose thew her hands on her hips and scolded, "Who the hell told you my last name is Claypool?"

"The shop owner, are you deaf?"

May Rose thought for a moment, then relaxed her face as she giggled. "You hear too much. And don't think you understand everything you hear. My last name ain't no Claypool." May Rose began to walk toward her house.

"Hold up now, pretty lady," Willie called out, doing a light jog to try to catch up. "Can I please come and keep you safe?"

May Rose stopped and grinned, turning around and saying, "Only halfway." She then turned back around and started walking off again. She didn't need him to walk her all the way. It wouldn't take her that long to handle her business.

Willie razzle-dazzled her the entire walk home with their conversation. That should have been the first sign that working Willie was gonna be trouble.

"Guess we need to wake the girls up and tell them."

Willie's words pulled May Rose out of her daydream.

"Yeah, I guess we should," she replied.

He joked, "That little smart-ass crazy African-acting Ginny will be over in the back with the rest of the crazy Africans jumping up and down once we tell them."

May Rose laughed. "Ginny loves you, Willie. She is going through her woman thing right now, which makes her a little mean."

"No, that makes her a decedent of your mammy," Willie said.

"Well, if that's what it is, then I hate to tell you, but we got two more coming up right behind her."

"Then I suppose working away from home couldn't have come at a better time."

May Rose pulled her hands from Willie's. "Go on and wash up to get ready for breakfast. Get those girls up, too." She held her head down in sadness as Willie walked away. She glanced up after she felt his breeze go past her bare legs.

She stood, paused for a moment, and then started to swing her body from left to right. Within seconds, she was in an all-out dance. She danced around in a small circle and whispered, "My ass is going to be dancing with Ginny and the Crazy African Sisters, too." She burst out laughing and said, "Ginny, baby, Momma just might be teaching you more about a woman's business than you thought."

"A fish and a bird may fall in love, but the two cannot build a home together."

African Proverb

Chapter 4

❧

THE CEREMONY CONT.

*I*t had been over a week since Willie went off to the coal mine. Back at the Jones home, just like he suspected, Ginny and the Crazy African Sisters celebrated the African way about the news of him leaving for extended periods of time. What he would be surprised to know was that May Rose and the other two girls joined in the celebration.

"If I'm being honest," Florence said to Lynette as they sat off on the side eating some jollof rice and fish stew that Nana made for the celebration dinner, "I'm going to miss Daddy."

"Me too," Lynette said.

Florence snapped her neck to the side and gave her little sister the side-eye. "Then why was you just dancing and clapping a minute ago with everyone else?"

Lynette shot back the same confused look. "Same reason you was, I suppose. It's a celebration. Ain't that what we supposed to do at a celebration? Celebrate?"

The girls stared at each other for a few seconds more and then each started chuckling, sounding like two wild hyenas.

The next day, it was a cool and rainy Saturday morning. Ginny was in her bedroom with her writing tools and paper on the floor. She continued adding to her list of questions and answers for the second part of her ceremony, which was happening in a couple days.

Not only did Ginny simply feel more grownup since her ceremony, but she even looked more grownup. She took more care with her hair, taking her time to gently brush through it instead of rapidly racking through it in order to hurry up and go play what she now referred to as 'childish games.' She even sat on the floor differently. Before, she might have sprawled out no differently than a boy—flat on her belly, legs spread as far apart as they possibly could, even if she were wearing a dress. But now, she sat on her bottom, feet cupped under her behind and back arched as straight as it could be while she leaned slightly over to write.

Whether it was mental or the ancestors called upon during her ceremony watching over her, reminding her, and shaping her into the woman she now was, Ginny had grown in maturity and become more aware of her femininity in just a matter of days.

There was a loud knock on the front door. It was so loud that Ginny jerked her head with fear, so startled that she dropped her writing utensil.

May Rose had been in the outhouse but was making her way back into the main house when she, too, heard the knock on the front door.

Ginny slowly headed down the steps, wondering who was making such a ruckus.

May Rose had entered the back through the kitchen and was drying her damp hands on her apron. Her waist-length flowing hair looked happy and free to be out of its usual everyday bun.

She spotted Ginny coming down the steps through the doorway. "Who is it?" she yelled.

"I dunno," Ginny spat, a bit irritated that a caller was interrupting her writing. She reached the front door and put her hand on the doorknob to open it.

"Child, you betta not just open the front door without knowing who it is."

"It's probably just Nana."

"Momma and my aunts do not knock that way. It is not them," May Rose said, coming through the kitchen and into the living room. "Plus, I would have seen them coming from the back because I was just out back." May Rose had moved through the kitchen and toward the living room so fast, she was out of breath.

Despite her warning and order for Ginny not to open the door, it was too late.

The knob was turned.

The door was open.

"Greetings, beautiful Jones ladies," the uninvited guest announced, walking inside with the rickety screen slamming behind them.

The apron dropped from May Rose's hands. She stopped in her tracks as if she'd seen a ghost. The only time their uninvited guest ever showed up at their doorstep was to deliver bad news.

"Is everything okay?" May Rose asked in a panic. She took a hesitant step forward. "Is First Lady Ramona all right? Is the baby all right? Is it ready to come?" May Rose took another step, this one with more intention. "Good Lord, did it come already?"

"Calm down now, Mrs. Jones," said their guest. "Everything is fine." He removed his slightly worn black hat and did a half-bow, one toward May Rose and the other toward Ginny.

"Hello, Minister Smith," Ginny greeted, eager to head back to her writing. Normally, she would have hung around as long as she could before May Rose kicked her out, warning her to "stay out of grown folks' business."

"You sure all is well?" May Rose asked before deciding to completely let her guard down and treat Minister Smith's visit like a regular call.

Minister Smith's teeth lit up his entire face, as they looked extra white against his dark skin that always stayed good and shiny. Nana and her sisters would joke that "Minister's skin so glossy, you'd think the man bathes in cooking lard."

And in that very moment, May Rose had to secure the chuckle that remained lodged in her throat just thinking about her elders' words. She swallowed the laugh and then looked up at the very tall man, waiting for his response.

"No, no, no, Rosie, she is fine for now," Minister Smith reassured her, "but it seems like it could be any day we'll need you to come by and catch that little one stewing in her belly." Minister Smith let out a hearty laugh.

"Then if all is well," Ginny said, "I bid you farewell, Minister Smith." She turned to head back to her room and finished preparing her questions.

"I'll see you at Sunday school?" Minister Smith called out to Ginny's back.

"Yes, sir, you will," Ginny shot over her shoulder. As she walked past her mother, she mumbled under her breath, "Rosie," mocking the minister. She then made a kissy face, switched by, and went back to her room.

If their God-fearing guest hadn't been standing smack in the middle of the living room, May Rose would have given her eldest child a smack right in the middle of her tail. But the last thing she wanted to do was show her own tail in front of her minister. With her attention back on their guest and the fact that he was there on a social call since nothing was going on with the missus, May Rose began patting and fixing her hair, something lots of women did subconsciously whenever someone of the opposite sex was in sight.

"So, uh, yes, Minister Smith," May Rose stuttered, "how may I help you, sir?"

He answered in a serious tone as he rocked back and forth from heels to toes. "Willie came by the house before he left."

May Rose's eyes widened. "Is that so?" She nervously began messing in her hair again. "What did he want?"

"Yeah, we prayed together," Minister Smith confirmed.

May Rose exhaled.

"He also asked me to check on you and the family from time to time. So, here I am. Checking on the family." Minister Smith smiled.

"How thoughtful of my Willie," May Rose said. "And how kind of you to do so."

"The pleasure is, indeed, all mine." Minister Smith gave another charming smile and nodded. "And there was one other thing we talked about I feel led to share with you."

"Oh?" May Rose said, wondering what on earth Minister Smith could have talked to Willie about.

Willie had done a bit of celebrating himself before he headed off. She wondered if it was Willie who had been doing the talking to Minister Smith or the moonshine. God only knew what words could have come out of Willie's mouth. God and Minister Smith, of course. And now May Rose would know, too, as Minister Smith proceeded to inform her.

"Yep, he told me that when I did come see about you and the girls, to make sure I stay away from the Crazy African Sisters."

All May Rose could do was exhale deeply before she feigned a childish giggle.

Minister Smith, on the other hand, had cracked himself up and laughter erupted from his throat. He went on to say, "You know our church anniversary is next Sunday." He gazed up as if he was staring at the heavens. "It was founded fifty-five years ago," he said proudly. He then looked back down at May Rose. "Me and the missus would like you and your family to be the special guests at our table at Sunday's anniversary picnic after service. You, Willie, the girls…" He cupped his hand around his mouth and leaned closer to May Rose. "…and even your momma and her sisters." He laughed once again as he stood up straight. "I mean, you all do so much for our community. You catch all the babies here and two towns over. The elders do the healing. You teach at the schoolhouse. And ya always sewing garments for me, Sister Ramona, and all six children of ours."

May Rose blushed, mighty proud to hear all she and her family were doing for their neighbors. "It's nothing." She crossed her arms down in front of her, cupped her hands together, and started swinging her body from left to right like a schoolgirl.

"Your children, your momma, and your aunts go and press all the women's and young gals' hair in our community. Why, May Rose, we'd be shamed not to honor you at this special occasion."

"Thank you, Minister Smith," May Rose said. "I'm mighty fond of such an acknowledgement."

"You deserve it. 'Specially when it comes to sewing and all." He chuckled. "You use potato sacks from the general store and scraps from your paying customers to sew for yourself and your family. I don't think the town could survive without you all. Y'all are like a whole business, you know?"

And how did May Rose know.

"Matter of fact, you know what?" He threw his fists to his waist. "Go on and get ready. I'll be back in one hour." He leaned in proudly with his eyes closed as he said, "I'm taking you to the dress shop downtown to pick out dresses, hats, and shoes for everyone to wear to the anniversary." He opened his eyes with a huge grin as he stood erect. "We can even grab ole Willie a new suit and shoes in case he is able to make it back to town."

May Rose's mouth dropped open in shock. Before she could refuse the offer, Minister Smith continued. "Please let your momma know we are going to town. If my baby number seven needs catching while we are gone, she'll need to tend to it."

May Rose smiled and said, "You don't have a thing to worry about. Tell your children to run to get Momma right away if help is needed."

"I'll do just that." He turned and started walking away. "Rosie, set your timer for one hour now." He held up his index finger for good measure. "Because I'll be back in an hour on the dot."

May Rose rushed past Minister Smith so that she could open the door for him. "Yes, Minister."

He sauntered ahead and had to brush past her, who was holding the screen door open for him.

She couldn't help but close her eyes and inhale the scent of his cologne. She thought he smelled as good as he looked. Six feet and four inches, with jet-black hair that laid back straight with a part on the side. He had a mustache and sideburns, along with a broad chest and back just like an oak tree. And according to the way May Rose's woman-parts were responding, not just any ole oak tree but one she would love to climb and wrap her legs around. And even slide back down.

May Rose's nipples hardened when he brushed against her breasts as he walked out the door.

"I'm so sorry for being in your way, Minister Smith," she said bashfully.

Minister Smith looked May Rose in the eyes. "There is no need to apologize in your house." He turned around and placed his hat back on his head. "One hour," he reminded her.

"One hour," she repeated as she watched him turn on his heels and trot off the porch.

She exhaled, closed the door, and then leaned back against it. "Lord, have mercy." She started fanning herself.

Once May Rose pivoted to walk toward the back of the house, she heard snickers and giggles. She then heard a whisper that sounded like Ginny. "One, two, three."

All three of the girls shouted, "Rosie!"

May Rose squealed. "You all are some silly-ass geese. Get on out of here." With one hand on her hip, May Rose used the other to start swatting at the girls.

Lynette hollered, "Quack, quack, Momma." She started flapping her arms like wings. "I'm a geese."

"It's goose, silly girl," May Rose said. "When it's only one, it's just a goose."

Lynette quacked and flapped over to her mother. "Then I'm a silly goose."

"That you are, little girl." May Rose smiled and bent over to rub her nose against Lynette's. "That you are." She stood up and started fussing and shooing at all the girls. "Go on and mind your business. Doing whatever you were doing before you got into mine."

"Aww, Momma." Lynette pouted.

"'Aww, Momma,' nothing. Get on," May Rose said as the girls fled.

She skipped over to the kitchen stove like a schoolgirl and set the hourglass. She then went into the washroom, where her bath water awaited her. She had drawn hot water from the cast-iron potbelly stove and warmed her water prior to heading to the outhouse. She'd only planned on doing her business and then running back inside to finish bathing, but she got distracted with Minister Smith coming over unannounced.

She put a couple drops of perfume into the water. It was the bottle her mother gave to her, which she had received from the white man that had taken a liking to her. Nana complained so much about the smell of the bottle Willie had gifted May Rose for her past birthday, she gave this one to her.

"Man can't even pick out a bottle of smell-good for you right," Nana had complained when she handed over her own perfume.

"Damn!" May Rose said, stepping into the chilly water. She slowly sank in, getting her body used to the cold temperature one inch at a time until she was totally submerged. She didn't have time to warm it if she was going to be ready when Minister Smith returned.

May Rose leaned her head against the back of the bathing pot and closed her eyes. Within seconds, she was replaying visions of her brief encounter with Minister Smith in her head.

His bright smile.

His beautiful teeth.

His dark, smooth skin.

The way he stood tall and mighty.

"Girl, what is wrong with you?" she asked herself, opening her eyes. "Stop lusting over another woman's husband." She shook her head. "Plus, you have a husband of your own. He's a man of God. May Rose, do not make a fool of yourself. And don't give the good Lord no more reason to send you to hell." May Rose laughed at her one-way conversation and began washing.

She lathered her hands with soap and began cleaning her body with her sudsy palms. She started with her shoulders then made her way down to her breasts. Once again, her eyes were closed and before she knew it, she wasn't just washing her breasts, she was caressing them...to the tune of the scene of her and Minister Smith playing in her head.

"It would be so amazing to have a man touch me like this," May Rose whispered with desire lacing her words.

May Rose enjoyed her husband's touch but felt it was always a little rough. "Willie pulls and tugs on me like a hunk of wood," she would say.

She stood up out of the water and twisted her beads around her waist. Once standing, the water was up to her lower calves. She picked up the sponge and began drying herself off. The locks of hair that had escaped her bun were dripping wet on the ends. The sponge brushed down her breasts, and she compared it to Minister Smith brushing by her just a few moments ago.

A loud, sudden crack of thunder shook May Rose out of her indecent thoughts. She looked up to the heavens. "Alright, already. I hear you, God." She laughed, then stepped out of the bath to get dressed. She decided to put on a dress made with some of that burlap Minister Smith had complimented her on being able to make her own dresses from. The design, details, and structure were so perfect, it looked store-bought and as if it were made with regular clothing fabric.

"Girls, I'm going to be heading out soon," May Rose shouted.

A few seconds later, Ginny peeked her head from her room. "We know, Momma... I mean, Rosie."

"You trying to lose your teeth, little girl?" May Rose asked. "Then you'll really be looking like your daddy."

Ginny made her way to the top of the steps, laughing the entire time. "How did you say Daddy lost his tooth again?"

"I didn't," May Rose said sharply, "but nice try."

Whenever Ginny went fishing around about Willie's missing tooth, she never even got a bite, let alone the fish.

So, Ginny's reply was going back to her room and slamming the door behind her.

"Those damn girls and their mouths," May Rose murmured, shaking her head. "If they ain't take nothing else after their grandmomma, it was that mouth of hers."

She headed to the kitchen and walked over to her timer. With a few minutes to spare, she looked at the window over the stove.

"The sky done opened up." It was pouring rain. She looked down at her open-toed shoes and then out the window again, specifically to see if puddles had formed, which plenty had. The last thing she wanted was to get mud all over her feet and in her toenails. She looked at her feet again. She didn't want to muddy up Minister Smith's black 1925 Model T-Ford Coupe automobile either. He was the only colored man in the community to own one. As a member of the Black Southern Baptist Convention, it was gifted to him. They took loving care of their preachers.

May Rose stood in the kitchen, indecisive about what shoes to wear. Her anticipation of her outing with Minister Smith was starting to get the best of her. She hadn't been out and about the town with a man besides Willie in as long as she could remember. Not only that, but she'd never ridden in an automobile, not one like Minister Smith's, and she never thought the day would come where she would.

"Momma's got a boyfriend. Momma's got a boyfriend."

Florence's teasing pulled May Rose from her thoughts.

Next, Ginny blurted out, "Momma's got a boyfriend."

May Rose rolled her eyes and replied, "Yes, I do got a boyfriend. Your damn daddy!" She stuck out her tongue at the girls.

The girls giggled as May Rose swept past them and headed up the steps to her bedroom. The girls followed her.

May Rose started fussing with her hair as she bent over her foot chest, looking for the only pair of black church shoes she owned. The only pair of closed-toe shoes. She jabbered, "Momma always says, 'A husband should make sure his woman has assorted pairs of shoes even if he doesn't have but one pair himself.' I am starting to understand what she meant." She held the church shoes and stared at them. "I should have understood this clearly before now."

"Nana and the elders don't skimp on details," Ginny said. "I'm sure they must have made it clear, Momma."

May Rose looked up at Ginny and then back at the shoes. "Yeah, they did. But that Willie made me fall." She exhaled in regret, but she kept her thoughts in her mind. *Once my babies complete their coming-of-age ceremonies, I will make sure they understand what they must require from a man often.*

May Rose closed the chest and went to sit at the makeshift vanity Willie made out of some old crates. Another piece of furniture in their home that needed upgrading.

May Rose lit up with excitement. Ginny and Florence gave each other a look and a grin.

"Don't be making no faces," May Rose said. "I'm just excited that we all getting new fits and shoes is all."

"Mmhmm, Momma. We know," Ginny said. The girls giggled again.

"Ahh," May Rose said, snapping her finger as she jumped up from the vanity table, remembering something her mother had taught her to do. The same bottle of perfume she used to scent her bath she used to put a few drops on the front neck trim of her dress and on the back hem.

"Momma why are you putting smell-good on the bottom of the back of your dress?" she laughed.

"A gentleman always allows a lady to go first," May Rose started, then realized Lynette and Florence were just as tuned into her words as Ginny was. And what she had to say was only for Ginny's ears. "Florence and Lynette, go look out for Minister Smith for me, would you? I wouldn't want to miss him calling and have you girls miss out on new dresses."

The girls gladly galloped out, leaving May Rose and Ginny to themselves.

Ginny stood with arms crossed and toe tapping. "Now that the *girls* are gone, can you finish telling me about the business and why we gotta put that perfume all over us?"

May Rose shook her head. "Woo, girl, you don't miss a thing, do you?"

"Nope, not now that I'm not a girl anymore but a woman," Ginny replied matter-of-factly.

May Rose rolled her eyes. "Anyway," she continued, "like I was saying, child, a gentleman will always allow a lady to go first." She did a little sashay. "And when he does…" She bent down in Ginny's face and got real serious, repeating words her mother had shared with her. "The men will smell you with every step you take coming and going. They will be curious to get to know you because of your beauty and your scent."

With her closed-toe black church shoes on, and smelling as fresh as a bouquet of roses, May Rose headed down to the kitchen with Ginny on her heels.

"Let me grab my umbrella, hat, and coat and get to the door." As she did just that, she said, "I don't want to make him wait." As soon as she picked up her coat, there was a soft knock at the door.

The girls started jumping up and down, screaming.

"Momma, I want a yellow dress," Lynette said.

"Momma, I want a pink one," cried Florence.

"You two want baby colors," Ginny said. "I want a purple dress to show my royalty, Momma."

May Rose winked at Ginny, approving her choice in color.

"If you all do not let me get out this door, no one will get any color." May Rose hurried over, patting down her dress while calling out, "Coming, Minister Smith."

With the girls on her coattails, May Rose opened the door, and there he stood with his hat in his hand, carrying an umbrella. The wind from the door opening waved his aftershave straight to May Rose's nose. She unknowingly smiled, which showed all her teeth. May Rose noticed Minister Smith was freshly shaven.

"Timeliness is godliness," he said.

"I thought it was cleanliness," May Rose corrected.

Minister Smith thought for a moment. "I'd say it's both. Wouldn't you?"

She laughed.

He joined her in laughter. "Come on, Rosie. Are you ready to go?"

"Yes, sir," she replied.

"Then, shall we?" Minister Smith took May Rose by the hand and walked her to his car. It had pretty much stopped raining, but still, he held the umbrella over them the entire time. Once they were only a couple feet away from the car, he sped ahead and opened the door for her. He bowed and extended his hand.

May Rose went to step toward the car.

"Oh, wait just one second." Minister Smith closed the umbrella, leaned into the car, threw the umbrella into the back seat, and pulled out a small stool from the passenger-side floor. He placed the stool outside the car door. "There you go."

May Rose felt like royalty. Minister Smith was pulling out all the stops for her...and stools. And it made her feel good. Made her feel like a woman.

Minister Smith grabbed her hand as she stepped onto the stool. He then pushed her coat and dress around her before she could do it herself.

Although it was only for a millisecond, May Rose enjoyed Minister Smith's arms around her. She grinned slightly and said, "Thank you, sir."

He nodded.

Right before May Rose stepped into the car, out of the corner of her eye, she could see her mother and her two aunts coming across the field. The girls were on the porch watching for May Rose to pull off. Once they saw the elders, they ran to meet them.

May Rose completely spun around to get the full view and then began to mumble, "Look at those loudmouth little gals of mine." She shook her head as Minister Smith followed her eyes to give his attention to whatever had hers. "They are telling Momma, Aunt Bertha, and Aunt Etta everything."

"There goes our surprise then, I suppose." He looked at May Rose. "I can't be rude. Better make my way over there and greet everyone." Minister Smith walked over to greet the elders. "How are you beautiful ladies doing this chilly and misty day?"

"It all depends on where you are taking my May Rose," Nana spat playfully. "A beautiful woman like her with a fine, good-looking man like yourself..." She looked him up and down as her words trailed off. "Why, unless you made it perfectly clear where the two of you are heading off to, one's mind could assume all kinds of places." Nana looked over Minister Smith's shoulder at her daughter. "And May Rose is awfully dressed up to be heading out to catch anybody's baby."

Minister Smith chuckled and shot back, "Rosie and I are going to buy Sunday dressings for some exceptionally beautiful ladies to be the church's special guest for our fifty-fifth anniversary tomorrow."

Realizing what the minister was alluding to, Aunt Bertha responded, "Dresses for all of us?"

"Well, it was supposed to be a surprise, but yes, all of you," said Minister Smith.

"If that's the case," Nana said, "then how come we all are not coming along?"

Minister Smith looked from one lady to the next. "Well, my automobile—"

"And a fine automobile it is," Nana interrupted.

Minister Smith looked back at his car and then returned his attention to the women. "Thank you, but, uh, like I was saying, my automobile won't seat everyone. Plus, who is going to catch me and missus' baby if it decided to come if everybody is with me?" He laughed.

Nana paused, giving Minister Smith's explanation thought. "You are surely right, sir."

Minister Smith felt like it was judgement day, and he'd just said the right thing to get into Heaven. He turned his attention to the only other adult he hadn't yet spoken to. "Sister Etta, we will make certain all of you who will be left behind will get the prettiest dresses." He kissed the hand of each of the adults and then patted the girls on the top of their heads. He looked to Nana. "My older boys have been instructed to run like hell to get you if the baby is trying to make an entrance while we are gone."

Nana nodded.

"All right, well, we must run now. I'll see you ladies tomorrow, yes?"

"In our Sunday's best, compliments of you, preacher man," Nana said with a wink.

On that note, Minister Smith tipped his hat and headed back to the car.

Once he got May Rose nice and comfortable in the passenger's seat, he climbed in after putting the stool in the back seat.

Once inside, he started the car and put his hands on the steering wheel, taking a deep breath before shifting the car into the gear to pull off.

May Rose smiled and put her hand atop Minister Smith's. "Minister Smith, I apologize for the circus you just had to endure."

He turned to face her. "Rosie, I love those ladies. When I need to set some congregation members straight, I know who to call. They really give Willie the business, that's for sure."

"That they do." May Rose chuckled as Minister Smith pulled off.

"So, Rosie, what's been going on with you? How are you? How are you faring with Willie being gone for lengthy periods of time? He told me it could be a month or more at a time he's away from you."

"I'm doing fine. I'm actually more concerned about the danger of the job than him being gone." May Rose stared out the window. "When the bossman brought the paper for us to sign, a large majority of the papers talked about the dangers of

Willie's job and those coal mines. Initially, I was all for Willie taking the job until I saw all the stuff that could happen to him. I'm sure it's no surprise to you, or anyone else for that matter, but Willie drinks too much moonshine. He cannot be safe if he is drunk or not feeling his best from drinking the night before." Her expression reflected the sadness she felt inside thinking about something bad happening to Willie in those mines.

Minister Smith responded, "I know about Willie's drinking. He has had this problem since we were teenage boys growing up together. I thought once you two married, had some babies, he would stop that behavior."

"Yeah, me too," May Rose said.

"I will continually pray for Willie and your family." He placed his hand on her knee. "And you, too, Rosie."

May Rose tingled at the minister's touch, and she changed the subject. "Sir, how are you and your family? Are you ready for the new baby?"

He sighed deeply and stopped the car on the side of the road.

May Rose was a little confused about what was going on, until he started explaining it to her.

"Rosie, can I be honest with you? I do not share my household going-ons with my parishioners, but you and your family are so much more to me… Rosie, can I trust you?"

"Pardon me?" May Rose was now more confused as to where the conversation was going.

"Can I trust you?" he said with intensity.

She responded fearfully. "Yes, sir, Minister Smith. I was raised up to treat secrets secretly as they are meant to be."

Minister Smith paused and then said, "I admire the way you, the elders, and the girls carry yourselves."

"Thanks so much for your observation of us. If you do not mind me continuing, sir, people may have a lot of terrible things to say about my crazy African women, however, they have never lost their class and royal manners from their homeland of Ghana. They have made sure it all continues to transcend to the generations coming behind them. And that includes me, Minister Smith. So, again..." May Rose twisted her body so that it was facing Minister Smith. "Whatever you share with me, it stays with me...until death."

"Only a fool tests the depth of the river with both feet."

African Proverb

Chapter 5

THE PROSPECT/THE CANDIDATE

*M*inister Smith listened to May Rose's words, and he believed her, so he continued without hesitation to share the secrets of his heart. "You, uh, know my wife, Sister Ramona." Minister Smith stammered out of embarrassment.

May Rose kept silent to allow him to continue speaking when he was good and ready. Something she learned from her mother. Let a man speak without interruption, even if it means him sounding like a fool.

"Being the young woman she is, the youngest of twelve siblings, she really didn't have anyone to raise her the proper way. Unlike with you being an only child and all. Her mother was too busy tending to the other twelve and their daddy. Besides, you know how it is with us folks. Once we get to child number four, the older children are expected to raise them up."

"Oh, yeah, I done seen how that works plenty of times with plenty of families." May Rose recalled one time catching a baby and the momma telling her to hand it to the oldest gal instead of her.

"Right, so then you know what I'm talking about."

May Rose didn't confirm. She didn't want to make it seem like she was speaking bad about her first lady.

"You know, like how your mother and her sisters did with you," Minister Smith continued. "I mean, Ramona's mother was an old woman when she gave birth to her. By the time Ramona was born, her momma, Mother Vivian, was tired from chasing all twelve of them other children around. Sick to death from raising them to put any womanly wisdom and knowledge into the last of the children. So, Ramona was left to be raised by the dozen siblings before her."

Minister Smith took a breath. "Ramona does the best she can with what she knows about being a woman. She has blessed me with these six babies and a seventh on the way. And I say all this to say..." His words trailed off as he looked May Rose in the eyes. "How have you done it, Rosie? You have *only* three girls, who are all well-mannered, and it's been some time since you birthed one, while my wife is birthin' 'em back-to-back. I love them. I love all my children, even the one yet to be born, but..." Once again, Minister Smith's words trailed off as he pieced the next ones together carefully. "It's just that...what if I don't want any more?"

May Rose kept a stoic face. She wasn't surprised by his comment, yet she was surprised. No man, not one, had ever asked her this question before. And telling any man the answer was like giving away the secret ingredients to the family's hot, buttered bun recipe that had been held close to the chest for years.

"You think I'm just awful, don't you, Rosie? An awful man who calls himself a man of God. Why, they might as well just take this here automobile back from me." He punched the steering wheel, grimacing with shame. Perhaps even wondering if he should have shared his inner thoughts and feelings with May Rose. "What kind of man deserves such an honor for being a servant of God when he is practically telling God he doesn't want any more of His blessings?"

May Rose could no longer sit there and let Minister Smith beat himself up thinking she thought the worst of him. Not when, in all actuality, the very act of preventing—or more like controlling—how many of those living gifts from God came through their wombs was part of a woman's business.

May Rose responded respectfully, "A woman dictates the number of children she has, sir. However, I had to learn these things."

Minister Smith looked over at May Rose with his interest piqued as high as a mountain's peak.

She smiled and continued, "You can start by curbing that bedroom business of yours. It is not all of Sister Ramona's doing."

He grinned while nodding. "You're right. You're right." He let out a bashful chuckle, again, mixed with a tad of embarrassment. It wasn't proper for a man to publicly talk about him and his wife's business in the bedroom.

But, again, May Rose was in her element, jumping at the opportunity to impress Minister Smith with her feminine knowledge. "Sir, there are syringes with acidic solution for douching and antiseptic spermicide sold at the pharmacy. I know these things because the pharmacist gave us this knowledge, along with the Ghanian traditions."

Once May Rose started pouring out the details, she couldn't keep from sharing every last ingredient of the family recipe. "Further, we have to get supplies from the pharmacy to help us catch healthy babies and take care of the mommas. They keep us educated so the white doctors do not have to help us catch. Some of the money you give me for the schoolhouse supplies, I also use it for the pharmacy supplies. I even asked Sister Ramona if she would like to try the douching supplies."

The minister turned his body sharp and swift toward May Rose in shock.

"Did you know?" she asked.

"I did not," he replied. "Well, what did she say?" His silent prayer that his wife would agree to this concoction to help keep another bun from getting in the oven spoke through the expression on his face.

"Well," May Rose started, "she informed me she wants a houseful of babies just like Mother Vivian."

Minister Smith's body deflated as it sunk into the seat of his car. It made him look two feet shorter.

"Sir, if that is not what you want, you need to clarify it with her." May Rose shrugged. "Perhaps you could start using the pull-out method before you put those dirty suds in her." She nodded toward Minister Smith's private parts without shooting her eyes in the same direction. "You pull your man-part out and put in a towel full of pig fat and finish in the rag. Also, you can use what they call the rhythm method. You don't touch her when she is due to have her rag. She is off-limits to your man-part the day her rag starts because that day is considered the first day of her ovulation. The egg is usually fertile around the fourteenth day."

"So, I do have some control over this, too?" Minister Smith straightened up. His eyes filled with hope.

"Indeed, you do, sir," May Rose assured him with a confident nod.

He grabbed her by the hand and squeezed it tight. "You're my savior, Rosie." He picked up her hand and kissed her palm. "My real, live savior."

May Rose chuckled, glad and proud she could help. "Now, now, Minister Smith." She patted his hand a couple times and slipped her hand from his. "You have about two more months before you have to worry about making another baby anyhow." She gave him a wink.

It took Minister Smith a moment, but he finally caught on to what May Rose was insinuating, which was that he and his wife could do all the business they wanted to in their bedroom for the next two months without the worry of putting another bun in the oven.

"We should be close to the dress shop by now, huh?" May Rose began looking out the window, her way of putting Minister Smith's mind back to the reason for their outing. Which surely wasn't just to get out of May Rose how him and his wife could have as much fun in their bedroom as they wanted without the worry of ending up with another mouth to feed.

Or was it?

"I forgot where we were going." Minister Smith chuckled.

"We're headed into town for dresses," she reminded him.

"Oh, yeah." He shifted the gear and then paused. "One more thing, Rosie."

"Yes, Minister?" May Rose waited with blinking eyes.

Minister Smith looked May Rose up and down for as far as his eyes could see. "Willie is one lucky man." He winked, made sure the road was clear, and then pulled off.

May Rose got warm all over at her minister's gesture. Let her body tell it, this man had been flirting with her all day. Even the way he said her name, Rosie, seemed intentional. The way he choreographed it to roll off his tongue like a runaway ice cube from the icebox sliding across the kitchen floor on a hot summer day. He'd called her Rosie plenty of times, but what was it about the way he said it today that hit May Rose's spirit different? Even her girls had picked up on it, with all their teasing.

There was never a moment when May Rose ever felt this connected to Minister Smith in her life. Nonetheless, she was mindful that this was just that...a moment. As the automobile rolled down the road, a sudden fear overcame her. Unless Willie came back home a completely changed man, she might never experience a moment like this again, because it was one Willie hadn't made her feel since their early years of courting.

As the car came to a near stop, May Rose's heart dropped from the cloud she was floating on. She looked over at Minister Smith, who wasn't paying her a lick of mind. He was too busy focusing on getting his car parked just right. It was clear that this was a one-sided moment. Had to be. He pulled over the whole car just to talk about his missus. May Rose laughed to herself thinking she must have looked ridiculously silly to Minister Smith, him staring off into space with the world's biggest smile, probably thinking about the fun he was going to be able to have with his wife the next two months. And May Rose was staring off into space, thinking about how she was the fool who told him how to do it.

"Rosie, Rosie," Minister Smith whispered close to May Rose's ear. "Wake up."

May Rose had been so far out to space that Minister Smith thought she was asleep.

"I am so sorry I bored you to sleep," he said, having parked the car.

May Rose hadn't even realized the car had come to a complete halt and was snug in its parking spot, with the owner ready to exit the vehicle.

"Oh, sir, I'm so sorry," she replied, gathering her bearings and bringing her thoughts back to reality. "Absolutely not, sir.

I was just trying to remember if there were any more details I needed to give you. You know, about you and First Lady Ramona's situation." May Rose cleared her throat, swallowed hard, and said a silent prayer to God asking for His forgiveness for the lie she'd just told Minister Smith.

"Well, were there?"

"Excuse me, sir?" May Rose asked, confused.

"Any more details. You said you were trying to remember if there were any more details. Well, were there?"

And just that quickly, May Rose had forgotten all about the lie she told. She responded, "No, sir, um, no. But if I think of anything, I will let you know right away."

"I'd be mighty obliged to it, Rosie." Minister Smith tipped his hat, smiled at her, and got out of the car.

He walked around and opened May Rose's door. Right when she went to step out, he stopped her. "Shoot, I forgot about the stool." He stretched his long body across her and reached into the back seat for it.

Once again, what felt like a gust of wind when he reached over May Rose, leaving his scent to linger beneath her nostrils, took her to a place in her mind where they lied in the woods under a big oak tree. They sat on the most beautiful, quilted blanket with a basket of dinner separating the two. In May Rose's vision, Minister Smith took a strawberry and playfully, gently rubbed it across her lips, daring her to catch it and bite into it.

May Rose mumbled, "Stop all of that carrying on."

"What did you say?" Minister Smith asked. "I didn't hear you"

She snapped out of her daydream to see Minister Smith standing outside the car door with the stool in his hand. She said the first words that came into her mind, even though they sounded nothing like the words she actually said. "I said I am so excited to go shopping for Sunday dresses." May Rose feigned a smile, hoping Minister Smith bought what she was selling. She didn't even look him in his face to see if his expression confirmed it or not. "I can't remember the last time we were able to buy new dresses." May Rose used the stool to step out of the car. "Gonna give me a break from having to make everyone new things for such a fine occasion as the church anniversary." May Rose kept running with the lie, hoping its legs wouldn't tire and let Minister Smith find out that she was having ungodly thoughts about a godly man.

"It's my honor and pleasure." He grabbed her hand as she stepped out. "You all deserve this and so much more." He picked up the stool after she stepped down and placed it in the car. "Let's go, beautiful lady." Minister Smith extended his elbow to May Rose.

She latched on to him as he escorted her to the first store they came to. The shop was owned by Mr. and Mrs. Day, but Mrs. Day ran it for the most part. It had been some time, though, since May Rose had stepped foot in the shop.

Fortunately, it had stopped raining, so May Rose didn't have to worry about getting wet…at least not by Mother Nature.

Minister Smith opened the door to the dress shop, making the bells ring and alerting the owner that a customer was coming or going. In this case, coming.

An older white lady came from the back of the shop and hollered out, "Minister Smith, you finally arrived."

"I did indeed, Mrs. Day," Minister Smith said, removing his hat. "Just like I told you I would."

Mrs. Day looked at the clock hanging behind the store counter. "I was expecting you a little bit ago, though. I thought the missus might have gone into labor or something." She looked to May Rose. "But seeming you got who you say is the best baby catcher in town on your arm, I reckon I'm wrong."

"Hello, Mrs. Day," May Rose greeted, blushing at the compliment Minister Smith had passed on to Mrs. Day about her.

Miniter Smith replied to her original comment. "No, Mrs. Day, no baby yet." He looked to May Rose. "According to our midwife here, May Rose Jones, like you said, the best baby catcher in town—and two towns over, might I add—we should have a couple more months left."

By now, May Rose was glancing around the shop like she was in a candy store. Had it not been for her not wanting to be rude, she would have run off and let her eyes taste every dress there.

Sensing May Rose's eagerness, Minister Smith said, "Mrs. Day, would you start by showing us the dresses for young girls?"

"Oh, absolutely, Minister." Mrs. Day started toward the appropriate section. "Those gals of yours are, what, ten, eleven, twelve?" she guessed.

"Yes, except for Ginny just turned thirteen," May Rose said, following the other woman.

Mrs. Day stopped and looked over her shoulder. "Well, she's practically a woman now then, ain't she?" She started off again toward the dresses without waiting for a reply.

"She is, indeed," May Rose agreed.

Mrs. Day flipped through a few dresses. She massaged one between her index finger and thumb, then looked back at May Rose. "They are all about the same size as their momma, huh?"

May Rose nodded. "Except the oldest. She's a bit taller than my other girls."

Mrs. Day continued, "Being the oldest gal, she's not going to want to be looking like the younger two."

"You're right," May Rose confirmed. "Ginny, the oldest, wants purple. The other girls would like pink and yellow."

Mrs. Day strolled over to a rack separate from the others. "Now, Minister Smith, you know you can only shop from this colored rack. However, when you told me you wanted to buy six dresses and six hats, I did a little ordering of some extra things." She winked.

"That was truly kind of you, Mrs. Day," Minister Smith replied. "We will appreciate whatever you have available for us."

May Rose wasn't as appreciative as Minister Smith with the measly selection being made available to them. She mumbled under her breath, "I will have my momma send your name to our African ancestors so they can visit you and this miserable store. You will then understand we are a royal people."

"And I'm sure you'll agree these extra pieces are just as divine." Mrs. Day beamed.

Minister Smith chimed in. "Understood, Mrs. Day. And we thank you kindly. I'm sure I speak for all the lovely ladies we are buying dresses for today." He motioned to May Rose. "Rosie, come on over here and find your dresses and hats. I am going over to the men's shop to pick up Willie's things. I previously ordered them. First Lady Ramona was ever so kind to get his measurements when he stopped by the place. I told him to keep y'all's special invite a secret. Not to go missing you like any man with good sense would go missing his wife, write you a letter or something, and slip up and tell you."

May Rose smiled. "You all are full of surprises."

Minister Smith once again tilted his hat with a schoolboy expression before exiting the shop.

May Rose began looking through the rack specifically for colored girls, whispering to herself, "The value of these dresses are expensive." She looked over at the rack Mrs. Day initially passed by, touching one of the dresses and realizing the fabrics on the rack for colored girls weren't nearly as beautiful or high quality as the others. "Besides, I can sew better dresses than this out of potato sacks," May Rose fussed under her breath.

If it weren't for this being Minister Smith's treat, May Rose would have walked straight out that store and got some much better fabric from the Windsors, who visited D.C. every so often and brought goods back to sell. It would have been better than what that white woman was trying to push on them. "I ought a push her in the face." May Rose whispered the idle threat as she continued flipping through the dresses. She huffed and puffed the entire time. "Let me hurry up and get out of here before I end up in the county jail."

May Rose was trying her best to get what the girls wanted, but all the colors were dark and not celebratory. She reminded herself once again under her breath, "I could have made our dresses way better than this." May Rose wished Minister Smith would have allowed her time to make their clothing.

She grabbed blue dresses for the girls and a black-and-white one for herself. She picked out the elders three different shades of gray with plain black hats and shoes with thick square heels. She opted out of buying a pair of shoes for herself because she already had a pair of the only style being offered for colored women. She did find the girls cute patten leather shoes off the "colored" shoe rack. May Rose was delighted about this, because the girls wanted patten leather shoes like the minister's daughters. The shoes made up for the lousy dresses.

"I would like to have these things," May Rose said, laying the last of the items on the counter.

Just then, the bells over the door started jingling as it opened.

May Rose looked over her shoulder and shouted, "Just in time, sir! Mrs. Day is packing up our things."

"Did you get everything you wanted?" Minister Smith walked over to the counter and admired the boxes and bags full of women's clothing and accessories.

Rose commented with joy and gratitude, "Absolutely, sir!"

Mrs. Day smirked and said, "That will be sixty-four dollars," as if to suggest they didn't have anything yet until they paid up.

Rose's body jerked with shock at the cost. She immediately told Minister Smith, "We can wear what we have. This is a cost of a big ole fat hog and a few chickens, too."

"I will hear nothing of the such." He counted out what must have been the sixty-four dollars. May Rose wouldn't have known because she'd never seen that much money in one man's hand in her entire life.

Minister Smith managed to grab all the packages and then bid Mrs. Day farewell.

"I'll see you next time, Minister Smith," Mrs. Day called out as she counted the money a second time.

May Rose, on the other hand, didn't as much as give Mrs. Day a good-bye wave. She was on fire that the woman had just raked in all that cash for those basic garments and had the nerve to try to butter them up by talking about ordering extra stuff. She could have sent it all back as far as May Rose was concerned. But Minister Smith was wearing a look as proud as the one he wore the last time May Rose caught one of his babies. So, she wasn't about to fix her mouth to say anything negative.

With arms full, Minister Smith still managed to open the door for May Rose.

"Thank you, sir. And thank you, again, for these beau—" May Rose couldn't bring herself to tell the lie that wanted to roll off her tongue. "—for such a beautiful gesture."

"Mmhmm," Minister Smith said, giving May Rose a knowing look.

"What?" May Rose asked as they exited the store.

"Your face don't lie, Rosie," he said. "Whew, wee! What did I miss? She must have done something to fry your skillet. I like to think you were going to set that store on fire with your eyes."

May Rose couldn't hold her tongue. "You paid too much money for me to start complaining. Still and all, she is a nasty wench who needs to be taught a lesson. Trying to make us think that stuff she got in there is so special. Like she ordered something special," May Rose spat. "Please don't take what I'm about to say next the wrong way, because, sir, I promise you I'm so very grateful and thankful for everything you are doing for me and my family, but, Minister..." She stopped and stomped her foot. "I could have made everything she has in that shop, even the 'white women's' rack!" She stormed off. "And with much better fabric, too." May Rose rolled her eyes so hard, it was a surprise they didn't go out into the road and stop traffic.

"It sounds like we need our own," Minister Smith said in deep thought.

"No, there is no way I can make all that stuff now in this short amount of time."

"I mean our own dress shop. One for coloreds. With the best dresses in town, even if they're made from burlap."

"I agree," May Rose huffed. "Because I was saying the same thing under my breath back in that store. That I could have made dresses better than that out of potato sacks. Sold 'em before they even got off the machine. I'm talking a wait-list of orders months in." May Rose strutted and laughed at the thought as she trotted on to the car. It took her a moment to realize she didn't feel Minister Smith's presence behind her anymore. She turned to see he had stopped a couple feet behind her.

"Exactly. Rosie, what do you say? What do you think about doing that? I could help. I mean, not with the dressmaking and all, but with setting up the business and stuff like that."

She frowned. "They will never let us have a shop of our own downtown."

"It does not have to be downtown." He started walking again toward the car as his mind entertained the possibilities. "It can be on the church property. We already have a name."

"Minister Smith, you and the church have done way too much for us. You are spoiling us. I mean, I can see the missus agreeing to do this gesture for me and my family," May Rose said, referring to the dresses, hats, and shoes. "But a business, sir. Why, I can't imagine any wife would allow her husband to—"

"Rosie," Minister Smith interrupted her. "Where are all these negative thoughts coming from?" He brushed past her and managed to get all the packages into the car. He was fussing the entire time, even as he pulled the stool out and extended his hand to help May Rose up to it. "You yourself ain't modest about how well you sew. Every woman in the town—heck, the state—would be lined up for you to make them some outfits." He looked up at the sky and painted it with his hands. "I can see it now. Rosie's Dresses. The finest in town."

May Rose chuckled at Minister Smith's antics, but then she realized he wasn't joking. "Sir?"

"I'm serious, Rosie." He placed his hand on the small of her back and gave it a slight rub.

May Rose looked back at him and tensed her shoulders. She then climbed into the car. She was speechless. Buying her a dress was one thing; buying her a dress shop was an entirely different animal.

Even once May Rose was tucked comfortably in the car, she watched Minister Smith walk around to the driver's side still huffing, puffing, fussing, and if he weren't a man of God, he would have been cussing, too.

The ride home started off in complete silence. Minister Smith was the one who decided to break it. "Rosie, I am just a man called to serve the Lord and His flock. I still have the same desires of every other man. Please do not hold this against me. I admire everything about you. I think all that you and Willie got going on is fine. I'm in no way trying to insult you or your husband. Nor anyone in your family. I'm just trying to bless a family who has been such a blessing to so many people. And how that blessing can continue to bless so many others. You should've seen how your eyes lit up when you walked into that store. Well, don't you want to do the same for other women and girls?"

May Rose took in Minister Smith's words. She shook her head. "It's just that... What would Sister Ramona think? And Willie?"

Minister Smith exhaled. "You've let me be honest with you up until this point, so I don't see no need in stopping now." He focused on his driving as he continued. "I was not being very thoughtful when I married Ramona."

May Rose had no idea how this had anything to do with a dress shop, but she waited to see which way the conversation was going to turn, the same way she was waiting to see which way Minister Smith was going to turn the car.

"The church dictates a man should take a wife. I was just seeing a young girl that I would have on my arm strutting around town." He paused before continuing, "She has been a major disappointment."

Rosie cleared her throat and gathered her words. She was sympathetic to Minister Smith's plight. She began sobbing because in that moment, she started seeing Minister Smith as

being the man she wanted, needed, and desired. She began saying through the tears, "We can't do this to them."

He responded loudly, "Do what?"

May Rose thought carefully and then said, "Do not play
games with me. You know I am well equipped with the rules
of this game. I appreciate that ever since you've known me,
you have never spoke on anything bad about me or the African
sisters. You've been nothing but respectful to me, and I to you.
But, Minister Smith, if we are going to go into any type of business, and I do mean business, then you know it goes without
saying that I call all the shots."

If May Rose didn't know any better, the switch in her
demeanor from submissive to standing on business seemed to
turn Minister Smith on.

He licked his lips and wiped the corner of his mouth before
the drool could seep out.

May Rose could say she was surprised about Minister Smith's
proposition, and she was, to some degree, but what she wasn't was
crazy. This little *thing* that was going on hadn't been one-sided,
with May Rose thinking the minister's actions were meaningless
and unintentional. Her mother was right when she'd voiced her
suspicions about their minister's behavior toward May Rose.

"That preacher man think he's playing you like a fiddle,"
she'd told May Rose one summer evening over iced tea. "But
when all is said and done, you better make sure he's dancing
to your tune."

May Rose had brushed her mother's words off as nonsense,
but they were starting to make more and more sense by the
moment. So much so that May Rose was now convinced her
mother had been right all along.

All this time, Minister Smith had been teasing May Rose.
Now that Willie was away, he was turning up the fire. May Rose

wasn't built to get burned. So, it was time she turned down the flame a bit. Things didn't need to cook so fast.

"You may not be in love with your wife, but I proclaim I love my husband." May Rose would never admit to Minister Smith that things were really hard in her marriage. She had been thinking about "the business" a lot lately. Ginny's ceremony only triggered it more, and it had been coming up to the forefront a lot. She wanted her girls to see the best of the woman's business coming from her, not weakness, pain, and constant sorrow.

"I assure you, Rosie, I will not interfere in your marriage. But I know you ain't no dumb woman. I know you be seeing the little breadcrumbs I've been laying out over the years. Well, now I want the whole loaf of bread." He licked his lips again. "But if I can't have the entire loaf, I'll just take a piece. And you know I would never tell a soul. And we already determined on our ride to the dress shop that I trust you. I know you would keep our business close to your chest. *All* of it."

May Rose was doing exactly what a woman was supposed to do her first day on the job, which was listen.

"Rosie, please be as much of mine as your heart can manage. I will protect you, the girls, the elders, and Willie from the church gossip. After all, Willie is my good friend, and I am just looking out for his family."

Minister paused for May Rose to reply, but she was still a woman on the job. She was all ears. God had given her two ears and one mouth for a reason. That reason was to listen twice as much as she talked so that she could get twice as much out of this man than if she had opened her mouth and said the wrong thing to ruin it all.

Minister Smith took May Rose's silence as her being uncertain about whether to go into business with him. "Just think about it." He gave her knee a friendly pat, as if patting away the tension that had built up in the car. "But in the meantime, please prepare a short speech for the church anniversary. You know the church history from when my grandfather founded it in 1870."

May Rose giggled and shook her head. "You are a bag full of surprises. Do you think I will be rested enough to give a church speech? Between thinking about you trying to climb all over me, hearing chatter from my girls and the elders about their gifts, and thinking about the decision I need to make about how I am going to manage this so-called business… David, please!" This was the first time she called him by his first name since he had become a preacher, and it felt liberating. And Minister Smith seemed to like it, too.

"Talk dirty to me." He laughed.

"You tickle me!"

"Oh, woman, I'm going to tickle you alright." He playfully began to tickle May Rose's side as they made their way back to her place.

As they pulled up to the house, May Rose could see the shadows behind the curtains. She could already hear the giggling and the teasing of her girls.

Minister Smith got out of the car, walked around, and grabbed the stool for May Rose to exit the car.

She stepped down and said, "I hope one day I can learn how to drive a car." She looked in his eyes. "The ride was very relaxing. Can't wait to ride again. But I imagine it would be even more relaxing if I were the one in control."

He grabbed May Rose's hand and squeezed it. "Maybe, I can teach you soon." He looked her up and down. "Real soon."

"You better escort me back into my home, Minister Smith, before we both end up committing a public sin." She stepped down from the stool and then moved toward her house.

Minister Smith grabbed the bags, as he needed them to cover his male part that was expressing the effect May Rose had on him.

She entered the house and he soon followed, with packages galore in hand.

The girls came flying to the door like a horde of buzzards. They jumped up and down, shouting, "Momma, which one is mine? Can we try them on now?"

May Rose hollered, "Where are your manners?" That instantly silenced the girls. "Speak to Minister Smith and thank him for the gifts, young ladies."

He chimed in and said, "Oh, don't be so hard on them, Rosie. I understand their excitement." He began doling out the packages, which the girls eagerly relieved him of.

"I am sure you are tired and probably need to go check on First Lady Ramona," May Rose said. "So, let me walk you to the door."

The girls were too busy ripping through packages to take note of the way May Rose sashayed to the door with her arm looped through Minster Smith's.

"Thank you for everything," she said once they approached the door. "By the way, I've thought about it, and my answer is yes."

Minister Smith jerked his head around so quickly, it was a surprise it didn't roll off his neck. "Really? What is it?"

"It's yes. Yes, I will have a short speech ready for the church anniversary tomorrow."

He chuckled. "Don't play with me, woman."

"Oh, Minister Smith, I don't play. I'm all about business."

"I'm sure you are, and hopefully when it comes to going into business with me, your answer for that will be yes, too."

"Momma, I don't see a purple dress," Ginny called out, interrupting May Rose and Minister Smith's moment.

"I better go tend to these girls. Which means I'll have to tend to you later." She winked.

"You may not play, but, woman, you sure do tease." Minister Smith bit his bottom lip so hard he nearly drew blood.

"Serves you right for all those years you played with me."

"Momma!" the girls began to call when they couldn't find the dress color they requested. Before they embarrassed her and said something ungrateful for what they did get, May Rose ushered Minister Smith out the house and onto the front porch.

"As far as the speech, you can prepare a standard twenty-minute sermon."

"If twenty minutes is all you need, Minister, then twenty minutes you shall get," May Rose flirted.

May Rose watched Minister Smith get in the car and drive off. She could hear the girls' complaints getting louder and louder, but her mind just drove off into the sunset...with Minister Smith.

"Those that pray for rain must be prepared for the mud."

African Proverb

Chapter 6

※

MINDING MY BUSINESS

"May Rose Jones, would you please come and give us some history about our Washington Street Baptist Church on what is our fifty-fifth anniversary?" Minister Smith announced from the pulpit.

May Rose took a big gulp and stood with a nervous smile. A regular attendee of Washington Street Baptist Church, she was in the front pew. Thank goodness her dress was ankle-length, so no one could see her knees knocking underneath it. And thank goodness the room erupted in applause, so they couldn't hear her knees knocking either.

A regular church member, yes. A regular spokesperson for the church, no. It took everything in May Rose to make it to the altar and behind the podium. Thank goodness the usher was instructed to seat her family in the reserved front pew, so she did not have far to walk.

Minister Smith smiled broadly as he extended his hand and assisted May Rose up the two steps leading to the podium.

"Thank you, Minister Smith," she said coyly, avoiding eye contact.

'Eyes are the windows to the soul,' her mother always told her.

The last thing May Rose wanted was for the entire congregation to peer into the container that stored her lustful feelings for their minister. Her hand slipped out of his, and if she didn't know any better, it happened in slow motion. Her fingertips lingered a few seconds too long on his. Perhaps they didn't need to look into her soul. All they needed to do was just look.

May Rose flattened out the invisible wrinkles from her dress. She cleared her throat and began by saying, "Thank you, Minister Smith." Her eyes traveled to his wife. "First Lady Ramona." She gave her a respectful nod. "I appreciate you both for allowing me the opportunity to speak before your congregation." She swallowed hard and then exhaled. "I'd like to welcome Bishop Ellis, who is with the National Black Baptist Convention."

Bishop Ellis stood.

May Rose continued. "We appreciate you joining us in this celebration of our fifty-fifth church anniversary. So, Washington Street First Baptist, let's give Bishop a warm welcome."

The church, once again, erupted in applause.

May Rose waited until the thunder ceased and Bishop Ellis took his seat before she began speaking again. "Before we get on with today's program, allow me to share some of our history." She looked down at the piece of paper she was requested to read from that sat on the podium, just where she was promised it would be. "The church was founded in the year 1870, five years after the Emancipation Proclamation. It was founded by Reverend Amos Smith, the grandfather of our minister, David Smith. The people of our town were and still are people who seek the Lord's heart. Reverend Amos Smith knew he had been called to give the colored people of Bedford what they needed.

The land where our church sits was purchased by Reverend Smith from the money he saved from going to plantations after Emancipation, showing the farmers who did not have share-croppers how to grow okra and tobacco. The enslaved people grew it, and the farmers never bothered to learn to tend their own crops."

May Rose used her index finger to follow the words as she read. "The farmers still depended on the previously enslaved people to grow their crops. They would rent a portion of land for them to grow crops and pay the farmers with crops yielded. Not Reverend Smith." She shook her head adamantly. "He refused to grow crops for the farmers because he was going to have his own land. He made them pay for his help. The share-croppers fed him and his family until this land was purchased." Now May Rose used her index finger to pound the podium as hard as she could without breaking a nail.

"Here we are today, a growing and thriving church," she continued. "Minister David Smith has accepted the vision of his grandfather, Reverend Amos Smith, and he's done a fine job of it. If you agree, then say amen, Church. Thank you for your ear." May Rose said her last line at the tip of everyone's chorus of amens.

She started walking toward the steps to take her seat while looking at her mother, who nodded in approval while giving her a big smile and a wink.

Minister Smith swiftly stepped behind the podium and said very quickly, "Rose, please come back here."

She stopped immediately, and her stomach started grum-bling with nervousness. Had she done something wrong? Had she forgotten to say something she was supposed to say? Maybe something was written on the flip side of the paper. She didn't stop to think about that. Not sure why Minister

Smith wanted her to come back, May Rose did what was asked, turning around and walking back to the podium where she stood next to her minister. His eyes were glued to her. She could feel them burning a hole through her, setting her soul on fire. His desires for her were so evident—at least to her— that he might have said so to the entire congregation. That's when May Rose's heart began beating so fast, she thought it might pump right out of her chest and land smack dead on the altar. Maybe that's exactly what he was going to do, confess his undying love for her.

When May Rose reached him, he turned his attention away from her and called on Bishop Ellis. "Bishop, would you like to share any remarks?"

Bishop stood, a sign that he would, indeed, like to say a few words, although he said nothing as he started walking. His face was hard and stoic.

May Rose mumbled toward Minister Smith, without turning her body or face away from the congregation, "Why do I need to be here?"

He kept his eyes on Bishop Ellis, ignoring May Rose's inquiry. The bishop came up the steps and walked toward May Rose and Minister Smith. She was terrified by then. Bishop Ellis was not the friendliest-looking man, so she didn't know whether to take the darts he was throwing at her with his eyes personal, or if it was just part of his natural demeanor. Rumor had it that he heard from God better and more clearly than anyone else. And nothing could be hidden from God. Had God told the bishop about May Rose and Minister Smith's antics?

May Rose tried her best to get out the path of the storm coming through in the form of Bishop Ellis. He was noticeably short with big, bushy eyebrows that were only a centimeter away from being considered a unibrow, and a mustache so thick, you could not see his mouth. In spite of his short stature, he was larger than life.

He nodded at May Rose as he brushed past her, his face still hard. One would think he had never smiled in his life, like the corners of his mouth wouldn't know how to raise to save his life. His pupils were black as coal and extremely small, something she noticed for the first time as he turned to face her.

"Mrs. Jones," he said, doing a slight bow and then taking her hand, holding it tight, all while leaning in and kissing her cheek.

"Bishop," May Rose replied, doing a slight curtsey herself.

As Bishop Ellis turned to face the congregation, May Rose looked directly at her family. The girls had their mouths covered while they giggled. Her mother's jaw was in a dropped position, while her aunts had their own reactions to what they were witnessing between the two men on the podium and their niece. Aunt Bertha had her handkerchief over her mouth, and Aunt Etta was turned completely around in her seat as if she were experiencing second-hand embarrassment and couldn't stand to watch.

May Rose shook her head. There was no second-hand embarrassment about it. She was first-hand embarrassed. "I've got to have the most ignorant family I know," she mumbled under her breath.

There wasn't a chance that anyone else heard her comment, as she did it while Bishop Ellis was simultaneously clearing his throat with a deep grumble. He then began speaking with a commanding tone, one no one would expect to come from such a little man. He roared, "Minister Smith, First Lady Smith, May Rose, and the Washington Street congregation, we at the Southern Baptist Convention are proud of the work you are doing in this community."

Hearing Bishop Ellis say her name with Minister Smith *and* First Lady Ramona made her wonder if she was supposed to be part of some package deal. This made May Rose feel like she was the second lady. Minister Smith had voiced that he would settle for just a piece of May Rose. He clearly meant her as a *side* piece.

"We come to you today with greetings and continued well wishes," Bishop Ellis said. "The history of this church is a rich one. Under Minister Smith's leadership, your church owns more land than any other church in the southern region. Your church also has the highest membership in this region as well. Your church allows more members to grow crops on its land. Your church has a large schoolhouse, with Sister May Rose teaching the children, as well as her beautiful momma and aunts catching all of the babies for this town and the next town over, which is aiding in membership growth of this fine church."

"Amens" made their way through the room, accompanied by several nods.

May Rose's curiosity and nervousness were replaced with gratitude.

Bishop Ellis turned his head slightly and threw his words over his shoulder at her. "Sister Rose, I understand your oldest girl, Ginny, is in training to become a midwife."

Ginny hunched her shoulders bashfully and blushed. Florence, who sat next to her, gave her a congratulatory nudge. The two sisters shared a loving smile. Ginny would never admit it, but the proud look her little sister gave her warmed her heart.

Bishop Ellis faced the congregation again. "And the other two will learn when they become of age, yes?"

Florence and Lynette giggled and looked at one another.

"And further," Bishop Ellis said, "your husband, Brother William Jones, is away working in one of those dangerous coal mines. I trust, Church, you all are saying a daily prayer for this family."

The congregation confirmed with gestures and verbally.

"I knew as much." Bishop Ellis turned to face Minister Smith. "I wouldn't expect anything else from sheep with a shepherd as fine and God-fearing as the one standing here in the form of Minister David Smith."

His lips threatened to smile but didn't see it through as Bishop Ellis continued. "At this time, I would like to present Minister Smith with this." He reached out to his right side, where he was handed a beautiful, black velvet robe with purple cuffs and trim going down the front and back. "You will now be called Bishop David Smith."

The congregation stood and erupted in applause for what seemed like ten minutes. Minister Smith was completely surprised, or at least he was doing one heck of a job pretending to be.

"May I do the honors?" Bishop Ellis held the robe up in front of Minster Smith, who was staring at the robe with stars in his eyes.

"Of…of course," the minister stammered.

Bishop Ellis placed the beautiful garment on Minister Smith's back and said, "Bishop Smith, you and your congregation have shown you to be worthy of this title. Also, I have heard about all of the work Sister May Rose here and her family does to help the expecting women. And that specifically First Lady is keeping her mighty busy. She seems to be with child every year."

And just like that, Bishop Ellis did something May Rose thought she'd never live to witness. He laughed. "Figured we need to start keeping you busier with your new duties as bishop."

Bishop Smith dropped his head in embarrassment as the congregation laughed.

"Sister May Rose," Bishop Ellis said, "I also would like to present these keys to you." He dug a ring with two keys dangling from it from his pocket. "There is a 1925 Packard Holbrook Limousine parked in the church lot. Just big enough for a family of ladies, and young ladies, to get about town catching babies and fulfilling all their other obligations to the community."

"Lord have mercy!"

May Rose recognized the sentiment—as she fell to her knees—to be the voice of her mother. With her hand covering her chest, May Rose shook her head in both disbelief and refusal. "No. No, Bishop. You don't understand." She looked up at him. "We do these things because it is the nature of the African women. It's our duty."

Elma was standing up, nodding in agreement, as she listened to her daughter's true and heartfelt words.

"Through the generations, we have been taught to uplift our people with pride," May Rose said, her eyes filling with tears. "I teach these ways to mine, and they will teach it to theirs."

Bishop Smith helped her stand. Her shoulders bounced up and down as she wept almost uncontrollably. "It's okay, now, Rosie," he said. "You deserve it." He looked out to the congregation. "Everyone, let Sister May Rose know just how much she and her family deserves this."

Members of the congregation—still on their feet—began to clap, stomp, and shout. Taking in everyone's reaction made May Rose cry that much harder. She turned and looked Bishop Smith in his eyes with an intense stare while she wiped away the tears. "You knew this all along, didn't you?" she asked. "This is why you wanted me and my family all dressed up with new dresses, shoes, and hats, isn't it?"

A mischievous grin covered Bishop Smith's face as he replied, "I told you; you deserve to be blessed."

May Rose was in such a state at that moment, she could not see anyone but Bishop Smith.

"Sister May Rose." Bishop Ellis's voice pulled her out of her trance. "I know you cannot operate a car yet. For this reason, Bishop Smith has been requested to start teaching you to drive immediately after the church picnic..." Bishop Ellis inhaled. "...that smells like it's about ready to be served."

A few chuckles rang about the church sanctuary.

"So, why don't we convene service and go break bread with one another and fellowship, and more importantly, celebrate?"

The congregation cheered even louder as they began to gather their belongings to head out back for the anniversary picnic.

"Will someone go out and ask the cooking committee if we may start to come out now?" Bishop Smith asked, to which a couple of the church members obliged him.

May Rose walked back to the pew while people ran to hug and congratulate her.

The girls were the most excited, jumping up and down as they squeezed their mother tightly. For a minute there, May Rose thought her mother and aunts were going to break out in one of them African dances, they were so beside themselves.

After a moment or so, Elma turned May Rose around by her shoulders until they stood face-to-face. Elma gave her daughter a tender kiss on the cheek while whispering in her ear, "It's time to get to work, queen." She pulled back and looked at May Rose. She might as well have had dollar signs in her eyes.

"You couldn't hold that until you got home, Momma?"

"No more than you could hold that look in your eyes you had for Minister—pardon me, Bishop—Smith." Elma snickered. "I knew it was only a matter of time before you tired of that do-nothing husband of yours whose sorry drunken behind didn't even bother showing up for such an important day for his family." She let out a 'tsk' as she rolled her eyes and dropped her hands from May Rose's shoulders.

Regardless of how May Rose's body had been responding to Bishop Smith as of late, she went into instantaneous defense mode for her husband as the concern about Willie's safety jumped right in her spirit and out of her mouth. "He's out working for his family, which includes you," May Rose was quick to remind her.

"Like hell he is!" Elma whispered harshly.

"Momma, really!" May Rose exclaimed. "In the house of the Lord?"

"You and Bishop Smith didn't care about showing your emotions in the house of the Lord, so never you mind if I show mine."

"Look, Momma, I understand. Everything boils down to a woman's business," May Rose mumbled, "but not in the Lord's house, please."

Elma giggled. "You are going to be doing it in the church, the vehicle, and in the Bishop and First Lady's bed for that big ole gift you got today. And let us not forget the gifts from yesterday."

May Rose tightened her lips and shook her head in dismay as she scooped the girls together and led them to the exit door. Willie stayed on her mind the entire trek, prompting May Rose to even consider going to Willie's job to check on him. He knew about the anniversary and them being honored, yet he didn't show up. May Rose had just explained away his absence to her mother, but deep inside, she thought with it being Sunday and all, Willie could have managed to show up.

Negative thoughts about something being wrong on his job started to swirl through her mind. The paperwork Willie signed for the job stated she would be notified within 24 hours if there was an accident at the mines, whether Willie was involved or not.

Suddenly, May Rose thought back to when Bishop Smith told her she was being negative. Perhaps he was right. And the last thing she wanted to do was be negative on a day where she should be overflowing with gratitude.

"What a beautiful new automobile you got out there," Sister Sarah said, entering the church as May Rose and the girls exited.

And just like that, May Rose decided to live in the moment and enjoy her new gift. And it only added onto the pressure of her needing to sit down and start strategizing a plan to deal with Bishop Smith's offer.

May Rose stepped outside, where several churchgoers were congregating. She glanced to her left and saw the first lady detouring around people trying to greet her while she headed in May Rose's direction. She had all six babies hanging all over her in some fashion on the other. Whether they were attached to her arm, leg, or hip, all six babies were accounted for, including number seven inside her. Behind First Lady Ramona was her elderly mother, Mother Vivian, and all twelve of her sisters and brothers. It was safe to say that dang near half the church membership was kin of some sort.

"Sister May Rose," First Lady Ramona said as she reached out to give May Rose a hug. "You so deserve the blessing you received today. It will surely help us all."

"Thank you kindly, First Lady," May Rose replied. "All of this was such a surprise, indeed." She looked over First Lady's shoulder. "Good afternoon, Mother Vivian and family."

They returned May Rose's greeting as most of them carried on about their business.

"Looks like I'll be catching that little one almost any day now." May Rose looked down at First Lady Ramona's protruding belly. "Hopefully not before I learn to drive that there automobile so I can get there in time to catch it." She looked out to the parking lot, where a crowd was gathered around her gifted vehicle, oohing and ahhing.

"Momma, come on." Lynette pulled on May Rose's arm. "I want to go see the new car. Please, Momma, please."

"Hold on now," May Rose said. "Don't be rude to First Lady Ramona."

"Oh, let the babies go on and check out what they'll be riding around town in style in."

"See, Momma, can we, please?" Lynette cupped her hands in a prayer position and interlocked her fingers. "First Lady Ramona said she don't mind if we're rude."

That made Ramona chuckle.

"Go on over there, girls. I'll be over soon," May Rose said.

"Yay!" the girls cheered and galloped off. Even Ginny, who tucked away her newfound womanhood for a moment and let the little girl in her skip over to the car.

Once the girls were out of sight, First Lady Ramona leaned toward May Rose and snarled, "And I hope Bishop don't think I'm going to let what went on up there at the altar today slide."

May Rose's body froze. She should have known that if her mother noticed the energy going on between her and Bishop Smith, then most certainly his wife would as well. May Rose wasn't prepared for a showdown with First Lady Ramona on church property. She hadn't even technically opened for business with Bishop Smith. Looks like this job was going to end before she even had her first official day at work.

"First Lady," May Rose started, not even knowing how she was going to finish, "I, uh—"

"I know, I know. I saw your face," First Lady Ramona said. "You were in a daze. Just as shocked as I was to hear Bishop Ellis out me and David's business like that. Him and everybody else needs to mind their damn business about the number of children me and my husband have. It is our business."

May Rose tried her best to control the deep exhale she instantly blew out of her mouth when she realized that *her* business wasn't the same business First Lady Ramona had her panties in a bunch about.

"I don't know who is running their mouth," First Lady Ramona continued, "but the folks in this town better watch themselves."

Although relieved First Lady Ramona wasn't on to her and Bishop Smith, based on what she just said, May Rose wondered briefly if Bishop Smith shared the conversation they had during their car ride about how to prevent a woman from becoming with child.

First Lady Ramona went on and on while rubbing her stomach, all the while May Rose's wheels were spinning, trying to think about how to respond. Finally, she replied, "You are absolutely right, First Lady. It is you and your husband's business. You can have as many babies as you like, and I will be honored to catch every single one of 'em." She nodded with finality.

"Thank you, May Rose," First Lady said, using the hand she was just rubbing her stomach with to rub her shoulder. "By the way, I love all of you all's dresses. The girls look absolutely like the little darlings they are. I'm just so glad we were able to do that for you. Would have hated for you all to have to wear sacks and rags, literally, on such a special day."

And there it was, that condescending remark First Lady Ramona was known to deliver. Every Sunday, she chose her victim precisely. She'd be sweet as butter slithering down an ear of corn to everyone else, but it was as if she had to throw salt on the corn in order to make her day. And this Sunday, she was throwing the salt at May Rose like she wanted her to turn into a pillar like Lot's wife in the Bible.

May Rose hadn't been on the other end of First Lady Ramona's negative insults in some time. First Lady loved to be the only woman at the church getting attention, and May Rose had stolen quite a bit of her usual thunder. So, May Rose, instead of giving First Lady Ramona a bite of the corn with one of her own slick comments, decided not to go on the attack but to respond kindly instead. "Oh, First Lady, all of your beautiful dresses still make all of ours look like rags."

First Lady Ramona gave May Rose a very warm smile. It almost looked genuine. And perhaps it was. May Rose remembered what it was like to be swollen with child, feeling unattractive. This was, perhaps, something May Rose could use to her advantage. She could keep the compliments coming. That way, First Lady Ramona wouldn't care about the additional time her husband and May Rose would spend together on the driving lessons. As long as May Rose played herself down, First Lady Ramona would think she thought far less of herself and wouldn't even think about trying something with her husband. Besides, as far as May Rose—and the entire town, for that matter—thought, all First Lady Ramona wanted and cared about were them babies.

"Momma, come look at it," Ginny's voice called from the church parking lot.

"First Lady Ramona, if I might excuse myself..." May Rose said.

"Oh, honey, go on." Ramona shooed her off. "If the shoe were on the other foot, you are the last person I would have stopped to talk to in route to see my new automobile."

May Rose discretely rolled her eyes while biting her tongue, using the last bit of self-control she had to not just throw salt back at her first lady and to not—once she did get in that car and learn to drive it—run over the woman. May Rose excused herself from the conversation and went out to the parking lot. She stood by Bishop Ellis and Bishop Smith. Her family had already made their way to check out the vehicle.

"We have been waiting on you to get over here and see the car," Bishop Smith said. "Go on, walk around and admire it, Sister May Rose."

May Rose stepped away to go look at the limousine. It was long and green with yellow stripes and three doors on each side.

"Ain't it a beauty?" Bishop Smith asked, walking over next to her.

"Indeed, it is, Bishop Smith," May Rose replied, not taking her eyes off it. She was so in awe. Before this moment, she could have only imagined owning a car fancier than her bishop's. Of course, it was purchased by the church, pretty much for the church and to do church and community business. May Rose was smart enough to know that. But she still felt a sense of ownership, and she was happy. She was proud. She was grateful.

"Hand over those keys, Sister Rose," Bishop Smith said. He turned and looked to May Rose's family. "Get in, everyone. Let's go for a ride!"

The girls excitedly headed toward the back of the limousine to get in while Elma and her sisters walked around to the other side. May Rose handed her bishop the keys. He galloped around to the other side of the car and opened the door for Elma and her sisters. He then opened the door for the girls.

May Rose stood by the passenger door waiting for Bishop Smith to open it for her.

"Rosie, you come on over here and get in the driver's seat," Bishop Smith said as he headed over to the driver's side of the car. He was so excited that he didn't even realize he'd called her Rosie. Neither did anyone else.

May Rose, surprised at Bishop Smith's request, shook her head. "Not yet, Bishop. I don't even know how to start a car, let alone drive one." She let out a nervous laugh.

He paused, reading his church member's body language as well as her frightened expression. "Well, all right then. Driver's lessons begin tomorrow." Bishop Smith took on the responsibility of sharing with the girls and the ladies that May Rose wasn't quite ready to take them for a spin.

"Aww, Momma, come on," Lynette said as she stomped out the car.

"I know you're not gonna act up in front of the church," May Rose said, throwing her hands on her hips. "'Cause if you willing to do so, then you willing to go get a switch from the church tree and get your tail handled in the church parking lot."

After that comment, no one else dared to express their disappointment, and Lynette regretted ever doing so herself.

"Bishop Ellis," Bishop Smith said as he approached. "Can one of your assistants follow in my vehicle to May Rose's home after we fellowship?"

"Absolutely," Bishop Ellis replied.

"Great, then let's go eat, everybody," Bishop Smith said, throwing his arm around Bishop Ellis's shoulder and leading him toward the picnic area.

"I thought you'd never ask."

May Rose and her family walked behind the two bishops as if they were the first family of the church, and this was where they were be supposed to be. It looked picture-perfect. Only it wasn't. Bishop Smith had a wife and family, and it wasn't May Rose and her girls.

At least not yet.

"If you want to go fast, go alone. If you want to go far, go together."

African Proverb

Chapter 7

BEST (WO)MAN FOR THE JOB

*R*ight before the ladies approached the picnic area, Aunt Etta picked up her pace to place herself next to May Rose. She lovingly took May Rose's hand and squeezed it tightly while speaking soft and sweet into her niece's ear. "You need to get to work the way you were taught. Just remember, there's no love involved. You got this, Baby Rose." She used the nickname she used to call her when she was just a youngin.'

May Rose kept her eyes straight ahead, listening intently to her aunt's words.

"It's your responsibility to do your job and be an example for them babies walking behind us," Etta continued.

May Rose looked over her shoulder at her girls. They would be her reminder for what she was getting herself into with her bishop. If her conscience dared threaten to make her rethink her position, she would trump it with a vision of her girls and the life her efforts would prepare for them for their later years. She failed at her initial chance, and she was determined not to mess it up this time around. Yes, the African sisters, and herself, could tell the girls all about a woman's business, but she could show them better than she could tell them.

"Your place has been set. All you need to do is walk into it," Aunt Etta said. "We believe in you. We know you won't fail us this time."

It was her aunt's last sentence that turned the pep talk from sugar to shit. May Rose knew what she needed to do, if not for her sake, then for the sake of her daughters. The family pattern could not end with her. Not this way. She didn't want to show her daughters that love conquered all...including living life with a man they loved and who did well enough for the family to be comfortable but who was a drunk. If they were going to have to tolerate such behavior from a man, even if they loved him, the reward should be greater. But the main objective was to not allow love to rear its ugly head in the first place. Love only confused things. And God forbid it prevail and blind them from seeing the real prize, which was simply control.

Control the benefits of the relationship, control your sexuality and sexual acts, control your man's influence over the relationship, control the finances in a relationship, control the trajectory of the relationship, control the growth of the relationship, control the conflicts in a relationship, and most of all, control the number of children you give birth to.

Although her aunt's intentions were all well and good, May Rose didn't need her breathing down her neck about her role as a woman. As a matter of fact, the last thing she needed was the women micromanaging her. And more so, she didn't need her aunt's insults, no matter how much sweet syrup dripped from her lips when she said them.

It offended May Rose that the women just couldn't let her relationship with Willie go, and that they not only constantly threw it in her face, but they injected that poison into the veins of her daughters. It made her children look at her as a failure in the family business. As the black sheep of the family because she couldn't follow her job description to the tee.

When Willie came into her life, it was a time when May Rose was tired. She needed a break from working men. And it just so happened that Willie was easy on the eyes and light on the heart. May Rose was genuinely tickled by Willie's ways, including the way he loved her.

"Girl, you don't even know what love is!" Nana spat to May Rose the day she confessed that she wasn't playing games when it came to her feelings with Willie. That they were real. That they were in love.

"But, Momma—" May Rose started.

"'But, Momma,' my ass! You wouldn't know love if it put two lumps on the middle of your forehead." She used her index finger to mug May Rose's head.

"How do you know?" May Rose shot back, on the verge of tears. "You don't know how I feel. How can you tell me I don't know what love is?" By this time, a lone tear slid down her face.

Her mother walked up to her nose-to-nose. She was so close, May Rose could feel her mother breathing on her. It felt like a dragon right before it shot out a flame.

"Because I never taught you what love is." The words shot out as if they were fire, burning through May Rose's being. Making her question her decision to settle down with Willie until death do them part. But it was too late. She'd already said, "I do." It was done, and neither May Rose's mother nor her aunties would ever allow her to live that down.

That was, unless she could make up for it somehow.

May Rose looked over at her aunt and saw the glimmer of hope in her eyes.

"We believe in you," Aunt Etta said, giving May Rose's hand an even tighter squeeze. "We know you won't fail us this time."

She poured even more salt into May Rose's old wound. She hated that the women in her family had little faith in her. That she was probably going to be the one that future generations used as an example of what not to become. Of how to fall asleep—in love—on the job and risk taking the family business under.

How long were they going to keep reminding her that in their eyes, she'd failed them with her relationship with Willie?

As long as I allow them to, she thought. And it was in that moment she committed to changing the narrative...to changing the story of May Rose Jones.

She faced forward like a soldier, snatching her hand from Etta's. She rolled her eyes sharply at her as she picked up her pace. Her mother was monitoring the activity between her sister and daughter, as she was privy to the conversation taking place between the two. From the moment the sisters witnessed Bishop Smith whisk May Rose off for a shopping spree, they salivated at the mere thought that May Rose would get an opportunity to right her wrong. They couldn't get back into their house quick enough and start laying out their strategy to lead May Rose in the right direction this time.

The African sisters held a sense of failure over how May Rose's life turned out. After all, they were her teachers. A failed student meant that somewhere along the journey, they'd failed her. This was an opportunity for them to redeem themselves as well.

Elma gazed at May Rose in complete disappointment and mumbled, "Umph, umph, umph. The ancestors must be just as disgraced as I am." She and her sisters had to help May Rose get her control back at all costs. It didn't matter how pissed off it made May Rose; they were going to be relentless at doing so.

Once May Rose and her family reached the table assigned to the first family and their guests, they admired the setting. The table was beautifully decorated, donned with fine, white China. At the right angle, the sun bouncing off the sparkling silverware and crystal glasses was blinding, making the guests shield their eyes to focus on whatever was before them. The tablecloth was made of crisp, white cotton and trimmed in fancy lace with matching napkins. But the eyecatcher was the captivating centerpiece of large-petal red roses, caressed in baby breath and long stems of greenery.

"Bishop Ellis," Bishop Smith said as he stood, "I would like you and your armor-bearer to please take the head seats here at our table." He pointed to where he wanted the men to sit. He then continued, "Rose, you and your family are just fine seated across from me and my family. And we are honored to have you do so." He smiled at them.

It didn't go unnoticed to May Rose that his eyes rested on her just a few seconds longer than anyone else. Unfortunately, there were a couple other people it didn't go unnoticed by either.

May Rose and her family took Bishop Smith's direction. He and Bishop Ellis pulled out their chairs as the ladies began to take their seats. First Lady Ramona was visibly missing from the table. Three of her sisters were sitting next to Bishop Smith. All six of their children were sitting at the children's table with another one of the first lady's sisters.

The food was spread out between two tables. There was baked ham, barbecue pig belly, fried chicken, pork neckbones, black-eyed peas, collard greens, fried corn, lima beans, okra, rice, macaroni and cheese, cornbread, molasses, sweet potato pies, pound cakes, peach cobbler, and red drink. As was customary at church functions such as this, the head table's plates were prepared and served by the women of the church—aka, the unofficial hospitality committee.

After a few minutes of everyone digging into their meal, May Rose turned her attention to Bishop Smith and politely asked, "Will First Lady be joining us?"

"She's resting," he responded.

She sensed a bit of frustration in his response. "This has been a long day for her. This is the time of her pregnancy where she will require more rest. So, it's absolutely understandable why she's not present." May Rose didn't know why she felt led to defend the first lady being absent from such a special occasion, something that could be taken as sheer disrespect to the guest bishop.

From the look on Elma's face, she didn't know why either. If anything, May Rose should have been pointing out just how disrespectful it was for Ramona not to be present. That definitely would have shown May Rose, who did bother to be present, in a better light. Instead of gaining brownie points, she ate them and pooped them out. Elma shook her head as her fork loudly crashed onto her plate, making her disgust obvious to May Rose and her sisters.

When all the attention turned to Elma, she deflected by asking, "Bishop Smith, would you like me to go check on her? I can't believe we're all sitting here enjoying this wonderful food and our first lady, who should be eating for two, is off somewhere, probably famished."

This was a great cover, Elma had to admit herself. Everyone assumed her disgust and the slamming down of her fork was because of the lack of concern for the first lady of the church.

Bishop Smith replied quickly, "No, ma'am, her momma and sister are in there with her. We're not making this day about her. This day is for you ladies. You know, as part of the church body. Thank you kindly for your concern, but First Lady will be just fine for now."

Elma nodded her acceptance of Bishop Smith's stance, picked up her fork, and ate like it was the last supper.

All May Rose could do was shake her head. Not in embarrassment of her mother, but how good she was at manipulating a situation...and people.

"Bishop Ellis," Bishop Smith said while everyone else at the table chatted among themselves. "Rose and I discussed opening her a dress shop on the church property."

Hearing the mention of her name, May Rose turned her attention to the bishops' conversation.

"It was a God-awful experience for Rose shopping in town to pick out the dresses for herself and her family to wear to this grand occasion today. Why, they almost had to come here in their bedclothes, for crying out loud." Bishop Smith turned to May Rose for confirmation. "Ain't that right, Rosie?"

Bishop Smith calling her Rosie, which wasn't something he usually called her at church, shook her a bit, to the point where she didn't immediately respond to his inquiry. Rose, yes, but Rosie, almost never. It was just a bit too intimate, in May Rose's opinion. Clearly, she'd been so nervous about speaking in front of the congregation that she hadn't heard him when he slipped up and said it earlier.

Bad habits are sometimes hard to break.

"Ain't that right, Rose?" he asked again.

"Oh, uh, yes," she stammered. "It was a crying shame."

"She could only shop from the colored dress rack. And not only was the pickings slim, but the options could not touch Rose's designs. Not even the ones for the white women."

"Not to mention, they were way overpriced," May Rose added.

"And we figured at May Rose's shop, the designs will be much better, and they will also be reasonably priced."

She nodded in agreement.

"So, I'd like to know your thoughts on that," Bishop Smith said, giving Bishop Ellis the floor to respond.

Before Ellis could even respond, Elma cleared her throat loudly and pinched her sister on the leg.

Aunt Bertha almost jumped out of her chair. "Oh shit!" she shouted. She started rubbing her leg quickly, looking up to some awkward stares. Aunt Etta elbowed her and gave her a discerning look. Realizing she'd just sworn in front of the bishops, she threw her hand over her mouth. "Oops," she said after removing her hand from her mouth. "But, uh, some devil of a bug just bit me, and it hurt like he—" Etta nudged her again. "Heck. It hurt like heck." She gave Elma an evil stare for causing her to have such an outburst.

Her sisters forced smiles to hide their secondhand embarrassment.

Bishop Smith cleared his throat and feigned a smile, hoping Bishop Ellis didn't change his mind about the flock he was shepherding. "Is there, uh, something I can do to help, Sister Bertha?"

"No, Bishop." She rubbed her leg while looking down at it. "I have some roots at home that will take out the stinger of whatever that was that got me."

Elma's pinch, which was what led up to this disturbance, was due to her shock of hearing about the dress shop Bishop Smith wanted to build for May Rose.

Bishop Ellis, in an attempt to shift the mood, shifted the conversation. "May Rose, you are such a great asset to this church and this community. I can only imagine what kind of asset you are in your own home. Your husband must cherish you."

May Rose acknowledged Bishop Ellis's words by simply nodding. She didn't want the conversation to be about Willie. As a matter of fact, she wanted no reminders that Bishop Smith had a wife and she a husband. They weren't part of the business plan; therefore, they needn't be discussed.

"Willie and I grew up together," Bishop Smith interjected, keeping the conversation on the very topic May Rose wanted to avoid. "I knew about Rose from the first day Willie got sweet on her. I was dating a young lady from the schoolhouse. We all used to go on hayrides together. My gal couldn't touch Rosie in any way."

Bishop Smith managed to change the topic of conversation from Willie to May Rose, and she almost wished he hadn't. Actually, she wished he'd just shut the hell up. Could this man not see—no, hear—how the compliments he was giving May Rose could cause suspicion among everyone? He should have been comparing the gal he was dating back then to his wife, not May Rose.

"Willie used to tease me by saying, 'I got the smartest and the best-looking girl in town.'" He chuckled. "He still says it."

"And do you still believe it to be true?" Elma asked, practically forcing Bishop Smith to declare his feelings for her daughter. As far as Elma was concerned, why play games? Why should May Rose be the woman on the side? If Bishop Smith got rid of First Lady and May Rose got rid of Willie, it would be much better for business. It was called working smarter and not harder. Having to hide a relationship was more work than it was worth sometimes. Elma was, in her eyes, just trying to make May Rose's job easier...smarter.

Ginny spoke up. "Momma, you have a whole story to tell about your days as a young lady, huh?"

Elma replied, "And Bishop Smith is a part of it. He's always been just like a family member for as long as May Rose and Willie have been together." She looked at Bishop Smith knowingly. "Ain't that right, Bishop?"

May Rose was on to her mother's antics and quickly interrupted. "This food is delicious. The cooking committee stuck their foot in these collards, potato salad, fried corn, and barbecued pork neckbones. They showed off for Bishop Ellis." She looked around the table. "Everybody, dig in. Enough talking. Eat." She began shoveling food in her mouth hoping everyone else would follow suit. And shut up!

"They sure did," Bishop Ellis agreed. "I'm a dessert man, though, so I got my eyes on that pound cake and peach cobbler over there." He pointed at the dessert table.

"Oh, you'll love them, too," May Rose said with a mouth full of food. She knew it was bad table manners and unladylike, but she needed to keep that conversation going before her mother hijacked it. "Mother Vivian baked those. She is the best baker in town."

Bishop Ellis curtly responded, "That's wonderful." He turned to Bishop Smith. "Did she teach that wife of yours to bake like this, or is she too busy chasing them children?"

Elma started laughing extra loud, saying, "Bishop Ellis, I like you. You call it like you see it. You must have some African in you."

May Rose, noticing the hot look First Lady Ramona's sister was trying to cool off, hollered, "Momma, don't you see First Lady Ramona's sisters sitting here? I'm sure she don't think it's that funny, if funny at all."

There May Rose was again, defending the likes of what should have been her archenemy. Elma had enough already.

"Her kin know it's the truth. They know how to count them children just like the rest of us do. Besides..." She shot First Lady Ramona's sister a look that said, 'I wish you would,' and then stated, "Who gon' stop me from laughing at the truth? Folks know which side their bread is buttered on, especially First Lady and her kin. Ramona's family are living off of Bishop Smith's finances. Without his money, their entire family would be living an extremely poor life."

Bishop Smith interrupted before things got out of hand. "No, Bishop Ellis, Ramona doesn't cook or bake. I'm blessed to have Mother Vivian and her daughters there to feed me and the children good." He continued by responding to Elma, "Sister Elma, I know you're always going to speak your mind just like Bishop Ellis, and I'm grateful for the two of you, but Ramona is your first lady." He looked to Bishop Ellis. "And she is my wife. So, I kindly and respectfully ask you both to not speak ill of her, even if it is just a joke. The entire church laughed at her because of the joke made from the pulpit today about us having all these children. And if you want the God's honest truth, that's why your first lady is not here fellowshipping with us." He looked down at his plate and started pushing his food around with his fork. It was obvious he'd lost his appetite.

May Rose glared at her mother, tightening her lips and widening her eyes. She nodded twice toward First Lady Ramona's family, trying her best to nonverbally tell her mother to apologize.

Elma lifted her chin in defiance and said, "I'm sorry," to her first lady's sisters.

Before anyone could even respond, Bishop Ellis blurted out, "I ain't sorry for a damn thing. As a matter of fact, I could say more." He turned his body to Bishop Smith but didn't make eye contact with him, as if reading his lines from the table. He was focused. "Bishop Smith is my son in Christ, and it is my duty to straighten his path when I see him off course." His eyes finally met his protégée's. "I sent you to that fancy colored college, Howard University, to become the smart man you are. You could've made better life choices when it comes to racking up children. You got this here large flock to look after." He turned his body straight again and spread his arms wide. "You need to be mindful of how large the flock you create at home is. So, I don't apologize for what I said, but I do apologize for where I said it. I will admit, I should've done it in private, but that's it."

Elma rolled her eyes at May Rose and wobbled her head on her neck. She'd felt as if Bishop Ellis had redeemed her and did all but toot her nose in the air at her daughter.

Bishop Smith took in his mentor's words. "That's fair, Bishop." In an attempt to lighten the mood, he said, "Can we finish up this here food so we can get Bishop Ellis on his way home to Birmingham, Alabama?"

It was apparent by the mentee that the mentor had worn out his welcome.

"Rose, do you mind packing up some plates for Bishop Ellis and his armor-bearer for the trip home?" Bishop Smith said. "Elders," he said to the African sisters, "would you all please pack up food for yourselves, even enough for Willie in case he makes it home?"

May Rose's mother let out a harumph at the thought of fixing Willie a plate.

"Momma, not another word. You have showed off enough today," May Rose said in a hard whisper.

"Girl, I'm your momma, who are you talking to?" her mother asked, slamming her fist on the table.

Wanting to keep the peace, May Rose stood. "I'll fix *my* husband's plate, thank you very much." She walked away to the food tables to go pack up Willie's food.

"Hope he chokes on it," Elma said just low enough for her sisters to hear, and they began to chuckle.

After all the to-go plates were fixed, May Rose and her family headed to the parking lot.

Bishop Ellis and his armor-bearer, Phil, began to walk toward Bishop Smith's car. Ellis shouted, "Elma, c'mon and ride with me so we can talk about your bishop, first lady, and that brood of theirs in peace." A deep laugh came from his throat.

Elma shouted back, "I thought you'd never ask." She started skipping toward him like a schoolgirl who couldn't wait to gossip. Not only that, but the white man she'd been dealing with had been dealing more with his wife than Elma these days. So, if the opportunity and the need arose for her to replace him, well, she needed to be ready.

The girls and the elders were slapping their knees and stumbling with laughter.

Lynette screamed out, "I need to ride with you all so I can hear these jokes. I like jokes, Nana."

May Rose pretended she didn't hear the shenanigans going on between Bishop Ellis and her mother. She kept her head buried in the back of the car while packing the food into it.

"May Rose, keep your mouth shut," she told herself, just wanting to get the day over with. "I heard enough from those two terrors today," she said in reference to her mother and Bishop Ellis, who was clearly on a roll in spite of his fake apology earlier at the picnic table.

Bishop Smith called, "Brother Phil, please keep up closely behind me."

"Just remember, we're following you," Phil said before he got into his car and started it up.

Once everyone was all packed into their respective vehicles, along with the food, the caravan took off down the road.

In Bishop Ellis and Elma's car, they didn't waste any time talking their mess.

"Come on, Bishop Ellis, what you got?" Elma said in anticipation of all the cracks Bishop Ellis probably had up his sleeves regarding Bishop Smith and First Lady Ramona.

"Elma, stop playing with me, woman," Bishop Ellis started. "I ain't call you here to talk about your bishop and his wife." He leaned into Elma and said, "I wanna talk about your bishop and your daughter." He burst out laughing. "It didn't even take a spirit of discernment to sense what was going on today." His laughter died down. "What are we going to do about this madness between David and May Rose?"

"Why, whatever do you mean?" Elma played coy.

"You playing with me again, woman. But cutting to the chase, if you ask me, them two should be together. And if you as her momma thinks the same, well, with the influence you have over your daughter, you could probably make it happen."

Bishop Ellis would love to see Bishop Smith with May Rose because he saw her intelligence and drive. He believed May Rose could help Smith elevate to the man he expected him to be, while Lady Ramona and her family were keeping Bishop Smith from meeting the expectation for his life goals. "He always seems to stay stressed out, not to mention he's starting to lack focus at times."

Elma responded sternly, "Hold on, Ellis. What's in it for my May Rose? David still has to take care of Ramona, those seven babies, with possibly more, and all of Ramona's hundred family members. My girl don't just want and need some damn man-meat. That's all you men think, give a woman some man-sausage and she fall in love with you. That's not how we African woman operate. No, sir."

Bishop Ellis countered, "What's in it for May Rose is getting away from that drunkard husband of hers. It seems like all he is giving her is man-meat, as you call it."

Elma shot back, "Let me take care of him. You just figure out how my May Rose and her girls can live better than Ramona and her family."

Bishop Ellis shook his head. "Woman, you drive a hard bargain. Is this a deal?"

"I know you uppity Baptist Convention bishops got plenty of money. You do your part working on the finances and David, and I will do my work on May Rose and Willie's drunk ass. So, in other words, this is a deal."

Bishop Ellis clapped his hands together in victory. Scooting in a smidge closer to Elma, he said, "How about me taking care of some finances with you tonight?"

Elma gave Bishop Ellis the once-over and bit her bottom lip right before a devious smile spread across her lips. "Don't mess around and move your ass to Bedford so you can keep getting you some of this magic I'm sitting on here."

Bishop licked his lips, and placed his hand on Elma's leg. "Didn't I tell you, Sister Elma? I love to travel," he said as his hand traveled up her thigh.

*"If you are building a house and the nail breaks, do you
stop building the house or change the nail?"*

African Proverb

Chapter 8

❧

THE BLUEPRINT

Ginny woke up on a beautiful spring Saturday morning and ran to the window. The birds were flying from tree to tree as they chirped on key, singing their praises to Mother Nature. Ginny smiled when she spied a baby cardinal hanging out on their clothesline. Its head clicked from left to right, as if looking for its mother. "One day, you'll be all big and grownup like me," Ginny lectured the bird. "Then you won't have to worry about momma bird looking after you. You'll feel good flying about on your own." She chuckled. "You'll be as free as a bird."

That cardinal was a sign to Ginny that part two of her ceremony today was going to fulfill all of her dreams. She was not only going to feel like a woman, she was going to be a woman. Her mother, Nana, and great-aunts would feed her everything she needed to survive in this world.

Like one day the momma bird would no longer have to feed her child from her beak, the same would be true for May Rose and Ginny.

After today, she wouldn't have to look to them for a thing when it came to the business. Today, every part of the job was going to be instilled in her, and Ginny was ready to soak it all up like a sponge.

Just as Ginny was about to turn away from the window, she gasped in delight as something returned to her memory. She recalled what her mother taught her and her sisters about God sending a cardinal as a reminder of self-worth and staying connected to their faith and spirituality no matter what they were going through in life.

Just then, two more cardinals landed on the clothesline. Their yellow beaks opened and shut as they sang so beautifully. Ginny watched as they fluttered their wings but didn't leave the clothesline. They sang and danced their little beaks and feathers off.

She laughed when she compared the cardinals to her nana and great-aunties. "Today is going to be an extra special day," Ginny declared. She closed her eyes and began to hum in unison with the birdsong.

May Rose entered the room as Ginny stood oblivious to her presence, still synchronizing with nature.

"I thought I heard you awoke up here," May Rose said, pulling Ginny out of the chorus.

"Yes, ma'am!" Ginny exclaimed. "I don't even know if I really slept any, Momma."

"I see you're just as excited as I was on the second part of my ceremony. I mean, the initial ceremony is a huge milestone as well, entering womanhood and all. But it's something about the second part that finalizes it all."

"Yes, Momma," Ginny said, racing over to her mother. "That's exactly it. That's exactly how I feel."

May Rose nearly melted at the look in her eldest daughter's eyes. A look of excitement, maturity, and appreciation all rolled up into the gaze of a child. It was all the more touching to May Rose because she knew this was one of the last times she could look in Ginny's eyes and see those of a little girl. After today, she might as well be looking at herself in the mirror because Ginny was going to become what every woman in May Rose's family had been bred and molded to be.

"C'mon down to the kitchen with Momma before our excitement penetrates the walls and wake your sisters up." May Rose headed out and went downstairs.

Ginny gladly ran over and slid her feet into her slippers that rested on the floor. From the foot of her bed, she grabbed a beautiful yellow bed shirt May Rose made her especially for today. It was more mature than the matching one she'd made for all the girls that had flowers on them with lace-trimmed collars. This was a solid one with a slight V cut at the center. It didn't show as much flesh as some of May Rose's nightshirts did, but more than a young girl just reaching her teenage years.

Ginny ran down the steps as quietly and quickly as she could. She couldn't wait to be in the presence of May Rose. For some reason, she felt extra love for her mother this morning. She was bubbling all over herself with joy as she made her way over to May Rose, who was at the oven warming some bread, and threw her arms around her. She closed her eyes and stayed wrapped around her mother for a few seconds. But to Ginny, it felt like minutes.

To May Rose, it felt like hours. And again, she took it all in, considering this might be the last hug she'd ever receive from the Ginny she knew today, versus the Ginny she would know tomorrow.

May Rose giggled. "Girl, let me go so I can breathe," she finally said, "and so that I can get this butter out the icebox to spread on our bread."

When Ginny released her mother, May Rose retrieved the butter and placed it on the center of the table.

Ginny went to the cupboard and collected two plates. "Momma, when I woke up this morning and went over to the window, there was a cardinal hanging out on the clotheslines," she said as she set the table. "They were singing so sweetly." She did a short encore of the song she'd sang with the birds. "Remember what you taught us about a cardinal being present?"

May Rose winked and said, "Of course I do. Stay connected to God, your faith, your spirituality, and be peaceful no matter what the situation or circumstance you find yourself in might be."

"Well, Momma, guess what? There were three. Two more joined us."

"God loves us, and He sent the cardinal to remind us of just how much He does love us, and how He cares for us and is always there to protect us and get us through life."

Ginny laughed. "Yeah, well, they also reminded me of Nana and her sisters." She laughed again.

Instead of joining in on the laughter, May Rose got serious. She tilted her head in thought. "Actually, it might have been God showing you that was you and your sisters. Did you think of that?" May Rose opened the oven and checked on the bread slices she'd placed inside.

"Hmm, I didn't even think about that."

"Yeah, you're the oldest, Ginny. The same role Nana takes as head of the family business, one day, that's going to be you. Tomorrow isn't promised. You can't assume Nana and your great-aunties, or even me, will be the ones to train Lynette and Florence up. It might be you and Florence who end up having to train Lynette up."

"You're right, Momma, because the first bird on the line was a baby bird. And it was like the bird was calling out and then came the two other birds."

May Rose winked at Ginny again. "See there. I told you."

Ginny smiled even harder at the thought that God was positioning her to one day take over the ceremonies and teach the generations that came after her. Dazing off at what that future might look like, Ginny sat at the wobbly kitchen table. "Shoot, Momma, are we ever going to have nice furnishings in our home like Preacher Smith's home? I can't wait to start doing a woman's business. That's one of the first things I'm going to do. Get this place together for you." Her eyes lit up as she looked around. "As a matter of fact, I'm going to get you a whole new place! Like you did for Nana and the aunties."

"Listen, baby," May Rose started as she pulled the bread out of the oven and walked over to the table. "You must understand a woman's business is just a part of a woman's life. It's not just about getting things, buying things, showing off, and all that stuff."

A confused expression covered Ginny's face as she watched May Rose slide the bread onto their plates.

Noticing the look, she said, "We'll discuss all of this later. I don't want you jumping ahead of yourself. Your nana will have a fit if we break the order of things."

Although eager to learn all she could about a woman's business, Ginny nodded in agreement. "One more thing, Momma. What are you going to do about Daddy?"

Now it was May Rose who was confused, and her raised eyebrow reflected as much.

"It's like he has left us. We haven't seen him in almost two weeks." Ginny paused. "And you're spending a lot of time with Minister Smith."

May Rose shot Ginny a stern look. "It's *Bishop* Smith now," she reminded her.

She swallowed hard and then finished her thoughts. "Taking your driving lessons...and all."

May Rose rolled her eyes as she stood over the table and began buttering the bread. Ginny watched in silence, not knowing whether or not to change the subject.

After she buttered a slice of bread for them both, May Rose sat next to her daughter. But before saying grace or eating, she cupped Ginny's chin in her hand and looked her in the eyes. "Let's have this discussion later. I think you'll better understand what I have to say after the ceremony." She took a bite of her warm, buttered bread. "If I know those Crazy African Sisters the way I think I do, I'm sure it will come up at the ceremony." Between chews, she added, "And I'm ready for your asses when it does."

With a mouthful of warm bread herself, Ginny smiled and said, "That's the Momma I know and love." After swallowing, she continued, "But you do know you have to tell the truth, Momma, about everything. Nana says this is a family business, and we can only help each other when we know the truth about what's going on with one another."

May Rose shifted in her chair, a bit uneasy, and then replied with a loving smile, "I promise to tell you the truth about whatever you want to know, my sweet girl."

"Well, the truth and understanding circle begins at noon promptly, Nana said so," Ginny said, referring to the second part of her ceremony.

"Yes, so eat up and go get dressed. We should be at your nana's door by eleven-fifty."

Ginny started clapping her hands and singing. "Yay, Momma, yay, Momma."

"Shhhh!" May Rose threw her index finger over her lips. "Don't wake your sisters. The less time we have to deal with them, the more time we have to get ourselves ready for the ceremony."

Ginny ate the last of her food just as May Rose ate the last of hers. Ginny gathered up all the dishes, washed, dried, and put them away. She dried her hands and darted up the steps to start getting dressed.

May Rose heard the commotion on the steps. "Girl, are you crazy or something? I just asked you not to wake up your sisters."

"Sorry, Momma," she whispered as she headed to her bedroom. Ginny had been tossing clothes to and fro across her room since last night. Still, she couldn't find anything grown-up to wear to the ceremony. Nana mentioned at the first ceremony she would receive her very own Kente cloth dress and hat. This made Ginny now look at her clothing and how she should dress differently, which was why she was disappointed when she didn't get that purple dress she'd asked for.

"If Momma sees this mess, she's gonna be fit to be tied. Probably skin my behind good and clean." Ginny paused. "I wonder if me being a woman now means I can no longer get a switch taken to my behind." She made a mental note to add that to her list of questions.

"You need to clean that mess up before Momma sees it." Florence said exactly what Ginny was thinking as she peeked into her big sister's room. "She's gonna beat your ass. Nana, too, if she hears about it."

Florence was right.

"*A woman doesn't live messy,*" Nana always told the girls. "*How you supposed to be the cleanup woman if you don't clean?*" Although Ginny never knew what that latter part meant.

Another thing to add to the list. Ginny made a mental note to do so.

Hearing Nana's words circle through her head instantly made Ginny begin cleaning up the mess she'd made, organizing everything nice and neat back into her clothing chest.

"Don't worry," Ginny said to Florence as she finished straightening up her room. "Your turn is coming soon. You'll be just as excited making just as big of a mess, if not bigger"

"My turn is coming?" Florence repeated. "My turn to what? To clean?"

Ginny had forgotten that the girls were clueless about the ceremony, so she opted not to address her little sister's question. "I'm going to clean up like a woman because when I come back, I'll be a full-grown woman." She stood and then bent over and kissed Florence on the cheek. "I promise you I'll still play with you sometimes, though."

Florence pushed Ginny's face and said, "Catching babies does not make you a woman. So, when you and Momma come back from catching babies, you still gon' be an ugly little Black girl." Florence put her hands on her hips, bent halfway over while squeezing her eyes shut tight and sticking out her tongue.

Two weeks ago, Ginny would have shot back to Florence with a comment that would have cut deep to the bone. But she was a woman now. She didn't have time to go back and forth with a child like a child.

Ginny let out a chuckle. "You wish, little girl. You wish!" She shooed Florence away. "Now leave me alone so I can go take care of this business." She jumped up with a bundle of clothes in hand, everything she'd been tearing the chest up looking for, and ran downstairs into the washroom.

About a half-hour later, Ginny came out and hollered, "Momma, let's go. We can't be late!"

"I'm coming, I'm coming," May Rose said, exiting her room as she adjusted her breasts in her bra. "Let me go talk to the girls to tell them what to do while we're gone."

Ginny anxiously went out the back door and sat on the porch steps, staring at the elders' house in anticipation of what was to come. She was so excited, though, that she'd left her notebook in her room. "Dang it!" she said as she raced back in the house to retrieve her notebook and writing utensil from under her mattress...where she'd hid it from her nosey sisters. By the time she made it back to the porch, May Rose still was nowhere in sight.

A minute or so later, May Rose finally came out the door, walking slowly because she was looking down to button her sweater. She didn't want to trip right off the porch.

Ginny hopped up from her sitting position. "Momma, let's goooooo," she whined.

"I'm coming, I'm coming!" May Rose barked.

Ginny took off running to Elma's front door. Once she reached the door, she swung it open to a strong scent that she had smelled at Elma and the elders' house before but never had the nerve to ask what it was. She was about to find out.

Upon seeing her great-niece burst in, Aunt Etta smiled and announced loudly, "Our tribe's latest woman has arrived." She took Ginny by the hand and led her to a circle of some type of brown powder in the middle of the living room floor. There were three pebbles in the center. "Baby, you sit here on the right, inside of the circle of truth and understanding."

Ginny did as she was told, folding her legs across each other.

Everyone else sat to the right of Ginny with their legs crossed as well.

Ginny was so grateful that there were no pleasantries, that they were getting right down to business...literally.

Her eyes filled with moisture. Something was taking over her. In addition to being surrounded by two generations of women in her family, there was also a feeling of gratitude greater than any that had ever entered her body. Her soul was crying out, but only Ginny, and perhaps the ancestors, could hear it.

Her heart was making its own drumming sounds as her spirit danced to it. The sweet smell of the burning cinnamon gave her a sense of peace. The thoughts of the bravery and strength of previous generations of women raced through her mind. Ginny began to silently pray that she could live up to being the woman they were. She so desperately wanted to make her ancestors proud. Not only make them proud, but her mother, Nana, and great-aunts as well. Her mind kept screaming the word, 'leadership.' She now strongly understood that she must be the example and leader for her sisters, and it needed to begin now. She sat up straight and held her head high.

May Rose's inner being was trembling, and she didn't know why. Perhaps she was taking on some of Ginny's emotions or simply reflecting on her own when she once sat in this circle many years ago. It was even quite possible that her own spirit was lining up to be officially reintroduced to the family business. This time, a willing spirit. Like how she'd heard Christians say they were re-baptized after having been baptized at such a young age where it wasn't voluntarily, but just part of the family pattern or expectation.

Elma and Bertha were dressed in their Kente cloth dresses and headwraps just like Etta and May Rose. May Rose wore her garb under her sweater. Neither Florence nor Lynette had questioned her attire since it wasn't out of the ordinary for her and the elders to wear Kente cloth to catch babies.

Elma had set a silver tray with cups of water on the floor inside the circle in anticipation of a lot of talking. She was positioned to the right of May Rose, and Aunt Bertha was on the right of her. It was amazing to Ginny to see her elders be so limber while crossing their legs after they sat. They were all facing the middle of the circle.

Ginny leaned toward her mother and whispered, "Where is my Kente dress and hat?"

"Later," May Rose whispered back without looking in her direction. "Later."

Ginny nodded her trust and resumed her upright position with her legs crossed in front of her. She held onto her writing paper and utensils very tight. So tight, it was a surprise her fingerprints weren't embedded in them.

Elma rang a little bell three times and began to pray as if it was coming from her stomach. "Dear God in Heaven, please allow our ancestors to come forth and be present while we complete Abdebowale's womanhood rite of passage ceremony. Allow them to guide us elders so we can send her down the right paths to womanhood."

"Yes," Aunt Bertha said softly under her breath.

Elma continued, "We thank and honor you, our Lord. Amen."

Everyone repeated, "Amen."

"May the truth and understanding of a woman's business come forth to all generations now and those to come," Elma said. "We have had to change the ceremony to fit into these present times and this land that is not our own, but we know it will be honored and blessed just the same. Though our ancestors used alligator pepper to create the circle, the circle we sit in is made with cinnamon. In the Bible in Exodus 30:23, it is one of the ingredients of the holy anointing oil. So, again, we know this circle is blessed and anointed."

Everyone nodded in agreement.

"Also, in Proverbs 7:17," Aunt Etta added, "the sweet scent of cinnamon is a metaphor for the alluring nature of sensuality and temptation."

Aunt Bertha decided to throw in her two cents as well. "An old wives' tale says cinnamon can bring greater finances and opportunities to you. It will remove negative energies and can be a magnet for bringing positive energies."

Elma chuckled and said, "May Rose, you should have your floors covered in cinnamon with that mess of a man you got over there."

Everyone let out a hearty laugh, even May Rose. Had it not been Ginny's ceremony and not a time to play the dozens, May Rose would have shot back with a reminder that some good had come out of her and Willie's relationship. The elders had a home to live in, didn't they?

Elma continued, "The three pebbles represent the Father, the Son, and the Holy Spirit." She looked at Abdebowale. "They will provide protection, healing, and help you to pri-oritize your life. These words of wisdom from the ancestors and us, your elders, should be masterfully practiced in order to make a successful life for you and your offsprings. The woman and man relationship is so complicated, and it must be con-ducted as a business by the woman. To love a man will cause you heartbreak. If you don't manage your emotions properly, they can destroy your entire life. Because if you don't remem-ber anything else, it's that you are in control of your emotions. Your emotions should never control you."

May Rose's spirit was pierced by that last comment because if she was being 100% truthful, her relationship with Willie wasn't just about her being tired of the business. She did allow her emotions to get the best of her. This was the first time since marrying Willie that she was able to outright admit, accept, understand, and take accountability for her actions. Guess this wasn't called a truth and understanding circle for nothing.

May Rose exhaled at that revelation and relaxed as her mother continued speaking.

"You can care for the man you choose with that neighborly type of love the Bible mentions," Elma said. "If you give him that deep-rooted love from your soul, he's not capable of handling it the way it should be. Not only will he mishandle your love, but he will mishandle you." She wagged her finger at Abdebowale. "Whatever we share with you in this circle and out when it comes to a woman's business should never, absolutely never, be shared with any man, especially the ones you choose to do business with. You must never let a man know your sly ambitions. Do you understand?"

Abdebowale nodded.

"Good. We will now begin the truth and understanding ceremony." Elma clapped her hands and stomped her feet simultaneously three times.

"Abdebowale, please remember these details given to you and discussed on this day should never be shared with anyone accept your girl-children, with one exception regarding your boy-child that we will discuss later," Bertha reiterated.

"Now, please begin with your questions," Elma said. "And remember, there is nothing you can't ask us. And more importantly, nothing we won't answer." She looked to her sisters and May Rose. "Right, ladies?"

"Right," they said in unison.

Abdebowale took a deep breath. "Greetings, my beautiful elders. My first question is, how do you know if a man loves or likes you?"

"Well, what do you think?" Elma wanted to first hear if Ginny had done any thinking on her own. It was important that a woman know how to think for herself as well as seek counsel.

Ginny didn't even hesitate with her response. "I think a man likes you if he is kind to you, but a man loves you if he tells you and shows you he loves you. But what does that look like? What does that feel like?"

The women looked at one another proudly. It was obvious they'd done a great job educating Abdebowale thus far. She asked the most important question she could have asked had she truly been paying attention and was intentional and committed about learning the family business.

Elma could barely hide her smile. She cleared her throat and replied, "That's a great question and answer, Abdebowale. Let me add a little more so that you have a clear understanding." Elma rocked her bottom from side to side, adjusting herself for comfort. "A woman must first love herself with all her heart and soul. She must love herself with the love of God and with the same love she has for God. Otherwise, it is impossible for her to love any other human being.

"We as women have changed from the woman we would've become if we were still in our homeland. So, loving ourselves is a hard thing to do since we have been treated so badly in this country. Since we have been taught to hate ourselves and one another. But the Dear Lord loves a woman. He will help us love ourselves if we do the work. Please understand a man should never like a woman. He should care for her. A man is not capable of being in love with a woman the way she desires nor the way she deserves. So, the love for herself must exist to fill that void. That way, it doesn't really feel like a void. He may think he loves her, but he really thinks of her as a possession. He was created to be a hunter-gatherer. His goal is to have babies with a woman and own her body, and to hunt and gather all the women he can."

The other elders and May Rose nodded in agreement and from experience.

"Slavery added with that caused a bigger problem because it took the man away from his family," Elma said. "And in these days, men continue to leave their families. They also still believe this is the way it's supposed to be or that it's okay to do so. Otherwise, why would they do it? If a man has never seen, witnessed, or experienced affection in his own home, how will he be able to give it? How can a woman think she can withdraw something from a man that was never deposited in him? And even if he did see, witness, or experience affection, did he understand what it was? Did anyone ever sit him down and explain it to him like we are doing with you, dear child?"

Abdebowale exhaled. She'd been sitting there inhaling the answer to her question without even breathing. "Why do women marry and have babies if the man will leave and not take care of them?" She looked to any of the women in the circle to reveal the answer.

"A woman wants to be in love and be loved," Aunt Etta responded, "but it rarely happens. Not only that, but a woman wants to feel safe. A woman wants to feel taken care of. She wants to feel secure. Women want to feel a sense of family and belonging. Every married woman or woman with a man will experience the hurt of a man if she doesn't practice a woman's business. But for those who do, like the women in this family, they experience no hurt regardless of a man's actions. What he does. What he doesn't do."

"Which, if you don't play your role correctly," Aunt Bertha added, "can be a gift and a curse."

"Just ask your mother," Elma couldn't help but say no matter how hard she tried to suppress her digs at her daughter.

Oddly enough, May Rose didn't take offense. She herself was thinking what her mother verbalized. This explained why she couldn't see in her and Willie's relationship what the elders—or anyone else—could. She was immune to the things that should have caused her hurt and pain. To the things that would cause the average woman to leave a man regardless of the lifestyle he was or wasn't providing her. But May Rose had gotten complacent. The elders had seen that, but she hadn't...until now. So, in a weird way, the woman's business was a gift and a curse.

"You can remain in a relationship with any man," Aunt Etta said, "if you understand your role and the actions you must take to make yourself feel whole. Because remember, you never give any man so much power over you that it becomes his responsibility to make you whole. That you look in him for your happiness, self-love, and self-worth. That you look in him to find yourself. Because, honey, God removed the rib from Adam. You're no longer inside that man. That rib is no longer even a part of that man. You stand alone. You don't need that man to survive and breathe. That rib walks the earth just fine no longer attached to that man from which it came," Aunt Etta concluded as Elma chimed in again.

"The man will never change. You will need to take him as he is. You will need to understand the man will cheat, no matter what his mouth says. His actions will prove it. If a man is alone with a woman other than *his* woman, and that woman puts her tail in his face, he will take it because he thinks it's his birthright to indulge with whoever he wants. He thinks it's part of being a man and is therefore acceptable and excusable. And the world will normalize it by saying, 'a man will be a man' or 'he's a man first,' as if he shouldn't be held accountable for his actions.

He will blame his cheating ways on his woman, the woman, his mother, and sometimes his daddy. But he will never take blame, because he's simply being a man. He will blame everyone but himself and his desires to have who he wants.

"Abdebowale, you must take action to protect your heart. You must take action to protect your body. One action you take to protect your body is to never allow a man to put his hands on you or your children."

Ginny asked, "What if the man you choose doesn't have a lot of money to take care of his home and children? I think a woman must be patient with her man to get his finances together."

Nana responded, "If your home doesn't have all of the fancy fixings you need and want, and you and your children aren't dressed to the nines at all times, you must go out and find it. The way you go out and find that man who will make your house a beautiful home and keep you and your children dressed well is to carry a smile on your face at all times. Don't carry the weight of the world on your face, always look and smell delicious, keep your hair clean and beautiful, keep your weight neat, keep your home clean no matter what fixings you have, educate yourself, walk like royalty, speak well of your family and your ancestors, take yourself places where men with means will be, be the envy of every woman when you walk in the room and own that room. Pray for this man and be specific about what you want him to look like, what you expect him to have and do, and most of all, pray that that man loves the Lord and will lead his family to the Lord. Baby, know that God must remain in the center of your life and your relationship."

Abdebowale took everything in and then asked, "Ladies, once I find my special man, will I be happy? Based on what y'all are saying, relationships will always take work."

"If you're looking for happiness in a man, you're making a mistake," Elma reiterated. "Remember, happiness comes from you loving the woman you are. The woman God has made you to be. Before you go to work with any man, you must work on uplifting yourself, and that is a never-ending task."

Abdebowale fired off another question immediately, "Does the way a man does his business in the bed make a difference?"

"Always be very particular of the man you choose. Don't marry because he makes you feel good in the sack," Elma advised. "That will, in most cases, backfire. You could be giving it to him all day and several times at night, and that still won't be enough for him. He wants variety until his ass is sick, and his man-parts don't work anymore. Even then, he would try to get satisfied somewhere else if he could."

Aunt Bertha jumped in. "You must learn their pedigree before you even think about marrying them. Does he come from a family with money or has his own money? Does he have a family full of crazy folks? If he tells you he doesn't have any family at all, then stay away because something is wrong."

Elma took back over. "Most of all, you do the choosing. You take control of the relationship without him even knowing it. You must be strong in every situation and lead your life. Don't allow any man to lead your life. That's part of your duties, because the moment you give him control, you lose it."

"But won't me being controlling make him mad?" Abdebowale asked.

"You can be sweet and be in control at the same time," Elma said. "The control is delicate. You will always make sure he is satisfied in bed and always keep him with good home-cooked meals. All the while, you are controlling it all."

"When a man is courting you, he must always come bearing a gift. This will also let you know his pedigree if he does,"

Aunt Bertha said, "as well as if he doesn't. And should you decide to marry him, that type of behavior needs to continue. In other words, the gifts need to keep on being given."

Without even thinking, Abdebowale said, "But my daddy don't do that with Momma."

Elma grinned and said, "Take it away, May Rose."

Now that it was her own daughter asking the million-dollar question, and the truth had to be told, the elders would finally get the answer they'd all been dying to know. May Rose was forced to speak on it herself to Abdebowale instead of the elders having to share their opinion about it all the time.

May Rose came with guns blazing. She'd already warned Ginny that she was ready for the elders, as she knew her and Willie's relationship was going to be brought up. She just didn't know Ginny would be the one bringing it up. Nonetheless, she gladly took the opportunity to finally speak on how she felt. "Your daddy had potential to be a good man. Before you and your sisters came along, he courted me very nicely. His family owned this property." She looked around proudly. She hadn't all the way veered off course as much as the elders liked to tell her girls she had. "But he changed as he got older. And the bottom line is that, yeah, I could have moved on, but I stay because of you girls."

As heartfelt as that might have come off, the elders weren't moved.

"The hell with potential," Elma shouted. She looked at Abdebowale and said forcefully, "Do you understand me, child?"

"Yes, I do, Nana," Abdebowale replied, nodding.

"I can admit that I made a mistake marrying Willie on his potential. I broke a cardinal rule," May Rose said.

The elders looked at one another, pleased May Rose could admit her wrong and that she knew better. That the elders had taught her better. That they'd done their job just fine. She hadn't done hers. That gave them a bit of peace and maybe, just maybe, they'd let up on May Rose some.

"So, Momma, what's your plan to get back to the woman's business? Because it's hard to learn something if you're living dead smack in the middle of the opposite."

Abdebowale's question caught May Rose off guard. She wasn't anticipating this question to be asked of her. She knew the day would be filled with lots of questions, but she had no idea her daughter would direct one specifically at her. Especially not this one.

Before May Rose could answer, Abdebowale continued. "Us girls don't like him being drunk all the time, him cussing at you and pulling on you, not to mention he's doing all that in a raggedy house, and we're raggedy."

A hurt look appeared in May Rose's eyes.

"I'm not trying to say hurtful things, Momma, but it's the truth. We're clean, but we're raggedy. We see the preacher man and his family dressed sharp and crisp all the time. Not just on Sundays either. Sometimes, I be praying that could be us." Abdebowale paused and thought about whether she should say the next words that popped into her head.

"Come on now, child, speak your truth," Betha urged her.

Abdebowale took a deep breath and then continued. "And now that I see him winking and grinning at you, and calling you Rosie, it seems like he's sweet on you. And even though you might not be sweet on him, for our sake, I was wondering why you don't just handle your business." She looked May Rose dead in the eyes, demanding the truth and nothing but. "A woman's business. This family's business."

Here, May Rose had thought the elders were going to be on her case, but it was Ginny all along prepared to get on her.

She wondered if the elders had put Ginny up to this, if those questions were really written down in her notebook or just in her head. Or even worse, in her heart. How long had she been paying attention to how May Rose handled Willie, or should she say the way Willie mishandled her? Was this why Ginny demanded earlier that May Rose come to the ceremony prepared to tell the truth?

Elma started choking on the water she had taken a big gulp of. She, too, was surprised at how Ginny seemed to be coming for May Rose. She took a couple deep breathes and said, "All this time she's spending with him learning how to drive, I know damn well she is working on something."

May Rose ignored her mother's comment. "Abdebowale, when I grow up, I want to be just like you," she said, proud of how open, bold, and blunt her daughter was. A sure sign no man was going to walk all over her. "I do have a plan with the bishop. Regardless of what things look like, your momma always has a plan, trust me."

"And what about Daddy?" Abdebowale asked with concern.

"Your daddy is going to be just fine," May Rose said. "Matter of fact, I'm going to ask Bishop Smith for my next driving lesson if we can go see about him."

"What for?" the elders asked in unison.

"If he ain't minding you, ain't no need in you minding him," Elma said.

"I don't know." May Rose shrugged and stared off. "My spirit been somewhat vexed about him. He ain't been to visit. Ain't sent no word. I don't know. Just feeling led to go see about him is all." She looked to the elders. "Trust me, it ain't gon' interfere with nothing I got planned."

Elma exhaled, still not too confident about her daughter's decision, but she turned her attention back to her granddaughter. "Abdebowale, a woman's business can some-times be messy. I need you to promise us and your ancestors that if you give birth to a son, with a husband or not, please talk to him about a woman's business as well. He needs to under-stand his role in a relationship. There could be harmony in a relationship if he understands why he does the things he does. He may have sisters and daughters, so he should always be in tune with a woman. You would have to swear your boys to secrecy. Prayerfully, his daddy will teach him the right way, but it's your responsibility to teach him about your ancestors' homeland and our expectations."

Abdebowale smiled and replied, "I promise, Nana." Her face then got serious. "I have another question." She looked from one woman to the next. "How do you have sex? I've acci-dentally walked in and seen Momma and Daddy. I've also seen some of the older kids doing stuff behind the schoolhouse."

May Rose shouted, "When?"

"Rose, it doesn't matter when," Elma said, giving her a dis-couraging look for interrupting the girl.

"But it looks like it's done different." Abdebowale shrugged. "I don't know, like there are different ways and different things to do."

"I'll tell the baby what she wants to know," Elma said. "As a youngin' trying to do the do, you are sneaking, so it won't be as comfortable and good as it can be." She put her hand up. "Wait a minute. Let me back up." She looked at her granddaughter. "Abdebowale, do you know about the man's part?"

"I think so," Abdebowale replied with very little certainty.

"It's the weirdest and ugliest thing you will ever see in your life," Elma said with a frown. "It can smell bad, too. Especially if a man doesn't keep it clean. And if he ain't circumcised, it's twice as bad. Both the odor and the looks of it." Elma fanned her hand across her nose.

Abdebowale tried to smother her laugh under her cupped hands.

"That's why before you do the do with a man, you get a basin and fill it with warm water and put a capful of bleach in it. Then you clean around the head of the man's part. They will sometimes do the do with another woman before doing it with you. They can be nasty that way. You will keep your woman-part clean and safe from infection by douching with water and vinegar after each time you do the do. There are many reasons you don't want them to put the dirty suds in you other than to make a baby. They will carry the spirit of every woman they've did the do with."

"Some of those spirits can be evil and cause you grief," Aunt Etta chimed in.

Elma nodded and continued. "Ride them backward like a horse. You will control how he gets it. Don't look them in their eyes while doing the do. That will keep you from getting all caught up in emotions and falling in love. But if you want a man to think he wants to fall in love with you, keep yourself pretty, keep your body clean and smelling sweet, be smart, and make him think you would do anything in the world for him. Another very important thing is to never let a man think he's more prettier than you."

"Amen!" Aunt Etta said.

Elma continued, "You will be many women in your life-time. In other words, you will play many roles as a woman. We believe you should value most being a woman that will be a protector, a leader, an owner, a warrior, a believer, a conqueror, a thinker, keeper of secrets, and a maker. You will touch the lives of everyone you come in contact with, not always in a good way, but whatever way it is, they won't ever forget you."

Over the next few hours, Abdebowale went through every question in her notebook, and the women answered them as clearly and as thoroughly as they could. Unfortunately, the ones she'd only made a mental note of and had not written down were overlooked.

"As we conclude this ceremony, my sweet baby," Elma said to Abdebowale, "always remember the woman's business will change throughout the ages. And that your momma and your elders, for as long as we breathe, will always be here for you to stand on our shoulders. We'll be here to answer any other questions you might have. So, don't think just because you didn't ask them here today that they can't be asked. Do you understand?"

"Yes, Nana," Abdebowale said sincerely.

"As we prepare to depart," Elma said, "I want you to remember the word sankofa, which means, in our native Ghanaian tongue, to reach back. Reach back, acknowledge, and teach about your ancestors."

May Rose leaned over and gave her eldest daughter a loving kiss. "There will always be questions and uncertainty. Sometimes, you will need to think of how to handle a situation as it is happening, but by you studying men and asking questions of us while we're here to answer them, the day you become an elder, you will teach your children and your children's children the business. So, baby, from this day forward, go out and be the best woman you can be." May Rose concluded by saying, "In other words, handle your business."

Abdebowale looked at May Rose with such love and gratitude. Even more than she had displayed earlier in their kitchen. "Momma, Nana, and Great-Aunties, I'm so grateful to have you strong women leading me into the woman's business. I will make you proud of me. I promise." She wiped the lone tear that escaped her eye and slid down her right cheek.

Elma stood up from the circle, walked into the center, picked up the three pebbles, and placed them in Abdebowale's hand. She announced, "Abdebowale, whenever in doubt about anything in life, put your pebbles in your hands and rub them together and pray to the Father, the Son, and the Holy Spirit for clear guidance on the matter." She kissed her granddaughter on the forehead and waved toward May Rose, Aunt Bertha, and Aunt Etta to stand. They each stood and kissed Abdebowale on the forehead.

They all started humming loudly as they began walking around the outside of the circle. Abdebowale followed the women in their actions, knowing a woman's business was something she was now obligated to do for the rest of her life. And hopefully, unlike her mother, she wouldn't renege on that obligation. Once walking the circle had ended, Elma stepped out and walked to her bedroom to grab Abdebowale's beautiful orange, white, and green Kenta dress and hat. Elma came back to the living room and gifted Abdebowale with her garments.

Abdebowale's eyes lit up with anticipation when Nana started walking toward her. Elma placed the things in the young woman's extended hands and said, "Baby, these are yours to wear with pride and be sure you pass it down. These belonged to your mother from part two of her ceremony. May Rose wanted you to have them." Elma bent toward Abdebowale and kissed her on the cheek.

Abdebowale smiled, and then she turned and ran toward May Rose. "Momma, thank you for these beautiful clothes. I just love you so much! You're really my hero."

"You're welcome, baby," May Rose said.

"Can I try it now?"

With tears in her eyes, May Rose said, "Of course, my baby! By the way, you're my hero, too." She quickly brushed the tears away and cleared her throat. "You stay here and have lunch with Nana and your aunts. I'm going to send the girls over shortly."

"Why, Momma?" Ginny asked, confused. "Why are you leaving?"

"I have to go get ready for my driving lessons with Bishop Smith."

"Ohhhh," Ginny said. "Alright then, Momma. I guess I'll let you go handle your business, too."

> *"If you educate a man, you educate an individual,*
> *but if you educate a woman, you educate a family*
> *(nation)."*
>
> African Proverb

Chapter 9

❧

ANOTHER MAN'S TREASURE

May Rose rushed home after Ginny's ceremony so she could prepare for her driving lesson with Bishop Smith. The first thing she looked at when she walked in the door was the old wooden clock on the living room mantel. "He is set to arrive at four p.m. and here it's already three o'clock," she grumbled. "My mother and aunts never stopped talking. I should've been home and started getting ready."

She started taking her clothes off as she shouted to the girls, "Florence and Lynette, your Nana and aunts making a beautiful lunch today."

"Yay," Lynette said as she came out of her and Florence's shared bedroom and met her mother in the area right outside May Rose and Willie's room.

"They made some fried chicken, black-eyed peas, collard greens with fatback, and Aunt Etta's delicious upside-down cake."

"Yes, yes, and yes!" Lynette clasped her hands together and jumped with excitement.

"Now get going on over there." May Rose playfully swatted her on the behind.

"That sounds like a holiday dinner instead of lunch." Florence walked up, braiding up her left ponytail to match the right one.

Florence was the first one who trotted toward the door to head to the African sisters' house. Lynette was right on her heels.

Florence blurted out as she walked away, "Momma, how did it go? Is Ginny going to be acting even more different than she has the last two weeks?"

May Rose shot Florence a puzzled look. "What do you mean?" May Rose and Ginny had been careful not to tell Florence and Lynette about the ceremony. They didn't want either of them slipping up and telling Willie. But it seemed like every time Florence opened her mouth, it was as if she knew what was going on.

"Ever since she started catching babies with you, she done got the big head," Florence said.

Lynette jumped in before May Rose could respond. "Yeah, Momma. Are we gonna be able to stand her at all now?"

May Rose chuckled and replied, "Wait your turns. I'm not going to keep telling y'all this. Your time will be here before you know it." May Rose was now inside her room, changing clothes, as she yelled, "As far as Ginny's actions toward you two, I think it's more of her menstruation than anything."

May Rose stepped back out and said in a hard whisper, "You'll understand what she's going through real soon. Now, get to your nana's house. I'm getting ready to go take my driving lessons with Bishop Smith. We'll probably be gone for a several hours."

The girls looked at each other and busted out laughing.

May Rose put her hands on her hips. "I don't see the joke here. Y'all asking for me to grab my switch and light your asses up. I got time for a quick ass beating before I leave."

Lynette screamed, "I'm sorry, Momma. I won't do that again, I promise."

May Rose glanced at Florence and asked, "What about your smart ass, Miss Florence? You're teaching my baby all of this smart-mouthiness. I should get you just for that."

Lynette, once again not wanting to break the sisters' code, abruptly jumped in and said, "Momma, Florence don't teach me nothing. You taught us to be leaders and not followers. I lead me, like you taught us."

May Rose dropped her head to hide her smile. "I'm not messing with you all no more today. I'm getting ready to go to my driving lesson in peace. Get on over to your nana's now, and take a reading book, and don't be talking that grown talk with Nana and your great-aunts about my business."

"Okay, Momma," the girls said in unison as Florence opened the door.

"Wait a minute," May Rose called. "Your momma can't get no sugar before you leave? I said I'm going to be gone some hours."

The girls trekked to May Rose, where she placed kisses on their foreheads.

Florence and Lynette ran off to Nana's as May Rose went into the washroom and washed her lady parts quickly, then went into her bedroom that seemed so lonely since Willie had been gone. He hadn't come back home since he left two weeks ago. She was going to ask Bishop Smith to allow her to practice driving out to where Willie was at the coal mine. She had already asked him how far of a drive it would be, and he'd said about two hours. May Rose wasn't ready to take that drive alone just yet. And if it hadn't been for Bishop Smith giving her driving lessons, no telling when she'd see her husband.

May Rose sprayed the perfume Willie bought her all over her neck, arms, and dress, in hopes Willie would want to get a piece in his room while she was there.

Just then, May Rose heard that rhythmic knock on the door she had come to know in the last two weeks. She did a little shoulder shimmy and whispered softly, "Here is the man of the hour." She had to laugh at herself as she looked in the mirror to make sure everything was in order. "How quickly I done went from wanting Willie to jump my bones to shimmying for David. This is a woman's business at its finest." She bit her bottom lip. "If only my mother, aunts, and Ginny knew how smooth I really am with the business." She let out a harrumph.

The second rhythmic knock snapped her out of her thoughts.

She jogged to the door and opened it quickly. "Hey there, kind sir. Please come in. I need to grab my handbag." May Rose stepped aside for Bishop Smith to enter her home.

"Take your time," he said, looking around. "Where are the girls?" He thought he'd asked after not hearing all the commotion they usually made when he came calling.

She responded while walking to the living room closet. "They're at my mother's house having a nice ole lunch." She grabbed her handbag off the shelf. "I made a few fixings from the lunch to bring along on our drive."

"You're acting like we're driving to another city, girl." He walked up behind her and tickled her waist.

May Rose giggled. "As a matter of fact, we kinda are." She slowly turned around. "Remember when I asked how long it would take to get to Willie? Well, I was hoping you realized I was hinting that we go see him." The look of disappointment in Bishop Smith's eyes didn't go unnoticed. "It's just that I haven't laid eyes on him in a while. What would folks think if a wife didn't show some bit of concern for her husband?" May Rose reasoned, batting her eyes. "I just have to lay my eyes on him. I have just been sick with worry. What do you think?"

Bishop Smith responded with a puzzling look on his face. "Rosie, are you sure you want to just drop in on Willie unannounced? It's just a far ride. And we can't forget about the fact that—"

"I know," May Rose said, cutting him off. "As always, while you're giving me driving lessons, I have my mother and aunts on standby in case First Lady Ramona goes into labor. Did you tell your boys and in-laws to fetch them if necessary?"

"I did," Bishop Smith said. "But that wasn't really my concern. It was you dropping by on Willie."

May Rose smirked and plucked her finger on his collar. "There you go trying to cover for your friend again like when we were young." She shook her head and wagged a finger at him.

"No, not at all. I'm thinking about you, Rosie. You know Willie is under a lot of stress working that deadly job. You know he doesn't handle problems very well. If he ain't working…"

"He's probably drinking," May Rose finished his sentence and laughed.

Bishop Smith chuckled. "But if you want to go, we'll go. We won't have a lot of time since I'll need to get back in enough time to complete writing my sermon for service tomorrow."

"Sounds mighty fine to me, Bishop," May Rose said and then headed for the door.

"Good." He followed her. "Because you're doing all the driving there."

May Rose froze in her tracks.

"And I'll do all the driving back."

May Rose exhaled and relaxed. She would use up so much tension driving there, she didn't know if she'd be able to muster up the strength to do it both ways. She was relieved to hear Bishop Smith confirm he would take on the second leg of the trip.

"Let's just go past my house to let Ramona know about our plans." He brushed past May Rose and opened the door for her. She locked up behind them.

They started walking toward the car, Bishop Smith in front.

She called out, "David." When he turned around, May Rose hugged him around his neck and whispered in his ear, "Thank you for always looking out for us. I will always appreciate you." She pulled back and out of the embrace.

He stared into her eyes momentarily. "I will always look out for you and the girls. Like I said during the church anniversary service, you have done so much for me. You have sacrificed your entire life for others, including me and my family. You are an incredible woman, Rosie, and for so many reasons."

May Rose gave him a sweet kiss on his cheek before walking to the driver's side of the car behind Bishop Smith. He opened the door for her and instead of getting the stool this time, he lifted her into the driver's seat. Her driving confidence had grown since her previous lessons.

Bishop Smith closed the door, and May Rose started the car. He settled into the passenger seat as she put her foot on the gas, shifted the car into gear, and took off.

"Whoa, tiger, slow down," he hollered as he overexaggerated his expression by gripping the dashboard.

May Rose smiled and replied, "I'm just doing what you taught me." She looked over and winked at her passenger before turning her attention back to the road.

He smiled. "If you keep driving like that, you won't be driving me to the McDowell coal mine on this here day."

May Rose tapped him on the knee. "I'm just a little anxious about seeing Willie. This is the longest time we have been apart since we married, you know." May Rose couldn't keep the same temperature for five minutes. One minute, she was cold for Willie and hot for her bishop, and the next, it was vice versa.

"I get it, but you have to calm down so we can get there safely." He released the dashboard. "Do I need to just drive us there?"

"I got this," May Rose said as she looked over at him, frowning at his lack of faith in her.

"Watch out!"

Hadn't Bishop Smith yelled out, May Rose would have run head-on into the vehicle coming toward them on the opposite side of the road.

"Pull over on the side of the road up there." Bishop Smith pointed. "I have confidence you can drive, but you can't focus on driving now. You're too anxious about seeing Willie."

May Rose was so frightened by her near head-on collision that she was too afraid to even acknowledge his instructions. She had her hands gripped tightly on the steering wheel with her back raised off the seat, positioned so close to the windshield that she was almost literally keeping her eyes on the road.

"Come on now," Bishop Smith said, trying his darnedest to convince May Rose it was the right thing to do...to save both their lives. "You can drive us back. By then, all of your butterflies will be gone, and you'll still get your lesson in."

There was silence.

"Huh?" Bishop patted her leg.

May Rose exhaled, finally feeling it was safe for her to speak without losing control of the vehicle. "You're surely right."

He exhaled a gust of wind and rested his back against the seat. As May Rose pulled over, he closed his eyes and said a quick prayer of thanks.

May Rose was barely able to get the car in park before Bishop Smith jumped out and walked around to the driver's door. He flung it open and escorted her out just as quickly as he'd ushered her in.

He led May Rose by her hand over to the passenger door, grabbing her waist and lifting her up into the seat.

She started getting those tingling feelings down in her lady parts once again, and she squeezed her legs real tight to try to satisfy her craving for her bishop. By the time he climbed into the driver's seat, May Rose managed to calm the raging flames between her thighs.

As Bishop Smith drove back onto the road, he said, "While you're there with Willie, maybe you can ask him when he'll be coming home again. That way, we can start working on building your dress shop. I can start getting the building supplies together. Also, with your extra time, you can start rounding up your dress-making materials and get started making a few dresses to get the shop started."

May Rose grinned from ear-to-ear. "I can't believe I'm about to be a legitimate businesswoman," she said. Not that she felt the woman's business in her family wasn't legitimate, but she understood that not all women would condone a blueprint that went against so much of what the women in America were taught. But the thing was, May Rose's family business wasn't an American thing; it was her African family's culture, created by her ancestors. May Rose didn't know if any other African women or American women followed her family's pattern. All she knew was that her family bloodline did, and her girls would continue to do so.

"I will definitely talk with Willie about it," May Rose replied as they pulled up to Bishop Smith's home. "Knowing how he works when he's not drinking that devil's piss, he can get the frame of the building up in one weekend."

Willie was very handy when it came to building and using his hands, which was why she had no doubt he would be able to get things in their house fixed up at some point. It had just been a minute since they'd had any extra money to get the things needed to fix it. With the church handling the supply costs for the dress shop, that wouldn't be an issue.

Bishop Smith parked the car in front of his home. "Me and a couple of the men from the church can continue working on the building after that. We will soon have a church full of beautifully dressed women and girls."

May Rose smiled and said, "That would be another one of my dreams that would've came true."

He opened the door to exit the car.

"Should I come in to greet First Lady?" May Rose asked.

"She was sleeping when I left, and we wouldn't want to wake her," he replied. "I'm just going to run in quickly, let the family know I'll be on the road a bit longer than I thought, and to give the children their marching orders."

"Well, at least tell everyone I said hello," she said as Bishop Smith headed inside to do just as he'd planned. He returned just a couple moments later and sat back in the driver's seat.

The two connected via their eyes, and May Rose shot him a wink. He smiled and then pulled off, headed to their destination.

They had driven for a while when Bishop Smith suddenly grinned like a Cheshire Cat and growled, "Tell me about your wildest dreams."

May Rose looked at him sheepishly and replied, "Stop with your old mannish self. Did you forget we are on our way to see my husband?"

He busted out laughing. "We're going to continue this conversation one day real soon."

She also laughed. "If you say so, slick!"

Bishop Smith looked shocked. "No one has called me that since we were kids. You're really trying to make me pull this car over and jump your bones right here, right now."

May Rose switched the subject quickly. "How much further do we have to go?" She looked every which way out the window she could to keep from looking at him. She needed to save her juices for her husband.

He giggled. "We should be really close because I saw a sign back yonder."

The rest of the ride was pretty quiet and uneventful. That was until Bishop Smith shouted, "Look, May Rose, that sign says McDowell Mine, two miles."

She was in the process of dozing off, but his booming voice jogged her out of her stupor. May Rose sat up in the seat and then rubbed her eyes. "It sure does." With a nervous grin, May Rose went into a silent prayer. "Dear God, let this man be okay. I'd feel twice as awful lusting for another man while my husband is in trouble."

Upon arrival to the property that hosted the mine, Bishop Smith pulled into the dirt driveway. He read the sign as he passed it, "Management Office."

"Is this where we are supposed to go?" she asked curiously while looking toward the small building with chipping paint. Looked like something someone would find a family on the prairie living in. Not a business office.

"Well, let's at least start here." He pulled into a gravel spot in front of the office and put the car in park. "No need to be driving around blindly." He turned off the engine.

May Rose jumped out of the car like a little child that just arrived at a traveling carnival. Bishop Smith hurried out to catch up with her. "Now wait up a dang minute, Rosie. You didn't even let me open the car door for you."

She had already made her way up to the building and knocked on the door, waiting for someone to tell her it was all right to enter.

A rough man's voice shouted, "Come in if you dare."

The voice was so startling, May Rose jumped backward right into Bishop Smith's arms. He pulled her behind him, took off his favorite black hat, and opened the door. He walked in, pulling May Rose behind him by the hand.

"Good evening, sir." Bishop Smith introduced himself to the big, burly man that matched the big, burly voice that had boomed through the door and invited them in. "I'm Bishop David Smith from the Washington Street Baptist Church in Bedford, Virginia." He nodded toward May Rose. "And this is Mrs. May Rose Jones, and she's here to see her husband, Mr. William H. Jones."

May Rose nervously smiled and nodded at the man. She thought Bishop Smith had a big presence, but the man stuffed in the chair behind the small wooden desk separating them had a *huge* presence. In May Rose's eyes, he tended to tower over Bishop Smith while sitting down!

"He has been working here at this mine for about two weeks now," Bishop Smith continued. "She has not heard a word from him since he has been here. We don't wanna pull him from his work or anything, but we would like to know he's all right and even lay eyes on him if possible."

The fat, white, bald man with a pipe hanging out his mouth responded, "You can't come up in here with your uppity colored ways demanding to see anybody."

The shocked expressions on both May Rose and Bishop Smith's faces, the way their necks seemed to pull back in slow motion, as if dodging the spittle flying from the man's mouth, made it clear they were taken aback by the response they were receiving.

The man leaned forward with a scowl. "Some of these men don't make it home for months. For some of them, it might be up to a year. They like the good six-nineteen a day they are making, so they stay." The man paused, dang near daring either visitor to speak.

May Rose swallowed hard, figuring she should be the one to do so since Willie was her husband. "I, uh, don't mean no disrespect, sir. I just got food in the car and all and just want to make sure my Willie is fed a good meal so that he can be nice and strong and get plenty of work done for you, you know?" May Rose's head bounced up and down as she smiled and nodded.

When Bishop Smith remained silent, waiting to see what was going to shoot out of the man's mouth next, May Rose elbowed him hard and furrowed her eyebrows, all while keeping that nervous smile plastered on her face.

"Ain't that right, Bishop?" May Rose asked him, demanding he corroborate her statement.

The man grunted, looking from May Rose to Bishop Smith, then back to May Rose. "Woman, you lucky Willie just finished his shift about an hour ago." He rolled his eyes. "I'll call for him to come up from his housing area."

"Oh, thank you kindly, thank you so much, sir." May Rose was so grateful. She would have felt just awful having Bishop Smith come all that way for naught.

The man stood up. "And the next time, send a letter and request to visit him."

"Yes, sir," she replied as the man disappeared.

May Rose stood in front of the door with a glass window at the top. She wrung her hands together in anticipation. Bishop Smith stood back in the rear corner of the office. It seemed like it was taking Willie forever.

Next thing they knew, that booming voice shot across the whole compound. They could hear the man hollering in some kind of microphone and his voice shooting out speakers all over the place.

"Willie Jones, get your ass up here to the office, now."

May Rose shot a look at Bishop Smith, to which he simply shrugged.

A few minutes later, that man came shuffling back through the door, dang near knocking May Rose over when he opened it.

"You can't block that door," he huffed. "Move to the side"

She did as he said and went to stand as close to Bishop Smith's side as she could.

"What's wrong with you people?" the man said under his breath as he took his seat behind the desk.

A few minutes later, the door flung open and Willie came stumbling in.

Thank God the rude man forced May Rose to move from in front of it. Otherwise, she'd probably be laid out on the floor with a concussion or pinned to the wall behind it, as flat as a pancake.

"Bossman, I paid you what I owed you. What you summonsing me for, inflicting on my—" Willie let out a disgusting burp. "—my time off."

The man didn't even look up from his desk or speak to acknowledge Willie. He simply pointed toward May Rose. He did eventually say, laughing loudly, "Boy, looks like you're in more trouble than you ever could be in with me."

Willie looked around the room in shock and said arrogantly, "What yaw asses doing here?" He took a couple stumbling steps toward May Rose. "Rose, what's wrong with you?" His neck wobbled toward the direction of his bishop. "Dave, why did you bring her here? Y'all trying to come see after me? I'm not a damn child." He struggled to keep his balance. "I don't need to be checked on. I should beat both of your asses." He pointed at May Rose. "You lucky I don't hit women." He then pointed at his bishop. "But you..." He took a drunken charge toward Smith.

May Rose jumped in front of him and stopped him in his tracks. "You're not beating nobody with your drunken behind. Look at you with all of that dirt all over your body." She pointed her finger the length of Willie's body. "Your eyes are red as fire, and your nails have pounds of dirt under them. When's the last time you bathed?" She threw her hands on her hips and nodded to the white man. "What money did you owe? You have not yet brought any money home, so how you got money to be giving somebody else?"

The bossman said angrily, "Take that shit outside and keep the noise down."

Willie grabbed May Rose by the arm and pulled her out the door.

Bishop Smith tipped his hat at the white man and scurried out behind the couple.

May Rose snatched away from Willie and said, "Get your filthy hands off of me."

The bishop caught up with them. "Hey, man, slow down." He rested his hands on Willie's shoulders. "What the hell is wrong with you? Any man be'd happy to have his wife pay him a visit." He pointed toward the car. "She even packed you a homecooked meal over there."

May Rose didn't care nothing about what Bishop Smith was talking. She squeezed her way back in front of Willie. "You are taking your pay and borrowing money to drink. What about your family and our home?" She poked Willie in the chest as her eyes filled with tears of anger. She didn't care about having to do without for herself, but when it came to her children, all bets were off.

Before Willie could respond, two women that looked like prostitutes walked up. They each looped their arm through Willie's and stood on either side of him.

One wearing a green dress with the straps hanging off her shoulders spoke. "Hey, Willie, baby," she said, salivating at the sight of Bishop Smith, "introduce me to your tall, gorgeous friend." She ran her tongue behind her top front teeth. "Hey, handsome, do you want some satisfaction?" She shot a snobby look at May Rose. "Your wife there don't look like she can spin your wheels, like Willie told me his wife can't." She and her friend giggled. "Since you as fine as you are, let's say today you're in luck. We running a special. Two for one." She boldly walked up to Bishop Smith and slid her index fingernail down his tie. "And Willie done already paid, so your lucky day just got luckier."

Willie hollered, "You talk too much, you loud-mouth wench. I bet you don't get another damn cent of mine."

That's all May Rose needed to hear for her boiling blood to spill over. She pushed Willie so hard in his chest that if it hadn't been for the women gripping each of his arms, he would have toppled over.

"Willie Jones," May Rose hollered, "I will cut your filthy throat. Don't you dare bring your ass back to Bedford. I'll have something waiting on you if you do."

Bishop Smith stepped to May Rose's side and gently secured her by the arm. "May Rose, please take these keys and get in the car."

She was fuming mad, chest heaving.

He leaned in her ear and whispered, "Rosie, take the keys and go to the car."

"Yeah, Rosie, go on to the car," the woman in the green dress mocked.

May Rose's fist balled to her sides.

"May Rose!" Bishop Smith's voice boomed even twice as loud as the white man's in the office had, pulling her from her moment of being hypnotized by rage.

She slowly looked up at Bishop Smith.

"The keys." He dangled them in front of her. "The car."

She looked down at them.

"Go on now, May Rose. I got this. You go on."

May Rose looked into Bishop Smith's eyes that exuded protection and trust. All of a sudden, she was now hypnotized by his eyes. She slowly took the keys and headed toward the car. She looked back at Bishop Smith a couple times, and each time, he nodded her on her way.

The bishop exhaled and then looked to Willie. "Do you know what you have just done? You better be making it home to make things right with her."

Willie responded with a drunken slur, "Take her back home. You should've not brought her out here." He belched again.

"That woman loves your stupid ass," Bishop Smith said through gritted teeth, not understanding for the life of him why Willie would be messing up such a good thing.

Willie looked to the car where May Rose sat in the passenger seat. For a moment, Bishop Smith thought he saw a tinge of regret in Willie's eyes, but then Willie turned and said, "Let them crazy-ass Africans give her all the love she needs."

Bishop Smith shook his head. "That moonshine has ate up your brain. May Rose is a beautiful, smart, kind, and loving woman. She's aways been that way."

The words went in one of Willie's ears and got stuck on the outside of that mucky brain of his, never quite managing to penetrate and get some sense in there.

"Boy, you're going to be really sorry. Those prostitutes won't give you a home like your wife has. And what about your beautiful daughters?"

"What about 'em? Ain't like they gon' be out on the street or anything," Willie reasoned. "Those houses and land belong to me and May Rose ain't going nowhere. I'll come back whenever I want to, and her ass better be there waiting on me."

Bishop Smith let out an exasperated huff. "Man, I'm so disappointed in you. You see that car she just got in? The Black Baptist Convention bought it for her for all the work she does in our community. They're also going to build a bigger schoolhouse for the children, and the church is going to build a dress shop for her. All of those things because of the woman she is. The woman you somehow can't manage to see."

Willie rolled his eyes. He wasn't trying to hear none of what Bishop Smith was saying. "Get the hell out of here with all that. And don't come back. With or without her. I don't owe you shit, so you ain't got no reason to be coming to see about me. That's my broad. I'll do whatever I want to do with her, and she better like it."

Bishop Smith let out a harumph tinted with a chuckle. "You're delusional, Willie Jones, and you're acting like a hurt man." He asked him sincerely, "Who has hurt you like this?

Huh, Willie? Who has hurt you so much that you want to hurt others?"

A serious look spread across Willie's face. He opened his mouth but then decided to withhold the words. "Get on out of here with all that preacher man talk. What you gon' do next, pray for me? Huh, Bishop?"

"Nope," Bishop Smith replied, "because I already did." He positioned his hat tighter on his head. "Anyway, we're going to abide by your wishes. We're leaving, but you better get it together and come get your wife before you lose her and..."

"Before I lose her and what?" Willie asked. "Go on, finish preaching, preacher man."

Bishop Smith stopped in his tracks and threw a look over his shoulder at Willie. "Before you lose your wife and another man finds her." He popped his collar, turned around, and left Willie standing there in the dust.

> *"A wise man never knows all; only fools know
> everything."*
>
> African Proverb

Chapter 10

WORK SMARTER, NOT HARDER

ishop Smith leisurely approached the car, but he quickly picked up his pace once he could see what was going on inside. When he reached the passenger side, he flung the door open so hard and fast, it was a surprise it didn't fly off the hinges and across the parking lot.

"Rosie! Rosie!" he exclaimed as he leaned inside the car. "Rosie, you alright?"

May Rose's shoulders were violently heaving up and down as sweat poured from her forehead. She was panting like a dog running from a wolf. She opened her mouth to respond to Bishop Smith, but she couldn't form words.

"Dear God, she's hyperventilating." Bishop Smith frantically looked around for a few seconds, not knowing what to do. No telling what he was expecting to find to help him out in a brand-new vehicle that had nothing in it but the bodies it was chauffeuring. By this time, May Rose was having a full-blown panic attack. He wrapped his arms around her shoulders and lifted her body close to his. "Breathe, baby, breathe. Just calm down and breathe." He rocked and bounced like he had a baby in his arms he was trying to soothe from a tantrum. "I got you, Rosie. Just calm down and breathe."

May Rose closed her eyes and silently prayed as Bishop Smith continued to comfort her. Before she knew it, the words dancing in her head strutted out her mouth. "Jesus, help me. Lord, have mercy." She opened her eyes that were full of tears while still trying to catch her breath. Her face was planted in Bishop Smith's chest.

"You got this, Rosie." He continued to coach May Rose. "Just calm down and breathe."

May Rose took in and exhaled a few deep breaths until her breathing and heartbeat had stabilized. "Thank you, Jesus," she said softly, her voice full of relief. "Thank you, Lord." She pulled herself away and sat upright in the car, placing her hand over her heart.

Bishop Smith slowly released May Rose, with his hands still in position to catch her as if he was teaching her to ride a bike and there was a slight chance she could lose her balance. "You okay?" He slowly began to lower his hands.

May Rose nodded. "David, can you believe that fool? I swear that man better stay completely away from me or I'm liable to kill him dead. Him and his whores."

"I know you're hurt right now, Rosie, but just take a minute to get yourself together."

"Hurt?" May Rose said in the most indignant tone possible. "Hurt?" She let out a harumph and rolled her eyes. "I ain't hurt, damn it, I'm mad." She slapped the dashboard.

Bishop Smith flinched, then looked up to the heavens to thank God that wasn't ole Willie's face. Even he could feel the sting.

"Here I am worrying about him, thinking he is laying up dead somewhere in one of these here mines, and that low-down, no-good drunk is laying up between some whore's legs." She buried her face in her hands.

Bishop Smith rubbed her shoulder in a comforting manner. "I know this is hard for you, Rosie, but God is going to see you through this situation."

She slowly removed her hands from her face and stared at him, dumbfounded. "Bishop, I ain't worried about me," she said in a tone that expressed just how dumbfounded she was. "I'm worried about what do I tell the girls." A light bulb went off in May Rose's head. She took the palm of her hand and smacked it against her forehead almost as hard as she'd smacked it against the dashboard. "And my mother and aunts! What will I tell them?" She dropped her hand and her head. "Lord, they will never let me live this down."

Bishop Smith was finally catching on to where May Rose's feelings resided, although he wasn't sure why figuring out how to win her man back was the last thing on May Rose's mind— unlike any other woman. As a matter of fact, if he was reading things properly, May Rose's heart was unbothered while her head was on fire, and her blood was boiling. And not entirely at the fact that Willie had done her wrong, but more so that she had to tell her girls and the elders about it.

"Listen to me, May Rose," Bishop Smith said gently, "you say absolutely nothing for now. Let cooler heads prevail. I believe Willie will see that he is wrong and will come crawling back to you and his girls. That way, you may never even have to speak on this discretion of his to anyone."

"Never...I'll never take that man back, whether he comes crawling, walking, or running," May Rose spat quickly. "I've been the one holding our family together, not him. So, I'm done!" she said with finality. "The strong African woman's values that were taught to me says a woman should protect her family like a lioness protects her cubs and her territory. I will not let Willie Jones destroy me or my family." She looked to Bishop Smith and with every ounce of certainty in every bone in her body, she said, "David, please take me home."

Bishop Smith stood there for a moment, waiting to see if maybe May Rose would change her mind or if maybe he should even minister to her to help her change her mind. After all, he was good for telling couples going through issues that God didn't like divorce.

Just as he fixed his mouth to remind his congregation member of such, May Rose said, "And if you even think about telling me the line about how God don't like divorce, I say to you, Bishop, that He don't like murder neither. And unless you want to witness one or be an accessory to one, I'd advise you to hop your tail in this here automobile and take me home." She twitched her bottom to get comfortable and looked straight ahead, signaling that the conversation was over.

He politely closed the passenger door and carried himself right over to the driver's seat, starting it up and heading down the road in silence.

A few minutes later, May Rose finally said what had been wracking her brain for the last few minutes. "I have to figure out how I'm going to get this lie together to tell the girls and the elders. They're not stupid. They'll have questions. They knew we were coming to McDowell to see about Willie. They ain't gon' have nothing but a boatload of questions." She shook her head. "Thank God I make a few coins with my sewing and midwife duties. I should be able to keep up my home and the farm for a bit."

"That business about the dress shop is sounding better and better, huh?" he asked.

Not only was the dress shop business sounding better and better, but so was a woman's business, and now she was more hellbent than ever on her bishop being her first hire.

He continued, "Look, Rosie, you don't have a thing to worry about. Me and the church will come along beside you." He removed one hand from the steering wheel and placed it atop May Rose's hand that was resting on her left thigh. "Are you sure you're really ready to let Willie go?"

May Rose pulled her hand from under Bishop Smith's, slapped it over her mouth, and put her head down. Her shoulders bounced uncontrollably.

"Now, now, Rosie, I didn't mean to make you cry," he said. "It's going to be okay."

May Rose's shoulders continued to bounce as she muffled her holler.

"Oh, Holy Spirit, comfort Sister Rose," Bishop Smith started to pray. Tears began to pour out of May Rose's eyes, prompting him to pray that much harder. "Rosie needs you right now, Lord."

May Rose's muffled holler got louder. Bishop Smith, excited that his prayer was working and that the Spirit was moving through her like a wildfire, added some hooping to his prayer.

"Yes, lawda. Ha! Thank you for coming down to comfort Mrs. May Rose Jones, ha! We thank you, Lord, yessah!"

At this point, May Rose exploded. She threw her hands up and leaned as far as she could forward. Her mouth was open as wide as it could as the scream rose up out of her throat. She jerked her body back against the seat, threw her hand on her chest, and couldn't even catch her breath.

May Rose's actions scared Bishop Smith at first. He thought she was having another panic attack. But when May Rose was finally able to breathe again and a loud cackle rose up out of her throat that was so piercing the windshield nearly cracked, he was fit to be tied. His praying came to a complete halt when he realized May Rose was laughing so hard that she was crying…and that was the only reason she was crying.

When May Rose looked over at the bishop and saw the puzzled/offended reaction on his face, she managed to get her laughter under control. "I'm sorry, Bishop Smith. I wasn't laughing at you. You know the saying that sometimes you gotta laugh to keep from crying?" May Rose asked the rhetorical question and then continued, "Well, that's what I did. Once I realized I was crying over Willie," May Rose lied, "I just felt plum stupid. So, I figured I'd take up the saying and laugh to keep from crying, you know?"

She had to look away, unsure how much longer she could keep a straight face. She looked out the window as her shoulders began to bounce up and down again. This time, she feigned a crying sound. Before she knew it, she felt Bishop Smith's comforting hand on her shoulder. He was clearly buying her little act hook, line, and sinker. So, May Rose continued.

"I don't know what I want to do right now." She sniffled.

"Do you want me to turn around and go back?" He asked. "Maybe talk things out a bit with your husband?"

Her voice rose dramatically. "It's best we head on home because I still got hell in me, and I will go back down there and fight that fool and his whore with everything in me."

Bishop Smith fixed both hands back on the steering wheel in the eleven o'clock and one o'clock position. He shook his head with anger. He was glad May Rose's attention was outside the window because he didn't want her to know he could join her in beating up Willie and his whore.

"Rosie, I promise you the Lord will make it all right. Let's finish praying." He took her by the hand and started praying as he navigated the dirt road. "Heavenly Father, we come before you to thank you for everything you have done and all of the wonderful things you will continue to do in our lives."

With a bowed head, May Rose said, "Yes, Lord."

"Although we may not understand, our faith leads us to believe it's all for our good. In your Son Jesus's precious name, amen."

May Rose squeezed Bishop Smith's hand. "Amen, Lord. I thank you." She gathered her composure, wiping her face and patting down her hair. "All this mess I bet done worked you up an appetite. We still have the fried chicken, fresh-baked bread, string beans, mash potatoes, apple pie, and some red drink I packed for Willie." She looked around. "Do you want to find a park on the way home to eat? I don't know if I can eat, but I know you have to be hungry by now. Besides, there is no need for all that good cooking to go to waste. Amen?" She looked at him with doe eyes, batting her lashes.

"Sure, I can use a bite. My mouth was watering all the way to McDowell from the smell of the food." He chuckled. "I know you and the elders can burn in that kitchen, so I know it's going to be tasty."

"I put my foot in everything I cook for my man, but my mother and aunts cooked all of this," she said with a flirtatious smile.

Bishop Smith licked his lips, taking his eyes off the road briefly to give May Rose the once-over. His eyes couldn't lie that there was something about her in this vulnerable state that was getting a rise out of him. "I'm sure you do," he said, turning his attention back to the road. "I'm sure you do," he repeated under his breath.

May Rose didn't want to lay it on too thick, so she said, "And I'm teaching my girls to do the same." She exhaled, going back into her damsel-in-distress mode. "Oh, my babies, they are going to be devastated about that asshole of a father not returning home. I know they miss their daddy. He doesn't even care." May Rose sniffed and looked over at Bishop Smith. "Oh, I'm so sorry. I don't mean to keep going on and on about this."

"There has never been anything off-limits with us," Bishop said. "You can talk about anything with me."

"Yeah, well, you're right. I need to calm down. So, let's talk about that another time."

"Of course, whenever you're ready," he said. "I'm going to pull up the road there so we can eat."

She looked ahead. "Okay, that's good. I can use the peace and the breeze." May Rose closed her eyes and smiled.

'Remember,' she heard her mother's voice in her head. 'Work smarter, not harder. If a woman's workin' hard, she ain't doing it right. It should be easy.'

As far as May Rose was concerned, Bishop Smith was making her job oh-so-easy.

By now, the sun had begun to set. He pulled over near an open field and walked to the back of the car, opening the trunk and taking out the food basket May Rose had packed.

She opened her door before Bishop Smith could get to it, and he yelled, "Hey, girl, how are you taking away my duty of chivalry. You know I don't play about that."

May Rose covered her mouth as she chuckled. "I'm so sorry. You know my mind is all over the place right now."

"Yes, I know, Rosie, but we're going to leave all that commotion right up here on this old hill."

Carrying the basket in one hand, he took May Rose by the hand with the other. The two started off at a regular pace, then somehow ended up doing a light jog up the grassy hill while giggling like two children. Once they reached the top, Bishop Smith set down the basket and pull off his suit jacket, dropping it to the ground.

"I apologize for not having a blanket or something," he said, "so my jacket will have to do." He took her by the hand again and helped her to the ground, where she sat on his jacket with her legs curled under her.

May Rose grabbed the bottom of her dress and tucked it underneath her legs. Bishop Smith sat, rolled up his sleeves, and reached for the basket as he scooted closer and handed it to her.

"I'll be happy with a piece of fried chicken, a slice of that homemade bread, and a glass of red drink, if you don't mind."

May Rose responded, "Coming right up, sir," as she started reaching in the basket. She took out a fancy porcelain plate, a shiny fork and knife, a glass container, a silver drinking cup, and a freshly ironed napkin. She put a slice of bread and a big fried chicken breast on his plate, and then she poured the red drink in his cup and handed it to him with a warm smile.

Bishop Smith took the drink out of May Rose's hand. "I'm waiting on you to fix your plate before I bless the food and dig in."

She held her hand up. "Don't wait on me, please. I'll eat something later. Like I said before, I haven't much of an appetite right yet."

He dropped his head and said a silent prayer, then lifted it and began cutting into his chicken breast. He cut several pieces and picked up a piece with his fork, reaching over and gently grabbing May Rose by the chin. "Please eat for me, Rosie. You need to put something on your stomach. All that stress has probably upset it. The least you can do is feed it, wouldn't you say?" He held the fork to May Rose's lips.

She bashfully opened her mouth and took in the piece of chicken. She put her head down and giggled as she wiped a bit of juice from the corner of her mouth.

"Wait a minute, I got that," Bishop Smith said as he took the napkin and wiped each corner. "There you go," he said as he watched May Rose's lips move about in a perfect circle as she chewed. "Don't you let Willie's selfish ways steal your joy or your appetite." He smiled as he leaned in and kissed her cheek.

May Rose turned toward him and gave him a gentle kiss on the lips. He received her kiss, grabbed her hand, and put it on his chest. "Do you feel how fast my heart is beating right now?" he asked.

May Rose whispered a soft, "Yes."

"This heart belongs to you. It has always belonged to you. Now, I don't want to move too fast. I knew we was headed in some kind of direction even before this mess with Willie. But still and yet, I'm going to follow your lead with us. But I want you to know, Rosie, I'm here to catch you when you fall. Whether it's falling out of love with Willie or in love with me, I'm here to catch you." He lifted her face by the chin. "Do you hear me, woman?"

It was time for May Rose to get down to business. "David Smith, I hate to do this to you because I really like you and you're a damn good man, but I have to take care of my family, and the small pittance of money I get will keep us barely making it. And I surely don't want them wild African sisters terrorizing the men of Bedford." She laughed. "I won't be able to give you the attention you deserve. Not while I'm trying to figure out this stuff with my money and all. I can't risk letting my girls do without while I'm fancying after no man. But like you said, we're leaving all of that Willie commotion on this hill. I know what I want, and it has always been you. I just was doing what I thought was the right thing by being with Willie. As it turns out, it was all in vain." She picked up the fork and poked at a piece of the chicken until it stuck to the tongs. She put in in Bishop Smith's mouth and grabbed his man-part, rubbing it softly in sync with his chewing. They had a nice little rhythm going.

His man-part was pulsating and growing at the same time. He chewed slowly while staring May Rose directly in her eyes. By now, all of his senses were in play. His head was also spinning. He'd given May Rose permission to take the lead so that things could move at her pace. That pace was faster than he'd expected, but he wasn't mad about it. Not one bit.

She pushed Bishop Smith down by his shoulders and then laid on top of him while hiking up the bottom of her dress. She snatched his zipper and started tugging at it while squirming on him. She finally got the zipper down and then started working on the button. By now, she was steaming hot for Bishop Smith to be inside her. There was nothing in the rulebook that said a woman couldn't be pleasured while pleasuring the man. Wasn't any crime in cracking two nuts with one stone.

Bishop Smith started tugging at May Rose's undergarments. She cooperated by appropriately wiggling to help him get them down. Realizing he was having quite a time achieving his goal, May Rose rolled over and pulled her own undergarment down.

He was looking at her in amazement as she took control. His wife had never been the one to take the lead in their intimate moments. His man-part was peeking out of his zipper. So caught up in the moment of passion, neither one was the least bit concerned about who might decide to mosey on up for a picnic and catch them sinning.

She positioned herself right on top of Bishop Smith and straddled him, rocking herself back and forth on his manhood. She bent down and whispered in his ear, "Just in case you didn't realize it, I'm ready. I'm ready for you." She took his thick, throbbing man-part in her hand and slid it inside her. She simultaneously moaned, shivered, and panted as she allowed her womanhood to stroke him. "Take your time and make sure I get mine. Will you do that for me, baby?" she moaned. "Will you do that for me?"

Bishop Smith let out a groan as he pressed his pelvis upward. "Yes, Rosie. Yes."

"I know where it's at that makes me explode, and I will help you find it. And I don't want your dirty suds in me right now."

He grunted. "I understand. I will always make sure you are satisfied in every way." He grabbed May Rose by her hips and guided her each and every stroke. She was doing all the leading. He was just along for the ride, literally.

May Rose started grinding against him in unison with his strokes. "David, you are so good. I've been missing some good dick for so long. Ohhh. Baby, I'm almost there. I'm getting ready to let loose. You gon' come with me? Huh?" May Rose picked up speed, pressing her hands into his chest. "You coming with me?"

"Give it all to me. You're the only woman I have ever had that knows where she needs to be touched to make her explode." And May Rose was also the only woman not afraid to tell him what she wanted, how she wanted it, and how it was making her feel. He barely ever knew when his wife was being pleased, let alone how she wanted him to please her, and the only thing he could recall Ramona ever saying during their intimate moments was, "Are you done yet?"

It looked like May Rose made Bishop Smith's job easy for him as well.

She fell off him and took his man-part, quickly sliding up and down until the dirty suds that exploded had covered her entire hand.

Bishop Smith screamed out, "Rosieeee," like he was singing one of those church hymns.

She grabbed the napkin and wiped the dirty suds from her hand and his man-part. She bent over and placed a gentle kiss on the head of it. "I'm going to show you more than this. Just remember, I tried to warn you I ain't nothing to play with."

"We're going to get this right, because I have to have you permanently."

May Rose stood and started pulling up her undergarment. "You're dealing with a woman who will give it to you so good, you'll never want to touch Ramona ever again. Are you sure you want all of this?" She rubbed her crotch and licked her lips. "No matter what Willie told his whore, he never knew how good it was because he was always too drunk."

"You sure got my seal of approval, girl. And, yes, I want all of you permanently. Like I said before, I'm going to have you."

She smiled. "Dear David, we can't get sloppy with this. We have to do this right. You have a lot at stake, plus you now have a whole new family, and I expect all of the same benefits Ramona gets. If you don't think you can handle my package deal, tell me now and we can walk off of this hill as if nothing ever happened here."

She wasn't playing around. She had to show Bishop that she was in control.

He jumped up, fixing his pants zipper and button. "Let me manage this. You do your part, and I promise, I'll do mine."

"You've got a deal. Hell, you're gonna have me kissing on your man piece all the time." May Rose winked. "Anyway, let's get ready to head back. You might have baby number seven waiting on you."

Thank goodness Bishop Smith's man-part had gone back down to size. Otherwise, her comments would have done the trick. "Did you have to say that? You just knocked me down off the moon." He sucked his teeth and rolled his eyes.

She put on a pouty face and put her arms around his neck. She gave him a juicy, wet kiss. Her way of apologizing to him for the backhanded comment.

He slapped her on her behind. "All mine." He looked up as if howling to the moon. "Willie, you will never get her back." He looked down at May Rose. "Right, my sweets?"

She quickly said, "You've got that right." She started repacking the food basket, while asking, "Are you sure you don't want to eat some more food?"

"Not unless you're going to feed me some more of your tail."

She laughed. "How about I just stroke you all the way down the road, and you can play a little with me, too."

"You're so nasty," he said. "And I like it." He patted May Rose on the behind one more time before pulling away. "Let's go so we can start having some fun." He picked up his jacket and the basket, then he grabbed May Rose by her hand, and they made their way down the hill. Leaving all the Willie commotion behind as planned.

Only thing was, they forgot to tell Willie.

"Even the clever one is advised."

African Proverb

Chapter 11

BACK IN BUSINESS

Bishop Smith was grinning with joy from the decision May Rose made to give him a chance to love her the way he wanted to. The way he'd been longing to. May Rose, on the other hand, developed a pit in her stomach. What she was feeling was written all over her face.

He looked over at her and noticed her blank stare. Her eyes were wide open but looking at nothing, at least nothing that he could see. May Rose was envisioning everything she and the elders had discussed playing out, either in front of her eyes or behind them. She honestly couldn't decipher.

Even as a youngin', May Rose would often tell her mother that she'd see stuff happen and it was so real that she couldn't tell if it was happening in her head or in real life. Sometimes, she felt as though whatever she was seeing had already happened.

"Momma, I think it's what they call déjà vu," a young May Rose said to her mother.

Elma, who was stirring up a big pot of fish stew at the time, paused, turned to May Rose, and said, "It ain't déjà vu, baby it's called the spiritual realm."

"It's just like it already happened, like I've already been there." May Rose's confused voice matched her expression.

"It don't feel like it already happened," her mother corrected her, "it *did* already happen…in the spiritual realm." She stopped stirring once again and gave May Rose a knowing grin. "Now, how and whether or not it plays out here on earth in the natural realm is up to you." She started stirring again, but not before giving her young daughter a quick wink.

May Rose, not quite thirteen yet, said to her mother, "I don't know, Momma. It all sounds so confusing to me."

"Don't worry, baby. In a few more months when you turn thirteen, it will all make sense." She let out a chuckle and shook her head.

"Sweetheart, are you alright?" Bishop Smith asked, snapping May Rose from her thoughts.

"The closer we get to home, the more nervous I get," she said. "I have decided to wait until tomorrow to discuss what happened with my family." She shook her head. "It is too late in the evening to stir up that kind of negative talk. I need to get some rest and think on things a bit more." May Rose bit her bottom lip in thought. "Although I know the girls are going to be awake just waiting to hear how my visit with their daddy went." She threw her head back against the seat and groaned. "I just want to go home, bathe, get in my bed, and forget this whole day ever happened."

Bishop Smith looked straight ahead. "The entire day, Rosie?" His question was laced with disappointment.

May Rose looked at him, then it dawned on her how he had perceived her words. "Oh, no, David, I didn't mean it like that." She reached over and grabbed his hand, patting it to reassure him. "I'm just talking about the mess with Willie is all."

He looked at her, saw the sincerity in her eyes, smiled, and turned his attention back to the road. Once she felt he truly believed her words, she released his hand and turned back forward in the passenger seat.

"I'll hang around to support you in case the family bombards you with questions if you'd like," he offered.

"No, no, no. You gotta get home and go check on First Lady Ramona. She's getting very close to being ready to push." There were a few seconds of silence, then May Rose looked over to see Bishop Smith staring at her. "What?" she asked with a coy giggle.

"You're so sweet and kind for being concerned about Ramona and the baby, especially with what's going on with you and Willie. And that's exactly why I've always…" His words trailed off, and there was an awkward moment of silence. "Anyway," he eventually continued, "I'm going to do just that, but know that when I slumber, you'll be in my dream."

"Same here, David. Same here," May Rose said as they continued their ride home.

"Well, we're here," he said a while later as he pulled in front of May Rose's home. "Let's say a quick prayer." He took her hand and bowed his head. "Lord, we thank you for seeing us home safely."

"Yes, Lord," she said. Her head was bowed and eyes closed as well.

"We also ask you to forgive our sins, those we have knowingly and unknowingly committed. Dear Father, you know our hearts. Rosie and I love each other. And I know this may sound wrong, God, but I ask that you see that maybe someday, you can remove the sin from our relationship somehow and that she and I become husband and wife as you intend for us to be…" Bishop Smith rarely stumbled over his words during prayer, but this wasn't a usual prayer, especially coming from a minister. "We're trusting you, Lord, as we lean on our faith. In your precious Son Jesus's name, amen."

May Rose was silent.

Bishop Smith opened his eyes to look at her while keeping his head bowed. "Everything okay? Ain't you gonna say amen?"

Taken aback by what Bishop Smith prayed for, May Rose still felt they came from his heart, went to God's ear, and needed to be respected with an "amen." She looked up to see him smiling at her and couldn't help but smile back.

Their eyes were like magnets for one another, drawing them closer and closer, but then something made May Rose pause and look up. "Umph, umph, umph, I knew it."

"What?" he asked, a bit confused.

"Look at them damn curtains moving and the shadows in the window." She pointed.

Bishop Smith followed to where May Rose was pointing. "They're not going to let me get some more suga." He chuckled, but then his face immediately got serious. "That's a lie. I'm getting my suga tonight and every day from here on out." He leaned in to kiss May Rose, but she couldn't let that go down without first sharing her situation with Willie with the girls. Part of a woman's business was making sure that her youngin's did everything clean and neat. Not messy and trifling.

May Rose started laughing, gently and seductively pushing him away. "C'mon, man, and get this door for me before you start something you know darn well we can't finish." She then leaned slightly toward him and licked her lips. "And it would be the worst punishment in the world for me not to finish what you get started. And I think I've been punished by that low-down husband of mine enough today. Don't you think?" May

Rose let her head wobble on her neck from left to right as she batted her eyes.

That tactic didn't give Bishop Smith no time at all to get mad. Horny beat out mad.

"Now, come on before I jump out before you open the door. And you know you don't like that." She taunted him by putting her hand on the door handle, threatening to kill his chivalry.

"Oh, woman!" he huffed, opening his door and getting out.

"And please don't forget the picnic basket in the trunk," she called as the driver's side door shut.

Bishop Smith walked around and quickly opened her door. "You're going to let me spoil you and the girls every chance I get, from the smallest things such as opening the door for you."

May Rose smiled as he lifted her out of the car.

"Now, I'll get the basket," he said.

She watched as that tall hunk of man grabbed the basket from the car. He caught her watching just as he lifted the trunk and threw a sexy wink at her.

"May Rose, get it together for the girls," she said to herself, fanning her flushed face. She turned and walked slowly to the front door with Bishop Smith on her heels.

"Here we go," she said before opening it.

Lynette was the first face she saw and the first voice she heard. "Good evening, Bishop Smith and Momma." She nodded and did a small curtsey. "Momma, how was your driving lesson? Did you see our daddy?"

May Rose looked to Bishop Smith, cleared her throat, and turned her attention back to Lynette. "Chile, stop and take a breath. The lesson was good and so was your daddy. He sends all of you girls his love. He also wanted me to tell you all he'll be home very soon." May Rose looked over Lynnette's head. "Where are your sisters?"

Just then, Florence came around the corner and Ginny, who was lying on the floor where May Rose hadn't seen her, popped her head up.

"When?" Florence said. "I heard you say Daddy was coming home. When?" She stood next to Lynette.

Ginny sat up, yawned, and stretched. Her notebook laid next to her "Yeah," she said in a sleepy tone while rubbing her eyes. "When is Daddy coming home?"

May Rose started shaking her head. "No, we're not going to do this tonight. It's late, and we'll talk in the morning." Before any of the girls could protest, she continued. "All three of you say good night to Bishop Smith, go wash up, brush your teeth, and take your behinds straight to bed."

Lynette sucked her teeth and shouted, "See what you all did?" She frowned at her sisters. "Y'all should have just stayed put and minded your business."

"You should have minded your business," Florence shot back, which was the start of a few seconds of back-and-forth between the two sisters.

By this time, Ginny stood up with her notebook in hand. "You all know Momma was not going to want to talk tonight." She rolled her eyes. "Y'all such babies. Dang it, y'all make me sick." She stomped off. Midway, she turned around. "Good night, Bishop Smith and Momma." Then she continued to the washroom.

Bishop Smith replied, "Good night to you, too, Ginny." He shook his head and laughed.

"Good night, sweetheart," May Rose said. "And next time, don't display the dramatics in front of guests." She looked at him and mouthed, "I'm sorry." She turned her attention to her other two daughters. "Now, good night, everybody. Just wash your faces, brush your teeth, and get in bed immediately. And wait your turn for the washroom. I don't want to hear a word coming from up them steps at all tonight. Say good night, you two, and get up those stairs."

In a pouty tone with their heads down, both girls mumbled and groaned, "Good night, Bishop Smith." They marched up the steps.

May Rose shouted, "You all can keep being sassy if you want. I'll be up there shortly." She exhaled heavily and then turned to her houseguest. "Bishop, I apologize for the girls' rude behavior."

He nodded and replied, "I understand. Remember, I got girls of my own." He looked around. "Where would you like me to sit the basket?"

"Oh, follow me." She gestured for him to follow and led him into the kitchen. "You can just leave it on the kitchen table. I'll have to clean it out."

They could hear the girls upstairs switching around like they were in a race. May Rose giggled. "These girls are acting like they found some of Willie's moonshine. I'm going to need to check them out."

He let out a hearty laugh. "You and your girls are a hoot. This is what is needed in my home, some good ole laughter. I got all of them in-laws, wife, and babies, and all I hear in my home is crying and hollering. I got to get some of this at home." He winked at her.

And he wasn't exaggerating. There were twenty-one people living under his roof—First Lady Ramona, twelve of her thirteen siblings, his mother-in-law himself, and his own four boys and two girls.

She winked back at Bishop Smith and said, "Once the children get older, you'll get more peace at home, trust me. And speaking of home, get on home to check in on First Lady Ramona and the bun in the oven. You wouldn't want her to think you were up to no good. You know, doing something with me besides driving lessons." Her arms hung down with her hands clasped in front of her as she swung her body from left to right.

Bishop Smith grinned. "Yes, ma'am. I'm headed out now."

"Let me walk you to the door." As May Rose opened the door for Bishop Smith, she turned and asked, "Are we having our driving lesson tomorrow after service? Or do you think you might be too drained in the spirit after preaching your face off like you usually do?"

He coyly replied, "It will be my pleasure. I'll always have the strength for you, Rosie. So, let's say about four p.m. after dinner, if that's fine with you?"

She looked over her shoulder. After no signs of the girls, she smirked and grabbed his crotch. "I'll be ready."

"Like you said yourself, woman, don't start nothing we can't finish." He spun her around, hugged her neck from behind, and began grinding on her butt until his man-part started enlarging in his pants. He sweetly whispered in her ear, "All mine." He began rubbing his hands up and down her leg, lifting her dress.

Keeping in mind her girls were busybodies, May Rose said loudly, "Well, how do you think my driving lessons are going, sir?" She turned around and began to grind against him.

He cleared his throat and panted quietly. "You're doing just fine, but I have a few more things to show you before I turn you loose." He kissed May Rose passionately.

She pulled back. "Then I guess after service tomorrow, it's just me and you, Bishop." She added in a whisper, "See, you got your suga. Now, take your ass home to your wife." May Rose laughed as she gave him a warmhearted shove out the door.

Bishop Smith caught his balance, blew her a kiss, and mouthed, "Thank you, Rosie."

She reached out and snatched the kiss from of the air, placing her closed fist over her heart and blowing a kiss back. He duplicated her action and then walked away backward, turning only to step off the porch before facing her again, walking backward as if it was killing him to take his eyes off her.

He finally turned when he reached the car. He opened the door, jumped in, and started the engine. Before pulling off, he tipped his hat at May Rose.

Waving, she backed into the house and slowly closed the door, leaning against it and catching her breath. She felt like a schoolgirl dating the most popular boy in the schoolhouse, but that feeling wasn't long-lived. When her eyes wandered over to the wedding picture of her and Willing sitting on the mantel, and then a picture of Willie and the girls right next to that one, she started thinking about telling her girls about Willie's behavior and how she doubted he would ever come back home, at least not for a while.

So much had happened so fast, she really hadn't a chance to figure everything out just yet. And then, of course, there was her mother and the elders. Would she hear 'I told you so' a million times, or would they be so excited by the fact that she might finally get rid of Willie that they wouldn't even bother? Of course, that final verdict was still out, although she was certain the elders would do their best to persuade her to leave Willie's cheating behind. At least he would no longer be a bone of contention between her and them.

May Rose grinned as she fetched water from the well in the back of the house and walked into the kitchen. She filled a pot to put on the stove to heat her bathwater. She sat on a kitchen chair for a while as she rested her head on her fist, deep in thought as the events of the day rushed through her mind.

"This shit is too much for one person to experience in one day." But May Rose figured that was pretty much how life went. At least her life, anyway, considering she had just made it more complicated by starting to handle "a woman's business" with Bishop Smith.

The water started boiling, and the noise broke her concentration. "Let me get my ass in this tub right now."

She picked up her kitchen mitten, snatched the pot of boiling water off the stove, and carefully shuffled up to the washroom to pour the water into the tub.

May Rose continued her thoughts while tiptoeing to her girls' bedrooms to make sure they were sleeping or at least pretending to be asleep. As she peeked in at her beautiful girls, she couldn't help but think how their little family could possibly be no more. The same rage she had back at the mine erupted through her blood again. If Willie came back home any time soon, she would get her sharpest razor blade and slit his throat.

She thanked God there had been no need for a question-and-answer session tonight with the girls. Her anger probably would have prevailed, and the conversation would have been all bad.

She yawned as the drama of the day caught up with her. It would be morning in no time, and time for Sunday school.

Returning to the washroom, she began to undress and slowly got in the tub while swirling her right then left foot in the water to help cool it off. Soon, it was cool enough to sit completely down. She grabbed her homemade soap and sponge and started bathing, finishing in record time. She quickly dried off, went to her bedroom, and dived on the bed, pulling the covers back. May Rose let out a sigh of relief and said, "Finally!" She rolled over on her left side, which was her favorite, and was fast asleep within minutes. Not even the rooster woke her just a few hours later when it went off.

Ginny, on the other hand, woke up as soon as the rooster started cock-a-doodle-dooing. She wanted to get well water going on the stove so everyone could have a warm bath, feed the farm animals, and most of all, catch May Rose before her sisters woke up. As Ginny started walking to the steps which were right past her parents' bedroom, she could see the candle-light burning under the crack of the door.

She stopped in her tracks and thought, *What the hell did I miss?* She never knew her mother to light a candle unless May Rose and Willie were up to grown folk's business. "Please don't tell me my sorry-ass father done snuck his sorry self in here last night," she said under her breath. Ginny started tapping lightly on the door. "Momma, are you woke? Can I come in?"

May Rose replied with a very raspy voice, "C'mon in. Who's with you?"

"It's just me, Momma." Ginny slowly opened the door and found May Rose sitting on the side of the bed. She walked over and gave her a kiss on the forehead. "Good morning, my beautiful mother!" She could see the worry all over her mother's face. "Momma, please tell me what's wrong."

With a dim look, May Rose whispered, "Because you are capable of understanding it, I'm going to be honest with you."

"It's Daddy, isn't it?" Ginny guessed, hinting that the wool hadn't been pulled over her eyes. "Everything didn't go as swell as you led the girls to believe, did it?"

May Rose exhaled and then just blurted out the truth. Ginny was a woman now. She could handle the truth, especially about a man. "Willie was up there at that mine drunk with prostitutes. He's borrowing money from the company to buy moonshine and prostitutes before his payday, then he owes all of his paycheck back to the mine. He told me he will do what he wants, and I better be here when he decides to come back. I got something for him the day he steps into this house. I will chop him up into a million pieces and feed his ass to the animals on this here farm."

Ginny had started pacing and wringing her hands from May Rose's first words. It had taken all her might to bite her tongue, to keep from butting in and instead let her mother say what she needed to say. Once May Rose stopped talking, Ginny said, "Momma, I knew it. He does not deserve you. He's just a sloppy drunk and deserves whatever he gets." She stopped pacing and stood right in front of May Rose with her hands on her hips. "As a matter of fact, I will help you chop him up."

"Baby, I understand you're upset, but he is yo' daddy. Maybe I should have kept that to myself."

May Rose's words had gone in one of Ginny's ears and out the other. Her mind had already traveled down the road. "What's your plan for now?" She started pacing again, rambling. "You can also teach me how to sew so I can help you make dresses for your shop once it's built." She stopped. "You are going to let Bishop Smith and the church build that dress shop for you, aren't you?"

"That's the plan, sweetheart," she said. "Although Willie was gonna play a big part in getting it built." She sighed. "Oh, well. We'll be just fine. Bishop Smith vowed to continue to help us, and yes, the woman's business will play a major part in our survival. It won't take a lot of work because as you know already, me and Bishop Smith are sweet on each other. Now is the time that you study my actions closely. It will all be heavy on our business."

Ginny nodded.

"Your sisters will not be told the truth just yet. For that reason, you will watch every word you say around them about Willie and Bishop Smith. That's your job, especially around them old coots of ours."

"They know?" Ginny asked, surprised.

"Not yet, but you know I gotta tell 'em. But I'll instruct them not to be talking about what happened with Willie around the girls. I'm sure they won't listen, though. They don't care what they say and where they say it." May Rose added sternly, "You have to protect Florence and Lynette from hearing the truth. You got all that?"

"I got it, Momma. It sounds like a great plan. Plus, it sounds like our lives will soon be changing for the better." Ginny sat next to her mother on the bed. "You don't have to worry, Momma. I will look out for the girls." She rested her head on her mother's shoulder. "I'm going to go feed the animals and fetch water to get it boiled and ready for our baths. We gotta get prepared for Sunday school and get ready to see our new daddy." She looked up at May Rose and chuckled.

May Rose laughed softly, put her arm around Ginny, and pulled her in tightly. "Get your grown ass out of here. I'm going to lay here for a minute longer. I took my bath last night. Get yours, then wake the girls. I'll get up shortly and make some oatmeal for breakfast and go tell the elders about Willie."

"Yes, Momma," Ginny said, and then stood up to do as she was told.

May Rose grabbed her hand before she was out of reach. "Thanks for stepping into your role as a woman and leader of your sisters."

Ginny smiled and then walked toward the door. Before exiting, she stopped, turned around, and said, "Momma, maybe you should wait on telling the elders. Maybe I should tell them and let them know they can't let my sisters know. They may listen since I'm now a woman."

May Rose thought about Ginny's proposal and then shrugged. "I don't know. We'll see. For now, finish your chores, bathe, get dressed, and get your sisters up to bathe and dress. And remember, watch your words. Don't make your sisters suspicious. Especially that Florence."

Ginny nodded.

"Go on now, girl. Let me rest for a minute." May Rose laid back on the bed. "I need all my energy to battle with those crazy African women."

Ginny cupped her mouth to keep from laughing out loud, tiptoeing out of the room and gently closing the door behind her as May Rose closed her eyes. She peeked into her sisters' room like a young mother hen. They were still sound asleep, so she proceeded with her morning as planned.

Meanwhile, May Rose only rested for about fifteen minutes after Ginny left. She got up, went to the washroom, washed her face, cleaned her mouth with a cloth, and brushed her hair up in her usual bun. She sprayed her favorite perfume in the usual places, and then she went back into her room and pulled her favorite dress off the nail on the back of her bedroom door. She got her clean undergarment out of her foot trunk and held it up to her. "I need to look extra pretty for Bishop Smith today since we've entered into business."

She hurried and dressed, then started walking over to the elders' house. She opened the front door and walked right to the kitchen, where she smelled fresh-baked biscuits and fried bacon.

"Hey, Momma," she greeted.

"Hey, baby," Elma responded.

May Rose sat down at the kitchen table and quietly wrung her hands. "About my trip to see Willie..." she hesitantly started.

"Oh, girl, just spit it out. He showed his ass, didn't he?" Elma guessed correctly.

"I caught him with two whores, Momma," May Rose blurted out. And now that she'd started, she figured she might as well finish. "He was drunk as hell. He had no money because he's drinking it up and spending it on the whores. I left from up there before I killed him. Bishop Smith had my back, though. He didn't let me do anything stupid."

Elma screamed, "Etta and Bertha, get in here and hear this shit." She shook her head as her sisters entered the kitchen. "Just like we said, this bastard final showed his true self, and at last, May Rose understands."

The aunts ran over to their niece, speaking something in their native tongue that May Rose didn't understand. Bertha stopped and began relaying her words in English. "What the hell did he do?"

Elma went into the details while May Rose sat there, nodding in agreement when her mother relayed the truth and shaking her head when she was disgusted by the truth being relayed.

Once Elma told all she knew, which was very little, she started adding yeast to the mix and shared parts that weren't necessarily quite true.

May Rose stopped her. "Can I finish telling my story?"

"The floor is yours," Elma said, eager to hear more, which May Rose shared.

"What did the girls say?" Aunt Bertha asked. "Or have you not told them yet?"

"Ginny knows, but Florence and Lynette don't know anything yet, and I don't want them to know. I told Ginny don't make a peep about it to her sisters." She looked from one elder to the next. "So, I ask you all to respect my decision for them not to know as well. And before you ask me, yes, me and Bishop Smith are now officially in *business*."

The women began to cheer and speak excitedly in both English and their native tongue. They weren't the least bit mindful of whether May Rose's pain was their pleasure.

May Rose interrupted their celebration with her next request. "Please promise to hold your tongues. This is part of my business plan. And we still have to be respectful to First Lady Ramona, their children, and the congregation, including First Lady's family. One wrong move and everything can be ruined."

"We promise, Momma." All heads turned to see Ginny walking into the kitchen. "Don't we?" She looked to her nana and great-aunts.

The elders looked from one to the next and then simultaneously said, "We do," in both languages.

Ginny looked to May Rose, who proudly nodded her approval of how Ginny handled the situation, which was like the woman she now was.

"Hey, my beautiful family, what a beautiful day for some church, huh?" Ginny said, politely putting a period at the end of the previous topic and moving onto another.

"Indeed, it is," Elma said. "Got any prayer requests?"

"Just for forgiveness. Because when my daddy shows his drunken and cheating face at the house again, and my momma chops him up into bits and pieces, I will be helping her."

Aunt Etta started choking on her laughter. When she could finally catch her breath, she said, "We sure taught this baby well, didn't we?"

The elders laughed while May Rose kept a straight face. "We didn't teach her to be a killer." She wagged a disapproving finger. "Anyway, I'm going to see if my babies are ready for

Sunday school." She stood up from the table. "I'm leaving in thirty minutes, if you all are coming."

Ginny started skipping behind May Rose and said to the elders, "With respect, my mother has put me in charge of protecting my sisters from hearing the true story, so I'll be watching and listening to make sure we all keep our promise."

Elma snapped her neck back on her shoulders. "Well, I'll be damned. This girl is ready to challenge us now." She glared at Ginny. "You looking for a fight, youngin'? Don't let me show you how I used to fight grown men during them slavery days."

While just a moment ago it may have seemed like Ginny was getting too big for her britches, they seemed to fit just fine now as she ran out the door. "No, Nana, I'm not looking for a fight." And she wasn't. At least not with the elders.

"When spiders unite, they can tie down a lion."

African Proverb

Chapter 12

SCHOOL'S IN SESSION

*I*t was an early, sunny Tuesday morning in Bedford, Virginia. The sound of hammers and nails cracking on wood filled the air on the land behind Washington Baptist Church. Bishop Smith and six of his congregation's best carpenters were putting up the frame to May Rose's dress shop.

He hollered to the men, "Hey, gentlemen, please keep working. I'm going to run over to the schoolhouse to grab May Rose to show her our work. I'll be right back."

Climbing down his ladder and dusting off his overalls, he walked toward the schoolhouse. He was so happy deep down in his gut. Not just about how well the dress shop was coming along, but how well his and May Rose's relationship seemed to be coming along as well. He just wanted to do everything he possibly could to please her. So much so, he could just burst wide open with joy. Besides his ministry, May Rose was now becoming his life's work.

He reached the schoolhouse door and did his usual rapid three knocks at the top of the door before grabbing the knob and sticking his head inside. "God bless you, children." He looked to May Rose. "Mrs. Jones, may I speak with you outside for a moment?"

"Of course, Bishop Smith. I'm coming immediately," she replied.

He backed out as he said to the children, "Now, you all continue to learn good, ya here?"

"Yes, Bishop Smith," some of them said, while others still referred to him as Minister Smith. It was even taking some of the adults some getting used to.

May Rose instructed the children to continue their math assignment. "Ginny will help with any questions until I return. Is that right, Ginny?" she asked, looking at her oldest child.

"Yes, Mrs. Jones," Ginny responded, never referring to May Rose as Momma when she was working as a schoolteacher. "You go right ahead and handle your business." She winked at her mother and then focused her attention back on the assignment.

May Rose walked outside and closed the door behind her. Bishop Smith snatched her by the hand and spun her in a circle toward the back of the schoolhouse.

She giggled softly and whispered, "Silly boy, what are you doing? Only the entire town could catch us right about now."

He whispered back, "I needed to see your beautiful face this morning." Once they were good and hidden behind the building, he bent down and gave her a big ole wet kiss on the lips.

Once the kiss ended, May Rose kept her eyes closed. "Mmm." She licked her lips. A smile covered her face as if she was reminiscing about the kiss or some things she wished could take place next.

"Walk with me." He took her by the hand and led her toward the back of the church.

May Rose heard the hammering noise and began scream-ing with excitement. "No, no, you're not doing what I think you're doing."

Bishop Smith began jogging and pulling her along. They reached the back of the church, where she got a full view of the partial frame of what appeared to be the start of her shop.

May Rose threw her hands on her hips, with her legs spread wide under her dress. She shook her head in a mighty proud manner. "Well, Bishop Smith, you're not only a man of God, but you're a man of your word. I can't believe you and the men done got started and done got this far without me even catch-ing the slightest wind of it." She shook her head again, this time in disbelief. "I'll tell you the truth, Bishop. I didn't know if we'd still get started without Willie's help and all."

Bishop Smith let out a 'tsk.' "No monkey is going to stop this show," he declared. "The men and I have been at it since dawn. By the way, how many rooms will you need in this here dress shop?"

"Oh, Lord, I will need a sewing room big enough for two sewing machine desks, a small fitting room, a storage room, and of course, the display area for all the lovely dresses." May Rose got excited just talking about it.

"Aren't you forgetting a room?" he asked.

May Rose went deep in thought, saying with a quizzical expression, "I don't think so."

"What about a small bedroom in case you're working late? Or what if I have to come over and help you? Might get so late, I'll need somewhere to lay my head," Bishop Smith said with a big smile.

"You ole manly thing, you." She elbowed him playfully. "I guess I wouldn't want to turn down help from a big, tall, beau-tiful man that looks damn good in some overalls."

Bishop Smith looked down at his clothing. These overalls were actually something May Rose had made him a couple years back. They still looked new, as there weren't too many occasions that called for him to wear them. "Aww, girl, you starting something now. Why don't you say we meet at the schoolhouse at around seven this evening? I need to show you what you do to me."

"Bishop Smith," May Rose said, "won't First Lady Ramona miss you? It's not like we have driving lessons scheduled or anything."

"Don't you worry about her. I'm talking about you. Us. Me and you. Not what I got going on at home, which surely ain't no sweetness. Not like the sweetness you give me," he said. "Come on now, woman, don't make me beg. Will you please meet me or not?" He only had to wait a few seconds.

"I'll be there. I'll be there early," May Rose panted as she fanned herself.

"Mmmhmmm. I thought so." A conceited grin washed across his face before he continued a moment later. "By the way, Ramona has been complaining about back pain more often than usual. Would you ask Sister Elma to come by and check on her while we have our meeting?"

May Rose wasn't sure if her first lady really was suffering from back pain, or if Bishop Smith just needed an excuse to keep his wife occupied. She figured it was the latter by the sly grin he could barely hide. "Yes, sir, for sure. The baby may be trying to come early."

"I thought that, too. She seemed to have had a fever last night. I had her sister give her a cool bath."

May Rose turned just as serious as the conversation. "The fever had broken last night?"

"Yup." He nodded.

"I'll make sure to ask my mother to check on her right away. I'll pop my head in on the children, and then go over to get Momma now," May Rose said. "She can still go back and check on her this evening, too." No matter what was going on between her and First Lady Ramona's husband, May Rose was going to take care of her first lady all the same.

"We'll have your shop finished in the next couple weeks, I reckon, if the men keep up all this hard work," Bishop Smith declared. "We'll drive over to D.C. to Woodards and Lothrop department store and find you a couple foot-operated sewing machines. Bishop Ellis told me about them. You'll be able to make more garments with the machines instead of using your hands. When we start building the inside, you can tell us where you want the dressing room and platform."

May Rose was overwhelmed, but in a good way. Bishop Smith had a way with helping her keep Willie off her mind… and heart. And with the new dress shop and all, she wasn't going to have time to fool with Willie and his shenanigans anyhow. May Rose was grinning from ear-to-ear. "Thank you, sincerely, David. Thank you…" Her words lowered as she got choked up, but she wasn't about to cry on the job.

"Let me get back over to peek in on those children." She looked down and started brushing the invisible lint from her dress, blinking rapidly to get rid of any tears that threatened to fall. She hurriedly walked away, throwing over her shoulder, "And I won't forget to run down and get my mother. I'll see you this evening, Bishop."

May Rose entered the classroom to see Ginny sitting with Bishop Smith's oldest son, eight-year-old Junior. She was helping him with his math. May Rose smiled with such great gratitude and pride for being blessed with a child like Ginny. She could see the bravery and leadership her girl had displayed over the last couple weeks, and she was starting to realize that she didn't have to be concerned about Ginny messing up the woman's business at all. This girl had it in her blood. And not even love would conquer her mission.

When Ginny looked up and saw her mother, May Rose gestured her over. The younger woman nodded and mouthed, "Okay." She left Junior to tend to math on his own, then grinned as she walked to May Rose. It was written all over Ginny's face. She couldn't wait to hear the praise report from her mother about how things were going with Bishop Smith. She figured her momma was probably planning another getaway with him, but what Ginny really couldn't wait to learn about was when her mother was going to get into Bishop Smith's pockets.

"I'm going to pick up Momma and take her to check on First Lady Ramona," May Rose whispered.

Ginny frowned. The last thing she was expecting to hear about was Bishop Smith's wife.

"He told me she has not been feeling well the last couple days," she continued. "He believes the baby will come soon."

Now that put some excitement back on Ginny's face. "Momma, do you think I can catch the baby this time? I can do it all by myself. I know I can do it this time. I've been watching you and the elders long enough. Besides, you'll be right there to help if anything goes wrong, and—"

"Ginny," May Rose cut her daughter off. "Let's discuss this later at home, child. For now, let me hurry to get my momma."

The young woman's shoulders dropped along with her excitement. "Yes, Momma."

"Good." May Rose rushed past and said to her classroom, "Children, you can quietly get in line and go to the lavatory. Wash your hands after you are done, come back to your desk, sit back down, and start your lunch. I will be back before you finish." She headed toward the door but paused. "Ginny is still in charge. Ya hear?"

"Yes, ma'am," the children said in a chorus.

"Very well. Now, enjoy your lunch."

May Rose grabbed her coat and purse from the hook on her way out. At first, she started walking toward her mother's place, but then she realized she had the keys to the limousine that was in the church parking lot. She'd had enough lessons with Bishop Smith to feel comfortable enough to drive such a short distance alone. She pulled the keys from her bag and headed for the car. Once she got to it, she positioned herself behind the steering wheel. She made all the necessary adjustments, as Bishop Smith had been the last one to drive the car and everything was set to his height. Once comfortable and satisfied with her position, May Rose drove off.

Although it was a short trip to Elma's house, May Rose was in deep thought about how much Bishop Smith had done to elevate her life in such a short period of time. "Hell, the man done did more for me in a matter of weeks than Willie done did in all our years of marriage," she said to herself, followed by a 'tsk.' "Even in the year before our marriage when he was courting me, he did less."

May Rose continued to think about how nice it would be when the girls were able to live a better life once she started making money from the dress shop. Not to mention the love offerings Bishop Smith would provide. How could she have denied her girls the lifestyle they deserved waiting on Willie's potential? Oh well, it was better that it was happening now than not at all.

May Rose arrived at Elma's house and began blowing the car's horn. Etta ran out the door, out of breath and hollering, "Chile, what's wrong, what happened? The babies okay?"

May Rose rolled down the car window and yelled, "Is Momma out of the bed yet? I need someone to check on First Lady Ramona. Bishop Smith is concerned she may be ready to push soon."

Aunt Etta's initial response matched that of Ginny's when May Rose shared her concerns about their first lady after her stroll with Bishop Smith. She stopped in her tracks and slammed her hands on her hips. "I know you ain't got me out here 'bout to lose my breath 'bout no Bishop Smith's wife."

"She's having really bad back pain and fever," May Rose said, "but the fever broke last night. Her water has not broken, but she's about eight months now. She needs checking on, for crying out loud."

Aunt Etta, showing empathy and understanding, let her arms fall. "Alright. I'll just come since I'm here now." She crossed her arms, hugging herself and shivering. "But let me grab my sweater and some tools right quick. I'll be right back." She turned to go back into the house.

"Please hurry," May Rose called. "I still gotta get back to the children at the school."

Aunt Etta disappeared inside for just a few seconds and came right back with her sweater in one hand and a medicine bag in the other. She struggled to put the sweater on as she quickly made her way to the car, panting as she opened the door and got inside. She set the baby-catching bag with the tools in it in her lap and said, "She needs to hold that baby at least another two weeks, I think."

"Aunt Etta, you know that baby is going come when it's ready," May Rose said as she drove off, jerking slightly.

"Wait a minute. How well are those driving lessons coming along?" Aunt Etta asked with skepticism. "I ain't gon' end up being the one who needs help, am I?"

"Oh, Aunt Etta, my driving is just fine," May Rose assured her as they made their way to Bishop Smith's house.

Etta made sure to do very little talking. She wanted her niece focusing on the road and not on a distracting conversation.

"I'm going to let you off at the door. I need to go back to the schoolhouse and check on the children. Send someone from there to come and get me if you need me. I'll be back as soon as I let the children out."

"Will do," Etta assured her as May Rose pulled up to Bishop Smith and First Lady Ramona's house. She got out and ran up the steps to the porch, knocking on the door and hollering, "This is Etta, May Rose's aunt. I came to check on First Lady and the baby."

Within a few seconds, First Lady Ramona's oldest sister, Lawanda, opened the door. "Hi, Miss Etta, please come on in." She stepped aside, opening the door wide for Etta to enter. "She's upstairs, still in the bed." She closed the door behind them. "She's been uncomfortable for the last couple days. My mother has been rubbing her down with cool water all morning. Please follow me."

Aunt Etta followed Lawanda up the stairs. The sound of the beautiful, shiny wood stairs made her stop in her tracks after taking only a few steps. "Do I need to take off my shoes? I don't want to scuff up these beautiful steps."

"No, ma'am. One of us will shine everything up. With all these kids running around here, we have to clean them every day." Lawanda chuckled and continued her trek upward until they reached the main bedroom, which was at the very top of the steps on the right. They could hear First Lady Ramona groaning as soon as they reached the door.

Lawanda opened it quickly and announced, "Miss Etta is here to see about you, sis."

Ramona moaned, "Please help me, Miss Etta. I have never had this much pain this soon during my past six babies. And I'm not even in labor. At least I don't think. My water ain't broke or nothing."

The vision before Aunt Etta wasn't anything like the well-groomed, sophisticated first lady she was used to seeing at church. Even with the other six babies, she'd never seen her so unkept before.

Etta rushed over to her. "I'm going to check to see what this baby is doing in there." She paused as she got to First Lady Ramona's bedside. "Where is the washroom?" She looked at Lawanda. "I'll also need a couple clean towels as well."

Lawanda, who still stood in the doorway, pointed down the hall. "It's the second door on the left. I'll get the towels." She hurried out.

"Hurry, please!" First Lady Ramona screamed in agony.

"I'm coming, sis. I'm coming," Lawanda called as she ran to the hall closet and grabbed the towels.

Aunt Etta jogged past her to the washroom. By this time, Vivian entered the room. One woman was on each side of the bed.

Etta fiddled through her catching bag. "Help your daughter scoot down to the bottom of the bed," she told Vivian. Then to Ramona, "I'm going to need to put this towel under your tail. Then I need you to lift it so I can check inside you. It may hurt. I'm sure all this will come back to you soon. Okay?"

First Lady Ramona groaned and grimaced in pain as she nodded and got to scooting.

"I'm going to go inside of you now. Please move down some more," Aunt Etta instructed her patient and then proceeded to go inside First Lady Ramona's private part.

Ramona let out a chilling scream. "Mommy, please help me."

Vivian took her daughter's hand. "I'm here, baby."

Aunt Etta continued the exam, feeling around with one hand and lightly pressing the top of her stomach with the other. She removed her hand and then wiped both with one of the towels Lawanda had fetched. "The baby has turned down," she reported. "It's getting ready for the push. That's probably all the pain you're feeling."

Aunt Etta set that towel down on the night table beside the bed. "I would like you to hold the baby another two weeks if you can. That means you gotta stay in bed with your legs up on pillows. Only get up to go to urinate and defecate." She looked at Vivian even though she was giving the orders to First Lady Ramona, assuming Vivian was going to be helping her out some. "Use a bucket at the side of the bed if you can." She looked back at Ramona. "It can be any day now. We'll be over every day to check on you. Try to get as much rest as you can, eat, and drink lots of water. I'll let Bishop Smith know everything." She patted her hand. "Hang in there, First Lady. You know how this goes."

First Lady Ramona seemed comforted by Aunt Etta's words. She winced less as she spoke softly. "I'll do the best I can, Miss Etta. Thank you. I'm sure going to wait a while before I have the next baby." She shook her head. "Just don't let know Bishop Ellis know I said that. Wouldn't want him to think he's got anything to do with my decision."

Etta smiled. "Yes, my dear. Give your body a rest. You have time to have more babies way down the road. You still good and young. Heck, one day, women as old as grandmothers will have babies without a problem. So, don't you worry." Aunt Etta laughed, not believing her words but saying them nonetheless to give her first lady some hope and a reason not to go running off having another baby any time soon.

After Aunt Etta packed up her things and Lawanda showed her out, she made the short walk to the schoolhouse. She knocked on the door, opened it, and stuck her head in. "Hi, Mrs. Jones," she said to her niece. "May I speak to you for a minute?"

May Rose followed the voice to see her aunt. "Children, please greet our guess, Miss Etta."

The children shouted in unison, "Hi, Miss Etta!"

"Hi, children," she responded, then nodded for May Rose to follow her out the door and meet her outside.

"Look, May Rose," Aunt Etta started, "that child is ready to have that baby before this week is out. The baby has turned, and her cervix is very soft. She needs to be watched closely. I need you to let Bishop know."

May Rose exhaled. "I suspected that. I'll let him know. I'm going to let school out a little early because I haven't been able to focus all day. I been running in and out. Guests been running in and out. Heck, I don't think the children have been able to focus either. There's so much going on." She threw her hand over her forehead and shook her head. "Bishop Smith and a couple guys have started building the frame of the shop." She dropped her arm and looked toward where the men were working. "I was trying to be excited about that, but with him being concerned about First Lady, I can't really show my true excitement how I need to. The way a man needs a woman to be excited about his efforts to please her. He wants me to be excited, but not right now..." she tried to explain before her words trailed off.

Aunt Etta rested her hand on May Rose's shoulder. "Baby, I know. I know. But it will all work out. After she has this baby, everything is going to work out just the way you got it planned. By the way, Ramona told me she will be taking a break before she has baby number eight." Aunt Etta laughed.

May Rose's mouth opened wide in shock. "You must be kidding me. She's already talking about baby number eight."

She shook her head. "Let me go talk to Bishop Smith right away to give him the update. Will you walk my girls home? I'll be shortly behind you."

"Of course," Etta replied, removing her arm from May Rose's shoulder.

"Thank you, Auntie. I'ma go inside and announce to the children that they can go on and get to heading home." She walked back into the classroom. "Grab your reading books, children. Finish chapter seven and read all of chapter eight. We will discuss them tomorrow. For now, you all can head on home. I'm letting school out early. Have a good night and remember to wash up before you go to bed."

She didn't have to tell the children twice as they eagerly started grabbing their things.

"Good night, Mrs. Jones," they started to say.

"Hold on, now." She held her hand up in a stopping motion. "I ain't gon' just let y'all loose like a pack of wolves. Get in line and follow me out," May Rose ordered as she grabbed her own belongings.

She marched the children out of the door and rang the school bell. This let the parents know the children were on their way home.

"Walk home with Aunt Etta," May Rose told her girls, who had finished saying their good-byes to their classmates. "I'll be there soon."

Just then, Aunt Etta approached them, smiling and hugging each of her great nieces.

Florence kissed May Rose on the cheek. "Momma, thanks for letting us out early. I'm not feeling well. My tummy hurts." She rubbed her belly and frowned.

"You're welcome, sweetheart," May Rose said, "but I sure do hope you ain't catching that belly bug that kept Norma Jean out of school most of last week." She turned to Ginny. "Make your sister some sassafras tea and get her to bed. Heat up a towel and put it on Florence's lower stomach like I used to do you when you had a bellyache."

"It feels more like a cramp, Momma," Florence whined.

May Rose, Ginny, and Aunt Etta looked to one another.

"Sounds like Florence is getting ready to start her menstruation," May Rose surmised.

"Don't worry, Momma. I know what to do." Ginny rubbed her sister's shoulder.

Her mother could have stood there and stared Ginny down with admiration the rest of the day. She was so proud of the way her eldest girl was taking on her role as a woman. And the timing couldn't have been better. With everything going on, May Rose surely needed the help and support Ginny's spirit knew to offer.

"I know just how she feels," Ginny said. "C'mon, little sister." The pair locked arms and started walking home. Aunt Etta and Lynette walked behind them.

May Rose stood there watching her family. Her heart couldn't do a doggone thing but beat with so much pride. Again, although she could have stood there basking in the moment all day, she couldn't. She headed over to where the dress shop was being built. As she approached, she heard the hammers still pounding away. She spotted Bishop Smith on a ladder, doing his part and still looking fine and dandy in his overalls.

"Good afternoon, gentlemen," May Rose called out as she approached. "May I have a few words with you?" she asked David.

"Absolutely." He climbed down the ladder, landing him right smack in front of May Rose where she waited for him.

"Can we walk over to the schoolhouse to talk?"

"Let me grab my towel and a refreshing drink and I'll meet you over there. Can I bring you a drink, too?"

With a sheepish grin, she replied, "That sure would be nice, sir."

May Rose started walking to the schoolhouse while thinking she better get her time in with Bishop Smith now because in the next few days, he would have to be a doting husband and father.

He entered the classroom shortly after May Rose, carrying one glass of red drink.

"I thought you were going to grab you a drink as well," she said.

"I drank mine already. I hope you don't mind." He handed her the glass and kissed her on the cheek. "Please forgive me. I smell like a billy goat." He let out a laugh.

"My billy goat," May Rose softly purred, accepting the drink and taking a sip. "Aunt Etta examined First Lady and found the baby is ready to come. It could be any day, but we would like her to hold it for a couple more weeks. By the way, she's also planning for baby number eight, just to let you know."

"No, the hell she ain't," Bishop Smith hollered. "I will pack us up and leave here. Ramona is stark raving mad. Right now, I don't even want to see her face if something as crazy as that is coming out of it."

"Looks like you need some help calming down some." She walked over to the door and locked it. "And I think I know just what can do the job." She cupped her breasts. "Let me put these hotcakes on you to simmer you down." She winked and headed to the supply room.

Bishop Smith eagerly followed, already coming out of his overalls. As soon as they entered the small room, she pushed him up against the wall and began massaging the bulge in his pants.

"I know it's been a few days since I made you explode," May Rose crooned as she pulled her undergarments down and bent over in front of him. "Take it."

"Woman, you ain't got to tell me that." By now, his britches were resting at his ankles.

"It's going to have to be quick now, because you need to tend to your wife."

As Bishop Smith entered her from behind, she swayed her pelvis in a circular motion.

"What a beautiful surprise!" He lightly spanked May Rose on her bottom. "My sweets is giving it to me in the middle of the day." He squeezed her so tightly around her hips that she could hardly move. "I don't care how quick it's going to be, I'm going to make sure you are satisfied first." He held her waist with one hand while he massaged her clitoris with the other.

May Rose was in a trance. She could feel Bishop Smith growing inside of her. She reached back and grabbed his thighs, pulling him in deeper, if that was even possible.

He moaned. "I can feel you getting soaking wet." He continued pleasing May Rose with his manhood and his fingers. "Are you satisfied?"

She blew out a loud burst of air. "Oh, honey, you did your job." Whether he really had, he would never know, but she knew she needed to make him think he had. Her goal was to make sure that he was satisfied with the small bit of time they had to spare. He would have many more opportunities to satisfy her.

She kept moving her hips in sync with his thrusts. "When you're ready to shoot your dirty suds, remember you have to pull out. You know the rules. You can shoot it all on my undergarments on the floor. I'll clean it up."

"I remember," Bishop Smith assured her. "And I remember after all this time how you make me explode."

"Then do it, baby," May Rose encouraged as she sped up the pace, forcing Bishop Smith to speed up his.

He groaned louder and louder, as did the smacking sound of his flesh against hers. "Argh!" he hollered as he pulled himself out, biting his lip and shooting his dirty suds where she'd told him to. "You just took me on another adventure. I can't wait to get you in a bed so that I can take all of you all night."

May Rose stooped and picked her undergarments up off the floor. She then began wiping Bishop Smith's man-part ever-so-gently. She looked him deep in his eyes and said, "You haven't really seen me go to work. So, get ready." She winked. "Now pull up your pants and go see what's going on with your wife and the children."

He pulled up his britches and began snapping his overalls.

"I will ask my mother to come up and check on Ramona tomorrow. You know the routine if her water breaks tonight."

Bishop Smith replied, "Yeah, yeah, yeah." He kissed May Rose's neck.

She closed her eyes and enjoyed the loving gesture. "Damn, you done kissed one of my weak spots. Go on home now with your handsome self. I'm going to clean up around here."

"When I get you in a bed, I'm going to touch every spot on your body."

"I believe you!" She blew him a kiss.

Bishop Smith caught it and closed his fist over his heart, blowing her a kiss. She repeated the motion. This gesture was now their special good-bye to each other. Or rather good-bye-for-now. Because this definitely wouldn't be their last encounter.

Things were just getting started.

"Tomorrow belongs to the people who prepare for it today."

African Proverb

Chapter 13

❧

BE CAREFUL WHAT YOU PREY/PRAY FOR

efore heading home, May Rose stopped by her mother's house. Finding the door unlocked, she walked straight to the kitchen, where she heard voices coming from.

"Hi, Momma," May Rose greeted. "What are you up to?"

A month ago, it wasn't very likely May Rose would make a random stop to see her mother. She never wanted to willingly subject herself to the verbal whooping her mother and aunts put on her when it came to her marriage. But now that May Rose was back in business, her and Elma's relationship had improved. More talk about Biship Smith and less talk about Willie.

"I'm cooking up some herbs we may need to use to catch the Smiths' baby." Elma stood over the stove stirring, not turning away as she spoke to her daughter.

May Rose sniffed, inhaling the scent before acknowledging her aunt. "Hi, Aunt Bertha. You doing okay?"

"Better than ever." She stood up from the table where she'd been sitting, yapping it up with her sister. "Was just in here keeping yo' momma company. But now that you're here, I think I'm gon' go lie down for a spell. Get me some rest." She left the kitchen.

"What brings you calling?" Elma asked, looking up from the pot of herbs to her daughter this time.

"I actually came by to talk about First Lady Ramona. I was wondering if you'd be able to go over to Bishop Smith's house to check on her tomorrow as early as possible. I would do it, but I don't want to risk being late to school. I was in and out of that place a million times today. I need to stay focused tomorrow."

"Yes, that was my plan already. That's why I'm cooking up some yarrow in case of hemorrhaging and some Lythrum Salicata and Hibiscus Rosasinensis to give that silly girl to keep her from having baby number eight, which I hear she is planning to have already." She let out a chuckle as her shoulders bounced up and down.

"Momma, I never heard of the last two herbs before." May Rose's mind had been too stuck on the earlier part of Elma's words to focus on the latter about baby number eight.

"No, because I never had to give it to anyone before. Me and my sisters have drunk it throughout the years. You see it really works. Ain't none of us been birthing no babies. We need to stop that foolish girl before she messes up your business with the bishop."

"You got that right, but I don't believe he will touch her again anyway. He's so angry about her wanting more babies. That and the fact that I've been putting it on him like a winning racehorse." May Rose giggled.

Elma screamed, "That's my girl!" She raised her hand, and May Rose walked over and gave her a high-five. "I'll get her ass on the right track about having more babies."

"I know you will," May Rose said. "Well, okay, Momma, I'm going to go home now and get my babies fed." She let out a chuckle. "You so crazy, Momma." She kissed her mother on the forehead and left.

Once she walked inside her house, May Rose called out, "Girls, I'm home and getting ready to start dinner. Is those rooms clean and reading assignment done?"

Lynette came running down the steps. "Hi, Momma! I did everything you asked." She ran up to May Rose and wrapped her arms around her waist. "Ginny did good teaching us today. Can she teach us some more days? She was so much fun!"

May Rose pinched Lynette's cheeks. "Don't you like your momma's teaching?"

"Yes, Momma, I love your teaching, but Ginny taught us math by playing games with us."

"Is that so?"

"Mmhmm." Lynette stepped back and bounced her head up and down.

"Okay, Lynette, thanks for letting me know. I will let Ginny teach me how she did it and maybe we can do it again sometime. Now, let me get these neckbones and lima beans in the pot, and get this cornbread in the oven."

"Love you, Momma," Lynette said, heading back toward the steps. "I'm going to get my school clothes ready for school tomorrow."

After Lynette was good and up the steps, May Rose could hear her say, "Ginny and Florence, it worked! It worked! Momma's gonna let Ginny teach sometimes. Yay! Momma's gonna to let Ginny teach again sometimes. We can play math games. Yay!"

There was pittering and pattering as Ginny and Florence came running out of their rooms.

"Shhh!" Ginny said in a hard whisper.

"Be quiet, bigmouth," Florence added. "Momma's going to hear us talking about our plan."

"Okay, okay," Lynette huffed. "Ginny, you don't have to be so mean."

May Rose hollered up the steps, "Florence, are you feeling any better?"

"I'm better now, Momma. The hot towel helped," Florence replied.

"That's just what I wanted to hear. Now y'all follow suit from Lynette and get y'all's clothes ready for school tomorrow."

"Yes, ma'am," the girls said in unison and then did as they were told.

After dinner, May Rose rested in the sitting room, stretched out on the old sofa with snags on the fabric and sunken pillow cushions that had been there since Daddy John Jones and Mother Fanny Jones were alive and lived there. The girls were taking turns bathing in the tub with a couple drops of perfume each. May Rose loved teaching them about having the finer things in life.

She got deep in thought with her eyes closed, first thinking about how Willie deserted her and the girls. Although she'd kick his behind to the curb in a heartbeat, the least his sorry tail could have done was try to see about her and his children. She thought how she just wanted to wring his neck.

May Rose opened her eyes and mumbled, "The hell with Willie Jones. I've got some good business going on with David right now, and I'm not going to let Willie mess that up. Serves us all well if he stays gone."

With that thought, she dozed off to sleep. She woke up to the rooster crowing and realized she never bathed or made it to bed. She jumped up off the couch and ran to the washroom to see if the girls left her some water in the well bucket. She grabbed the bucket, looked inside, and said, "My angels was thinking about their mother." She was glad to see it full to the rim.

She ran to the kitchen to get a pot to dip water to heat on the stove. She then ran outside and quickly fed the animals, came back in, and put the hot water in the tub. "I must hurry so I can get to the schoolhouse early since I wasn't in the classroom most of the day yesterday. Dang it! Can't believe I'm running behind."

She undressed, took down her hair, and put her hand in the water. "Owww, it's still too hot. Let me let it cool off a little more." May Rose sat at her vanity and started brushing her hair.

She glanced at the window, where she saw a flash of a car's light. "Who the hell is this coming here this time of the morning?" She stood up, then slipped on her housecoat and slippers. She tiptoed down the steps and jogged to the front door, slightly cracking it open. To her surprise, she saw Bishop Smith getting out of his car.

"What's going on? Has this man lost his damn mind?" May Rose whispered.

For a moment there, she forgot all about the fact that he could be showing up at her doorstep at such an hour because his wife was about to have the baby. She waited for him to come on the porch before opening the door all the way. "Good morning, handsome." She kissed his sweaty cheek.

"Now, that's how a man should be greeted." He gave May Rose the once-over. "What do you have on under that housecoat of yours?"

May Rose feigned bashful and wrapped her arms around herself, swinging her body from left to right.

"Can I see?" He waggled his eyebrows.

She thought for a moment then quickly opened her housecoat to reveal her entire naked body.

"Well, I'll be..." Bishop Smith said as he stood in the doorway, dang near salivating.

"Come here." She signaled him in with her index finger, closing the door behind him.

If First Lady Ramona was about to have that baby, it most certainly was the last thing on Bishop Smith's mind.

She took his right hand and rubbed it on her breast.

"Lord have mercy," he moaned.

"And just what brings you by my place this morning?" May Rose asked. "I already know how to drive, so it can't be for no driving lessons." She chuckled. "You know my girls will be waking up for school shortly, and my mother and aunts will be getting up stirring around in a minute, too. So, whatever brings you over, you better make it quick," she said seductively.

He hurried and replied, "I would never risk your girls catching us being frisky." He placed his hands on her. "Although I sure wouldn't mind getting a little frisky now."

"I bet you wouldn't." She playfully swatted his hands away.

"But anyway, Ramona wanted me to see if you could come check on her. She said she knows y'all wanted her to hold the baby a couple more weeks, but she don't think it's up to her."

May Rose got serious. "I know you don't think your wife is about to have a baby and you over here trying to make one with me." She gave Bishop Smith a look of shame.

"Well, how was I to know you was gonna answer the door naked and distract me and such?"

"I fooled around enough yesterday in and out of that schoolhouse. Take yourself over there and get my mother. She was prepared to come to your house this morning anyway." May Rose rushed over and opened the front door. "Please tell my mother I'll be over to help her after I get the children settled in at schoolhouse." She grabbed Bishop Smith by the arm and started dragging him toward the door. He wasn't moving fast enough for a man whose wife was in labor.

"Okay, baby, okay. I'm leaving now," he said as he headed off the porch and to the elders' house.

"Shoot," May Rose started to fuss at herself. "Why didn't I just send the man out the back door." She let out a 'tsk' and shook her head. "And congratulations to you and First Lady Ramona," May Rose shouted.

"Yeah, yeah, yeah," he negatively replied, waving dismissively.

He walked up the steps at the elders' house and to his surprise, Elma swung open the door before he could even knock.

"I'm ready, let's go!" she said as she came charging out of the house with her baby-catching bag. "I knew that baby was coming today. I've been catching babies for over thirty years. I know when a baby is ready. I saw your car lights when you drove up. I said, today will be baby number seven's birthday," Elma said as she marched to the car.

Bishop Smith took a loud gulp. "Wow, baby number seven. That sounds so different when someone else says it." By this time, Elma was a long way ahead of him. "Okay, I'm ready. Let's go get baby number seven," he said, almost as if giving himself a pep talk as he put some energy into his step toward his car.

Elma was darn near at the car door before he picked up his speed so he could open it for her and put the stool down. Once he did that, Elma took his hand and climbed onto the seat. He picked up the stool, placed it behind Elma's seat, and closed the door.

Once Bishop Smith got in the car, he took off slowly, as if there was no reason to be in a hurry, which had pretty much been his entire attitude that morning. "By the way, Miss Elma, Rosie said she'll be over to the house once she gets the children settled in the schoolhouse."

Elma nodded. "Okay, thanks for letting me know, Bishop." She continued, "I think you need to get you a sip of that fine brandy you have at home in your office. You seem so very sad, like you need a boost or something."

Bishop Smith exhaled. "Thank you for your concern, Miss Elma. I guess you could say I kind of am a bit sad."

"Is that so?" she asked, deciding she wouldn't push if he didn't want to give her anything more than a 'yes,' although she wouldn't mind hearing more about what was going on in that head of his, especially if it were something she could carry back to her daughter that might hurry her plans for Bishop Smith along.

"Yes, it is," he replied.

There were a few seconds of silence, then Elma got her wish.

"I didn't want a houseful of babies or in-laws," Bishop Smith blurted out. "There are so many things I still want to do with my life. This wasn't my plan."

She remained silent, sensing he had a bit more he needed to get out of his system.

"Miss Elma, I think you already know this, but I'm going to say it anyway." He looked at her. "And I mean no disrespect whatsoever, considering she's a married woman..." He put his eyes back on the road. "But I love your May Rose, and I want someday for her to be my wife now since it seems Willie has thrown his hands up on his marriage," Bishop Smith said in a heartfelt tone.

"I hear what you saying about Willie, Bishop," Elma responded, "but first things first, let's get baby number seven born, then we can have a sit-down about you and May Rose. Because baby number seven, and the other six, got a momma. And that momma just happens to be your wife."

"Yes, ma'am. I know. I hear you." He sighed but quickly picked himself up and said, "But it still don't change how I feel about your daughter."

Elma took in Bishop Smith's words. "I'm sure as much as you both want each other and want to be together, you'll work this out."

He perked up like a bunny tail. "She wants me just as much as I want her. She said those words to you?"

She rolled her eyes. "Bishop Smith, it don't take neither one of ya saying much of nothing. I see how she sees you and without you even saying a word, I see how you see her. Neither one of ya gotta say much of nothing. But never you mind all that. Like I said, we got baby number seven to get to tending to. Now, hurry up and get us down this road before Seven beats us there." Elma pointed straight ahead.

"Yes, ma'am," Bishop Smith declared as he picked up speed. No one would have even been able to tell that just moments ago, he was as down in the dumps as a betting man who'd lost all his money.

When he pulled up to his house, Elma noticed how candles lit up every window. He jumped out and jogged over to Elma's car door, opening it quickly. Instead of getting the stool, he simply lifted her out of the car by her waist.

She couldn't help but notice how strong and manly Bishop Smith's hands were. As far as she was concerned, it was no wonder May Rose had the hots for him. She stopped her fleeting thoughts, clutched her catching bag, and trotted up the front steps. Having more of a sense of urgency than Bishop Smith from the moment he came to her doorstep, she was ahead of him. As he came up from behind, she stepped aside to allow him to pass. He pushed the front door open, and they were immediately greeted by First Lady Ramona screaming bloody murder.

"Please help me," she yelled. "I swear I'll wait a couple years to have another baby. Just get this one out of me!"

Elma and Bishop Smith ran up the steps. When they reached the bedroom, Bishop Smith shouted at the top of his voice, "Woman, you're really crazy. Shut your silly ass up and deliver this baby."

"Everyone, calm down," Elma shouted, then she began barking out orders. "Bishop Smith, please get me a washbasin full of warm water, clean towels, rubbing alcohol, and a couple clean blankets." She stood over First Lady Ramona and placed her hand on her forehead. "How often are the pains coming?"

"Hell, the pain has not stopped coming since it started two days ago." She held her belly with both hands, winced, and groaned. "Oh, Jesus, help me." She started huffing and puffing, breathing in and out heavily.

"Lawanda!" Elma called, not realizing Lawanda had come into the room and was standing right behind her, so it startled her when Lawanda answered. She ordered, "Open all of the windows. I can smell the fever from her."

Lawanda immediately did as commanded as Elma headed out the bedroom door. "Bishop, please hurry up with the rubbing alcohol." She ran to the washroom and washed her hands thoroughly. By the time she finished and headed back to see about her first lady, Bishop was entering the bedroom.

"Ramona, c'mon and get in position," Elma instructed her as she approached the bed.

She and Lawanda scooted First Lady Ramona down the bed, and Elma proceeded to check between her legs. "I'm seeing blood. We have to hurry to get Seven out. Bishop Smith, hand Lawanda the alcohol. Lawanda, rub First Lady Ramona all over her forehead and the back of her neck with it. Bishop Smith, have one of your in-laws go fetch my sisters. I'm going to need some help. Then you go have your brandy," Elma ordered, and Bishop Smith did just that.

Elma helped First Lady Ramona scoot a little bit closer to the edge of the bed, where her bottom was perfectly positioned on top of the towels. Blood was pulsating out of her like drops of water from a broken faucet. Elma's eyes became as large as plates, and First Lady Ramona could see the shocked expression. The midwife reached down to examine her patient, where she could feel the crown of the baby's head.

"What's wrong? Oh, God, what's wrong with my baby? I feel funny." First Lady Ramona slammed her eyes closed, but tears leaked out the corners.

"First Lady, you have to calm down," Elma said. "Let's get ready to push."

A few minutes later, Etta and Bertha walked into the room.

"Oh, Lord, thank you, God," Elma said, relieved she had backup. "Etta, get me some towels soaked in yarrow. It's in my catching bag. We have some hemorrhaging going on." She turned her attention back to Ramona. "C'mon, baby, let's push. Bertha, hurry and hike up her legs," she continued. "First Lady, are you still with us?"

First Lady Ramona moaned faintly, "Yes."

"Lawanda, you can step back. We'll let you know if we need you," Elma said.

Etta immediately stepped in where Lawanda had been.

"Etta, get behind First Lady to help push. She's too weak to do it on her own."

"First Lady Ramona, baby, give it all you got."

Elma calmly said to their patient, "Okay, when you feel your next hard pain, tell me so we can help you push. Remember your breathing. Don't forget to breathe."

Ramona screamed, "Here it comes, oh my, God, help me!"

Elma said in cadence, "One, two, three, breathe and push. One, two, three, push and breathe."

First Lady Ramona was panting and pushing as hard as she could. She laid her head back and rested between pushes. Her entire body began to tremble.

Elma reached for the beautiful pink satin and lace stool from First Lady Ramona's pink vanity. She placed it at the foot of the bed and sat on it. "We have to get this baby out of her right now," she told her sisters. "It looks like we're losing her. Bertha, stretch her legs out as far as you can. Etta, lift her head and push her back up. I'm going to pull this baby out now. First Lady, just one more really big push. I'm going to help you. C'mon now and push."

Ramona let out a loud squeal, and then her head dropped to the side as white foam began spilling from her mouth. By then, Elma had the baby out to its shoulders.

"My God!" Aunt Bertha exclaimed. "Our first lady is not breathing."

"And the baby is damn near blue," Elma added. "Etta, work on First Lady. Me and Bertha will work on the baby."

Etta started shaking First Lady Ramona and calling her name, but there was no reaction. "Dear God, she's turning ice cold," Aunt Etta cried nervously.

Elma and Bertha were busy tending to the baby.

Lawanda, in spite of them asking her to step away, raced back to her sister's side, but she couldn't help. There was nothing she could do.

It was too late.

"Elma, in Jesus's name, First Lady Ramona is gone," Etta cried.

Lawanda started shaking her sister. "Ramona! Ramona!" she called out as tears spilled from her eyes.

Elma couldn't attend to First Lady Ramona or comfort Lawanda because her focus had to be on the baby, whom she was repeatedly smacking on the back to try to get it to breathe. "My God, the baby is not breathing no matter how much I am smacking its back. This is about the worst case we have seen… Bertha, please run and fetch Bishop Smith." Elma proceeded to smack the baby on its bottom, trying to get it to cry.

Finally, her sister caught her hand mid-swing. "Won't do no good, sis. Won't do no good," Bertha said somberly. "He's gone."

Elma closed her eyes and said a silent prayer. "Please go fetch Bishop," she said to Aunt Bertha a second time. Elma started cleaning up the deceased baby boy with the water in the basin.

Bertha did what her sister asked and went and knocked softly, but rapidly, on Bishop Smith's office door. "Bishop," she whispered, "we need you upstairs right now." Before he could step out, she turned and ran back up the steps to the bedroom. She couldn't even look at him. He'd see that something was amiss from the moment he looked at her face.

Because he was not a regular drinker, not drinking enough to even be considered a social drinker, Bishop Smith was a little tipsy from his one small snifter of brandy. He even stumbled slightly in his attempt to catch up to Aunt Bertha. He felt like he was going in slow motion. All the way up the steps, he was mumbling, "It's about time. This time took much longer than the others. She finally calmed down all of that screaming she does, thank God."

Although Aunt Bertha was ahead of Bishop Smith, she stepped aside so that he could enter the room before her. Her head was down, and she didn't say a word. It didn't go unnoticed that she hadn't made eye contact with him. Neither had she said a single word about his wife or baby number seven.

Bishop Smith walked into the room and saw his wife lying in the bed with their new baby in her arms. A blanket covered them. As he drew nearer, Elma walked straight up to him. She looked just like her sister, Bishop Smith thought, in the sense that she wore the same expression and could barely look him in the eyes.

Elma took both of his hands in hers. "Bishop Smith, I'm so, so sorry." Her voice was shaky, but she kept her hands still. "First Lady Ramona and the baby boy passed away during childbirth. She had a severe infection, and the hemorrhaging would not stop. She lost too much blood."

Elma wasn't sure if he'd heard her clearly or not at all. He just stood there with a stoic and slightly confused face.

"Bishop, you alright?" Elma shook his hands in an attempt to shake him out of his trance. "Bishop?"

He pulled his hands from Elma's and went and stood over his wife and baby. He slowly started to shake his head. "No, no," he whispered softly.

"We're sorry, Bishop, so sorry." Aunt Etta offered her condolences from the corner, where she held an emotional Lawanda.

Bishop Smith looked up from his wife and baby to Aunt Etta and Lawanda. "No. Oh, no." He started shaking his head more frantically, and his voice rose. "What do you mean? No, it can't be. She… They… What am I supposed to tell my children?" He looked to Elma for answers. "Her family…" He pointed at Lawanda. "They're gonna be devasted." He laid his head on his wife's cold chest and pulled the baby from her. "Ramona, I asked you to stop doing this to yourself. We had enough children." Tears began to fill his eyes. "I will take responsibility for all the children. Father, please accept Ramona and my baby into your Kingdom. Amen."

Bishop Smith laid the baby back into his wife's arms after he kissed her cold forehead. He then looked from Elma to Bertha to Etta.

The women were prepared for Bishop Smith to give them a tongue-lashing. He was surely hurting and since hurt people hurt other people, they were certain he was going to slice them up with his words, blaming them for the death of his wife and child. But they were strong women. They could take whatever their bishop was going to throw at them, and they wouldn't take it personal. They understood that sometimes, pain's purpose was to heal by inflicting itself on others. It didn't know any better. Nonetheless, they braced themselves for come what may out of Bishop Smith's mouth.

"Thank you for ushering Ramona and my baby boy onto glory. I appreciate everything you ladies and May Rose have done." His next comment was directed at Elma, since she seemed to be the unspoken leader of the women. "Would you all please stay until I go tell Mother Vivian and her children?"

"Absolutely, Bishop," Elma said. "You don't even have to ask."

Bishop Smith nodded his thanks and then slowly walked to the door.

Everyone in the room could hear his sniffling and whimpering outside the door once he'd exited. He carried with him a burden larger than anyone knew, except for May Rose. She was the only one privy to his prayer about creating a situation or circumstance that would allow her to be his wife. But he had no idea his prayer would lead to this.

The African sisters had no idea that Bishop Smith would never blame them for what happened to his wife and baby, so that was a burden they could release themselves from. This was a blame he and he alone would carry. And just like with the prayer itself, no one would ever know. Just him and May Rose.

And God.

"Chance comes to those who know what they want."

African Proverb

Chapter 14

BUSINESS AS USUAL

Mother Vivian and her daughters, Lawanda, and Diane, all fell into Bishop Smith's arms. The other eight siblings and his own two-year-old daughter, Lou Lou, wailed all over the house. It had been an hour since everyone learned of First Lady Ramona's and the baby's death, but every minute felt fresh, like they were learning it for the first time. Every second, even.

"Excuse me, Bishop…" Elma stuck her head in the room. "Can the family please come in and bid their farewells to sweet Ramona and baby boy Seven?"

Bishop Smith looked at Elma and nodded. She returned the nod and left.

He pulled away from the family huddle and grabbed his white, crisp handkerchief with the initials D.S. out of his pocket. He gave it to Mother Vivian. "Y'all heard Miss Elma. We better go say our good-byes."

Everyone pulled themselves together as best they could, and Bishop Smith escorted them into his bedroom.

Elma had gathered the other family members, too, who were already in the room.

Mother Vivian screamed the moment she walked through the doorway. "Look at my babies! Lord, please help me accept this. I can't see out of your supernatural eyes. Will I ever be able to understand your purpose for this? Lord, Jesus, help me. Give me strength."

By this time, Lawanda had grabbed one of Mother Vivian's arms and Diane held her by the other. They continued to walk up to the bed, stopping once they reached the foot of it.

Mother Vivian loosened herself from their grips and walked up alone to the head of the bed. She bent down and kissed her deceased daughter all over her face, weeping the entire time.

Lawanda grabbed Mother Vivan around her waist and held her tight while she cried on her mother's back.

Diane went back to the door where Elma stood and hugged her around her neck. "Did she suffer?" she asked.

Elma softly responded, "It happened very fast. The infection traveled throughout her body quickly. I think she might have suffered more these last couple of days from just the labor pains than she did from the cause of her death." Elma looked toward the bed. "We did all we could."

"I know you did, Miss Elma," Diane said sincerely. "Thank you, Miss Elma. Thank you to you and your sisters."

Bishop Smith approached them. "Can we get a message to May Rose?" he asked. "Tell her she's needed here. Ask her to send all of the children home for the day and bring my five babies—Ode, Buddy, Alex, Daniel, and Denise—home."

"Yes, sir, Bishop," Elma replied.

"I will meet her at the door. I would go get my children myself, but if I go get them, they'll know something is wrong."

"I'll head out right now," Elma said.

"*I'll* go get *my* nieces and nephews," Diane snapped at him.

"You'll do no such thing," Bishop Smith replied sharply. "I understand you're upset and all, but you certainly will not disrespect my wishes. Elma can go fetch her daughter."

Diane grumbled, "Like you disrespected my sister when you felt like it?"

Mother Vivan swung around. "You will not disrespect the man of this house," she scolded.

"Thank you, Mother Vivian," Bishop Smith said, "but we will discuss this later." He turned his attention back to his sister-in-law. "As far as you, Diane, I suggest you stay away from me until after we put Ramona and my baby in the ground. In my state, I might do something that will make me lose my collar."

Diane fixed her mouth to speak, but Elma jumped in before any words could escape.

"We'll leave now to tell May Rose to bring the children from school," she said. "C'mon, sisters, I need y'all to go with me to get May Rose and the children." She gave Bishop Smith a smile as her sisters headed for the door. "Again, Bishop, I'm very sorry for your loss. We did all we could do." She marched over and retrieved her catching bag from the bedside table, and then she and her sisters walked out.

Bishop Smith pivoted and started walking behind them to escort them to the door.

"Ladies, can you please hold up for just one minute?" Knowing the ladies heard him and had paused before heading out, he did a light jog to his office. He returned in less than a minute with a white envelope. "I had this put up for you all for catching the baby and all of your visits before. I truly thank you so much."

Elma accepted the envelope and placed it in her catching bag. "Thanks, Bishop. First Lady's body just couldn't take bearing all those children back-to-back. Some of them less than stair-steps in age."

Bishop Smith lowered his head. "I know. I tried to tell her." He shook his head and sniffed.

"We tried to tell her, too." Aunt Bertha let out a regretful sigh. "She just wanted a big family, like her momma."

"Come on, ladies," Elma said. The sisters all filed out the door, but before walking off the porch, Elma turned and said, "We'll hurry back. But send one of your other children after us if you feel you might have to beat some ass tonight. That Diane didn't know me and my sisters were getting ready to African dance all over her smart ass. And we ain't got nothing to lose. Certainly not no collar."

"Thank you, Miss Elma, but my house is going to get cleared out real soon." On that note, Bishop Smith closed the door and went back to tending to his family.

The ladies whispered about the events of the day all the way to the schoolhouse door, including their remorse for the loss of their first lady and the baby.

The sisters approached the schoolhouse and headed up the steps. "Wait a minute," Elma said, stopping in her tracks. She turned around. "Etta, you go on in and get May Rose to come out. We'll tell her what's going on once she gets out here."

Elma and Bertha waited at the foot of the steps while Aunt Etta went to fetch May Rose. A few seconds later, they came out the door. The latter shut it behind them. Elma walked up to May Rose and grabbed her and held her arms really tight.

May Rose pulled away with a confused look. "What's wrong?" She could tell by the look on the sisters' faces, as well as the dark energy emanating from them, that whatever was going on was bad. Very bad. "Oh, Lord, is it David?" She began frantically looking from one sister to the next, not giving either of them the opportunity to respond before she said, "What is it? You all speak up now."

Elma swallowed hard and took a deep breath. "Ramona and Baby Seven passed away. She had a raging infection and heavy hemorrhaging. We did everything we could."

May Rose cried out softly, "Momma, what did you do? Please tell me you didn't have anything to do with this." She snatched herself out of her mother's arms and smacked her forehead. "Oh, my God. I told you I had this. I told you I would handle my business. But you just couldn't trust me on this, could you?" She barked at her aunts. "Any of you. Y'all just couldn't let my mistake with Willie go." She began pacing and shaking her head. She suddenly stopped mid-pace. "You told her to hold that baby inside." She pointed an accusing finger at Elma as she stepped toward her. "You knew what was happening." She looked to her aunts. "Any of you could have delivered that baby and just maybe—"

"You better watch your mouth," Elma growled, charging toward May Rose. She would have snatched her up good if her sisters hadn't grabbed hold of each arm and held her back. "I didn't have to do anything. That girl destroyed her own body, and you know it, having all of those babies back-to-back. And while you're talking crazy to me, you better take Bishop's children to him at the house like he requested." Elma leaned forward just enough to be nose-to-nose with her daughter. "In other words, you better go get your man. You know all the single young and old biddies will be on his heels."

May Rose shook her head in disgust. "You're a real piece of work, Momma. Who would think like that at this time?"

Elma grinned and shook her head, not in disgust but in shame that her daughter was still letting her feelings get in the way of business. "I would, your aunties would, hell, even Ginny would, because we are about business, come what may. You seem to be the only one who keeps forgetting how a woman's work works." She let out a 'tsk' as she rolled her eyes.

Aunt Bertha released Elma's arm and stood between her and May Rose. "The business plan has just ramped up! Don't be silly, May Rose. The work never ends. It comes rain or shine. So, just shut up and get to work, and go get that man's children up there. He's waiting on them." Bertha leaned in so closely that May Rose could smell her breath. "He's waiting on you." She stepped back to her sister's side.

May Rose's lips trembled with anger. "You all are unbelievable. Absolutely unbelievable." The women remained silent as May Rose stood their accusing them of the unthinkable. All the while, May Rose's trembling lips crept into a smile. "But wise as hell." She let out a chuckle that became so contagious, all the women found themselves chuckling. May Rose put her index finger across her lips. "Shhh." She looked around to make sure that no one was watching them. "We don't want to be seen kee-keeing at a time like this." She turned her attention back to the sisters, who each muffled their laughter. "I hate to agree with you all sometimes, but when you're right, you're right."

"And trust us," Aunt Etta chimed in, "we're right about this. So, we'll get the girls and take them home with us. We'll also tell them about Ramona and the baby's death. I'm sure you may not make it home tonight."

May Rose slapped her hands on her hips. "Really, not coming home tonight. Lady, that will not be the case. First Lady Ramona's family is still there."

"Not for long, though, according to Bishop," Elma added.

"Nonetheless, they're there now, and the last thing I'll be doing is spending the night there. So, be gentle with my babies.

This is not something that should be delivered with the lack of empathy like you just did with me."

May Rose walked over to the bell and rang it three times. She then ran into the schoolhouse and announced, "Children, school has been dismissed early today. The Smith children, wait for me to walk with you home. Jones children, your nana and great-aunts are waiting for you all outside. The rest of you children go straight home and look out for each other on your journey. Take a book to read tonight and read at least two chapters. We'll discuss the chapters tomorrow or the day after, depending." May Rose was certain she was going to return to her home tonight, but she wasn't so sure about when she'd be returning to the classroom. She was going to be there for Bishop Smith for as many days as he needed her...just not nights. Not yet, anyway.

Ginny walked over. "Momma, so Lady Ramona done had the baby? What did she have, a boy or girl?"

May Rose kept busy gathering her things so that she wouldn't have to make eye contact with Ginny. "Quit fishing and get on out that door. I'll see you in a little bit," May Rose sternly said. She grabbed her sweater and her purse, gathered up the Smith children, and they left.

The Smith children playfully walked up the hill to their house, where Bishop Smith was now in view, waiting on the front porch for them. He'd been standing there for the past few minutes, waiting for them to come into his eyesight.

He hollered, "C'mon, children, run." The children giggled and raced each other up the hill.

May Rose walked slowly, deep in thought. "What am I supposed to say?" she asked herself as she watched the children run ahead of her. She started to question whether this was the time for her to be present. If perhaps she should let Bishop Smith be with his family without her presence. "But he wants me here," she reminded herself. "Momma said he sent for me."

Just as she finished that thought, Bishop Smith called, "Rosie, please hurry. I need you here."

May Rose picked up her speed and galloped up the hill behind the children. Bishop Smith stepped off the porch. As the children arrived at his open arms, he put them in a circle around him. He sat on the grass and told the children to sit with him.

"Miss Jones, come join us."

May Rose leveled her breathing after hustling over to Bishop Smith and the Smith children.

"Children, you know Papa loves you all, right?" he asked.

All the children responded, "Yes, Papa!"

May Rose sat on the grass, too, directly behind the children.

He continued, "I will always protect and take care of you all. You know that, right?"

The children responded, either verbally or with nods.

"I have to tell you something that's going to make you sad, but just know you have so much love around you." Bishop Smith took a breath. "I want you all to look me in my eyes. I need to tell you that your mother and your baby brother went to be with God this morning."

The spirit of calmness drained from the children as chaos entered. They began crying, falling out, and running into their father's arms. They clung to his body, weak in grief.

"Their bodies are in the house in our bedroom, but their spirits are now with God." He looked at May Rose as if seeking her approval on how he was doing in relaying the situation to his children.

She nodded and gave him a soft smile.

"Me and Miss Jones are going to take you all inside to tell them good-bye like you had to say good-bye to my papa, Poppa Amos, when he went to be with God. Remember?"

"Yes, Papa," some cried while others simply nodded.

"I know this is not easy for you to understand, being as young as you all are, but some day as you grow up, it may be easier to live with."

"Momma," one of the children whined, missing their mother already.

"Do you think you are ready to see your mother and the baby?" Bishop Smith asked.

The children were wiping their tears and runny noses on their sleeves and on Bishop Smith's crisp, white dress shirt.

The oldest son, eight-year-old Junior, cried out, "Papa, I'm ready. Momma and our brother are in a better place with God, and they are preparing a place for us all with Grandpa Amos, just like the Bible teaches us."

Bishop Smith rubbed Junior on the head. "Junior, you are giving me strength. I see a calling over your life. Son, I believe God has just called you into ministry."

A small smile crept from behind Junior's look of grief, like the sun peeking from behind a dark cloud.

"I was twelve when I was called. Praise God! I'm going to have to start letting you teach some Sunday school classes and lead some prayers during Sunday service." He looked to his other children. "Does anyone else want to say anything? I want you all to be able to talk to me and Miss Jones. You can trust her, too, since she is your schoolteacher." He looked at May Rose. "Isn't that right, Miss Jones?"

She was a bit caught off guard with how quickly Bishop Smith was weaving her into their lives. She couldn't get any words out, but she nodded her confirmation.

Seven-year-old Regina spoke up and said, "Papa, can I sleep over Miss Jones's house sometimes to play with Florence and Lynette? Ginny always says she doesn't play with kids."

"Baby, you'll need to ask Miss Jones," he replied.

May Rose jumped in immediately. "Of course you can, Regina." She looked from one child to the next. "Any of you can."

"Let's go, children," Bishop Smith said. "Miss Jones, will you please wait here a spell? I'd like you to accompany me to the Mills Gray Funeral Parlor to make the burial arrangements and send off telegrams to my mother and Bishop Ellis. I will ask the deacons to notify the congregation of Ramona and the baby after the arrangements have been made."

He gathered up the children, and they all went into the house. May Rose sat on the steps to wait. This was a time for family, and she wasn't family...yet.

She went deep into thought, conjuring up all the many ways this thing could turn out. Even with First Lady Ramona out of the way, there was still ole Willie they would have to tend to. "There you go, thinking like them crazy African ladies," May Rose said to herself with a chuckle.

A little while later, Bishop Smith came out the door and down the steps. He planted his bottom on the steps next to her.

"How's the children?" she asked.

"My babies are brilliant and strong. We've taught them well. And when I say we, that includes you. My children are blessed to have the family and community around them that they do. And for that, I do believe they'll be all right."

"I ain't have nothing to do with that. Your children came to the schoolhouse with brilliance." She gave Bishop Smith a friendly and caring pat on the knee. "How are you holding up?"

"I'm doing better now. I have been thinking through my plans. You didn't know this, but I was in the process of buying the old Davis Farm over there in Roanoke for my in-laws. I knew it was time for them to go before this happened. That damn Diane showed her ass with me today. I'm not taking that behavior in my house."

"Emotions are raw now, so don't be too hard on Diane, and certainly don't take it personal. However, I understand your concern." She changed the topic. "How's Mother Vivian holding up?"

"She's doing the best she can. I'm going to make sure she is well taken care of. She has always been so sweet and kind to me and the children," he replied. "Rosie, I won't ignore that this must be hard for you to deal with because I know you have a caring heart. But I have to continue to live for my children, and you're going to be a part of this new life with my children."

"Bishop, I—" May Rose started before he cut her off.

"Rosie, don't you feel no way ashamed about nothing. This was God's will for Ramona and the baby. She was so hardheaded about having babies. Something was wrong with her mind. I truly wish I could have helped her understand," he said sadly. The tears started to stream down his face, but he quicky brushed them away, as if he didn't want May Rose seeing him show such emotions. He stood up from the steps. "Let's walk on to the car and go take care of the funeral arrangement business and send the telegrams." He extended his hand and helped May Rose to her feet.

"I got your back, David. Continue to cry if you need to. You were together a long time," she empathetically responded as they walked to his car.

"Rosie, please don't leave me ever. I don't know if my poor heart could take such a loss again."

She stopped walking and took his hand. "We're going to make this work. Our children love each other. My girls, my elders, and me, of course, will help you rear them."

Bishop Smith looked deep into May Rose's eyes. "Thank you. I always have to give you my gratitude because you're such a remarkable woman."

She wanted to embrace him at that moment, but by this time, a few of his in-laws and children had come out onto the porch. She quickly released his hand. "Let's get in the car and go now."

After he helped her climb into her seat, May Rose turned and waved good-bye to the family members on the porch.

Bishop Smith shouted as he walked over to the driver's side, "I'm going to see Mr. Mills the undertaker and have him come and pick up Ramona's and the baby's bodies. Would someone prepare lunch for the children? I'm sure after the congregation finds out, they will bring loads of food. But for now, let's get something in my babies' stomachs."

Mother Vivian shouted back to her son-in-law, "They sure will bring enough food to feed us for weeks. We'll get the children cleaned up and fed a little something in the meantime. You just go do what you have to do."

Bishop Smith got in the car and drove to the funeral home. He and May Rose made the arrangements and then went to get the telegrams sent off. One went to his mother, Marlene Smith, who lived in New York City with his baby sister Marnita. She'd lived there since Bishop Smith's father passed away six years ago. The other went to Bishop Ellis.

Next, they stopped at Deacon Green's house to share the news and give him instructions on notifying the congregation. The funeral services were scheduled for two weeks away.

They decide to go past May Rose's house to check on the children before heading back to Bishop Smith's place.

When they arrived, the girls greeted them at the door. Florence and Lynette ran to May Rose and grabbed her tightly around the waist. Ginny walked up to Bishop Smith and extended her hand. "Bishop Smith, I am so deeply sorry for your loss. I pray you will find comfort in your memories of First Lady Ramona. I offer my support to you and your family in any way I may help."

He shook her hand. "Thank you, young lady. You're incredibly wise. I will be taking you up on your offer."

Florence and Lynnette let go of May Rose and followed Ginny's lead. They let Bishop Smith know that the two of them would be there to help him and his family, too.

He touched them both on the shoulder. "Thanks, girls. We appreciate your offer." He continued, "Rosie, I'm going to head back home to spend some time with the children and be there when the undertaker arrives. You might as well stay here with your family. I think I've got things from here."

"Absolutely, Bishop," May Rose said. "Would you like us to come fix breakfast in the morning for the family?"

"No, Rosie, that won't be necessary. Please continue to run the schoolhouse tomorrow. All of the children will need a sense of normalcy. I would like to come over to the schoolhouse in the morning to have a talk with all of the children, if you don't mind," he said.

"Sure, come whenever you're ready," she replied.

He thanked her and bid farewell to the girls, and then he walked toward the door. May Rose walked behind him, and the girls followed suit. When he opened it, May Rose stepped aside while the girls went their separate ways. She turned to Bishop Smith.

He kissed May Rose on the hand. "I know this is uncomfortable for you right now. Things might move faster than we anticipated, but I will take it at your pace, okay?"

She nodded and blew him a kiss in their normal fashion... even though nothing from this point on would be normal.

"When the rhythm of the song changes, the dance steps must also change."

African Proverb

Chapter 15

⤜

THE HAUNT IS ON

*I*t was 11:00 a.m. on Tuesday, May 11, 1926, the morning of the funeral for First Lady Ramona Smith and Baby Seven. The entire congregation had been planning for this day for the last two weeks. The senior and children's choirs practiced up a storm the songs that had been selected for the service. "Burdens are Lifted at Calvary" and "When the Saints Go Marching In." The children's choir were all set to sing "This Train is Bound for Glory."

The planning committee planned the repast, the cooking committee prepared the menu, and the deacons spent time with Bishop Smith and the family—running errands, picking up the out-of-town guests, and setting up the tables and chairs on the church grounds. The church sanctuary was beautifully decorated with white roses, which were First Lady Ramona's favorite.

Bishop Ellis had gotten in late the evening before. With very few beds left to house any guests, Elma gladly accepted the request to permit Ellis to stay with her and her sisters.

"I don't trust the care of our beloved Bishop Ellis in the hands of anyone else," Bishop Smith had told Elma.

Once he arrived, Elma got him all situated for bed, and the two agreed to have a little talk in the morning.

Elma woke up when the roosters started crowing, which was her and her sisters' usual time to rise. She was in the kitchen making a hearty breakfast of pork chops, grits, scrambled eggs, breakfast potatoes, fresh bread, and some coffee. Bishop Ellis entered the kitchen and took a seat at the kitchen table, which was dressed in a beautiful white lace-and-linen tablecloth. Aunt Bertha had already gotten him everything he needed to wash his face and brush his teeth. He was still wearing his sleeping clothes, planning to get dressed after breakfast. He didn't want to risk spilling any food on himself.

"Top of the morning, beautiful Elma," Bishop Ellis greeted, getting comfortable in his chair. "Why are you doing all this cooking and you know all of those women at the church are cooking up a heap of food today trying to compete for David's affection?" He let out a hearty laugh. "But we know damn well that's May Rose's spot."

"You better know that's the truth," Elma said.

"By the way, please tell me how we're going to get Willie's rotten ass out the way to clear the path for our two lovebirds. Not that we had to get rid of Ramona. The good Lord handled that one." He shook his head. "I tried to tell them to take a break from having all those babies. And like you said, Ramona did this to herself."

"She kept allowing herself to get pregnant after just losing a baby four months before getting pregnant with this one. Her body couldn't take having any more children. I told her that the last time, with the one she lost, which was before she still decided to go ahead and get pregnant again!"

"We at the Baptist Convention have a special place in our hearts for David and the children. Me and all of the other pastors and bishops that belong to the convention have given a substantial amount of money for David to start his new life. I want May Rose and the children to hurry and start this life with him and his children. Not that First Lady Ramona was a bad woman, but she just wasn't the right woman."

Bishop Ellis went on to explain further why he was so vested in Bishop Smith and May Rose getting together. "May Rose exemplifies all of the characteristics of a forward-thinking woman. She's educated herself and her children to prepare for a successful future. She cares for everyone she comes in contact with. She will give Bishop Smith and the children all of the affection and love they need. She will also help Bishop Smith grow the ministry. People look up to and admire her leadership in the community."

"Ellis, you sure have just said a mouthful," Elma replied. "First of all, I know how to treat my gentleman callers. I don't depend on no other broad to feed a man calling on me. Secondly, you're right. Ramona did this to herself. We all tried to teach her to control herself from getting pregnant. Lastly, the ancestors have been called upon to handle Willie. It's just a matter of time." She walked over to the table.

"And what makes you so sure the ancestors will handle Willie?"

Elma shot him a knowing look. "They handled Ramona, didn't they?" She placed his food in front of him. "Here's your plate. Now eat while I go bathe." Elma headed out of the kitchen, but she paused before exiting. "If you feel you need a little touching, c'mon back to my bedroom after you finish eating. I got something else for you to taste on," she said with a sultry voice as she sashayed toward the washroom, which was on the bottom floor along with her bedroom and the kitchen.

"Woman, you're going to have me forget the damn eulogy, messing around with me this morning," Bishop Ellis shouted. He took a bite of his food and said to himself with his mouth full, "You know I'm a widower, too. You'll mess around and have me up in your face every day."

Not realizing Elma could still hear him, he heard her call out, "You mean you'll mess around and have your face up in me every day."

Meanwhile, over at the big house, May Rose and the girls were in an uproar while getting dressed for the funeral. Bishop Smith had given her money to buy everyone dresses. They all had their hair pressed real pretty, styled with long bouncing curls. They had never had so many curls before.

May Rose sat on the side of her bed and thought about how she and Bishop Smith should navigate from here. The town knew that Willie was away working, but what they didn't know was that he didn't plan on coming home, at least that's what May Rose had assumed since he hadn't bothered to return or send either word or money to them. She further thought she should divorce Willie as soon as possible. That's what Bishop Smith would want, and really, that's what she wanted. May Rose smiled at how well her plan was coming together. Things could only get better from here.

Ginny stuck her head in May Rose's room as usual when she wanted to be nosey. "Momma, things are changing for us already. I guess things will change even more after today, huh?"

May Rose snapped her neck to look at Ginny. "Child, you must be reading my mind. That is my very thought. I'm sitting here gathering my thoughts now, so can you please leave me with them? We'll see soon just how it all will unfold. Go finish dressing and put a little of my cold cream on you all's faces."

"Okay, Momma! You finish getting pretty, too. You'll soon be the first lady. Give them a preview of what they'll be getting." Ginny chuckled.

May Rose rolled her eyes. "Get your grown ass out of here right now, and you better not be saying stuff like that around my babies." She bent down and picked up her house shoe and threw it at Ginny, who took off running.

Over at Bishop Smith's place, he sat in his study, where he had been sleeping in his desk chair since First Lady Ramona and the baby passed away. He thought he couldn't wait until the funeral was over so he could get a whole new bedroom set. He was thinking that maybe he'd let May Rose decorate it to her liking since it would ultimately be her bedroom, too. But first, he had to hurry and get the in-laws out. He was so tired of pretending there was no friction between him and some of Ramona's family members.

The Smith children were getting dressed in the all-white suits and dresses Bishop Smith had May Rose pick out for them. In these times, children wore white to signify purity and peace. First Lady Ramona's siblings and mother were all dressed in black. In his normal Sunday attire, Bishop Smith had on a black, pinstriped three-piece suit, a crisp, white shirt with beautiful gold cufflinks with his initials engraved in them, and a freshly shined pair of wingtip shoes. His hair, goatee, and sideburns were freshly shaved. It was something his wife normally did for him, and he'd been two seconds from calling May Rose over to do it, but he'd done it himself. The last thing he wanted was them thinking May Rose was trying to take his wife's place...already.

Bishop Smith came out of his study and called all of his children by their names in order of age. "David, Jr., Amos, Regina, Frederick, Joseph, Lou Lou." The children all came running, looking like angels. "You all look so beautiful. Let's go and lay your momma and little brother to rest. We will always love them and remember that we will see them in Heaven when God decides to call us home. Your papa loves you all, and I will always keep you safe and protected. All I ask of you is to be the best in this life you can be. I will do the rest."

The children all hugged Bishop Smith and told him they loved him.

He led the children to the front door and then called for his in-laws to join them so that they could all head to the church together. With Bishop Smith leading the way, they walked through the newly cut grass toward the church. The siblings-in-law and Mother Vivian walked silently in a line behind the children. It was a beautiful sight to see. As the organist played a beautiful selection, Bishop Smith and family were greeted at the church doors by the women usher board, the deacons, and Bishop Ellis.

Bishop Ellis grasped Bishop Smith around his neck and whispered, "We got you and the children, son. Just keep doing what you're doing. The conference still has great plans for you. I have a love offering from all of the pastors and bishops in the conference. You may think about taking some time off to get things in order."

Smith humbly responded, "Thank you, sir. You have been such a great father figure since my father went on to glory six years ago."

The ushers seated the children and the in-laws in the first three pews. By now, the church was standing room only.

At the front of the church lay First Lady Ramona with the baby boy lying in her arms. She was dressed in an elegant, white chiffon gown. The baby was wrapped in a white chiffon blanket. The casket was white with shining gold hardware. Inside the casket were three white roses lined on each side of her, signifying each of her living children. There was also a white rose in her hands that rested on her stomach, which signified the seventh. The casket was surrounded by beautiful bouquets of white roses.

The bishops started walking up the steps to the pulpit. As soon as Bishop Smith took his seat, he began looking through the congregation for May Rose and her family. He asked her to sit as close to the front as possible and found them sitting on the left side in the middle of the row. She would have sat closer, but the church was already half-full by the time her and her family arrived.

Bishop Smith got up and walked to the podium. "Church, me and my family feel your love and support. The telegrams, flowers, and meals you have cooked for us were so greatly appreciated." He turned his attention to Mr. Gray, who was the undertaker. "You may start the order of service."

Mr. Gray walked over to the casket and closed it. The sound of crying and sniffling filled the air. The children could be heard crying over everyone else.

The senior choir began singing their first selection, "Burdens are Lifted at Calvary." The congregation was tapping their tambourines, rocking back and forth, clapping, and singing. The women were waving their hand-fans and shouting out "amen" and "hallelujah."

After the senior choir completed their selection, the children's choir stood up. Five of the six Smith children walked up into the choir stand with the others. The youngest sat in Mother Vivian's arms.

The children's choir began their song, "This Train is Bound for Glory," when the choir director began waving her hands and swaying from side to side. You could hear some of the people hollering, "Sing, children." The vibration of the church was so high from the children's joyous sounds. If you didn't know any better, you would've thought you were at a revival instead of a funeral.

As the children finished, Bishop Ellis took the podium. "Amen, Church. I have been charged with delivering First Lady Ramona's eulogy. I know you are wondering why me, because you know I was not her favorite person, and she sure wasn't mine."

There was a large gasp throughout the church as well as a few chuckles.

He continued, "Church, sometimes you don't have to like someone you love, and I'm okay with that, because I loved her because she loved my son-in-Christ and them babies. She and her family took great care of them babies. God knows she loved them babies." He looked to the Smith children and shook his head in sympathy. "As you know, I gave her a hard time for having so many babies so fast. She surely left here doing what she loved. She was a young seventeen-year-old girl when Bishop Smith married her. She had the first child David, Jr., exactly nine months after their marriage. She was a child having children. She only had the example of her mother, Mother Vivian, who herself had thirteen children. Ramona didn't know no better."

Once again, there were some chuckles, but also some gasps, especially by those who weren't privy to First Lady Ramona's and Bishop Ellis's love-hate relationship.

"Bishop Smith being the great man-of-God that he is," Bishop Ellis continued, "married Ramona and took her entire family into his home and took care of them as if they were blood. I know she loved fashion, and Bishop Smith made sure she dressed in the best fashions. I pray her sisters don't fight each other over those fine dresses."

The entire church giggled, even her sisters.

Bishop Ellis continued, "Church, continue to look after Bishop Smith and his family. You do such a good job of it already, but now, they need you more than ever. I'll be coming back often to check on them and don't want nothing but excellent reports. Now I'm speaking directly to the women of this church, young and old. Don't you bombard my son with your advances for his heart. When he is ready, he will choose his next wife. So, stay the hell out his face and his house with your nasty macaroni and cheese."

The church erupted into laughter. Bishop Ellis turned and walked over to Bishop Smith. "I had to do it, son," Bishop Ellis told his protégé.

"I ain't mad at cha, Bishop," Bishop Smith said. "Ain't mad at all."

Bishop Ellis took his seat.

Mr. Gray stood in front of the church. "The choir will now come to perform their final selection, 'When the Saints Go Marching In.' After the choir finishes, we will lead you to the church cemetery down the road for burial. Please fall in line behind the family. The repast will be on the church grounds immediately after the burial. Senior choir, please stand."

The choir started singing.

> *"Oh, when the saints (when the saints)*
> *Go marching in (marching in)*
> *Now, when the saints go marching in (marching in)*
> *Yes, I want to be in that number.*
> *When the saints go marching in."*

The congregation stood and began singing with the choir, clapping and dancing while some shook their tambourines.

The church was so filled with joy that almost nothing could have cut through it.

Almost nothing.

But all that changed when the church doors flew open and there stood Willie with his prostitute on his arm. He was his usual drunken self as he stumbled down the aisle. The woman was staggering drunk as well.

"Hey, Dave, man," Willie shouted out to the pulpit. "Why the hell you couldn't come and tell me about First Lady Ramona's passing away? You brought May Rose to my job to spy on me but couldn't drive your Black ass down there when it mattered?"

By now, the choir stopped, and the two bishops started walking down the pulpit steps. May Rose and her family started quickly walking out of their aisle toward Willie and his woman.

Bishop Smith yelled, "How dare you disrespect the life of my wife and child. Take yourself and your whore up out of my church before I throw both of you out."

"I ain't come here for you, yo' baby, or yo' wife. I want to see my babies." He searched the sanctuary with squinted eyes until he spotted his three girls. "Babies, c'mon and see Daddy and your stepmother."

"Sit back down, girls," May Rose said. Florence and Lynette obliged, but Ginny followed May Rose, her nana, and her great-aunties out of the pew and down the aisle. They circled Willie and the woman on his arm. May Rose reared her fist back and hit him dead smack in the mouth. Ginny crawled on the floor behind them on her hands and knees. Elma pushed the woman, while Etta and Bertha pushed Willie over Ginny's back. May Rose crawled on top of Willie and kept swinging, punching all over his face. He tried to block her blows, but she was swinging too quickly. His alcohol-blurred vision wasn't helping much either.

"You crazy monster. You're mad because I have me a new woman," Willie slurred.

At the same time, Elma had the woman's arms twisted behind her back and started pushing her out the door.

The folks in the sanctuary were frozen in shock. They couldn't believe such a disturbance was taking place in the Lords's house, let alone at a funeral.

Bishop Smith ran to May Rose and pulled her off Willie, who he then pulled up and pushed back toward the door. "Don't you ever set foot in this church again. As a matter of fact, don't let me see you in Bedford again, you good-for-nothing drunken clown. I don't even know what a woman could ever see in you to make you her husband. No woman deserves you." As bad as Bishop Smith wanted to say May Rose by name, he had to respect his wife, even if Willie wasn't willing to.

"The hell with your church and Bedford. I have a new life and don't need to come back here." His eyes roamed until they landed on his two daughters sitting in the pew as their mother had instructed them. "Florence and Lynette, Daddy is coming back to get you." He turned his attention to his oldest daughter. "Ginny, you're just like your momma and those crazy-ass Africans. They done got to you. Nothing I can do with you now. So, you stay right here with them."

Bishop Ellis ran up the aisle at Willie. "You lowlife drunk, leave now!" He punched Willie in his stomach, snatching the front of Willie's shirt and twisting it up so he could sling him down the church steps to where the woman was lying.

"I'm so sorry. I'm so sorry, Bishop Smith," May Rose cried. She was humiliated and hurt, not to mention ashamed for carrying on in such a manner.

Both bishops took turns consoling her as she kept apologizing and asking for forgiveness.

Bishop Smith nodded and said, "There is no need to be sorry for his behavior." He looked to the congregation. "Church, let's finish giving First Lady Ramona and my son what they deserve, which is a decent and respectful homegoing." He looked to the choir. "Choir, sing," he said as he began singing "When the saints go marching in..." as he walked up the steps to the pulpit.

Bishop Ellis followed right behind him as he straightened out his clothing.

The choir began to sing. The congregation started rocking, praising, and clapping again.

Willie had managed to scrape himself, and his woman, up off the ground and head back to the mine.

May Rose joined her family outside of the church after signaling for Florence and Lynnetta to come to her.

While trying to pull herself back together, May Rose was still huffing and puffing with anger. She told the children to go sit in the car until she called for them. Ginny didn't budge.

May Rose looked directly at Ginny and said, "You go, too. Tend to your sisters. I'll talk to you later about your behavior today, young lady."

"But, Momma, why are you mad at me? I was taught by you all to protect myself and my family," Ginny replied.

"Go to the car, damn it, now," May Rose said through clenched teeth.

Seeing May Rose was not playing, she ran to the car and jumped in. Her sisters did the same.

May Rose said to the elders, "I think we should go and let the Smith family mourn in peace. I'm so embarrassed. No way can I step foot back inside that church. Not right now."

Elma quickly responded, "That wasn't your doing. We did what we was supposed to do."

Bertha jumped in. "You surely beat Willie's ass into next week." She chuckled.

"And we took care of his whore." Aunt Etta gave Aunt Bertha a high-five.

"But more importantly," Elma added, "we just put those desperate women at Washington First Baptist Church and Lady Ramona's sisters on notice that you will fight for what belongs to you."

"Amen," her sisters agreed.

Elma continued. "Ginny has even showed them she is battle-ready. Don't be mad at her. She is becoming a strong African warrior woman. Hell, she might can take all of us on."

Aunt Etta started giggling and said, "She can take you on, but she won't take me on."

"Don't you think Bishop Smith will be disappointed when he doesn't see you? You can leave, but me and my sisters are staying. We'll keep our eyes on these hungry women, and I don't mean for food. Plus, I'm not leaving my special project up here." Elma smiled and winked at May Rose.

"Momma, please tell Bishop Smith if he needs me, I'll be at home. Please don't show y'all's asses no more today. I'll see you all when you get home," May Rose said somberly.

She went to the car and climbed in with her children. She took a deep breath, closed her eyes, and shook her head. Everything seemed to be going so well, then along came Willie. She could just spit. But instead, she started up the car and drove off. Bishop Smith would be disappointed, but she was not happy that he saw her behave like this. He'd thought so highly of her, yet she couldn't control herself. She could only pray that her actions didn't come back to haunt her later. Or that First Lady Ramona didn't come back to haunt her either.

"Don't call the forest that shelters you a forest."

African Proverb

Chapter 16

❧

AIN'T MISBEHAVIN'

On the ride home from First Lady Ramona's funeral, the car was initially full of dead silence, but May Rose had to speak on things with her girls. She could only imagine how they were feeling about everything that had just gone down with their daddy.

"I know you all are very hurt about your daddy's behavior. He has a sickness. The moonshine makes him do and say crazy things," May Rose said. She allowed a few seconds between her next words just in case one of the girls found a need to express themselves. When neither spoke up, she continued. "As your mother, through the years, I have tried to protect you from seeing these very things. I never wanted to see you hurt." And hurt was exactly what her girls were experiencing. She could tell by their expressions and their tear-filled eyes. This made May Rose shed a few tears of her own.

Florence was the first to respond. "Momma, you thought you were hiding Daddy's nasty ways from us, but we knew what he was doing. I would've rather you kicked him out than to stay with him and all of us being miserable. I think Ginny and Lynette agree with me." She looked from one sister to the next for confirmation.

Lynette wiped tears off her wet cheeks. "Momma, I agree with Florence. If Daddy took the money he spends on moonshine—"

"And now hoes," Ginny mumbled under her breath while Lynette finished speaking.

"And bought us a decent dress or two—"

Now Lynette was interrupted by her other sister. "Or even some nice fabric for Momma to make us some," Florence said before Lynette continued.

"Then maybe we wouldn't have to dress in raggedy clothes. And we do tell God thank you that we live in a house, Momma, but it got raggedy, old furniture."

Ginny jumped right in. "We have to tend a farm and farm animals. You have to work so many jobs, like catching babies, teaching, and sewing for other people just so you have enough money for us to eat. That ain't no woman's business. Humpf. Not in this family, anyway." Ginny smacked her lips and stared out the window after saying her piece.

"Let the elders tell it, Daddy the one supposed to be working his fingers to the white meat, not the woman," Florence said. "And you told us we should always listen to our elders."

Ginny smirked and let out a snort.

Feeling hurt and sad or not, May Rose snapped her neck to let the girls know they could express themselves, but they better watch their words while doing it.

She took a big gulp. "C'mon, Ginny. Go on and let it all out. I know you got more to say." She figured on second thought, she might as well let them say what they needed to while her hands had to stay on the steering wheel so she couldn't put them around their throats.

"Momma, it's simple to me." Ginny did not need to be told twice to continue speaking her piece. "Daddy made his choice. Let his silly behind be the drunken, whore-chasing bum he wants to be. As long as you and the girls are okay, I'm good, too."

May Rose nodded. "I hear you. I heard you all. And now that you all have said what was settling in your chest real tight, I don't want to hear another word about what happened today. If any of you want to have a relationship with Willie, I will try to make it happen, but your daddy and I are over."

Ginny and Florence rolled their eyes and shook their heads, implying they had no desire to have a relationship with Willie. Lynette sucked her teeth as if to say, "Yeah, right!"

"Now that all minds are free and clear," May Rose said, "let me hurry home to get started with dinner. I'm sure you all have some reading to do or would like to take a nap or something after all this mess of a day."

In unison, all three of the girls said, "Okay, Momma!"

May Rose exhaled, glad she'd gotten that conversation over with, then drove on home. But her mind couldn't help but wander back to what might be going on at First Lady Ramona's funeral.

Well, needless to say, Willie showing out put an end to the funeral. But back at the repast, which was on the church grounds, Elma and her sisters sat at the table with Bishop Smith and Bishop Ellis. Elma sat right next to Ellis. Bishop Smith's mother, Marlene, and his sister Marnita sat on each side of him.

Marlene said to her son, "David, I know it's too soon to know all your plans, but I would like to know if you need me and Marnita to stay for a while? Help you mind the children. Ramona's family gotta grieve, too. You know we're scheduled to return back home to New York by train tomorrow morning, but if you need us to stay, we'll—"

Bishop Smith interrupted. "Momma, I appreciate you for asking, but we're going to be good. I have plans set in place. The in-laws will be fine helping with the children. We'll definitely talk in the morning, Momma." He kissed her on the cheek.

Everyone proceeded to eat, then Bishop Smith cleared his throat. "Mother Elma, I'm so sorry May Rose felt it was necessary to go home. Ain't nobody blaming her for Willie's actions. Even if some do, who cares what these people think? May Rose has helped damn near every person who was at the funeral at one time or another. She has nothing to be ashamed of."

Elma hesitated for a few seconds before responding out of sheer surprise. Not at what he said but at what he called her... *Mother* Elma. He had always addressed her as Miss Elma or Sister Elma. She failed to hold back the thought that he was moving very quickly toward joining her family, and she loved every bit. She looked over at her sisters. They must have caught wind of it, too, because Aunt Bertha gave her a wink and Aunt Etta gave her a grin. Each elder was pleased that May Rose's business was finally moving along in the right direction.

"You know May Rose is a very private person," Elma said. "She's not like me, because I would have told these people to kiss where the sun don't shine and finished paying my respects."

The table erupted with laughter.

"We know you would have, Mother Elma," Bishop Smith said as his shoulders bounced with his laughter. "We know you would have."

Bishop Ellis chimed in. "The way May Rose whipped up on Willie, these people know they better not mess with her or any of y'all, even that oldest gal of hers." He belted out a laugh. "I thought I was going have to rescue Willie from getting killed."

Marlene replied, "Willie's a lowdown snake in the grass. I pray May Rose be done with him once and for all." She shook her head in disapproval. "Like you, Elma, as quiet as it's kept, I never liked him for her since they started courting." She leaned in and finished her statement in a whisper. "I have a sweet spot in my heart for May Rose and hoped her and David would've ended up together." She sat straight up and nodded definitively.

It was Aunt Etta's turn to lean in. "Marlene, we were all on the same page about Bishop Smith and May Rose." She sat back up straight and looked around to make sure no one was listening in whose ears the conversation wasn't for. "But they went their separate ways."

"There are hearts that need to be healed," Aunt Bertha said. "Once that occurs, maybe they can find their way back to each other." She said this to keep it from looking like they were overly anxious for May Rose and Bishop Smith to be together.

Elma added, "May Rose has to divorce that old damn fool Willie and go on about her life... Bishop Ellis, would you run us home now?" She looked to Bishop Smith, Marlene, and Marnita. "If the three of you would like, please come by our home tonight for a nightcap. We can catch up and look after Bishop Smith at the same time." Elma's plan was to get Bishop Smith in the vicinity of May Rose so their business together could continue as planned, definitely without the interruption of that ole fool Willie.

"Yes, Bishop Smith," Bishop Ellis added. "That way, you can get the envelope I have for you. I left it at Sister Elma's because I didn't want you to be carrying it around this afternoon."

"And I can check on May Rose," Bishop Smith replied. Not money, not even the death of his wife and baby, could keep May Rose off his mind. "Please have her come by, too." He looked to Elma. "Mother Elma, I'll make sure the children are in bed and come over about eight this evening, if that's not too late for you all?"

"Why, sure. Eight is just fine," Elma said. "I will also make sure May Rose is there as well." She turned her attention to Bishop Smith's mother. "Marlene, I hope to see you and Marnita, too."

Marlene responded, "Yes, we'll come by for a spell. I want to check on May Rose and hug her neck."

Bishop Ellis got up from his seat and walked over to Elma's chair. He took her hand and helped her up, then he did the same for Aunt Bertha and Aunt Etta. He walked over to Bishop Smith's mother, took her hand, and kissed it. He did the same for Marnita. Then, he walked over to Bishop Smith and grabbed him around his neck. "I'm so proud of you, son. You are handling this better than most. You will continue to be blessed in everything you do. The children will be raised up nicely with all of our help."

"Yes, sir, they will. I'll see you all later." Bishop Smith tipped his hat.

Elma and the elders walked off, and Bishop Ellis followed slowly. Once everyone got into the car, they began talking immediately.

"My Lord, May Rose was going to kill that fool Willie, for real," Bishop Ellis said, shaking his head. "If Bishop Smith didn't snatch her up off of him, I know she would have, for sure." He chuckled. "I didn't know that little lady could rumble like that. David better fly right if he knows like I know. But I won't worry too much because that man will drink May Rose's dirty bathwater."

Everyone in the car began laughing.

"Bishop Smith better act right, for sure," Elma agreed. "He doesn't want to lose my jewel and her beautiful daughters. All of our girls are equipped with everything it takes to make a happy home. They were taught by the best." She looked at Etta and Bertha. "Sisters, can I get an amen?"

Her sisters shouted out, "Amen!"

Bishop Ellis said, "Elma, what are we going to do about getting Willie completely away? You know there is a chance he might sober up and try to sweettalk his way back into May Rose's and the girls' lives."

"That's between me, my sisters, and our ancestors that I have summoned to assist," Elma assured him.

"Ancestors, huh? Not God?" Bishop Ellis inquired.

"Bishop, we call on our ancestors when we're in need," Elma said. "We know God is the ruler of all things, but He allows our spirits to live forever. That's why our ancestors never leave us. God also allows them to help shape our destiny. Don't worry, the ancestors will move when they see fit."

Bishop Ellis responded, "Well, just don't have your ancestors messing with me, that's all I know." He rolled his eyes.

Again, the car erupted with laughter. The women were amused by how seriously Bishop Ellis delivered his words. He may have feared God, but he clearly feared their ancestors as well.

"Bishop Ellis, please drop me off to May Rose's house. I want to tell her about the gathering tonight and to help her get her head right," Elma requested.

"Of course," he said. "I would like to nap a little, if you don't mind. I have to get ready for our business tonight."

"Yeah, you better rest up. I need you to be with full strength tonight, because I want you to miss this when you're gone," Elma said as she pointed to her crotch. A woman's business didn't slow down with age. And needless to say, Bishop Ellis was Elma's new prospect. The white man had officially been fired.

Aunt Etta giggled. "And keep all that moaning and scream-
ing down in there like two teenagers. I started to go over to
May Rose's house this morning to be able to sleep peacefully."
She rolled her eyes.

"I don't know if I can do that, Sister Etta. Elma is damn
good, and she puts it all on me," Bishop Ellis boasted.

Etta frowned and swatted his words away as if they were
about to hit her face. "Don't nobody want to hear all that...
literally!"

Elma laughed.

Bishop Ellis pulled up to May Rose's house. He got out,
opened Elma's door, and lifted her out of the seat. He kissed her
on the lips. "Get our girl together for tonight. I know Bishop
Smith and Mrs. Smith will be ready to love all over her."

"I got May Rose covered. Don't you worry one single bit."
Elma winked and then headed into the house. Elma walked up
to the front door and pushed it open, which was rare because
she usually entered through the back. "May Rose, where are
you?"

May Rose hollered from the kitchen. "Momma, you just
scared me half to death. I didn't know who was coming into
the front door."

Elma scolded as she followed May Rose's voice to the
kitchen. "You're going to have to start keeping that front door
locked. You don't know when that damn fool Willie might try
to come back."

"Hmm, I wish he would. His ass won't make it out alive.
But it ain't like he ain't got the key to his own house."

Elma let out a harrumph before continuing, "The repast
was nice, as expected. Bishop Smith and Mrs. Smith both
missed you not being there. As a matter of fact, I invited them
over for a nightcap this evening. They'll be by around eight,

and they are expecting you to be there. Put on one of them pretty dresses Bishop Smith bought for you and c'mon over to the house by seven so you can mentally prepare yourself. It's time to straighten up your back and get back to work. You have Bishop Smith's mother, sister, and spiritual father all on your team. What more do you need? It's all on you, my dear. It's time to seal the deal. And this time—"

"Here you go with this mess again," her daughter interrupted. When would the elders start trusting in her again? "Momma, I'm not in the mood for this."

Just then, Lynette let out a squeal from the living room. "Owww! Help me, Nana! There's a big spider crawling on my arm. Come kill it!"

Elma took off running to the living room while rifling through her bag for her change purse. "Lynette, you better not kill that spider. I'm coming." She reached the living room and found Lynette dancing around with the spider cupped in her hand. Elma opened her change purse and scraped the spider out of Lynette's now-open hand onto a small piece of brown paper bag. She then folded the paper at each corner until it was tiny and almost couldn't be seen. She placed it in her change purse.

Elma continued, "What you talkin' 'bout come kill it? Lynette, you know we don't kill spiders around here. They bring good luck, and God knows we need some good luck around here."

"But, Nana, I'm scared of spiders," Lynette said. "How do you know spiders are lucky? Where did you get that from?"

"Chile, I don't know where it started, but I know that's what I was taught as a child when I got to this country. The older women would fuss at me when I tried to kill a spider. I never asked why because they would be hoppin' mad about it. So, I did like I was told. But back in my village in Ghana, a spider represented the god of the knowledge of stories. I just adapted to the story about spiders being lucky because it was pushed in my face. So, now I'm pushing it in you and your sisters' faces. Don't kill no spiders around here, young lady. If the spider is trying to give us good luck, we gonna take it." Elma giggled.

Lynette shivered and scratched her crawling skin.

May Rose called Elma back into the kitchen. "Momma, stop with all that superstition stuff. If my baby is afraid of spiders, we're not going to make her catch them for you. I'm going to let her stomp the hell out of them." Elma walked in as May Rose continued, "Why did your sneaky little self set up this gathering with Mrs. Smith and Bishop Smith tonight?"

"Superstition, my behind," Elma said, deciding to address May Rose's rant about the spider before answering her questions about the evening's get-together. "You better make sure you keep telling them girls about not killing spiders. How do you think we have survived and continue to survive in this horrible country? The dear Lord and the luck of the spiders I have collected over the years. That's how."

"Momma, stop that foolishness. It's the good Lord alone who has kept us safe and well in this country," May Rose said. "I will be coming over to greet Mrs. Smith and David, but from here on out, please let me manage my business with Bishop Smith. I got this and have always had it. I mean it, Momma. And give the same message to my meddling aunties."

Elma barked, "Girl, I'm going to be quiet about all of the nonsense you just spilled out your mouth. You must've forgot I'm the matriarch of this tribe. All I know is, you better seal the deal tonight. Don't be a damn fool."

"Okay, Momma, go get ready for your company. I'll see you as you expect. I'll also make sure I'm dolled up, too. Don't get excited, there will be no proposal tonight. Bye, Momma, I need to finish up dinner for the girls so I can get ready."

Elma chuckled. "I've been put out of better places." She threw up her hand as if to say good-bye, then she slid her feet and swayed her hips as she walked toward the back door.

Lynette yelled, "Bye, Nana, thanks for catching the spider."

Elma yelled back, "You're welcome, baby. Tell your mother don't put me out again." She burst out laughing as she walked out the door.

May Rose finished up dinner, sat the girls down to eat, and went to get ready. She arrived at the elders' house at seven sharp, like Elma requested. Although she didn't want to admit it, she needed to test Bishop Smith's temperature to find out if her business plan was still in place. She was a little unsure after Willie's actions of the day.

She opened the elders' front door to see Bishop Ellis bopping his head back and forth to Aunt Etta singing a jazz song and playing the piano that had sat in the parlor for years. Etta always loved to sing. She taught herself to play the piano and dance. She was a one-woman show.

Shouting over the music, May Rose said, "Good evening, Bishop Ellis. Aunt Etta, you sound so beautiful. I love to hear you sing."

Etta stopped and replied, "Thanks, my sweetheart. You know I always love the opportunity to perform. I always wanted to be a flapper girl."

Bishop Ellis giggled. "Hi, slugger, we missed you at the repast. It wasn't the same, you not being there. Bishop Smith was really lost without you. He'll be happy to see you tonight. Don't you be the least bit embarrassed about you kicking Willie's ass. That's what you were supposed to do. You'll never have to worry about such thing with David. I know for a fact he loves you dearly and will treat you like nothing less than rubies and gold." He gave a crooked grin. "Just wait and see." He nodded and winked at May Rose.

She modestly responded, "Sir, the most important thing right now is for Bishop Smith to heal and focus on those babies. I'm going to give him the space he needs, but on the other hand, if he needs me, well, I'll be there for him."

"That's understandable," he said. He cleared his throat. "But in the meantime, we have to get you divorced from Willie, and I will personally make sure that happens...with your permission, of course."

"That's so gracious of you, Bishop Ellis. My goal is to divorce Willie immediately." May Rose felt comfortable sharing some of the details of her plan with him, as Elma had made sure to let her know she'd been working Bishop Ellis herself, and he was all for and all in with it.

"Good, now that's settled, Etta, give me some more of that 'Ain't Misbehavin' by Fats Waller."

Aunt Etta started playing and singing as Bishop Ellis requested.

The smell of the pot roast her mother was cooking led May Rose into the kitchen. "Momma, you got the kitchen singing, too, with that roast smelling good."

"Thanks, dear," Elma said, looking up from the stove to her daughter. "You sure look pretty." She admired the rose-colored lace dress with draped pearl necklaces that Elma had gifted her with.

"Where's Aunt Bertha?" May Rose asked, not ignoring the compliment, just choosing not to acknowledge it.

"She's laying down. Her spring allergies done jumped on her today. I made her some ragweed and dandelion tea. She said she'll try to come down later."

The conversation came to a halt when they heard Bishop Smith's usual knock. May Rose nervously hurried to the door. First Marlene entered, then Marnita, and standing like a big, beautiful statue behind them was Bishop Smith. May Rose grabbed and hugged the two women tightly around their necks.

"How are you, baby?" Marlene asked.

May Rose kissed Marlene on the cheek. "I'm okay, if y'all are okay." She looked from woman to woman for a response.

"We just fine, baby." Marlene tapped May Rose on the shoulder. "Just fine."

Bishop Smith ushered the women into the house, stopping in front of May Rose. "Look at you caring about everyone else first." He grabbed May Rose around the waist and whispered in her ear, "I missed you not being there with me, but you're here now, and I'm delighted." Afterward, he planted a big, wet kiss on her lips.

May Rose was afraid for Marlene and Marnita to see this behavior between her and Bishop Smith.

Marnita, either not noticing or ignoring Bishop Smith's and May Rose's intimate moment, handed May Rose a dish. "We thought this pound cake would be good to have this evening."

"Oh, thank you." May Rose accepted the cake. "It will go great with my mother's pot roast. Please head on into the parlor. Aunt Etta was performing some good ole jazz for us." She nodded toward the room. "I'm going to take this cake into the kitchen and get some slices made."

May Rose headed into the kitchen while the guests entered the parlor.

Bishop Ellis stood and greeted everyone when they entered the room.

Aunt Etta also stood and greeted everyone. "Please have a seat." She extended her hand toward the unoccupied couch and chairs. "I'm sure dinner will be ready soon. Can I make y'all a nightcap now?" She walked over to the bar area. "We have bourbon and some delicious homemade rose wine that was made by Bertha."

"Etta, may I try some of the wine?" Marlene asked.

Marnita spoke up. "Me too!"

"I'll take some bourbon, Miss Etta," Bishop Smith requested.

Elma entered the parlor with May Rose on her heels like a frightened child. Elma walked over to Marlene, hugged her neck, and greeted, "Good evening, good people. Welcome to our home. Dinner is served. Please join us in the dining room. We have some beef pot roast, mashed potatoes, and some hot water cornbread. Also, please forgive my sister Bertha's absence. She's feeling a bit under the weather. She sends her greetings."

Elma and May Rose turned and escorted everyone into the dining room.

"Miss Elma, you didn't have to do this," Bishop Smith exclaimed when he saw the spread smothering table. "We have so much food over at the house. But none of it, I'm sure, is as delicious as what we're about to partake in.

"We're happy to have you all. We don't entertain here often. Plus, Bishop Smith could use some breathing space from all those people for the last two weeks," Elma suggested.

"You sure got that right, Miss Elma. We pray Miss Bertha will be well soon," he replied.

"Everyone, please sit where you like," Elma ordered. "And then use the hot, lemon towels to cleanse your hands."

May Rose waited to sit. Although she wanted to sit next to Bishop Smith, she followed his lead.

Sensing her hesitance, Bishop Smith said, "May Rose, please sit next to me." He pulled out the chair next to the one he'd stood in front of. "Nobody's judging. I don't think anyone at this table is a stranger to how I feel about you. The feelings were there before Ramona was called home to glory, and ain't nothing made them go away after."

May Rose looked from face to face, trying to gauge if Bishop Smith truly was speaking for everyone. The fact that everyone was paying more attention to the spread on the table than the words that had come out of Bishop Smith's mouth said it all.

"I'm going to have one of my D.C. lawyer friends start working on the divorce as soon as he possibly can." Bishop Ellis stopped halfway sitting down. "That is, if that's what you want, May Rose."

"Uh, yes, of course." May Rose nodded her approval of Bishop Ellis's offer to help.

Once everyone sat and Bishop Ellis said grace, all that could be heard was the clinking and clanking of silverware hitting the dishes.

"It seems like we'll have a wedding around here soon," Bishop Ellis said. He looked to Bishop Smith. "Looks like you won't have to be a widower too long."

Bishop Smith and May Rose remained silent. They simply smiled coyly at one another.

"I'm just going to say it," Elma said. "May Rose and her girls deserve to be in a wonderful family such as yours, Bishop Smith."

"Mother Elma, it will be an honor to become a part of your wonderful family as well," he said with a smile.

Elma made the biggest smile she had ever given and told Bishop Smith, "Thank you!"

Bishop Smith took May Rose's hand under the table and squeezed it tightly. She was so excited inside, but she still had First Lady Ramona and the baby in her heart. Everything was going better than she thought. Almost too good. She couldn't help but feel that it was too good to be true. That something like Willie not agreeing to the divorce would mess everything up. What would her and Bishop Smith do then?

Bishop Ellis asked, "Son, when will the dress shop be finished? I know there has been just a little work being done these last two weeks. Do you need me to send some carpenters over here from Montgomery? Those boys over there would've had it done."

"Thanks, sir," Bishop Smith replied. "You might can send a couple good men until I get the ex-in-laws out my house and over to their new home. Then I can continue to help. Me and May Rose will go on over to the department store to get the fancy sewing machines, and I need to order more lumber. I'm thinking about another month should do it before we officially open the doors."

Marnita cleared her throat. "Brother, do you think it will be good for the children if the Williams leave your house so soon?" Her question was laced with uncertainty.

"Hmm, you make a very good point, sister, but if that Diane stay any longer in my house, I may have to kill her and leave town." Bishop Smith chuckled.

Marlene grabbed Bishop Smith's left cheek and pinched as hard as she could and shouted, "David, you stop that crazy talking."

"Momma, she's walking around my house like she owns it," he declared, sounding more like her little boy than grown son. "She is challenging my manhood. I can't have that. She's lucky I'm going to allow her to live on the Davis farm. I know I must do what's best for the children, but I'm not taking Diane's smart talk."

"David, do what you have to do, but make sure the children are all right. You can bring them to us after school lets out for the summer. I want to be a part of their rearing, too," Marlene said.

"Of course, Momma, I will make that happen."

"And we'll help him make it happen, if need be," Elma chimed in. "Won't we, Bishop Ellis?"

"Indeed, we will," he agreed sternly, confirming he would enforce backup if needed.

May Rose said a silent prayer that it wouldn't be, but something told her there was a force praying for just the opposite.

That force being Willie Jones, a man well known for misbehavin'!

"Sticks in a bundle are unbreakable."

African Proverb

Chapter 17

❧

THE NEW NORMAL

*I*t had been a few weeks since the death of First Lady Ramona and Baby Seven, and everything was falling in place with Bishop Smith and May Rose, which meant the elders—or anyone else, for that matter—didn't have to interfere with the process. The dress shop had been completed. All of the supplies needed for May Rose to start making dresses were in place as well, and she'd been sewing like crazy. So much so that any baby catching was reserved for the elders and their apprentice, young Ginny.

In between catching babies, the elders also assisted with the sewing. The shop's grand opening was in three weeks. May Rose was hellbent on making sure there was a wide enough selection so that every woman and girl could leave with something if they chose to do so.

May Rose and Bishop Smith had been inseparable, especially after First Lady Ramona's family had moved into the new farmhouse. Diane chose not to move in. She went to take up with an old man over in Roanoke, Virgina. Bishop Smith was happy not to see her face again, and the children were adjusting well. Bishop Smith could now take up with May Rose openly.

The Smith children went to New York with Mrs. Smith and Marnita after school let out for the summer in the second week of June. May Rose's girls were enjoying their new lifestyle with all the pretty new clothes and their new extended family. There was always joy and laughter wherever they were.

The congregation had even stopped whispering about the kerfuffle that took place the day of the funeral between May Rose and Willie. Speaking of Willie, there were a few church members who didn't bite their tongue about how they could understand why May Rose no longer wanted to be married to him, but nevertheless, she was. They also warned her of what others might say about her flaunting around with their Bishop.

"Sounds like to me I already know what folks are saying," May Rose shot back, "because you in my face saying it."

And with that, anyone bold enough to step to her with their opinion would quickly get to stepping right on out of her path. Unfortunately, it never stopped them from keeping Willie's name in their mouth whenever they encountered her.

"Hey, May Rose, how's Willie doing?" they'd inquire.

It got to the point where she wouldn't even acknowledge them. She'd turn up her nose and keep on walking. Funny thing was, everyone knew better than to say those things to Bishop Smith.

One lady named Lizzy, the church's mess-starter, came into the dress shop one evening trying to get under May Rose's skin. Little did she know, Elma and Bertha were in the backroom sewing as well.

"Hey there, *Rosie*," Lizzy said, mocking Bishop Smith as she entered the shop with her nose so far up to the heavens, she could probably smell the angels' butts. "I mean, May Rose." She snickered.

"Ain't open for business yet." May Rose responded without even looking up from the ties and bowties she was laying out on the counter. Those men accessories were the elders' ideas.

"A woman handling her business knows that when she out shopping on her man's dime, she best bring him back a nickel worth of something," Elma had told May Rose.

"Yeah, and a man don't mind half as much breaking his woman off something extra 'cause he knows he's gonna get a treat as well," Aunt Etta said.

"Plus, if a man come in looking to buy his lady something," Aunt Bertha added, "you got nothing to upsell him on otherwise. And what man don't need a tie for church? Hell, even Willie shows up when hell freezes over."

The women had burst out laughing. But on the serious note, May Rose took heed and added ties for the men to the inventory.

"Come back in a few weeks, Lizzy," May Rose said, still not making eye contact with who could have been her first customer. "That's the official grand opening."

"Oh, come on now, May Rose, what's it gonna hurt if I get an advance sneak peek?" She strolled over to a rack and started fingering through some of the dresses. "Will you be making dresses for curvy ladies like me?" She ran her hands up and down her waist and hips. "You know, real women?" She looked over her shoulder, giving May Rose the once-over as if to suggest May Rose wasn't a real woman since she was more on the slim side.

"Oh yes, Lizzy, we will be making dresses in all sizes, even girls' sizes." May Rose responded like the professional she was.

Now, had she seen the look Lizzy was giving her, her response might have differed some.

"By the way, I love the name of the shop, The Modern Woman Dress Shop," Lizzy said. "I guess you can consider yourself a modern woman since you and Bishop Smith have started courting and all." She swung her body around abruptly and placed her index finger on her chin. "Oh, wait a minute. You can't be courting Bishop Smith. You're still a married woman."

Now that comment made May Rose lift her head. Her mouth opened, but before any words could come out, Elma and Bertha came running from the back.

No questions asked and no regrets, Elma smacked Lizzy on the face and then poked her forehead.

Lizzy balled her fists at her sides.

"I dare you to jump, you evil-ass snake," Aunt Bertha warned. "I will scrub this beautiful wood floor up with you."

"So, you better take your raggedy ass back to that cave you crawled out of. You are messing with the wrong person," Elma said through gritted teeth. "I knew you wanted to try May Rose because she has more beauty, intelligence, and class than you. But guess what? She doesn't have to deal with you, you lonely-ass dustcloth." Now it was Elma giving the once-overs. "Me and my sisters got her covered like Bishop Smith covers her with his big, beautiful body at night while they sleep."

Lizzy's mouth saved her butt a good whipping by staying shut. Although by the way her face turned red and her lips tightened, it wasn't the easiest thing for her to do.

"Now, get on!" Elma released her. "Bishop Smith don't want you, so get your ass over it and don't come back in this shop unless you're shopping."

Lizzy had tried to cozy up to Bishop Smith on numerous occasions, even before the death of his wife. She was known for stepping in front of First Lady Ramona to greet him and was one of the women Bishop Ellis spoke about in his eulogy.

Lizzy made her way to the door, crying and startled. She stepped out and yelled, "Elma, you're one mean-ass broad. I was just joking around with May Rose. You and your battleaxe sister can't even take a joke."

Both Elma and Aunt Bertha charged toward Lizzy, who took off running, leaving a heap of dust behind.

Laughing, May Rose yelled, "Aunt Etta, please come out here and get yo' crazy sisters."

Etta, who had also been in the backroom, had been so focused on putting the finishing touches on a dress, she hadn't heard anything that was going on out in the shop. She hadn't even noticed that her sisters had left the room. "What? What's going on?" she asked worriedly as she hurried out.

"Your crazy sisters are going to chase our business away, that's what's going on," May Rose replied.

"Who? What happened?" A confused Aunt Etta scanned the room for a sign of trouble.

"That ole heifer Lizzy," Aunt Bertha said, rolling her eyes. "She in here talking silly."

"Plus, she was talking about May Rose and Bishop's bedroom business," Elma added. "So, you know she is running her mouth to other people if she bold enough to run it in May Rose's face."

"And God knows we can't afford for somebody to go messing up May Rose's plans now that she's finally handling her business the right way." What was meant as a compliment made May Rose tighten her lips and scowl.

Aunt Bertha decided to quickly intercede. She broke out laughing. "Me and Elma done chased Lizzy halfway to her house. I didn't think we still had it in us."

Just then, Bishop Smith appeared in the doorway. "Is everything all right in here? I just saw Lizzy running like a pack of wolves were on her hide."

The women each looked at one another, and then they were all laughing.

"You know what, Bishop? That ain't too far from the truth." May Rose snorted.

As clueless as could be, he shook his head. "Clearly, I missed something really good."

"You did, Bishop," Bertha confirmed, "but I'm sure your Rosie will tell you all about it."

May Rose settled down her giggling. "It's nothing. Just Momma and my aunts doing a little overkill."

"Humph," Elma said. "Not enough killing, if you ask me."

"You're always taking everything to the edge, and you know it," May Rose said.

After a few moments, Bishop Smith asked, "Uh, Rosie, have you heard anything from Bishop Ellis's friend, that big ole attorney James A. Singleton sitting up in the White House? The one who is supposed to help you get your divorce finalized?"

"Yeah," Elma jumped in, "so these nosey people around town can shut up." She untied her apron and threw it on the countertop. "I'm getting ready to go home. I'm worn out. Way too much action around here than I saw coming."

"I'm going to head to the house as well," May Rose said.

Her mother snickered. "Which house, madam?" She sucked her teeth. "It's a good thing me and my sisters know how to drive, because otherwise I can see you making us walk home in the dark so you can get to your big cheese." She discreetly but not so discretely nodded toward Bishop Smith.

Everyone laughed.

"Good night to you, bad girls," May Rose said, snatching off her own apron and tossing it on the countertop. "I'm going to my big daddy's house. That's what house I'm going to, since you nosey like that."

"Do we need to see about the girls?" Aunt Bertha asked, willing to play whatever role she needed to play to make sure her niece handled her business.

"I'll have you know," May Rose started proudly, "the girls are at Bishop Smith's house taking care of some chores."

"And me, not knowing how late their momma would be at the store," Bishop Smith said, "already planned for them to sleep over at the house."

"Is that so?" an impressed Elma asked, looking at her sister, nodding with approval and delight at her daughter's progress with Bishop Smith.

"And so it is," May Rose said. "Now, if you all don't mind, lock up tight for me." She grabbed her sweater and purse and exited with her arm looped through the bishop's.

When May Rose and Bishop Smith arrived at his house, she was met by the girls the moment she walked in the door. They were all bouncing up and down with excitement.

Lynette said eagerly, "Momma, Bishop Smith is going to take us to D.C. to see the White House. He said we have to work around your schedule. Please, please, please, Momma, can we go tomorrow?"

Ginny chimed in, "Momma, Bishop Smith said we have to go as a family. So, you have to go. He also talked to us about going to one of the Black colleges. He even asked us what we want to do with our lives when we grow up."

It was Florence's turn next. "He is so nice to us, Momma. He cares about us all as if we were his very own. We never had fun like this with…" Florence allowed her words to trail off. She didn't want to go and ruin all the excitement by mentioning her father.

"Please, Momma, can we go to D.C. tomorrow?" Bishop Smith jokingly mocked Lynette.

Everyone laughed loudly at his impression.

"I forgot to mention that me and the girls made dinner," he said. "We ate already because we didn't know when you were going to get home. That's actually what I was coming to the shop to tell you. C'mon and get washed up for dinner. I'll fix your plate."

May Rose looked at the girls and waggled her eyebrows. Ole Willie had never had a meal waiting on her, let alone fix her plate.

"We have some good ole fried pork chops made with love by Ginny and me," Bishop Smith said. "Florence and Lynette made the fried cabbage, the creamed corn, and cornbread with love as well. Go on now and get yourself ready to eat."

"Yes, sure, I'm going now," she said. "Thank you for everything." She blew him a kiss in their usual fashion and marched up the steps to the washroom.

The entire time May Rose got herself together, she smiled thinking about the happiness the girls were now experiencing. She could never let the girls live the way they did with her and Willie's mess. Of course, she wondered if a different decision would have meant the girls enjoying this lifestyle a long time ago. But she couldn't let the what-ifs eat away at the what-is.

After she finished, May Rose walked into the dining room to her plate, a glass of wine, and a beautiful bouquet of freshly picked flowers.

"Oh, honey the flowers are exquisite," she told Bishop Smith. "You're so good to me."

"Your beautiful chocolate self deserves every bit of it," he replied, "and I can't wait to make you, my wife." He kissed her cheek and pulled out her chair. She sat and he continued, "We may need to get another lawyer if Mr. Singleton can't find some time to get your divorce filed. Is that all right with you?" He took a seat for himself.

"Of course. That's just fine with me. But as far as going to D.C. tomorrow, we sure can. Can we go around one? I want to get Momma and my aunts going at the shop."

"Yep, we sure can. Speaking of your mother and aunts, what the heck went on with them and Lizzy Thompson? But before you get started, let me bless the food for ya." He did so and then continued, chuckling, "What did Lizzy do to set them off? I can just imagine."

May Rose couldn't help but laugh as she recalled the incident. "Stop it, now. You just made me almost spit out my food." She finished chewing. "She brought her tail in the shop talking about she guess I'm a modern woman because me and you are courting, and I'm still married."

"I knew it was something foul because of the way Mother Elma chased her out of that store. Boy oh boy, if she had gotten her hands on Lizzy, we would've had to get the undertaker to pick Lizzy up tonight."

"Yes, it's very foul, but guess what? I don't care what she or anyone says. We are here to stay, right, baby?" May Rose asked as she picked up Bishop Smith's hand and held it in hers.

"Yes, indeed, my love." He lifted her hand to his mouth and kissed her fingers. "So, finish up eating so we can have our touchy-feely time. I missed you really bad today. Oh, I forgot to ask you something. What do you think about me expanding the size of the house?" He looked around. "Do you think ten bedrooms and three washrooms is enough for the girls? My children are already used to it, but I figure it might take some getting used to for your girls to live in this space with my six children. And I just want them to be comfortable."

May Rose's appreciation for his concern showed all over her face. "Yes, we will need the extra room, especially having teenagers coming along. I'm thinking soon, Willie will want his houses and land back. We may need to find somewhere for Momma and the elders to live."

"I thought the same thing." He stared off in thought for a moment. "We still have plenty of land to build on. I'll have the gentlemen from Montgomery come back and bring a few more men with them to knock out the expansion fast before my children return the beginning of September. I'll probably need to move in with your mother and the elders to get out of their way while they work. Also, I'll have them stay here while they work."

May Rose nodded her agreement while she ate. "The food is delicious, honey."

"Thank them fine young ladies of yours. I was basically standing in their way. They're so delightful. I love having them around."

May Rose continued to enjoy her meal until she had just a few bites left on her plate.

"C'mon, let's go take care of our business. We'll ask the girls to clean the kitchen. I'm going to start giving them a weekly allowance for doing their chores. I'm also going to hire some help with the housework around here. I can't have my sweets stretched out too far trying to keep up with an eight-room house."

She finished eating, and he pulled out her chair and helped her up before taking her plate and wine glass to the kitchen.

May Rose went to the parlor where the girls were. "Okay, ladies, thanks for such a tasty dinner. I'm so proud of you! We will be going to D.C. tomorrow afternoon. We'll be leaving at one, so please clean up the kitchen, do the dishes, get your baths, and get to sleep. I don't need no lazy bones in the morning."

"Yay, Momma, you're the best," the girls cheered and threw in a little dancing right along with it.

"Good night, my sweet babies. Thanks for the dance moves, too." May Rose gave each one a kiss on the foreheads and a big hug.

Bishop Smith entered the parlor. "To D.C. we go tomorrow." He pulled a wad of cash out of his pocket. "I'm going to give you girls one dollar each."

The girls started cheering again.

"This is called an allowance." Bishop Smith started counting out one-dollar bills. "You will get it every week for completing your chores without your mother needing to tell you to do so."

May Rose intercepted, stopping him mid-count. "Hold up now. How about we start with fifty cents each? Then once we teach them a bit more about finances, we can increase it up some." She looked to Ginny, giving her a knowing look. "Right, Ginny? As the eldest child, wouldn't you agree that a woman needs to learn what to do with that much money?"

Although Ginny would have much rather received a whole dollar, she understood why her mother felt that might be a bit too much for a child yet to be educated on the value of money. Otherwise, she might frivolously spend the funds like some child. And a child she was no more.

"Yes, Momma," Ginny agreed with very little excitement. Her sister's expressions mirrored her own.

But it all changed when the coins landed in each of their palms. Going from nothing to something was still exciting.

"Well, you heard what your momma done said," Bishop Smith said after giving the girls their money. "You can do whatever you wish with the money, but all I ask is that you save a portion of it every week for your future. By the time you become a young adult, you could be well off and don't have to start adulthood while in college from scratch."

"Yes, sir. Thank you," they said with one voice.

Everything suddenly got quiet as Lynette stood in front of Bishop Smith with her head hanging low, her arms crossed in front her and fingers intertwined as she swung back and forth. She looked just like the little girl she was. Because all the girls were so wise and mature for their age, it was easy to forget that Lynette was just that, a little girl.

"Yes, Lynette?" Bishop Smith asked.

"I was just wondering something, Bishop Smith."

"What is it, sweetheart?" he asked in a genuine, caring voice.

She looked up at him with her baby doll eyes and little girl's voice. "Can I give you a hug?"

May Rose exhaled, not even realizing she'd been holding her breath, worried about what was about to come out of the mouth of babes.

Even his eyes lit up in relief. "You sure can, baby, you sure can." He squatted and opened his arms.

Lynette didn't hesitate to run into them and give Bishop Smith a big, warm hug. He looked up to see Florence and Ginny standing there with a look that said they weren't taking too kindly to being left out.

"As a matter of fact," Bishop Smith said, "I have enough hugs for everyone." He opened his arms even wider, taking all three girls in.

May Rose didn't even realize she was crying until she felt the first tear slide down her cheek. All she'd ever wanted was her girls to know what this kind of love felt like coming from their father. Willie was not able to deliver that, and May Rose knew deep in her soul he never would be.

As David hugged the girls, he continued, "Thank you for changing my life and making my heart happy. I honestly don't think I would have been able to handle the loss and huge hole of a void in my heart if you girls weren't here to fill it." He looked up at May Rose. "That includes your momma, too." He winked at her, cheeks already wiped clean of any tears and now blushing as her eyelids fluttered. "We will be one big, happy family."

"We sure will," Ginny agreed as the girls fell out of the hug.

"You girls go on and get to bed," May Rose ordered. She needed for the scene to play out to the end before she turned into a big ball of tears, which was not part of her plan.

"Good night, girls," Bishop Smith said, standing and stretching out his legs. "And don't forget to say your prayers."

"Yes, sir" and "we won't" and "good night" could be heard all at once, followed by "Good night, Momma and Bishop Smith."

Within a few minutes, the entire house was asleep in bed.

At least the girls were asleep in bed.

May Rose and Bishop Smith were in bed all right, but sleeping wasn't exactly what they were doing. And that *was* part of May Rose's plan.

It was early Saturday morning, and May Rose was up fixing a big breakfast before they headed out to D.C. Since they would be doing a lot of walking, she wanted everyone's bellies full. She made bacon, fried apples, grits, and hot, fluffy biscuits. She also planned to wrap up and pack last evening's leftover pork chops and some biscuits in case anyone got hungry. But when she spoke of her plans to Bishop Smith, he told her there was no need to do that because there were plenty Black-owned restaurants on U Street, which was known as the Black Broadway. "There are also nightclubs, a concert hall, and a department store," he informed her. "It's where Black folks in the area go to dine and get entertainment like Cab Calloway and Pearl Bailey, as well as to shop." This was something Bishop Smith was certain both May Rose and the girls would enjoy.

She got dressed for the day and after breakfast, she went to her house to check on it. She was also going to tell her mother and aunts the plan for the day and ask them to continue working in the shop.

May Rose stepped into the house and looked around. She didn't feel an ounce of love as she stood there, and she had to ask herself if she'd ever felt any love in there. Sure, the girls loved her, and she loved them. Sure, she had love for Willie, and he had some love for her. But still, there was this certain feeling of love that the home simply lacked. And maybe she hadn't missed it because she didn't know she was missing it. But after feeling it in Bishop Smith's home, well, now she knew what she'd been missing...and it was definitely missing from that home.

It actually felt eerie to her. She thought how glad she would be when Willie came and took all of it. She didn't need anything that man had to offer. Not anymore. Not now that she had Bishop Smith in her life exactly where she wanted him.

Where she needed him.

For her girls.

Smack in the middle of May Rose's thought, she looked out the front window and saw a dust storm. "What the hell is this?" she asked, not having seen dust kicking up like that since Lizzy had gone kicking out of the dress shop yesterday. She chuckled a little just thinking about it.

"Lord, let me hurry up and get out of here," May Rose said to herself a moment later. It would be just her worst luck for Willie to decide to show up while she was there checking on the place. As she opened the front door, she saw three cars filled with white men.

By this time, Elma and her sisters were running toward May Rose's house with their shotguns.

"What the hell the law want with this place?" Elma said as she cleared the corner and was now just about four feet away.

May Rose squinted in confusion, but a knowing expression covered her face just a moment later. "That ain't no law, at least one of 'em ain't," she said as she recognized one of the men as the fat one from the coal mine. "He's from Willie's job."

Elma lowered her gun. "Jesus Christ, what has his crazy ass done did now?"

"Well, whatever it is, they bet' not be coming looking for me to fix or repair it. I ain't no longer got nothing to do with that man. Period," May Rose said as she watched the men get out of the cars and walk to the front porch. Elma and the elders followed right behind them. Two of the men were well-dressed in black suits and black hats. They actually did look like lawmen.

May Rose started the conversation with fear in her tone. "How may I help y'all?"

One of the men in black asked, "Are you May Rose Jones?"

Aunt Etta spoke up. "Yeah, that one right there is. State your business."

The man removed his hat.

May Rose's heart started beating out of her chest. "Someone go get Bishop Smith," she stated, looking down as her chest heaved. She fumbled to get her keys out of her purse. "Right now! Please! Somebody please go get David right away." She held her keys out for the taking.

Aunt Bertha snatched them. "I will right now." She raced down the steps, hopped in the car, and sped off, leaving a trail of smoke behind.

Meanwhile, the man who had removed his hat continued. "Mrs. Jones, unfortunately, we're here to inform you that your husband—"

May Rose started crying out before the man could even finish his sentence. "No, God, please, no. This is too much." She fell in Elma's arms. "Death wasn't supposed to be part of the plan." Her words were muffled against Elma's chest.

"Ma'am," the man continued, "I'm sorry to inform you that at approximately 6:50 p.m., William H. Jones was killed in a mine explosion at the McDowell Coal Mine."

Everything went dark, and May Rose's body became just as lifeless as Willie's, wherever he rested in peace at that moment. She slid out of Elma's arms and hit the porch. "Where? Where is his body?"

May Rose's devastation was no act. Even if her and Willie's marriage had turned sour, she still didn't want him dead. He was the only man her girls had ever known as their daddy.

Elma pulled her back up off the porch and held her hand.

"He's under the rubble now, and it's not safe for search and rescue yet," Willie's boss answered. "There has been a war between the coal workers and the mining companies. We're suspecting the blast was intentionally done by the opposition side. The blast occurred at the entrance of the mine. It looks like someone started a fire that made the gases inside to explode."

The man in the black suit jumped back in, fiddling with his hat. "Ma'am, there probably won't be any remains at all."

Willie's boss took over again. "We had nine men down there with Willie. It may take years to get someone back in there." He continued, "We're aware you knew Willie had a female friend that he was spending time with."

"You mean a whore he was spending time with," Elma corrected. "What the hell do she have to do with this? How dare you even bring her up in this moment."

"Ma'am, if you let me finish, I'll tell you." He rolled his eyes. "Her name is Pepper Bunch. She gave us a note that Willie wrote to you and your daughters. A lot of the miners do this. She asked if we would see you get it. We also have what's left of Willie's last pay, along with your widow's pension money, which is twenty dollars. Pepper asked to keep Willie's personal items. She has been informed that we would need to get your permission since rightfully, they belong to you."

Bishop Smith and Aunt Bertha arrived, and they both jumped out the car, leaving it running. He ran up the porch steps straight to May Rose and held her tightly. "I'm here, Rosie, I'm here." He rubbed her head, looking at Elma in anticipation of her telling him what the heck was going on.

"It's Willie, Bishop," Elma answered, "he's gone."

A heap of wind exited Bishop Smith's mouth like it had been knocked out of him. He quickly gathered his composure, though. He had to be strong for May Rose, whose weak body rested against him, and he pivoted his attention to the group of men. "Gentlemen, I'm Bishop David Smith of Washington Street First Baptist Church. Is there any additional business needed with Mrs. Jones? She needs to give the news to her children."

Willie's boss focused on Bishop Smith's face and started nodding. "Oh, yeah. I remember you from when you and Mrs. Jones came to the mine."

"Oh, yes, that's correct," Bishop Smith replied.

Willie's boss continued, "We're waiting for Mrs. Jones to let us know if she will allow Willie's female friend Pepper to keep his belongings. It's just dirty clothes—one suit, a hat—and some pictures they took together. If you want to go through his things first, I can go get the trunk for you." He nodded back toward his car.

May Rose straightened her broken body, as if Bishop Smith breathed life into her. "Sir, please take all of that alcohol-smelling stuff right back to Pepper. And please tell her I've done released Willie to her and I'm so sorry for her loss." She brushed the invisible dust off her clothes as if she were dusting away anything left of Willie. "Thanks for the information, gentlemen. Now please excuse us, but me, my children, and this big, fine man right here are going to have a family day. Please have an outstanding day like we're going to have."

The men tipped their hats, walked off to their cars, and then pulled away.

Of course, Elma, Bertha, and Etta started doing one of their African dances right away.

"Momma, y'all don't have to be so happy," May Rose fussed, shooing at them. "That is the girls' daddy."

Ignoring her daughter, Elma said, "Correction, *was* their daddy." She shouted, "Hallelujah, thank you, God and the ancestors."

The aunts were dancing and singing hallelujah as well.

"That man is dead. Don't make fun of the dead. Y'all know better," May Rose said, swatting the air as if swatting the elders, but they paid her no mind and continued dancing and singing.

"Well, we're taking the girls and spending the day in D.C. Would you bad girls please go to the shop and finish up the dresses we were working on last night? And most of all, don't let anyone in, because you might start fighting them, too."

The elders started jumping around and throwing punches, as if they were boxing.

"In the words of Willie, 'y'all are crazy-ass African women,' and just think, you won't have to hear it again unless he comes and haunts y'all in your sleep." May Rose started laughing so hard, her eyes watered.

"Whatever, girl, go on about your business, because soon, y'all got some decisions to make," Elma said. "Oh, and would you all send a telegram notice to my buddy Bishop Ellis? I need him to get here right away. Tell him I said his lawyer friend Mr. Singleton took too long. The ancestors were allowed to honor my request. Also, tell him he needs to get his money back and come put it in my pocketbook."

Bishop Smith chuckled. "Y'all are not to be played with, that's for sure! Me and Rose got most of the plans for our future in the bag already. We're going full steam ahead."

Elma shot him a look of approval.

"Well, okay, we're going to run." He turned his attention to May Rose. "Let's go, my sweets. We don't want to leave too late going to D.C., and you need to talk to the girls first." He looked to the elders. "We'll see you all soon." He clenched May Rose's hand as they walked to the car. He opened the passenger door and lifted her up into the seat, straightening out her dress. While doing so, he noticed how in just that short distance to the car, May Rose's demeanor seemed to change. "Baby, it's all going to be all right. Don't have no guilt or shame, you hear?"

May Rose nodded.

"Now we're free and clear to become that one big, happy family I talked about." He kissed her on the cheek and then closed the door, making his way to the driver's seat. "There are so many things we need to talk about," he said as he drove back to his house. "Like, we have to plan the engagement announcement and party. I'm now thinking we should add a ballroom to the house. What do you think about that?

May Rose was deep in thought as Bishop Smith rattled on. All she was thinking about in that moment was talking to the girls and how their life truly was about to change forever.

"Rosie, my love, are you with me?" he sang, shaking her knee to get her attention.

"Oh, honey, I'm sorry. I was just thinking about the girls right now. Whatever you were saying, can we talk about it tonight?" she asked.

"Sure." He tapped her knee and then placed his hand on the steering wheel. "I better calm down all my excitement in front of the girls. I don't want them to think I don't respect how they feel about their daddy passing away," he said as they pulled up to his house. He turned the car off and looked over at May Rose. "Well, we're here. Tell me what you want me to do."

She exhaled. "Just have my back as always. I'm just not sure how they're going to handle this."

"You have brilliant girls. I'm sure they will handle it well."

"Just don't be surprised what you hear from them. They are pretty angry with Willie."

"I know they have been hurt by him. It will change with time."

After they exited the car and entered the house, they went inside to find that the girls were all dressed for their outing. They sat on the couch waiting with puzzled expressions.

"Hey, girls, are you ready?" Bishop Smith asked, to which the girls each replied in the affirmative. "Good, but first, your mother needs to talk to you about something."

"What happened now?" Ginny was the first to ask. "Why did Aunt Bertha rush in here to get Bishop Smith, telling him he needed to get to our house quick?"

Florence added, "We know it's Daddy. What did he do today?"

"He's going to ruin our trip, isn't he?" Lynette whined.

"Stop it now, girls, and let me talk," May Rose said, her head spinning with their chattering. "I have some very bad news. Your daddy is dead. He was killed in a coal mine explosion yesterday."

There was complete silence as the girls looked at each other.

"Well, does anyone have anything to say?" May Rose asked.

"I do," Ginny answered. "May he have a wonderful journey to Hell while we have a wonderful journey to D.C. Can we go now, Momma?"

"All right, Ginny, that was too much," May Rose scolded. "You may feel a certain way, and that's just fine, but you got your sisters' feelings to consider. He was their daddy, too."

"It's alright, Momma," Lynette said. "He didn't want us anyway." Her eyes became wetter at this thought than the fact that Willie was dead. "That's too bad for his girlfriend, though."

Florence growled, "You can't miss nothing you never had." She threw her hands on her hips. "Are we still going to D.C., or is Willie Jones still ruining our fun from the grave?"

"Florence Jones!" May Rose said. She looked to Bishop Smith, who made sure he didn't make eye contact. He had her back, all right, but it was way back. He hadn't anticipated the girls' reactions being so unbothered.

"Babies, I know he hurt you deeply, but you don't have to be so hateful," she said. "I don't want you to grow up being bitter women, do you understand? Don't go hating your daddy on my behalf, because that's not what I want."

"Yes, Momma," they unconvincingly mumbled.

"Fine, then. Now, are you sure you still want to go on this trip? You may feel you're okay now, but later, it my hit you."

Ginny responded on the girls' behalf. "Yes, we still want to go to D.C., and, Momma, I want to know when are you and Bishop Smith going to get married? Will Bishop Smith adopt us? And can—"

"Ginny," Bishop Smith interrupted. "We're not going to discuss marriage today, but I will say yes to all of your questions. Now, if it's okay with your momma, we can leave now." He looked to May Rose to see if she was fine with that.

She nodded and before she could even think about changing her mind, the girls rushed to the porch with elation.

"We'll see y'all in the car," Florence shouted, leaving the adults standing in the living room, quite dumbfounded at the girls' reaction but also relieved that they weren't taking the death of their father hard.

"I thank God for you, David. You are allowing me and the girls the life we always dreamed of," she said.

"The best is yet to come, Rosie. You just wait and see," he replied boldly.

They had a long, passionate kiss before they headed out the door and joined the girls in the car, waiting for the day they would officially be joined in holy matrimony.

"When one is in love, a mountaintop becomes
a flat field."

African Proverb

Chapter 18

❧

IT'S SHOWTIME

May Rose stood there, her hands trembling. The only noise was the crunching sound of the envelope she held as she gripped it so tightly, it was just about crumbling in her hands. Her fingers left their sweaty print where they touched.

It had been several months since Willie died, and May Rose had not yet read the letter he left for her in the event of his death. Life with Bishop Smith had been going so well, she simply hadn't been in the mood to risk Willie haunting her from the grave. However, the thought of the unknown was starting to nag at her. She prayed over the letter and asked God for guidance. She decided she would read the letter and just keep what it said to herself. Secrets were a common thing for May Rose throughout the years.

She stood in the living room of her old house with Willie because that's where she'd left it, since she never wanted the children or Bishop Smith to stumble upon it. She walked up to the bedroom she once shared with Willie, closing and locking the door behind her. She didn't anticipate anyone would be showing up unannounced, but she didn't put anything past the African sisters.

May Rose lay across the bottom of the lumpy mattress. It couldn't compare to the lavish mattress she was now accustomed to at what she and the girls referred to as the Smith Mansion.

She stared at the envelope for a few seconds as her hands shook nervously. Eventually, she did it. She ripped the envelope that read "May Rose Jones" open. Inside was a couple of stained yellow pieces of paper that reeked of moonshine. She closed her eyes and shook her head. *That damn Willie has found a way to annoy me even in his death.*

"Let me hurry up and get this over with," she moaned.

She slowly read the letter aloud as her emotions began to take over her. "May Rose, if you're reading this, I must be dead. Don't get happy so fast. Tell your mammy and them other crazy African broads to get the hell out of my house. Speaking of the house and the land, since my brother Logan signed everything over to me because he would never come back south again after leaving to live in Alaska chasing after the gold mines, the houses and property will now belong solely to you and the girls. Now your stinking elders can stop saying I ain't never did nothing for ya."

She shook her head. Ole Willie was still cussing her elders from the grave. "You better not move that sneaky Negro David Smith in my house with you since you both are now free and clear to rip your clothes off each other like he wanted to do when we was youngin's. I may have been a drunk, but I ain't stupid. David couldn't keep your name out of his mouth. All the men in town wanted to take a shot at ya. You know there were stories that Ginny was old man Claypool's child. After all, you and them crazy elders were living in his house when I met ya. Your mammy thought she was going to end up with his house and property, but his family put the brakes on that. Ha!"

May Rose tightened her lips at Willie's continuous shots at her mother and aunts, but she managed to continue even though she wanted to ball up that letter and burn it. "During that time of you getting pregnant with Ginny, you were living in his house. He threw you out because he knew we were courting then, too. You told me Ginny was my child, but I really thought she belonged to Claypool.

"That's why I couldn't get close to Ginny. Every time I asked you if I'm her daddy, you would just start crying and tell me to stop the drunk talk, but I didn't forget you never answered the question. Your mammy didn't want us to get married, and my mammy definitely didn't want us to be married because she heard the rumors about you and Claypool, too. She didn't trust you or your elders.

"That's when I asked Minister and Mrs. Smith if you could live with them until I could convince my mother to allow me to marry you and move you in my house. Plus, they had that big, old house with several empty rooms. They agreed, of course. Little did I know then I was sending you to the arms of the man that would end up stealing your heart and who you would end up with in the end. Hell, for all I know, Ginny could be David's child. We wasn't romping in the bed all that much back then. You got the ways of them crazy Africans. You're just sneaky like that. Y'all do what you have to do to win. Ain't that right?"

May Rose let out a smug snort to match the smug look on her face. "Ya got that right," she said, and then continued reading the letter. "Have a nice damn life. I'm out of here. By the way, my whore, Pepper, accepted me just as I was, drunk and all. I was just never good enough for you."

By the time May Rose finished, she was shivering like a wet dog out in the cold. She screamed, "Willie, you no-good so-and-so." She balled her hands into fists, the letter crumpled in her right one, and jumped up off the bed. "You mistreated my baby on purpose. I should've never allowed my babies to be subjected to that clown of a man."

She brought the letter up to her eyes and fussed at it like she was fussing out Willie. "You're damn right you were never good enough for me! It's not that you couldn't have been, you just didn't want to, fool!" She threw the letter across the room.

Her mind started racing, thinking about what Bishop Smith must think about the rumors of her and Claypool. What people didn't understand was that Claypool was taking her every chance he could. He would get drunk and start pulling on her. May Rose was using the roots and the spermicide shots Elma would give her. But what didn't work on Claypool was May Rose's physical strength. She fought him like a lion would've fought a predator trying to attack its cub. Sometimes, he would eventually get tired, stop pulling on her, and fall asleep. But other times, well, it would be May Rose who tired out and would just let Claypool have his way.

Elma was outdone when May Rose ended up pregnant.

"Child, how in the world could you let this happen?" Elma scolded May Rose, who was in tears. "I been wasting my time giving you stuff from becoming with child and you ain't been using it?" Elma threw her hands up and started pacing at the foot of the bed where her daughter sat crying.

"But I was taking the stuff, Momma," May Rose promised. "I was putting savin and pennyroyal in Claypool's food, too."

Elma stopped pacing long enough to ask, "Well, any idea who the daddy might be?"

"Willie's," May Rose said instantly and with confidence. Willie was the man May Rose loved and willingly gave her body to, not Claypool. Therefore, in May Rose's mind and heart, and most certainly in her body, Willie was the father of the child she was carrying.

Elma gave May Rose a good side-eye. Then, May Rose declared Willie as the baby's father, and a few months later, May Rose gave birth to Ginny.

"You know the saying," Elma told May Rose after catching Ginny and then laying her on May Rose's chest, "Mama's baby and Daddy's maybe."

May Rose sat back down on the bed, inhaled deeply, and exhaled as she looked up at the ceiling. "Lord, forgive me," she said. This moment was the first she'd ever felt even an inkling of remorse about telling Willie that Ginny was his, knowing there was a chance he couldn't have been…and more than likely wasn't.

Willie would've acted a damn fool about it, but clearly, his gut already knew the truth. And as cold as it might have sounded, May Rose was glad his behind was buried six feet beneath the earth. "And that's exactly where it's gonna stay," she said as she proceeded to do just what she'd been thinking to do with the letter all this time, which was to burn it.

As May Rose watched the letter turn to ashes, she decided she would simply continue to live her wonderful new life with Bishop Smith and all of the children.

The pulpit was full of beautiful baskets of red roses, which were May Rose's favorite flowers. It was a surprise for her. She thought they were only going to see the new organ, but as they entered the church, Aunt Etta was sitting in the choir stand, playing the new organ, and singing "Honeysuckle Rose" by Fats Waller. Bishop Smith had asked May Rose and the family to follow him to the choir stand as they all swayed to the music. He began singing as he took the steps.

Every honey bee
Fills with jealousy
When they see you out with me
I don't blame them
Goodness knows
Honeysuckle rose

When we're passin' by
Flowers droop and sigh
And I know the reason why
You're much sweeter
Goodness knows
Honeysuckle rose

Don't buy sugar
You just have to touch my cup
You're my sugar
It's sweet when you stir it up

When I'm taking sips
From your tasty lips
The honey fairly drips
You're confection, goodness knows
Honeysuckle rose

Everyone applauded and cheered as the song ended.

"Darlin, you know this is my favorite song," May Rose said, her eyes full of tears. "You have such a wonderful singing voice. You can sing to me any time."

Bishop Smith winked at May Rose and then turned his attention to the congregation. "Everyone, take a seat," he said, and everyone did as they were asked, including those on the pulpit with him. "Except for May Rose, Ginny, Florence, and Lynette," he added, stopping them in their tracks.

Before he could say another word, Aunt Etta blurted out, "Thank you, God. You are the author and the finisher." She shook her head, clapped her hands, and rejoiced all the way to her seat.

Once everyone was seated, Bishop Smith bent down on one knee and looked at the girls. "Girls, it's been such a joy making you a part of our family." He looked out into the congregation at his own children. "Ain't that right, children?"

His children affirmed both verbally and with nods.

Turning his attention back to Ginny, Florence, and Lynette, he continued, "I would like to ask you for your mother's hand in marriage. Will you allow me to marry her, and will you allow me to be your father?"

The three girls looked at each other, and Ginny led with, "We thought you'd never ask."

The congregation giggled, and then the girls each responded with a "yes."

"Thank you, babies." He looked back out to the congregation at his six children, who were now back home after spending the summer in New York City with his mother and sister. "Smith children, front and center." Once the children circled him, he said, "Children, will you allow May Rose to be your new mother, her girls to be your sisters, Mother Elma to be your extra grandmother, and Aunt Bertha and Aunt Etta to be your extra aunts?"

The children started jumping up and down and shouting, "Yes!"

The members of the church couldn't contain themselves as they started celebrating as well. But there was still one other person who had to say yes. That's when Bishop Smith turned his attention to May Rose.

May Rose, in shock, had both her hands covering her mouth. He pulled them away, taking them in his, and stared into her eyes. "Well, Rosie, we can't disappoint the children, can we?" He laughed. "You gotta say yes now."

She also laughed. "But I still need to hear you say it."

"May Rose, my Rosie," Bishop Smith said as he bent down on one knee again, pulling a ring from his inside suit pocket, "will you marry me? Will you take my hand in marriage and be mine for the rest of my breathing days here on earth?"

She smiled as one tear slid down her face. "I will."

Bishop Smith slid the ring on her finger.

May Rose exhaled.

The pair got right into planning their engagement party, which was set for October 5th with the actual wedding to be held December 31st. They decided to bring in the New Year as husband and wife.

The reception was going to be held in the newly built ballroom in Bishop Smith's house, which had beautiful crystal pendant lights that hung all over. The additional bedrooms and washrooms had also been added and furnished. The house now looked nothing short of a mansion; hence the nickname May Rose and the girls had given the home. By now, May Rose and the girls were permanently moved in.

May Rose, to save money, was willing to make her own wedding gown, but Bishop Smith wouldn't hear of it.

"I want you to spend time planning the wedding without worrying about finding the time to make your own gown," he said.

Obliging her future husband's wishes, the elders helped May Rose pick out a nice, fancy wedding gown from an upscale dress shop in New York City. She did not want to wear white since she had already been married and had three children, a clear sign she wasn't a virgin white kind of gal. The gown she selected had a beige lace bodice and sleeves with nude-colored beads. The bottom of the gown was a pleated nude color as well. May Rose always had exquisite taste, just never the income to feed it. She was simply delighted when Bishop Smith told her money wasn't an issue when it came to his wife having the gown of her dreams.

By the time May Rose arrived in New York, she didn't have to do a bunch of dress shopping. She'd already picked out the one she wanted from the high society section of the newspaper. It was one of her guilty pleasures whenever she would go to the town pharmacy to pick up the baby-catching supplies. She always dreamed that one day, she would actually be one of those women she saw in that section of the paper. And that day had arrived.

However, May Rose was growing very weary. Even at this late-night hour as she lie in bed in the middle of the night next to Bishop Smith. A secret she had been hiding for many years was haunting her, Willie's letter from the grave pushing it closer to surface. She was starting to doubt whether she could marry Bishop Smith without being completely honest with him.

She was contemplating taking the matter to her elders to get their wise counsel, something she hadn't done before marrying Willie, and look how that turned out.

She played out the woman's business principles with Bishop Smith to a tee. Everything was going so well. This was not a time to take risks, so what did May Rose have to lose by talking with her elders? Upon the conclusion of that thought, she decided she would speak with them as soon as possible.

The elders would be proud, but shocked, and nothing surprised them. She contemplated including Ginny in the conversation as well, even though an explosive secret would be revealed. Ginny was still just a young girl, which made May Rose question whether she was woman enough to handle the conversation.

Whether she was woman enough to handle the truth.

Well, if May Rose was finally going to be woman enough to tell her, Ginny would have to be woman enough to hear it.

Ginny was now considered a woman in their family, but that still didn't alleviate May Rose's concern about her knowing and processing such a deep secret. May Rose suddenly felt like her life could blow up in her face. The truth must be told.

She woke up the next morning and crawled from underneath Bishop Smith's strong arms that tightly gripped her. She bent over and whispered in his ear, "Me and Ginny are running over to Momma's house to discuss some more wedding plans." She wasn't lying, as she would be sure to mention wedding plans just to make sure she wasn't lying to Bishop Smith. "I'll fix a little breakfast first. I will need you to get the children up for breakfast if I'm not back in a couple of hours. Okay?"

Bishop Smith yawned and moaned, "Yeah, sweets, I will. I love you."

"Thanks, honey. I love you right on back." May Rose stared at him as he fell back to sleep. She thought how this could possibly be the last time she heard him tell her he loved her, if the truth prevailed…and he couldn't handle it.

She went into the washroom and closed the door behind her. She looked in the mirror and frowned. "What the hell did you do?" May Rose scolded herself. "Girl, this tops everything you ever heard your mother and the elders talk about that they have done."

After getting cleaned up and dressed, May Rose went to Ginny's room. "Sweetheart." She gently shook Ginny awake. "Will you throw something on and come go with me to Nana's house? We have some business to discuss. I'm going to whip up some breakfast real fast for the family before we head out."

Ginny sleepily nodded then May Rose turned and headed for the door, stopping in her tracks when Ginny spoke.

"Why so early in the morning, Momma? I'm tired."

Usually, Ginny would have sprouted out of bed at the sound of getting to be a part of grown folk's business, so it surprised May Rose to hear that Ginny was too tired to join them. Perhaps this was a sign that Ginny shouldn't be part of the conversation.

"You don't have to come," May Rose said. "You can stay right here, but don't ask me later to talk to you about what we discussed." She continued to the door.

Ginny jumped up out of the bed. "Okay, Momma, I'm coming." She was not about to miss this show. Or showdown. She didn't know which, but she did know she wasn't going to miss it.

" Mmhmmm, thought so," May Rose said knowingly as she left Ginny's room.

She went to the kitchen and started frying some sausages and making scrambled eggs. She retrieved some homemade cinnamon applesauce Aunt Etta had made from the apple tree in the back of May Rose's house. She brewed coffee and left Bishop Smith's weekly Black-owned newspaper, *The Richmond Voice*, on the kitchen table. This was the way he educated himself, his family, and the congregation on what was going on with other Black people across the country. Bishop Smith was slowly but surely becoming a big figure in the state for advocating for equality.

"You're just in time to grab a quick bite to eat," May Rose informed Ginny as she entered the kitchen.

"I'll just have a couple sausages. I'm sure Nana and the elders are up banging them pots in the kitchen. I can get breakfast over there. I'm ready to go now. I'm real curious to find out what this is all about," Ginny anxiously replied.

"Okay, I'm ready, too," May Rose said, removing her apron and hanging it on the hook by the pantry. "Let's go." Trying her best to hide her nervousness, she picked up her sweater and pocketbook off the coat rack at the front door.

Ginny was on her heels, following suit.

The drive to the elders' house was completed in silence. However, May Rose had all kinds of noise going on in her head. She worried how Ginny was going to take everything more than she worried about the backlash from the elders. Bishop Smith's reaction to her secret was something she didn't want to think about but couldn't help doing so. Her brain was consumed with the fact this could possibly destroy their relationship. More and more, she questioned whether, like Willie's suspicions, she should take it to the grave with her.

When they arrived at the elders' house, Ginny jumped out of the car, ran up the porch steps, and busted through the front door. May Rose walked slowly, like she was on her way to a firing squad.

Ginny stuck her head out and shouted, "C'mon, Momma. Why are you walking so slow?" She went back into the house and straight to the kitchen, where she knew the elders would be. Plus, that was the usual meeting spot at their house. She greeted them all individually with a hug and a kiss on the cheek.

Aunt Bertha smiled. "What do we owe for the presence of our beautiful young queen this early morning?"

"Momma is calling for a wise council meeting," Ginny replied. "Whatever it is, it has her acting really strange."

"Is that so?" Aunt Etta asked, shooting her sisters a peculiar look.

Ginny threw her hands on her hips. "I've been in here about five minutes and she hasn't come in the door yet. She's walking like she's got molasses in her—"

"You betta watch your tongue." Elma wagged a disapproving finger at Ginny.

"Nana! I would never disrespect your house," Ginny said, feigning innocence. "I was gonna say her tail. Like she's got molasses in her tail."

Elma turned her lips up. "Mmhmm. Sure you was, gal." She rolled her eyes and put her face in her cupped hands. "Anyway... Lord, what has May Rose gone and done now? Please tell me she's not having second thoughts about marrying Bishop Smith."

"Oh no, she better not. She can leave. I'm staying right there," Ginny angrily noted. "Let me go and get her."

As Ginny walked to the door, May Rose appeared.

"Momma, what's going on with you? You're scaring the crap out of me." She wore a scowl shadowed by worry.

"Hush your mouth, girl. I'm still the momma around here," May Rose scolded right back, brushing by Ginny as she made her way into the kitchen. "Blessed day, my beautiful elders. I'm here to call on the wise council for direction on a serious matter. May we convene now?" May Rose went over to the table, throwing down her purse, taking off her coat, placing it over the back of the chair, and sitting down. Legs crossed. Hands on knee. Back straight. Chin up. A sure sign that, regardless of what the elders said, a meeting was about to take place, indeed.

"Let me run to use the washroom really quick," Etta said. "I can't hold myself any longer. You're being all formal. I think this is going to be a long council." She hurried out.

Elma barked, "Be quick about it, Etta. This girl looks like she's ready to burst. You're getting ready to miss it because in a minute, we're going to start without you."

Aunt Etta shouted from the washroom with the door open, just in case they did start without her, "Just give me a damn minute. Sisters, y'all got old lady bladders, too."

Ginny couldn't help but snicker until the two African sisters shot her the side-eye.

May Rose, anxious to get this meeting going, tapped one of her feet on the floor.

"Oh Lord!" Elma threw her hand over her forehead. "The girl is tapping her foot like she does any time she's in the way of trouble." Elma let her hand drop to her side and said, "This ain't gon' be good."

Elma's comment only made May Rose start tapping her foot that much faster.

"Momma, stop it," Ginny frantically shouted. "You're making me nervous." She rolled her eyes.

"Let's go, May Rose," Elma finally ordered. "Etta is taking too long. Speak your mind."

"Dang it, you don't even want to give me a chance to wash my paws." Etta stormed back into the room with wet hands, drying them on her clothing. The eerie silence in the room made her look up, where she found all eyes glued to her with a look of disapproval. "What? I could barely get my hands washed. I knew you impatient heifers wasn't gon' let me dry 'em," she barked, slamming her bottom down in the kitchen chair with an attitude.

Once again, Ginny laughed.

This time, Elma was gon' give her more than a talking-to. She raised her hand and started marching toward Ginny, who immediately stopped laughing and held her hands up in defense.

"Will you all cut out the shenanigans?" May Rose pleaded. "This is serious business!" She stood up beside her chair and began speaking. "Wise council, I am here seeking your counsel for a truth that will have complications. I'm starting at the beginning in order to fill Ginny in." She looked at her daughter but quickly looked away. This just wasn't a conversation she ever wanted to have with one of her girls, yet here she stood having it. "It all started with Mr. Claypool. He was an old, widowed man closer to seventy than sixty years old at the time."

Now she was able to put her eyes back on Ginny and keep them there long enough to address her. "Ginny, me and the elders lived in his house with him for a short stint before I married Willie. He took a liking to me. He used to climb up on me at night when he got drunk. There were rumors flying around town when I got pregnant with you that you were Claypool's child. Willie and his mother were the main two people who started the rumor and kept it going. I was finally able to convince Willie you were his child."

"Convince?" Ginny raised an eyebrow.

"You see, Claypool put me out of his house when I started showing. Willie's mother would not allow me to move in with them because she swore you belonged to Claypool. Willie went to Bishop Smith's family and asked them if I could move in with them in their big ole house until he could get the thought of you not being Willie's out of her crazy mind."

"You used to live with Bishop Smith before?" Ginny asked, her other eyebrow rising. She was making sure she had clarity on everything her mother was saying. Her gut told her this was not the time to get confused.

May Rose nodded. "We've been friends with Bishop Smith and his family since we were children. Minister Smith and Mrs. Smith had always took a likin' of me, thank God. Otherwise, I would have ended up on the side of the road somewhere." She sighed, caught her breath, and continued, but not before contemplating as to whether she could leave the story where it was at...just a rumor. She didn't really have to confirm or deny anything at this point. May Rose was slick with words. Surely, she could lie without lying. After all, wasn't that what she'd been doing all along?

May Rose looked to the elders. "Y'all never gave me credit for properly conducting the woman's business principles with my relationship with Willie." She looked at each woman real good and then said matter-of-factly, "Well, get ready to stand up and applaud me."

"The child who is not embraced by the village will burn it down to feel the warmth."

African Proverb

Chapter 19

STANDING OVATION

The sisters looked at each other, confused. Aunt Etta and Aunt Bertha looked at Elma like she should know what was going on, considering May Rose was her daughter.

Elma shrugged at them, then they all turned their attention back to May Rose.

"I was using the roots savin and pennyroyal the whole time I laid with Willie and when Claypool would try to take me," May Rose confided. "Plus, they both would be so drunk, they didn't realize that most of the time, they were never inside me."

The three sisters gasped. In that moment, they were becoming quite familiar with the neighborhood May Rose was driving them through with her words. Ginny, on the other hand, still stood at the fork in the road, confused. Of course, the elders were much wiser, older, and had been around the block and in the business long enough to know just how explosive the bomb May Rose was about to drop was.

"What?" Ginny asked the elders, who remained silent. She could tell by the sound that simultaneously escaped their mouths and the expression on their faces that they knew what

309

her mother was getting at. "What?" This time, she spoke louder and shot her words at May Rose.

"Baby girl," May Rose said with trembling lips, grabbing Ginny's hands with her own trembling one.

Now, what the elders might see as a win for May Rose in this here game, Ginny might think otherwise about. That was what had May Rose trembling like the last leaf on an autumn tree with a windstorm on its way.

"I'm here to tell you, all of you—" She looked to the elders and then back into her daughter's eyes. "—that the rumor ain't true. Not at all. Claypool is not your daddy."

Ginny closed her eyes as she exhaled. "Gosh, Momma. I thought it was going to be something bigger than that. I never believed—" She went to pull her hands from May Rose's, but May Rose gripped them tight, keeping them in place.

"Ginny, wait, that's not all," May Rose said.

Now Ginny felt, once again, uneasy.

"Willie ain't your daddy neither." May Rose braced herself for whatever response was coming her way from any of the women.

Ginny's mouth dropped open, but no words fell out. She started shaking her head. "I... I don't understand, Momma," she stammered. "If Claypool or Willie ain't my daddy, then w—" Before she could even finish her sentence, the answer came to her. May Rose saying it out loud only confirmed it.

"Ginny, baby, David Smith is your daddy. He's all you girls' daddy." She paused and waited on a response, especially from Ginny.

There was dead silence for what seemed like forever, then suddenly everyone's attention went to a pounding sound. Elma banged her fist on the table. Her mouth was wide open as she rocked back and forth, only nothing was coming out. After this went on a few seconds, May Rose raced over to Elma and started patting her on the back.

"Momma, are you okay?" she asked nervously. "Momma, say something. Are you okay?" May Rose knew her secret was one that would take her mother's breath away, but just figuratively, not literally.

A screeching howl erupted out of Elma's throat. It was a scary, piercing sound. May Rose didn't know what was going on. And then tears started pouring out of Elma's eyes.

"Grab some water!" May Rose exclaimed to Ginny. "I think she's choking or something."

Elma quickly started shaking her head and waving her hand. Another roar came up from her throat. "Ahhhhhhhhhhhhhh, haaaaaaaaaa, haaaaaaaaaaaaaaaaaa, haaaaaaaaaaaaaaaaaaa!" It took a few seconds, but then it was clear that the only thing Elma was choking on was her hysterical laughter. Pretty soon, it became contagious. Bertha burst out, and then Etta.

All May Rose could do was exhale as the fear her mother was about to choke to death left her body. She looked at Ginny to make sure she was okay. Ginny was just staring at her elders like the Crazy African Sisters they were.

"You surely knocked my socks off." Elma was finally able to speak. "Whooo wheeeeee. Now that's how you win a war. That's how you shut some crazy old ladies up."

"You got that right," Aunt Etta and Aunt Bertha agreed.

"Child," Elma said, now that she was able to get herself under control, "you have just earned the right to be called an expert of this here woman's business." She looked to her sisters. "Agreed, ladies?"

"Hell yeah," Aunt Bertha said.

"I just can't believe you didn't pull out that bullet and shoot us with it years ago," Aunt Etta said. "That would have got us off your back for sure."

A serious expression took over Elma's face as she held her arms wide to silence everyone. "Wait a minute. Does Bishop Smith know about this?"

"Yeah, does he?" Ginny chimed in.

May Rose couldn't quite tell how her daughter was feeling about all this. Her tone was even, and her expression was flat. "No, he doesn't know, and that's my dilemma, baby." She left Elma's side and took Ginny's hands into hers again. She stroked them hands tenderly. "That's why I'm here for advice from the elders. I don't want to mess up the good thing we've got going. More importantly, I don't want to mess you up, you know?" May Rose dropped Ginny's hands and turned away, fanning the air in exhaustion. "I know just like the elders, you thought I was messing up the woman's business legacy. But then when you saw how things were working out with David... You seemed so proud." She shook her head as she got a little choked up. "I just didn't want to mess things up for anybody."

"Momma, I still am proud. Hell, I'm more proud now than even before. Like the elders said, you could have burst everyone's bubble with your truth. But you kept it." She took her mother's hands and placed them on May Rose's chest. "You kept it close. You kept it tight. You used self-control. And didn't you tell me that's the truest sign and most valuable characteristic of a woman? Self-control?"

May Rose stared at Ginny for a moment. "Yeah, you're right. I did say that, didn't I?" She had some confidence about her now. Her neck and back straightened up, and her head was held high. It was as if Ginny pressing on her chest was pressing her into position.

"Yeah, that's the momma I'm talking about. That's the momma I know." Ginny clapped her hands and smiled.

May Rose smiled and nodded. Her little girl, indeed, was maturing. After a moment, the smile faded. "Well..." She turned her attention to the elders. "Do I tell David now? Do I tell him later? Do I tell him ever? I mean, y'all saw how he was about Ramona wanting to keep giving him babies. It's clear the man don't want no more babies."

"But, Momma, we ain't babies," Ginny said.

"And besides," Elma chimed in, "he said he didn't want no more babies with Ramona." She stood up, walked over to her daughter, and rubbed her chin with her thumb. "And you ain't no Ramona."

May Rose nodded. "I hear you, Momma. I hear you."

Elma smiled and sat back down. "I know you called this meeting to get our advice, May Rose, but—and I'm sure the sisters will agree with me—we trust you. We trust you to make the right decision without our influence, help, or even wise counsel."

May Rose looked to her aunts for confirmation.

They each mumbled their agreement while nodding.

She turned away from everyone, walking away and pacing as she wrung her hands together. She'd finally gotten the respect and trust from her mother and aunties she'd wanted for years, but this was a time when she wouldn't have minded them telling her what to do.

"What are you thinking, dear?" Bertha asked.

She sighed, stopped pacing, and turned toward everyone. "Well, I have always wanted to tell him. I told myself I would, but not until I could get away from Willie. I also was calling on the ancestors to remove Willie from me and my children as far as the east is from the west." She took a breath and continued,

"I knew if I had children with David, my children would have a better life. But it needed to just be me and him. Telling him while he had a wife wouldn't have done me no good."

The elders listened intently, but there was something about those words that gave Ginny pause. May Rose didn't notice it, though, and went on.

"He always told me that he would never be far away from me, and he would always make sure me and the girls were alright," May Rose said. "He told me that not even having the slightest idea his blood ran through their veins." She shook her head in disbelief. "We loved each other just that much, although we both went our separate ways. We agreed to be respectful of our spouses. I kept trying to conduct the business principles by trying not let the love I felt for David overrule my common sense." She looked at the elders accusingly, "Like you all fussed at me about for doing so long with Willie."

The elders looked away, guilty as charged.

It was now clear that, yes, love and other emotions did get in the way of a woman's business for May Rose, but it wasn't all feelings for Willie as much as it was for Bishop Smith. As a matter of fact, if May Rose was being 100% honest, which it was clear she had never been, she forced her feelings for Willie just to keep them away from David. All the while, Bishop Smith was who she really wanted to give those feelings to.

May Rose continued. "But David has always been my heart-throb. I've always thought deep in my spirit, we would someday be together."

Ginny stood up, shaking her head slightly. "How the hell did you do this to us, Momma?" Her sudden outburst surprised everyone in the room. It was as if something in her had been brewing and now she was spewing it out like venom. After all, not less than five minutes ago, she was telling May Rose how proud of her she was. Now, she was treating her like her worst enemy.

Ginny's words shocked May Rose and were piercing at the same time. "We could have done had a better life with Bishop Smith," she said, everything May Rose was saying registering clearly now. She glared at her mother. "But you let us live this tortured life with Willie. Why? Why, Momma? Why not just tell him? If not for yourself, for your daughters?" Ginny's eyes began to fill with angry tears. "Why play games with *our* lives? Why didn't you just be with Bishop Smith? If he loves you as much as you say he does and you love him the same in return, wouldn't he have left First Lady and you left Daddy to be together? To give us a better life. Or even when you know you was carrying his child in the first place, you could have just told him then. Your lie cost us a better life. It could have been—it should have been—us marching behind Bishop Smith as the first family, wearing the prettiest clothes in town, living in the best house, eating the best food, and driving the best car. We could—"

"Watch your mouth, little girl." May Rose cut Ginny's words off because they were cutting too deep. "For your information, Willie was not going to walk away without a fight. It wasn't going to be as easy as just telling him I was carrying another man's child—David's, of all people. You don't understand the history." She grabbed Ginny by the shoulders. "I suspected you would be hurt, but I need you to look at the big picture. David was always in your lives. He's always done right by you all and done good things for you. No, maybe it wasn't the life you should have had, but you have it now."

Ginny snapped back, "Yeah, but we should have had it then. But no, we wore his wife's rags and burlap potato sacks as dresses. What kind of madness is this?" Ginny smacked herself upside the head, knocking May Rose's hands off her shoulders.

"Now you're getting ready to blow up the marriage. When he throws you out his house for lying like the devil, me and my sisters are staying right there with our real daddy."

"Hey, hey there, smart-mouth girl." Elma jumped up from her chair. "You better stop while you can. You're getting ready to get your teeth knocked out of your mouth." She pointed her finger only one inch from Ginny's nose. "And that's only if you're lucky, because if they fall in the other direction, you gon' choke to death on 'em."

Ginny fell in Elma's arms and sobbed. "Nana, what am I supposed to do with this information?"

Aunt Bertha responded, "You're supposed to live with it, that's what. The same way your Momma had to live with it. You think it was easy for her carrying that inside all these years? You and your sisters are now bearing the fruit of your mother's smart labor. You are now living an abundant life because of your mother's strategic planning and keeping her mind focused on y'all's future. And damn it, it's better late than never!" Aunt Bertha was furious at what she felt was Ginny's selfish reaction. Maybe they were wrong about Ginny being able to handle and understand the business just as much as they had been wrong about May Rose not being able to handle it.

Aunt Etta looked directly at May Rose, smiled, and said, "I salute you, May Rose. You unselfishly focused on all of our futures. We have all been set up with an abundant life. We have this house free and clear. Bishop Smith has had things fixed up inside our house. We now have an inside toilet, a big, beautiful tub, and plumbing with running water. New kitchen and dining furniture thanks to Elma's loverboy, Bishop Ellis. What more could we ask for? May Rose, you did a good thing. And I know Ginny's words ain't too pleasing, but one day, she'll understand."

"And even if she don't," Aunt Bertha added, "I bet it ain't gon' stop her from reaping the benefits of it." She rolled her eyes at Ginny. "She already done said herself, she'd choose to stay in that big ole house with Bishop."

Ginny's tear-covered face had been wiped with one of Elma's beautiful lace handkerchiefs, gifted to her by Bishop Ellis.

May Rose asked, "Ginny, baby, is it starting to make any sense to you now? I brought you because I believed you could handle the truth now. I have faith in you." She looked to the elders. "The same way they have faith in me."

Ginny looked to the elders. She could see May Rose was right about how they now felt about her. There was a new look of admiration in their eyes toward May Rose that Ginny had never witnessed before. "I guess so." But it was evident Ginny wasn't changing her feelings much. She still felt deprived.

"If you still have questions, please speak your mind," May Rose said.

"Momma, I just don't want you to mess things up. We finally got the life we've all been dreaming of. Even if it is a life we should have had."

"That's why I'm here asking for counsel." She looked to her elders. "Do you all think David loves me enough to not call off the wedding and end things with me? I don't think it's fair to not tell him about the children any longer. I won't be able to watch him love on the girls and he doesn't know they are his. It's not fair to the girls either. And it's certainly not fair for me to ask Ginny to hold a secret from her sisters that has worn me down over the years."

"You know the saying, May Rose," Aunt Bertha said. "Momma's baby, Daddy's maybe. This happens all the time for one reason or another. But everyone has not done it as well as you have, honey."

May Rose asked in desperation, "What should I do now? I don't want to mess things up like Ginny said. I didn't think the moment of truth would come so fast and under these circumstances."

"Then why, Momma, why now?" Ginny asked. "If you think it might mess things up, why not just let things be?"

"Your daddy... Willie... He left me a letter," May Rose said. "Basically telling me he had wind of, or at least suspicions about, my secret. It's like he dug my secret up from the grave from his own grave." May Rose shook her head. "David is a good man. He's the type of man that will make you throw all of the women principles out the window and make you fall deep in love with and give him your complete all."

Elma's tune instantly changed when she heard May Rose going on about this love thing. "Hold your horses, young lady. Remember all of the foolery you and him were doing behind that fool Willie and Lady Ramona's backs. Don't let love blind you or make you stupid. You can't trust him, and he won't trust you. You better remember that. The principles don't change; they just get a little softer," Elma said. "It's of my opinion that you and Ginny keep your mouths shut until y'all are good and damn married for a long, long while."

May Rose let out a harrumph and put her hands on her hips. "So much for trusting me to handle my business." She sucked her teeth and rolled her eyes.

Bertha added, "You asked. You have everything you want and need right now and so does the girls. Why risk losing it all? You'll not only lose his trust, but you'll lose Mrs. Smith's, Marnita Smith's, and Bishop Ellis's trust. And most of all, you may lose the girls' trust. You see how Ginny received it. If you tell him, you'll have to tell the girls. He won't let the lie continue. You may end up losing your children."

Now that's something May Rose didn't think about—Bishop Smith taking the girls from her. After all, he would have right to them. They were his flesh and blood. "I can't live with this lie any longer. I'm so confused. I can hardly look him in the face right now. He keeps asking me if I'm getting cold feet. He knows something is wrong." May Rose started wringing her hands again.

"Look at you getting sloppy, Momma. You're getting ready to mess everything up," Ginny said.

"I just can't lie to David anymore. If he loves me truly, he'll love me through this, too," May Rose declared. "Not all men deserve the woman's business beat over their heads."

"Oh Lord, I hope we didn't speak too soon," Elma said as her sisters mumbled and groaned those exact sentiments.

"I have been them all," May Rose said. "A wife, a girlfriend, and the other woman. I asked you all to help me figure this out. To be honest, your thoughts have made it almost clear to me that I can't allow this wound to fester any longer." She snatched up her belongings. "Ginny, let's go." She stormed toward the kitchen exit.

"Momma, I'm not coming. I don't want nothing to do with this mess you are about to make." Ginny stood with her arms folded in the most defiant manner she could muster up.

May Rose stopped but didn't even turn around to face her daughter before she threw the words over her shoulder, "Well, stay your tail right there."

"I don't know why you're mad at us," Elma yelled. "We told you the truth. Don't let your silly anger tear up you, your children, and our lives."

May Rose stomped out of the kitchen, ignoring her mother's words. She stopped at the door and shouted, "Whatever the good Lord leads me to do during my drive home, that's what will be done."

"May Rose, don't be stupid," Elma called, chasing after her daughter. "You have lives in your hand. You took care of the woman's business like it was supposed to be conducted. Don't blow it in the end. Please think it through."

May Rose spun around in anger. "You all—all of you, including Ginny—are just thinking about yourselves." She walked out the door and slammed it shut. "I should have known better."

Tears poured out of her eyes as she made her way to the car. She prayed silently during the entire ride home, asking God for forgiveness in her decision to deliberately get pregnant by Bishop Smith not once but three times, and then not tell him to this day that her girls were his. She prayed for guidance on what to do now.

Yes, May Rose might have done everything she needed to keep Claypool and Willie from giving her a baby. But not when it came to her David.

She pulled up to the house and saw a couple of the children playing in the yard. She sat and gathered herself in the car for a few minutes after waving to them. She got out of the car, shaking on the inside.

"Hi, babies, have you had your breakfast yet? Have your beds been made? Where is your daddy?" May Rose rambled on out of nerves, not even allowing enough time in between her questions for the children to answer her.

The youngest child, two-year-old Lou Lou, who was so mature for her age, sweetly said, "Yes, ma'am. We ate. Made beds." She pointed to the house. "Popa in study."

May Rose bent down and kissed Lou Lou on her forehead. "Thank you, Little Bits." That was the nickname she gave her. May Rose thought as she walked into the door, *God knew Lou*

Lou was going to need to grow up fast so she could help keep them older children in order. May Rose loved all the Smith children, but Lou Lou had a special place in her heart.

She slowly walked to the study, singing, "Honey, where are you?" She still wasn't sure what she would do up to this very second. She knocked on the door and softly asked, "Honey, can I come in?"

"Sure, you're right on time to give me some sugar," he said as May Rose entered.

She walked over to give him a kiss, and he playfully pulled her onto his lap.

"You better stop before we end up upstairs for a quick one." She laughed.

"Is that an invite?"

"Later, my love! We need to talk." May Rose couldn't count how many times she'd said that to him the past couple weeks.

"You keep talking about we need to talk. You really got me worrying. I wish you would spit it out. You got me thinking you want to call off the wedding."

"No, I would never do that. You're mine forever." She was still sitting in his lap and playing with the goatee he had grown. Just then, there was loud screaming from the front porch.

"Lou Lou, wake up! Wake up!" they heard.

May Rose jumped off Bishop Smith's lap. Thank goodness she did, otherwise she would have landed flat on her behind with the way he popped up out of his chair at the sound of one of his children in distress. He ran to the porch with May Rose on his heels.

Lou Lou lay on her back with her eyes closed and blood flowing from the back of her head. May Rose went and checked her pulse. She was all right from that perspective. She then lifted Lou Lou's head, where she discovered a small gash. She took off her sweater and laid it under the girl's head.

Lou Lou opened her eyes and cried out, "Miss Rose, no leave me. I scared."

"I'll be right back, baby girl," May Rose assured her. "I'm going to get stuff to clean your head up. Your daddy is right here with you."

David was standing over May Rose and Lou Lou in deep worry.

"Honey, she's just fine," May Rose said. "She's just a little afraid. Hold her hand until I get back."

He did as May Rose instructed while she headed back into the house. By this time, all of the children were on the porch to see about Lou Lou.

David yelled, "Junior, what in the hell happened to my baby? You better speak now. You're the oldest out here. What happened?"

Junior was sniffling and saying, "I was teaching her to do the backflip. She fell on her head when she landed. Popa, I didn't try to hurt her. She was doing good at first."

"Don't you teach another soul in this house to ever do that again. As a matter of fact, don't you do another one in or around this house or the schoolhouse," David ordered.

As May Rose was gathering supplies out of her catching bag, she wondered if this was a sign from God to keep her mouth shut. She'd silently prayed on the ride home, "God, make it clear. Please tell me what to do. I don't want to lose my beautiful family. And if your will is for me to tell it, please make David receive it well. But if I'm not supposed to tell it, give me a sign."

As far as May Rose was concerned, this was her sign.

She exited the house and returned to the porch with all the supplies she needed to clean Lou Lou up. The little girl would be okay. May Rose and her husband-to-be would be okay. Her family was going to be okay. All of them.

Willie had taken the suspicions to his grave, and it looked like God wanted May Rose to do the same with the truth.

Yep, everything was going to be okay.

With that thought, May Rose got Lou Lou cleaned up and the household back in order.

Later that evening, May Rose lay next to David in bed.

"Rosie, what was it you were going to tell me earlier?" he asked.

May Rose paused for a moment. "I know you got designs on a big wedding and all, but would you be mad if I said I didn't want to wait to have a great big, ole wedding? If I said, let's call Bishop Ellis down to marry us? Or better yet, we go to him?"

"You mean we elope?" he asked, confused.

"Yes!" May Rose exclaimed. "David Smith, I've waited to have you and for me to be yours for my whole entire life, and it's like death making me wait one more day. Please don't make me," she pleaded, as always, handling her business to the tee. The sooner they got married, the sooner she wouldn't have to worry about him finding out the truth and not marrying her.

"May Rose, you ain't said nothing," David said with excitement. "Consider it done."

And with that, May Rose was able to exhale. Soon enough, it would be a sealed deal, and she would live happily ever after.

Unbeknownst to May Rose, while she slept like a baby that night knowing everything had come together just like in her business plan, that everything she'd been through was paying off, Ginny was wide awake in the next room, planning her payback.

"Nana, what am I supposed to do with this information?" Ginny had asked her grandmother just hours earlier.

Well, now, Ginny knew exactly what to do with it.

"A secret only remains a secret if only one person knows it."

African Proverb

ABOUT THE AUTHOR

*T*racy Mungo is an American author who pays homage to things learned from her African ancestors through her heartfelt tales and bold adventures. Tracy is an inspiring and passionate literary artist whose work spans from mystery to romance. Known for her unique trait of creating relatable characters, weaving intricate plots, and blending humor and heart, Tracy's stories will captivate readers with her key qualities of vivid storytelling and emotional depth.

When not writing, Tracy enjoys researching family history and genealogy, while drawing inspiration from her research and the love of talking with her senior family members, extracting and deciphering her family history. Currently residing in Atlanta, Georgia, Tracy is hard at work on her next book, a screenplay, and an exciting new series.

To contact Tracy, email her at tracybmungo@gmail.com. Be sure to visit her website, www.authortracymungo.com, to learn more about her, her writings, and to sign up for her newsletter.

READER DISCUSSION QUESTIONS

A Woman's Business
Discussion Questions

1. Does the banter that Ginny and Florence have about skin color still happen in modern day households among siblings?

2. Is it possible that Willie loves Ginny like he does Florence and Lynette?

3. Why do you think Willie went all those years without telling May Rose what he suspected about her relationship with Bishop Smith?

4. Why do you think May Rose didn't tell her elders about the woman's business she had with Bishop Smith earlier in order to keep them off her back about Willie?

5. Do you think Willie's decision to go work at a coal mine was a way for him to surrender to May Rose and Bishop Smith's love for one another?

6. Do you feel Elma and her sisters did all they could do to save First Lady Ramona's life during her delivery?

7. Would you consider some of the rituals performed in this book a form of witchcraft? If so, which ones?

8. Was Ginny mentally ready to hear May Rose's secret? What do you think she plans on doing with the information she has? What would your reaction had been if you were Ginny?

9. Did First Lady Ramona conduct a woman's business with Bishop Smith? If so, in what ways?

10. Do you feel the principles of "A Woman's Business" is a form of gold digging or using a man? Why or why not?